Runes of Deception

By

Jack Cullen

Dedication

This book is dedicated to my wife Sonya who tolerates my insistence that Bad Penny writes herself.

Acknowledgements

A heartfelt thanks to Jocelyn for continuing to put up with me.

A big thanks to my editor Megan Harris and to my beta readers who helped make it a better book.

Bob Beloin

Keith Berube

Aaron Kinder

Jay Levasseur

Sarah Veader

Editor: Megan Harris: www.mharriseditor.com

Cover by Jocelyn Cullen

Published by SpellBinding Books

Table of Contents

Dedication

Acknowledgements

Chapter One: The Stakeout... 7

Chapter Two: A Conversation with a Dragon... 22

Chapter Three: The Battle for Bacon... 26

Chapter Four: Q Gets a New Toy... 33

Chapter Five: Culain's Guests... 40

Chapter Six: Sex and Magic... 48

Chapter Seven: Eddy Brunching Badly... 72

Chapter Eight: Dating and the Undead... 85

Chapter Nine: Late Night Visits... 97

Chapter Ten: A Lack of Pants... 109

Chapter Eleven: Police at the Door... 114

Chapter Twelve: Another Morgan… 122

Chapter Thirteen: Officer Down… 129

Chapter Fourteen: Breadcrumbs…143

Chapter Fifteen: Dracula's Lair… 157

Chapter Sixteen: Enter the Muse… 167

Chapter Seventeen: One Last Errand… 184

Chapter Eighteen: The Reading… 191

Chapter Nineteen: The Contents of the Envelope… 209

Chapter Twenty: A Mutual Exchange… 218

Chapter Twenty-One: Paraphrasing Jeffery Combs… 225

Chapter Twenty-Two: Arrogance and Cheap Cologne.. 239

Chapter Twenty-Three: Pawn takes Knight… 244

Chapter Twenty-Four: You Don't Tarnish the Badge… 248

Chapter Twenty-Five: No Geeksplaining… 255

Chapter Twenty-Six: Forging a Deception… 268

Chapter Twenty-Seven: Volunteers Needed… 291

Chapter Twenty-Eight: Winners and Losers… 298

Chapter Twenty-Nine: SOS… 304

Chapter Thirty: Mike's Big Reveal… 314

Chapter Thirty-One: Latin Class… 319

Chapter Thirty-Two: Soul Swapping… 326

Chapter Thirty-Three: The Big Plan… 343

Chapter Thirty-Four: Enter Silas... 362

Chapter Thirty-Five: A Bad Coat of Paint... 371

Chapter Thirty-Six: Kitchen Witches and Staff Twirlers... 375

Chapter Thirty-Seven: The Candy Store... 381

Chapter Thirty-Eight: Origin Story... 386

Chapter Thirty-Nine: Best I Can Offer... 397

Chapter Forty: Losses and Revelations... 405

Cast of Characters... 416

Author's Note... 427

Chapter One

The Stakeout

I hated stakeouts.

Rookie Officer Penelope "Bad Penny" Harper snored softly and shifted in the passenger seat to use my shoulder as a pillow *again*. The crick in my neck and the drool stains on my uniform shirt were testaments to her inability to stay awake.

Her eyes snapped open, and she bolted upright when the Chief's left rear door opened. "I was just helping Emma find her top!

The ancient Vampire Lord known as Valentine slid into the backseat of my car. "Excuse me?"

"Nothing," Penny said as she wiped the drool off her face.

I raised my eyebrows. "Stone or Roberts?"

"Stone." She sighed, grabbed some napkins from the dash, and began dabbing her handiwork on my shoulder.

"Her voice?"

"Right? It's just…wow! You know?" She tossed the napkins in the trash bag on the floor and leaned back with a sigh. "I hate stakeouts! Are they ever getting here?"

"I told you to stay at home."

"And miss meeting Dracula? No way!" She paused. "Stakeout for Dracula. Heh heh heh."

Valentine eyed us for a second before speaking. "As a matter of fact, that is why I returned. They should be here momentarily."

As he spoke, we could see two sets of headlights preceding down the road on the other side of the river. The lead car stopped before the red bridge. Valentine snorted. "That's a 1961 Lincoln Continental limousine."

"So?" I asked, blinking to switch my runic eye to night vision.

"Same year and type of car your President Kennedy was killed in."

"Coincidence?" asked Penny.

"Unlikely." As Valentine spoke, two men and a woman exited the lead car and approached the bridge. One of them wore a dress shirt and slacks and was gesturing angrily at the bridge.

I frowned. "What's the problem? The spells on the bridge should only keep Normals from venturing across it. They shouldn't have any effect on vampires."

Valentine nodded. "The one with the mustache is Vlad Tepes. He is complaining they didn't tell him that they would cross a river."

I shook my head. "They are too far away for me to make out such details. You mean the one waving his arms around?"

"Yes. One of his many idiosyncrasies is he has a phobia of crossing running water. Doesn't your metal eye have telescopic vision?"

Oh yeah. I'm an idiot.

I frowned. "I thought that was all vampires *and* I thought it was bullshit."

"No, many of the incorrect myths about my kind can be traced back to his… habits."

Penny lifted a pair of binoculars. "That's him? Bit of a letdown. The mustache is kinda goofy looking. He looks like Mario. Where's Luigi? You sure he's not Italian?"

Valentine stiffened. "I assure you, he is not from my homeland."

Penny lowered the binoculars and turned to him. "That's another thing. If you're from the boot originally, why is your accent wrong?"

"I do not have an accent. My English is flawless. As is my French, German, and Russian."

"You have an English accent."

"The English invented the language, hence its name. Therefore, it cannot *be* an English accent."

"But there are plenty of accents in Britain. Cockney and um… Whatever John Lennon spoke and… um, Cockney."

"I do not dispute there are various accents in the British Isles. However, what you are referring to as my accent is called standard English or the Queen's English and therefore is not an accent but the proper way to speak English. You, in fact, are the one with the accent."

Penny finally caught on that he was putting one over on her and made a face at him.

"Can we get back to work?" I asked. "I recognize Seward." About four months ago, a good chunk of Dracula's vamps had migrated to Llewelyn with Jack Seward overseeing them. This was the first time Vlad Tepes, the vampire known as Dracula, had shown up. "Who's the woman?"

"Katrina Bathory. Her father Stephen put Vlad on the throne of Wallachia and was the one who Turned him."

I studied the dark-haired woman. "Any relation to Elizabeth Bathory?"

"Yes. Elizabeth was a grandniece of some sort and her protegee."

Bathory was now attempting to coax Dracula back into the car. "Protegee?"

"Yes. It's complicated. I'll explain later. I need to depart before they sense me." In one quick motion, he was gone. Just in time, too, as whatever Bathory said must have worked because they all got in the car, and it raced across the covered bridge at a high speed.

"Perfect." I tabbed my badge. "They just zipped across the Red Bridge. I'm going to pull them over for speeding."

"Roger that," replied Detective Ulysses Khan. "We'll be there in a moment."

"Light 'em up, buddy." I tapped on the dash of the car. The Nova I named the Chief started up by itself and took off down the road towards the Lincoln. As we got close, the Chief's headlights shifted in to rotating blue and a siren roared to life under the hood.

The Lincoln and its companion vehicle, a 1960s panel van that looked like it should have four meddling teenagers and a Great Dane in it, pulled over to the side of the road. I edged the Chief out a little to the left to shield me from any other cars coming down the road.

I tabbed my badge and read off the vehicle descriptions and license plates to Dispatch. "Four males in the van, two males and two females in the limo."

"Copy, Sergeant," Crystal's reply came from my badge.

Penny and I both exited the Nova. Penny, acting as cover officer, stopped at the passenger corner of the van as I moved to the driver's window. I stopped just short of it, causing the driver to have to crank his neck to look back to see me. "Evening. Llewellyn Police. You fellers seem to be in a hurry. Clocked you at well over the legal speed limit for this road."

I shined my flashlight around the inside of the van, trusting Penny to tell me if anyone got out of the limo. "Please turn your dome light on and hand me your license and registration."

The driver was the beefy bodyguard type and looked confused. "You said Llewellyn, right? We're in the right place?"

"This is Llewellyn. That's correct."

"Then why do you want my license?"

"Because you were speeding."

One of the meatheads in the back sighed. "Just give it to him, Karl."

Still looking confused, the driver handed me his license and registration. "Van's a rental."

"Sure." I looked at the license. "This is a fake."

"Of course it's a fake. I'm a hundred and twenty-one years old. You think I still use my original?"

I peered down at him with my best cop face. "Just because you're a vampire doesn't mean you can break the law."

"Oh, this is some bullshit!"

"You were doing at least sixty in a thirty plus the fake license. Keep the dome light on and all four of you stay in the van. You exit the van, I assume you're coming to do me harm and will respond in an appropriate fashion. You get me?"

The driver looked me up and down. "You think a couple of meat sacks can slow us down?"

"You must be new in town."

"What's that mean?"

The same voice from the back sighed again. "Karl, look at the nametape on his uniform."

Karl stared at the name on my shirt and looked at me. "Brennan? You're the one they call Blood Drinker's Bane."

"So I've been told."

"I don't care what they call you. Do you know who's in that limo?"

"Yes, I do." I dialed in my cop voice. "Now stay in the van before I'm forced to end you."

He shrugged. "Whatever, man. Your funeral."

I moved forward to the limo and tapped on the tinted rear window. "Lower all your windows, please."

Once they did so, I moved up to the driver. "Evening."

Dracula and Bathory were in the back. An unknown female was in the front passenger seat. She looked to have been in her late teens when she was Turned. Dr. John "Jack" Seward blinked up at me from behind the wheel. "Hello, Sergeant Brennan. Is there an issue?"

"Both vehicles were speeding, and your buddy back there has a fake license." I shined my light in the car.

Both women gave me sullen looks, but Dracula never looked up from the folder he was reading. "Dr. Seward, I have some concerns regarding the latest publications in the image rehabilitation program."

Oh my God, he really sounds like that. Blah Blah Blah Blah Blah.

"What seems to be the problem, sir?"

13

"The author from New Jersey. Does he have to be so vulgar? Why is the protagonist so…?" The vampire lord looked over at the unknown female. "What is the word, my dear?"

"Nerdy," she answered with a British accent.

"Ah yes, nerdy. That's it."

Seward shifted uncomfortably in his seat. "I believe that's part of the humor of his series. He has quite a large following for one of our thralls."

"Really?" Dracula's eyes took on a predatory gleam. "Are we considering Turning him?"

"Um, no sir, not that type of followers. I was referring to readers and fans."

"Pity." He flipped to another page. "I'm baffled by this other writer."

"Which one, sir?"

"The female author from Massachusetts. The one that uses her initials. I am no means prudish, but this idea she has concerning certain… bodily fluids of our kind…" He closed the folder. "Is this the route we want to take? We are still dealing with the whole sparkly vampire fallout."

"Apologies, my lord, but the author in question is not one of ours."

The so-called Prince of Darkness raised a single eyebrow. "She writes this of her own free will?"

"That is correct. She also has a loyal following and I've found her take on our kind to be intriguing."

"I do not know if that means the program is a success or spiraling down another rabbit hole." He tossed the folder on the seat next to him. "Very well, Doctor. Please introduce us."

Seward shifted again in his seat and gestured toward his Boss. "Sergeant Michael Brennan, I present to you Vlad Tepes, Prince of Wallachia and Head of the Line of Dracula."

"Hey." I nodded casually at one of the most notorious monsters that ever lived. "How are you doing tonight?"

"Good evening, Sergeant. I was looking forward to meeting you. I just didn't think it would be so soon."

Dracula has heard of me. That... that can't be good.

"I actually have a gift for you. I heard we have a hobby in common." He gestured towards a soft leather briefcase on the floor by his feet. "May I?"

Somehow, I don't think Dracula is going to pull a gun on me. Rip out my throat maybe...

"Slowly, please."

He lifted an item protected in a glassine bag out of one of the side pouches and handed it to me. Inside the bag was a Dracula comic book from the 1970s.

I shined my flashlight on it. "Issue number one. These are rare."

"I took the liberty of signing it for you."

"Sorry, we're not allowed to take personal gifts." I gave it back to him. "Besides, I'm more of a *Werewolf by Night* fan anyways. Didn't know you were a comic book guy."

He chuckled slightly as he ran a hand across the protective cover. "Oh yes. The epic stories of good and evil, the artwork. And of course, the capes."

"The capes?"

"Regardless of how many actors portraying me would hide their bad acting behind their capes, I always preferred them and was sorry to see them go out of fashion." He sighed. "Oh well. How may we be of service, Sergeant?"

"Leaving and never returning would be a good start."

Dracula leaned back in his seat. "Oh, he's every bit as delightful as you said, Doctor. This is going to be most amusing."

I flashed my light around the car again. "Let's start by introducing the rest of the people in the motor vehicle."

Seward waved a hand towards Bathory. "Lady Katrina Bathory of Transylvania."

He turned back towards the woman sitting beside him. "And this is my wife, Lucy."

I looked at her. "Do you have any identification?"

"I'm afraid not." She smiled at me. She had what my profession called *crazy eyes*.

I continued to move my flashlight around the inside as a 1970 plum colored Dodge Challenger pulled up behind the Chief. "Please put your dome light on and stay in the car. I'll be back in a moment."

Dracula smiled at me. He had crazy eyes of his own. "Of course, Sergeant."

I nodded to Bad Penny to keep an eye on them as I approached the Challenger. Ulysses Khan, our only detective, exited the driver's side, his badge pinned on the lapel of his leather coat which hid the hand cannon of an automag he kept in a shoulder holster. Khan always looked like he stepped out of a blaxploitation movie. Valentine had some theory about Khan using the clothes of his time to remember who he was. Personally, I think he does it to fuck with people's perceptions.

"Evenin', Sarge." Quintrell Faraway stepped out of the passenger's seat. His drawl gave away his Texas roots. So did the completely unauthorized black cowboy hat and the jeans he wore with his uniform shirt. Like me, he was a gifted Outsider. Also like me, he had been in law enforcement when he first encountered something from the magic world. But where I had been a cop, Q had most recently been a Deputy U.S. Marshal, one of the many careers he's had over the centuries. I had to bribe him with magic items to get him to come work for us, but it was worth it.

"Your timing is perfect. They're not denying who she is, but I still need you to I.D. her. Khan, you're with Penny. Q, come with me."

He spit out some chewing tobacco and nodded. "Let's do this then."

We walked back to the limo. Q strolled over to the passenger side with his head down, the brim of his hat hiding his face. He slowly raised his head. "Evening, Lucy."

Both Seward and his wife recoiled at the sight of Q. Dracula said nothing, but I noticed him running his right thumb over the fingers of the same hand. It appeared more like a tic than counting.

Lucy tried to compose herself. "Quincey, what are you doing here?

"I haven't used that alias since the dust up with your boss there. I'm using my real name here, so it's Quintrell or Q. Or, if you want to be formal, Officer Faraway." He leaned in to look at Seward, his hands resting on the .45 colt and the cross drawn Bowie knife attached to his belt. "Hey Jack. How yer doin?"

"Did you know he was working here?" she asked, turning to Seward who shook his head.

I was watching Dracula during Q's big reveal. His grin had faded into a scowl, but he made no comments. Fexts and vampires don't get along. You have to die to become one or the other, and fexts are often confused as vampires by mortals, but the two races are very different. If vampires represent death, then fexts represent life.

My understanding was Q being a fext is why Dracula Turned Lucy during his pursuit of Mina Harker. In the end, that hadn't worked too well for him.

Q investigated the back seat, the fingers of his left hand tapping a beat on the handle of the Bowie. "Been a while, Vlad."

Dracula's eyes were drawn to the Bowie. I wondered if he was experiencing phantom pains in that thing he called a heart. "You replaced your knife."

"I did." Q slowly drew if from the sheath and angled the blade so the runes I placed on it gleamed in the light. "This one won't break as easily."

"Okay. That's enough." I cleared my throat. "Officer Faraway, do you recognize the woman sitting in the passenger seat of this vehicle?"

"I sure do, Sarge."

"Please identify her and how you know her."

He tilted his hat up slightly. "The woman seated before me is Lucy Westenra Seward. I knew her back in 1890. We dated briefly before she became engaged to marry my friend Arthur Holmwood. At the time I was using the alias of Quincey Morris. Shortly afterwards she was Turned into a vampire by Vlad Dracula."

I looked at Lucy. "Is what he said true?"

She frowned, trying to figure out our game. "Yes, that's true. It was before Jack and I were united for eternity."

"Lucy Westenra Seward, as a vampire known to prey on infants and children, you have been deemed by the council of Llewellyn as an undesirable." I slid a paper out of my shirt and handed it to her. "Here is a writ of banishment issued by the council. You are to leave the city immediately and if you return, you will be killed on sight."

I turned to Dracula. "Be aware that the Living Temple is currently above us in the sky. Should any of you attempt to interfere in this banishment, she will unleash her full power upon you."

I looked at the sky for a second and then back down at him. "I'm not sure even a vampire lord can survive that. But just in case you can, I have other assets in the field waiting to be deployed."

He studied my face for a moment and nodded. "Lucy, it seems you will not be joining us on this venture. Take the other vehicle and please return to Boston. We will contact you shortly."

She crumbled the unread writ in her fist. "You're going to allow this? From a dirty human and a fext?"

"Fexts are treacherous creatures, my dear. That is why there are so few of them in this world. Their machinations are never tolerated for long. His time will come." He gestured to the door. "Go, I will not tell you again."

"Yes, my Lord." She glared at Q as he opened the door for her. Without another word, she stomped over to the van.

I waited until the van drove back over the bridge. "As for the rest of you, I've got no reason to throw you out. Yet! I don't know what drama is going on in the vampire world that has made you come here, but I will not let it affect my city. Is that understood?"

"Oh yes. I understand much now." The Vampire Lord's eyes blazed with fury, but his voice was calm, almost lazy. "Are we free to go?"

I stepped back. "You are."

"Very well. Sergeant, Faraway, I'm sure I'll see you both soon." He leaned back into his seat. "Drive on, Doctor."

Khan and Penny stepped up to us as we watched the car drive away. Khan shook his head. "You two are playing a dangerous game. That guy's not right in the head. He scares other vampires and you're messing with him? He could have killed us all before Gabby had a chance to react."

"I'd have lived." Q shrugged. "Would you have done it any different?"

"Yeah."

I looked at Khan in surprise. "Really?"

"I'd have done it with more style." He turned on his heel and walked back to his car.

"Now what?" Penny asked as she waved at Sergeant Gabby Zhao, who floated high up in the sky. Gabby gave a lazy salute and flew off.

"We head home." I turned towards the Chief as I spoke to her. "You should catch up on some sleep before the shift starts."

She frowned. "What are you going to be doing?"

"I gotta see a dragon about a boy."

Chapter Two

A Conversation with a Dragon

The dragon stared out at me from behind the eyes of the boy.

WHY DO YOU KEEP RETURNING?

As always, its voice in my head created a dull ache at the front of my skull. It could have been worse. If the runes on my helmet weren't protecting me, the power of the creature would have crushed my mind in a second.

It had been six months since David warned us of the dragon. Six months since he slipped out of the house under the control of the creature. Six months of me entering the edge of the druid's forest to try and deal with the thing that took him over.

I shook away the ache. "Voices, please."

A frown appeared on David's face, the voice coming from him sounding strange and alien. "Very well. Now answer the question."

As it spoke, many of David's creatures creeped out of the darkness of the trees, now under the control of the dragon.

I resisted the urge to step back and sighed. "Just like every other time, I want you to release David."

"I have refused each time. Why do you think this time will be any different? I have left your city alone and remain in my woods. Realize your good fortune and leave me be."

"Let's face it. You're a dragon. Which means you have a price. Last time I offered you twenty-five magic items. Why don't you just counteroffer so I know what I'm working with?"

"This boy gives me access to the creatures of these woods and all the treasures they possess. You have nothing to compare with that." As he said this, some of David's creatures emerged further from the dark woods and took slow, menacing steps towards me. I spotted griffins, centaurs, and one minotaur.

"Careful there. We wouldn't want any accidents." I waved an index finger at him as the Vargar came up from behind me to stare down the dragon's creatures. The descendants of Fenris were somehow immune to the dragon's influence. One night after the dragon took over David, the entire pack showed up at my house and have been living on my property ever since. "What do you care about what nuts a squirrel has stashed away? I thought you dragons were all about gold."

The blank look on David's face turned into a sinister smile. "Treasure is treasure. All that matters is that something values it."

"Wait, what? Can you explain that better?"

I TIRE OF THIS. LEAVE OR BE DESTROYED.

I winced as the voice thundered in my head and motioned the wolves back. They stepped slowly back, pacing themselves with my movements.

I glared at the dragon as I turned away. "I'll be back. You're not going to keep him."

The Dragon moved David's body back into the shadows, his creatures mimicking him.

I nodded at the wolves as we began the long trek back to my house. "Thanks, guys. Appreciate the backup."

As usual, they ignored me. As far as they were concerned, this was a temporary alliance in order to get David back. The problem was none of us knew how to do it. Very little was known of dragons. Most of it was legend and myth and not reliable.

This one had slumbered in the druid's woods for untold generations. The working theory was that the Druid Hywel brought it over from Europe. David accidently woke it with a psychic link when he was rallying the creatures of the woods to defend Llewellyn from Harrow's army. By all accounts, it should have sacked the town as soon as it was awake. Instead, it slowly broke down David's will until it had him under its control.

Once it commanded him, it used David to control the various creatures of the woods. Since then, Llewellyn had been storing up its defenses against an inevitable dragon attack.

Well, that and dealing with more and more political bullshit from the fallout of Harrow's attack and Joubert's attempt at killing the ruling council.

I sighed. "Going to be another long day, my furry friends."

Chapter Three

The Battle for Bacon

I caught a few hours of sleep before it was time to head back to work. Everything ached as I slowly got out of bed, all my joints creaking as I did so. Even with healing potions, I was starting to feel the culmination of the years of abuse my body had taken. In a normal department I'd be nearing the end of my career. Llewellyn was worse. I was constantly punching above my weight class with various supernatural bad guys, and it was taking its toll. Many of them were nigh immortal, while I was a normal guy aside from the blood runes and the ability to make magic weapons. Even with my toys, I probably only had a few more good years before I needed to retire.

The stark reminder of my mortality brought another issue to my mind. While I aged normally, Zoe didn't have to. As a witch, she had the ability to age slowly or even become immortal. She already looked ten or fifteen years younger than she was. What happens when I'm a doddering old man and she's still young with decades or centuries ahead of her? That's not fair to Zoe.

I sighed and shook my head as I headed to the bathroom.

Probably won't ever become an issue. The way Llewellyn is going, I'll be lucky to survive the year.

After a shower and shave, I headed downstairs to find organized chaos. The smell of bacon permeated the kitchen as my wife added a skillet worth of bacon to a dish with scrambled eggs on it. Her apprentice, Emala Delgado-Finnigan, was arguing with Bad Penny and Morgan on whose turn it was to do the dishes. Sonny, our bull mastiff, was hiding under the table, alert to any scraps that might fall into his domain.

My wife handed me the plate and studied my face. With an understanding nod, she added a couple of extra strips on my plate. "Did it at least say anything useful this time?"

"Maybe. It mentioned something about it collecting any type of treasure. That it would add anything to its hoard considered valuable to someone, and that included the animals of David's forest. Didn't make a lot of sense. I don't know, I'll run it by Martin later." I slid into my seat at the table and blocked Bad Penny's attempt to steal some of my bacon. This unfortunately left me open to an attack of opportunity from Morgan who deftly relieved me of two slices. "Thief!"

"You snooze, you lose, Daddy!" She broke a small piece off and gave Sonny his tithe.

Zoe snorted as she poured herself some tea. "And this is why I already ate."

I gave a mock glare at Bad Penny. "Don't you have a stove in that camper of yours?"

"Yeah, but I hate cooking and your wife loves to. So… here I am." Penny lived in a vintage camper behind our carriage house. Since she returned from the police academy, she seemed to always be at the house these days. I looked around at all the females seated at the table and then down at Sonny. "We are vastly outnumbered, buddy."

"I have to study." Emala stood and put her empty plate in the sink. She was days away from earning her hat. While she would still be an apprentice, the hat would mark her as a member of the powerful Morgan coven. "Leave the dishes in the sink. I'll do them on my next study break."

Emala had a penchant for wearing colorful tights. She wore red and white striped ones under a black goth style dress. Purple was the color of the week for her hair. My wife frowned at her apprentice as she scrambled up the stairs to her room.

I raised my eyebrows. "What?"

Zoe shook her head. "Too much time on that broom. Now she has to cram at the last minute."

Emala had a natural talent for broom flying. She was fast and fully planned on breaking the current speed records. Any off time she had found her up in the sky. I shrugged. "You were never a big flyer?"

"It's fun, but firegating is much easier." She snagged a piece out of my dwindling supply of bacon, much to the delight of Morgan.

"You're looking at it wrong." I found myself guarding my food like I was in prison. "Your methodical in your study habits and that works for you. So, you're viewing how she study's as wrong because it's not how you do it. But cramming last minute works for her. She does it every test and you freak out each time, but she's done consistently well."

"Maybe." My wife mulled over my words. She looked at the clock over her head as I shoveled down the rest of my food. "Morgan, time to get dressed."

"Okay, Mommy." My daughter slipped off her chair and took her plate to the sink before giving me a kiss goodbye. "Love you, Daddy. Have a fun day at work."

"Love you, too. Behave for your mother."

"No promises." She high fived Penny and scrambled up the stairs.

"What was Dracula like?" Zoe asked after Morgan was gone.

"Not what you'd think." I raised a hand to cover the fact I still had food in my mouth.

"How so?"

"He's got this goofy 70s porn stache and you could open a soup can with his nose." Penny chortled.

I ignored her. "He seems charming, intelligent, and bat shit crazy all at the same time."

Zoe took a sip of her tea. "That's a bad combination."

"Yup. Kicking Lucy out really pissed him off, but he refused to show it. Oh, and he really doesn't like Q."

29

"The whole London encounter or because he's a fext?"

"A bit of both I think." I swallowed. "Currently, I'm just trying to figure out what the Bathory woman is doing here."

"Bathory?" Zoe added a little creamer to her tea. "There are Bathory vampires here?"

"Yeah, Katrina Bathory. She rode in with Drac." I shoveled more eggs onto my fork. "Don't know much about the Bathory line. Valentine says she's related to Elizabeth Bathory. There seems to be some story there, but he didn't go into it."

Zoe took another sip. The creamer must have done the trick because she immediately took a deeper drink. "From what I can remember, the Bathory line is from the same part of the world as the Dracula line. They've been both allies and opponents of each other over the years. The Bathorys are supposed to be weird, even for vampires."

"Like Dracula weird?"

"I wouldn't go that far. Something about pain, I think. Can't remember."

"I'll get more out of Valentine later." I shrugged. "Either way, I'm keeping an eye on her."

Penny shook her head. "I'd say that Lucy is the one to watch out for."

My wife cocked her head at her. "More than Dracula? How did you come to that conclusion?"

"So, Vladdie boy may have a few screws loose, but he seems to be able to keep it together. I mean, he's on the

30

vampire board of directors or whatever it's called, right? That means he can compromise when he needs to. Knows which battles to fight and which to avoid."

I nodded at her. "Right."

"I spoke with Lucy when she was getting in the van. She's big time broken. That's one who can't control herself. Not really." Penny snagged a muffin and started buttering it. "I'm betting the only reason she listens to Drac is that he can Compel her. He's got a freaking psycho on a lease and if she ever slips her collar, all hell is going to break loose."

Zoe turned to look at me, arching an eyebrow as Penny bit into the muffin. I took a sip of hot chocolate and put my mug down. "I'd say that's a pretty dead-on description of her. She's definitely not right in the head. She's like Archibald Campbell. She won't quit unless she's won or put down."

Zoe stared at me a long time. "Yeah, don't know anyone like that."

I was about to ask her what she meant when Penny snorted. "It's worse. She enjoys the madness, embraces it. Mark my words. We haven't seen the last of her."

"You're not wrong. Not unless Dracula Compelled her to leave which I don't think he did." I finished my drink and looked at my watch. "Penny, you ready?"

Penny stuffed the remains of her muffin into her mouth and gestured to the police uniform she was wearing. "Waiting on you."

I ignored the crumbs that sprayed out of her mouth. "Time to go to work."

Chapter Four

Q Gets a New Toy

The Chief pulled up to the police station and Penny and I got out. I grabbed a box from the backseat and looked down at the Nova while Penny unloaded a bag of breakfast sandwiches and a tray of coffees. "We're going to be here a while. Get comfortable."

The driverless car beeped once at me and pulled into a parking spot with lots of sun. As Bad Penny and I approached the station, Cassie pulled her shopping cart along the sidewalk. The elderly bag lady had a knack for showing up when we had food.

She stopped in front of us. Penny did a balancing act as she dug out a breakfast sandwich and coffee for her. Cassie straightened up and looked me in the eye. *"Deception abounds! You must gather the piece needed to play the great chess game that will fre-* Two creams, one sugar. Thank you, sweetie. Where was I? Oh yes. *That will free the chosen of Artemis. Beware the breath of the dragon and keep safe the Child of Fire and Steel, for the Great Serpent must not claim her."*

"Un huh." I sipped my hot chocolate. "We have to go to work now, Cassie. See you tomorrow."

Cassie gave us a look of pure frustration and placed the coffee in a cup holder strapped to the side of the cart. She squirreled away her sandwich and pushed the cart down the sidewalk while shaking her head.

Penny adjusted her load and walked up the stairs. "She's a nice old lady, but the gibberish she sputters sometimes…"

"I know. Just ignore it. Everyone else does." I held the door for her as we entered the station.

After the city of Joubert's assassination attempt and the looming threat of the dragon, the city council had allowed us to hire more officers—not near the number we needed, but it was a start. Commissioner Culain Gowan and I had tried to get people that already had policing experience. One of these was Q, who was waiting for us in the break room.

Penny set up the food for everyone at a table and slipped the bill into the accounts folder. "This is bullshit, you know. Why do I have to always pick up the food for everyone?

"Because you're the rookie. Be glad we don't make you pay for it, too." Q looked at the box I held and smiled. "Is that them? Are they done?"

We had worked a few cases over the years, and my phone call to him came one day after his retirement from the

34

Marshals Service. It had taken some serious sweet talking and a large bribe to get him to hire on with us. The second part of the bribe was currently in the box he eyed hungerly.

"Penny, go check in with Dispatch. We're going to be a few." Q followed me into the sergeant's office. I placed the box on my desk and sat down, waving at Q to do the same. Once he did, I grinned and slid the box over to him. He pried opened the top and slowly lifted the rune covered tomahawk. It was a match for the Bowie knife I had already made for him. "This is beautiful," he said.

"Thanks." The shaft of the tomahawk was two feet in length and weighted for throwing. Traditional tomahawks usually had shafts made of hickory, ash, or maple, but this one was designed more as a tactical tomahawk and had a metal shaft instead of wood.

He flipped it around to study the hammer side. "No pipe bowl?"

"Um, no." I paused. "I didn't know you wanted one."

He smirked as he gave a couple of practice swings. "I'm messing with you."

"You're going to have to test it out. Any bugs, let me know."

He nodded and slipped it back into the box. "Thanks. This is great."

"Can I ask you a question that's none of my business?"

"Depends on what it is." He brushed a hand through his steel gray flat top.

"Why a tomahawk?"

"My mother was a member of a tribe native to Texas. I grew up using one. It was quite common to fight with a tomahawk and knife combo." He laughed at my surprise and waved a hand in my face. "What? You thought this was a tan? Surprised the book left out the part that the guy who stabbed Dracula was half Indian?"

I shrugged. "It's just that you've never talked about being Native American."

"It's a fext thing. You don't want to give too much away. Besides, how often do you go around telling people you're white?" He spun the tomahawk in his hand. "I had a set that had been spelled by the medicine man of my mother's tribe. He did a good job, but he was no runesmith and spells fade over time. Lost the 'hawk after a fight with a spellslinger, and I snapped the blade of the knife off in Vlad's heart."

He shook his head. "I really thought I had killed him. It was a couple of years before I heard he was still creeping around."

"How could you know? On another note," I reached into my drawer and drew out a gold badge and tossed it across the desk at him. "That's yours now, by the way."

He held it up. "Sergeant? What about Khan?

"He doesn't want it. Prefers the whole detective thing. Culain and I spent days trying to talk him into it."

"Gee, thanks. Always nice to know you're the second choice."

"No reflection on you. Both of you would be outstanding sergeants. But he was here first. Seniority counts. Just ask the rookie you made fetch the food."

He slipped the badge into his pocket. "Now what?"

I grinned evilly. "You know how you were excited to cycle off nights and onto days?"

"Oh no, what the hell?"

"We're moving you off Gabby's shift and have you replace me on Alpha Shift." We had been working as two shifts. I had been running Alpha Shift, and newly minted Sergeant Gabby Zhou had been running Bravo Shift. Two weeks on days, then two weeks on nights. Bravo Shift had just finished up doing their two-week stint on nights and were about to cycle to days.

"Where's that leave you? Bumping you up to Lieutenant? Going days with weekends off? Finally, be a REMF?"

I shook my head. "Putting together a Special Operations Unit. As our only detective, Khan will fall under it. Mickey as well, since he isn't exactly a normal street cop. Haven't put the rest of the team together yet."

Q frowned. "We don't have enough officers for two shifts and you're creating a sperate unit?"

"You catch that cat burglar last night? How about those terrorist cells Joubert has been funding?"

"Well, no."

"That's why we're putting together an SOU. These are specialized cases. It's not fair to expect patrol cops to have the time to track them down. Not when we have such a high call volume. We need a unit that can be proactive instead of reactive."

He tilted his head to the right for a second. "Yeah, I guess that makes sense. Who else is on the team?"

"Still sorting names. It's going to be small, though."

He pursed his lips. "You're going to make a mistake."

"Really? Do tell."

"You're not planning on putting Bad Penny on the unit because she's fresh out of the academy and you don't want to show favoritism, what with you living together and all."

I sighed. "We don't live together. She lives in a camper on our property. She's a tenant."

"Does she pay rent?"

"Well, no."

"Uh huh." He waved off my next comment." That's not the point. You're going to be so worried about projecting an image of impropriety you're going to pass her over. Which is a mistake because she would be highly effective in that type of unit."

He tilted his head again. "Why are you scowling?"

"Because when I broached the idea of forming an SOU to Culain he made the same argument. In fact, he made her being on the unit one of the requirements before he would sign off on it."

Q leaned back in his chair with a satisfied smile. "Wise beyond his years, he is."

"Yeah? How many years is that exactly?" I shook my head. "Never mind. Come on. Let me go see Culain to find out when he wants to swear you in as a sergeant. In the meantime, you need to find some stripes for your uniform."

Chapter Five

Culain's Guests

"Come in," came the reply as I knocked on the door to Culain Gowan's office. I stepped into the office to see the police commissioner wasn't alone. Two men in suits sat in the old wooden chairs in front of Culain's desk. Culain motioned me to shut the door. "Sergeant Mike Brennan, this is… Mister MacCian and Mister Donarson."

The chairs creaked and the room suddenly got exceedingly small as both stood up to shake my hand. I'm a big guy in height and in weight. Both guys were only a couple of inches shorter than me. Donarson had a shaved head and a bushy red beard. He was built like a tank and even through his suit I could tell his muscles had muscles.

MacCian, on the other hand, was tall and lean with curly blond hair. With an Irish lilt to his voice, he said, "You're the one that killed the wendigo then."

"That's right," I said as they sat back down. "With the help of others."

"This city of yours has had some trouble in recent years. I understand you are having trouble with a Jörmungandr now." Donarson's accent was from one of the Nordic countries. I wasn't sure which one.

"A what now?" I asked, confused.

"It means huge monster. He's referring to the dragon," replied Culain. "He has some experience with them. I had hoped he could share some light on our current predicament."

"You fought a dragon?" This sounded promising.

"No, but my father had several battles with one. Neither survived the last encounter." Donarson studied my face and sniffed several times before angrily turning to Culain. "He stinks of the wolf. When you said one of my uncles, you did not mean the adopted one, did you? He does not count and would harm your cause."

"No," answered Culain. "The silent one."

"Ah. That is promising, then." Donarson appeared slightly mollified. "But why does he stink of that wolf?"

"The dragon drove out the Vargar. They currently reside on Mike's land."

"Mmm. I don't like it." His chair creaked again as he leaned back, struggling to contain his bulk.

"I'm not following you guys." Annoyed, I looked around the room. "It feels like you're purposely talking over my head."

"It doesn't matter." MacCian waved his hand. "What part of Ireland are your people from, Sergeant Brennan?"

"Ballymote in County Clair." I felt like a lab rat as both of them studied me closely. "What does this have to do with dragons?"

"Oh, I just like to know who I'm dealing with. Culain and I haven't always gotten along so I'd rather judge you myself than rely on his words. I believe that Ma—that is to say, Mister Donarson —feels the same way."

"Aye." Donarson turned back to Culain. "He's a big one. But then the Silent One's mother is of my mother's people."

"For my part, I see all three factions of Ireland upon him," stated MacCian. He leaned closer as he studied me before giving a disappointing sigh. "I also see the runes of the berserker on him. He's ruined! Why would you do that? You know it caused problems for my son's journey as well as... Alcides and several others. There is a reason we have discouraged the use of blood runes."

"I had nothing to do with it. He did it to himself when I was in Faerie. I admit it's caused some complications, but we are dealing with it."

Three factions of Ireland? Is he talking religion? Catholic, Protestant, and who? Pagan? I'm missing something here. What's wrong with the blood runes?

"What are you talking about?" I asked, trying to understand. "How do the two of you know Culain?"

Culain stirred in his seat. "I've had dealings with Mister Donarson's family. Mister MacCian and I lived in the same

42

area for years. In fact, his son worked for me for a summer back when he was a teenager to pay off a debt. But enough of that. Let's get back to the dragon."

MacCian glowered at Culain after the son comment. Donarson gave me one last long look before nodding. "Fine then. The first thing you need to realize is that a Jörmungandr is not just a physical beast. Like Winter's Spirit of Hunger, it exists on more than one plane at a time."

I looked at Culain who rolled his eyes. "He means the wendigo."

"Oh. Is that why it controls David? It needs a body to exist on this plane like the wendigo?"

MacCian shook his head. "No, it's physical form is here on the plane. Why it retains the boy is beyond me."

Donarson nodded in agreement. "Its form is in this plane, but it feeds and gains power on an emotional plane. It's a creature of avarice."

"Then why is it hiding in the woods?"

Donarson shrugged. "The ways of Jörmungandrs are a mystery. No one knows how many there are or what motives they possess outside of greed."

MacCian drummed his fingers on is armchair. "Has it given you a name yet?"

"No."

"Mmm. Too bad. If we knew which one it was, we could have at least studied it's past behaviors." He continued to drum his fingers, lost in thought.

"Well, what can kill it? Will a magic sword do?" I summoned my sword in a flash of light.

Donarson stood and held out his hands. I gave him the sword and he held it close to his eyes, studying every inch of it. He even licked the blade before shaking his head. "No, it is a fine blade, but it is no match for a dragon. What do you call it?"

"I call it my sword. It doesn't have a name."

"Nonsense!" replied MacCian. "All magic weapons have names. Who was the smith who created it? They will have named it during the forging."

"I forged it myself, and I didn't give it a name."

"You're a runesmith?" remarked MacCian as both turned and glared at Culain. "Well, isn't that interesting. Culain forgot to mention that. I thought you were just a warrior."

"I'm a cop." A thought struck me. "No name, but it's been called Blood Drinker's Bane."

"No," corrected Culain, "they call *you* Blood Drinker's Bane. The weapon is called *The Sword with No Name.*"

Donarson muttered that to himself a couple of times and his face brightened. "I like it. It has just the right amount of drama attached to it. What is a cop?"

"A peacekeeper tasked with catching criminals," answered MacCian.

"So, a berserker warrior then." Donarson handed me back the sword which I dismissed. "One who forges his own weapons and follows the path of justice. Who has killed both a Body Thief and Winter's Spirit of Hunger?"

"If you mean a dybbuk and a wendigo, then yes, but both were group efforts."

Culain waved a hand at me. "In both instances, Brennan fought the final battle alone. He also slew a Lord of Hell and he did it with *The Sword with No Name*."

Damn. I could practically hear the italics when he said that. I think I just lost the no name fight.

MacCian's eyebrow went up at that last bit. "You mean he banished it back to Hell?"

"No, he killed it," Culain corrected.

"You lie, Forger!" Donarson growled. "I have tasted the mettle of that blade. It could not do so."

"He coated it with his own blood," Culain informed him calmly.

"So, it's true. Another one walks the earth then. It's been a long time." MacCian said. "That *is* promising. Still, I am not yet convinced to support your cause. Regardless of the family connections. You have been down this path before. The berserker runes worry me. It did not bode well for my son or the others."

"Yes," agreed Donarson. "We will see how Jörmungandr problem turns out. Then… maybe. You will still have many arrayed against you. Few remember you fondly after what you did."

Culain shrugged. "I have always accepted responsibility for my actions."

"Yes, but never remorse," said MacCian. "You wear your penance like a badge of honor!"

Culain's eyes narrowed. "Are you saying, you thought what they did was right?"

Donarson shrugged. MacCian, on the other hand, started to turn red. "Of course not. But it should have been war! There should have been a proportional response. What you did was... insane."

"To paraphrase a movie quote, they put one of yours in the hospital, you put two of theirs in the morgue."

"What are you talking about? It was a hell of a lot more than two! And on top of that, you sided against your own kind in the aftermath."

"It had to be done." Culain stood. "Now, are you going to hold old grudges against him because of me or judge him on his own merits?"

MacCian calmed himself with a visible effort. "No. That will not factor into my decision. It would not be fair."

Donarson put a hand on his shoulder. "Enough. This visit is too short. I do not want to spend it all arguing in this tiny room." One minute they were there, the next they were gone. No smoke, noise, or flash of light. Just gone.

"What the hell? Who were those guys?"

"It doesn't matter. I'm sorry. I had hoped to get more information about dragons out of them, but old arguments wouldn't stay buried." He sat back down in his desk, opened a desk drawer, and took out a folder. "There was another burglary last night. I need you to follow up on it. I want you to meet with the victim."

I sighed as I took out my notebook. It was always smoke and mirrors with him. I motioned him to continue and settled down to deal with mundane police work.

Chapter Six

Sex and Magic

The Chief drove down the long driveway to a mansion that looked like it belonged in 1940s Hollywood. As the car pulled to a stop, I studied the building and surrounding grounds. "See any obvious ways our thief could have made entry?"

Bad Penny shook her head. "No. The windows have bars, and I'm sure there are plenty of magical protections I can't see."

For several months now, the magi had been victims of a cat burglar, one who overlooked many valuable items in favor of singular objects. The only connection to the objects was that they were all magical. This particular victim was the Head of House Davenport.

I looked over at Bad Penny and suppressed a grin as I was about to ruin her day. "Grab your magic glasses and scour the outside. Once you're done, wait in the Chief."

"W-what? You're not letting me come inside?" Penny sputtered. "Why not?"

I tapped the stripes on my arm. "Because I said so, rookie."

"Oh, that's some bullshit."

"What's the matter? You usually prefer to stay in the car for, what did you call it? Oh yeah, *The boring part*."

"Yeah, well, those don't normally involve a leading practitioner in sex magic."

"This is a follow-up investigation, not a social call to get tips to up your game."

"No reason a girl can't do both."

"It's not too late to partner you with Eddy."

She slumped down in the seat. "Fine. I'll wait outside."

This time I openly grinned as I exited the car. She leaned out the window. "Mikey, wait. What the hell am I supposed to do when I'm done? Just sit here twiddling my thumbs?"

"I don't know, read something."

She looked around the car. "What?"

I pulled out the notebook I kept on me to jot down ideas for runes. "Here, look at the pretty pictures. Maybe you can even understand a word or two."

She gave me a one-fingered salute as I walked toward the house.

A male model wannabe who had apparently lost his shirt answered my knock at the door. "Llewellyn Police. I'd like to speak to the Wizard Davenport, please."

He looked at me and pouted. Seriously. This guy appeared in his late twenties, was about 6'2 with no body fat. He made Brad Pitt look ugly, and he was pouting like a three-year-old. "Do you have an appointment?"

"Hey, Zoolander, just show me to her."

He looked like he wanted to argue, but instead turned on his heel and started walking away. "Wipe your feet."

I followed him down a hall that had marble floors, walls, and nude statues. "I guess she likes marble, huh?"

Silence.

Okay then.

He stopped at a pair of double doors and opened them. "Toria, there's a rude policeman here to see you." He gave me a look.

"Come in, Sergeant Brennan." The voice was reminiscent of Kathleen Turner. I looked around the room.

Or perhaps Lauren Bacall.

In a city where many of the inhabitants used magic to ward off aging, it was often difficult to determine how old someone was. I found that their houses often reflected the time period of their twenties and thirties. The room, like the house, had a 1940s feel to it.

Victoria Davenport's platinum locks flowed over the shoulders of her dressing gown. She was stretched out on a white chaise lounge sipping from a champagne glass.

Sitting in a chair next to her was another woman, and while Davenport appeared in her forties, the other woman seemed in her mid-twenties and wore jeans and an olive-colored blouse. She didn't exude the *va-va-voom* feeling coming from Davenport. In fact, I'd put money on her being a vampire. I was fairly certain that wasn't wine in her glass.

I walked down the marble steps to the sunken portion of the room they were in. Davenport waved her hand over to an ottoman. "Please. Sit down. Would you like a refreshment?"

"No, thank you." I awkwardly sat down on the ottoman.

"Very well. Tomas, another round for the two of us."

Tomas gave me another look and left in a huff.

"What's his problem?" I shifted around on the ottoman, trying to get comfortable. At my age, I prefer my seating to have back support.

"Oh, my spouses and I announced we were looking for another husband. He thinks you're a suitor and is a bit jealous."

"Ah…"

She laughed. "Relax, Sergeant. I don't poach. Besides, you're a bit more rough-hewn than I normally go for."

"What a nice why to call someone ugly." I ran my hand over the branch like scars that traced down the right side of my face.

Both women laughed that time. The vampire finished her glass and said with an English accent, "That's not what she meant. Victoria prefers her men less alpha and more willing to let her be in charge. Besides, those scars are far from ugly. We both come from a time where scars added a rugged charm to a man."

"If you think I'm the person in charge at home, you haven't met my wife."

Davenport laughed again. "I've known Zoe for years. I was, what's the word? Frenemies? Yes, her mother and I were frenemies for many years. What the two of you have is a partnership. I'm too much of a diva for partnerships."

The vampire leaned forward. "May I ask what caused such a strange pattern?"

"Lightning. I'm sorry, you would be?"

Davenport swirled her champagne glass around. "I apologize. I'm being a dreadful host. Mike. May I call you Mike? You must call me Toria. Anyways, this is my friend Wila Moray."

Tomas entered with two full glasses on a serving tray and leaned over so the woman could exchange their old glasses with full ones. He turned on a heel and departed without a word. I watched him leave. "Toria, do you always have your husbands acting like the butler?"

"Goddess, no. Tomas isn't one of my spouses. He's my apprentice." Toria took a sip and lay back down on the chaise lounge.

I nodded and looked pointedly at Wila's wine glass. "So, are you of the Unaligned or are you of the line of Dracula?"

She smiled over the glass. "What makes you think it's one or the other?"

"Lately, those seem to be the only game in town when it comes to vampires."

She nodded. "I'm of the line of the Muse."

Valentine had told me of the Muse. A former Vampire Lord, her preference to make musicians, artists, and actors into vampires had gotten her kicked off the vampire council when she made too many famous ones.

I shifted on the ottoman again. "I've met one of your line. Rather famous. Likes to wear white jumpsuits and sing about blue moons."

She smiled. "He's going by Jesse these days. It was a whole thing. He's here somewhere if you want to speak with him."

"He wanted a peanut butter and banana sandwich." Toria shuddered. "I sent him to the kitchen."

"Anyways, it was my understanding that the Muse likes to turn her progeny loose and that's why... *Jesse* is with the Unaligned. So why do you refer yourself as being of the line of the Muse?"

"Because while I am friends with and admire Valentine, I have no wish to follow him. Vlad, even less so. You've met him?"

"Dracula?"

"Yes. What did you think of him?" Her voice was calm as she spoke.

I studied her face for a moment. It was serene. It was also an act. Her left hand was gripping the arm of her chair so tight I thought the metal would bend. She and Drac had a history, and it wasn't a pleasant one.

"I only met him for a few moments. In that short time, he was charming and polite."

"But?"

"But I don't think you can become a Vampire Lord without being cunning and ruthless, and I can't help but remember he was called The Impaler *before* he was Turned."

"Astute."

I nodded and turned to Toria as I pulled out a notebook. "You had a break-in."

"Yes. Very odd. Went right through my wards and none of my alarm spells went off."

"Yes. We've been plagued with a cat burglar for weeks now. They seem to have a way to circumvent wards. What was taken?"

Toria frowned. "That was the odd thing. She got into my vault, but all she took was one magic item. She left everything else behind."

"She?" My eyebrows went up. "Why do you think the thief was female?"

"I- I don't know. Just a feeling." She gave a confused look at Wila.

"Perfume," said the vampire.

Toria frowned again. "Perfume?"

"I smelled it when you had me look. I thought you had, too, but now that I think about it, it was faint enough that as a human you probably only registered it subconsciously."

Well, that's a lie. But she told it awful smoothly. Think I need to watch these two closely.

"Alright, then. What was the item stolen?"

"It was a silver jewelry tray." Toria seemed to relax at my question.

"What is it spelled to do?"

"It will recharge the magic on anything I place on it."

"That's a neat idea." As a runesmith, when I create a magic item, I link it directly into the ley lines in order for it to always have power. Wizards and witches can't do that. Any item they bespell has to have the spell reinfused with magic after a while. The tray would save her some time and effort and she would only have to recharge the tray. It was also a ridiculously powerful item that a lot of casters would want to get their hands on.

"Thank you. I got the idea from those charging mats they have for cell phones." She lifted a folder from the table next to her chaise lounge. "Here's a photo of it."

I slid the photo out of the folder she gave me. A square silver serving tray with handles on the sides. Looked to be about one foot wide and two feet long. I slid the photo back. "May I keep this?"

"Of course. That's why I had it brought out." She drained her glass. "Can I ask you why you left your partner outside?"

She laughed at my surprise. "I'm not only the Head of House Davenport, I'm also a senior member of one of the strongest wizard organizations in the city. You don't think I'm aware of what takes place on my property?"

"Cat thief excepted?"

"Ah... Yes, and I will close whatever loophole she used once I find it. So, about your partner?"

"Penny is new to the force. She's not ready to be in on interviews like this."

"Like what? Interviewing the sex fiend in her lair?" Toria's tone was light, but just a bit self-mocking.

"I didn't say that. Your professional reputation is flawless."

"Professional. Nice double entendre." She smirked.

"Not what I meant in the least."

"I'm teasing. I long ago came to terms with how many view sex magic." Toria curled a strand of hair around her finger. "Few realize how potent the energy created during sex is. When harnessed properly, it can be used as another reservoir for magic. Separate from a caster's internal reservoir. Similar to your wife's fire magic reserve."

She motioned to her face. "Its regenerative effects are peerless."

"You're leaving out the dark side to it. The Succubi and Incubi Those who kill through sex magic. Drain their victims of their life during sex."

"That's death magic cloaking itself as sex magic. Short-sighted fools who kill for immediate gains. My partners are willing participants who enjoy making the energy and harness it with me." She shifted gears with a wave towards the entrance. "The one outside. Bad Penny? Are you sleeping with her?"

"What? No!" I let my annoyance creep into my voice.

"You should. She likes you. I can feel it. You would make great magic together even if you were unable to cast it."

I gave her a flat stare and said nothing. She shrugged. "Well, is Zoe sleeping with her, at least?"

"No, Zoe and I are married."

She tilted her head to the side. "You said that like it's the end of it. A marriage doesn't have to be between two people. I myself have five spouses and, as I mentioned, am currently looking for another."

I frowned. I was past annoyed with how personal this had gotten. "We have very different outlooks on marriage."

"When you say 'we,' you mean you, correct? Zoe grew up in a coven that had a variety of different types of relationships. To be clear, this is *your* hang-up."

I leaned forward, causing the stupid ottoman to roll slightly. "You've met my wife? You think she would be willing be part of a harem? You wouldn't be able to find the ashes of anybody stupid enough to suggest it!"

The two glanced at each other and Wila shook her head slowly. "Typical male thought pattern."

I stared at her a moment trying to puzzle out her meaning. I looked back at Toria. "What are you talking about?"

"Why would you assume it's a harem?"

"Well, what the hell else would it be?"

"Ever hear of the term *throuple*?" Toria took another sip of her drink.

"I— huh. Well —" I paused to gather my thoughts. "Our marriage is fine the way it is."

"The idea of it makes you uncomfortable?"

"Yes. It's not how I was raised, and it sounds like a midlife crisis to me."

They both started laughing. I felt my face getting red. "What?"

Wila wiped a tear from her eye. "From our perspective, you are barely out of a crib."

Toria finished her glass and placed it down. "So, you admit it's your hang-up. That's a start. If Zoe were interested, would you consider it?"

"No!" My voice was full of exasperation. "Penny is a subordinate. It wouldn't be appropriate. That would be like you sleeping with your apprentice."

"I do more than sleep with him." Toria gave me a mocking smile.

"Wait, what?"

"Sex magic, remember? How else do you think I could teach him?" She frowned for a moment. "Though he needs to get over his preference for men if he's going to progress further. Limiting yourself to a single sex is to limit one's power."

"Umm..." Once again, I found myself grasping for words. I shook my head and angrily stood up. "Okay, what the hell is this really?"

Wila took a dainty sip of the red liquid in her glass. It was taking a massive effort on my part to ignore the fact that it had to be blood. "What do you mean, Mike?"

"A patrol officer could have taken this report. Culain told me Toria insisted that I was the one to respond. Why?"

Toria hid another smirk. She was enjoying this way too much. "You don't think as a city council member I don't rate a sergeant?"

"No, I don't. A council member should be treated as fairly and equally as anyone else in the city. No more, no less. And you didn't ask for a sergeant, you asked for me specifically. You're holding something back on the robbery, and for someone I've barely ever met, you've been asking a lot of personal questions regarding my family life. So, I'll ask again. What the hell?"

They both started laughing again. I threw up my hands and headed for the exit. "The hell with both of you."

"Wait, wait." Wila came over to me and tugged on my left arm. "Please, come back. We'll explain what we can."

I let her pull me back but refused to sit on that ridiculous ottoman again. Toria fanned her face with her hand as she tried to stop laughing. "Okay, okay. I'm sorry. What do you want to know?"

"Why did you want me to take the report?"

"To get to know you., Toria replied.

59

"Why?"

"As you know, one of the things you need to pull off your little plan is a vote from one of the Houses. Culain asked for my vote, but I don't know you enough to blindly agree."

"Oh." I felt the anger drain out of me. What we were planning was a well-guarded secret. If she knew, it's because Culain had informed her. "Well, he could have told me."

Toria shook her head. "I wouldn't let him. This way I could see the real you."

"What about her?" I pointed at Wila.

"I don't know what the vote is for, just that you need it," the vampire replied.

Toria shrugged. "I trust Wila, but Culain asked me to keep it a secret."

"What was all that crap about Penny and my marriage?" I grumbled.

"Well, I felt the energy between you and Penny and couldn't resist. Besides, I always thought Zoe would have had great potential in my field of practice. Witches always bring an exciting dynamic to the ceremonies. And the idea to combine fire and sex magic... Oh, the possibilities!"

I eyed her suspiciously. "Ceremony? Is that code for orgy?"

"Come to one and find out." Toria leaned forward and gave me a *come-hither* look. "Make sure you bring Zoe. As I said, I don't poach."

I looked over at Wila. "Are you part of her sex club?"

"No." She sat back down and picked up her glass. "I'm a bit Victorian in my nature. But I do like her passion. She's an artist in her outrageousness and like the Muse, I've always been a patron of the arts!"

I changed the subject. "So, what aren't you telling me about the theft?"

They carefully avoided looking at each other. Wila drained her glass and dabbed a napkin to the corner of her mouth. A crimson stain spread across the satin white napkin. "Whatever do you mean? We told you everything you need to know."

What I need to know? Not everything you know. Okay then. Silly games it is.

"That's a lot of bull, but whatever." I snapped my notebook closed and put it back in my shirt pocket. "Well, Toria. You got to know me. What do you think? Did I pass your test or whatever this is?"

"Your plan… It's never been done that I'm aware of. It's going to create a lot of ripples through the city. That alone, I'm in favor of it. Still…" She drummed her fingers on the table next her as she studied my face. "Why do you want to do it?"

I rested my hands on my duty belt. "The council won't pull the trigger. You lot keep letting politics and power grabs get in the way. Joubert should have been dealt with by now. They attacked our city and killed a lot of people. Instead of going to war with Joubert, you keep trying to broker a deal with them."

Toria held up an index finger. "To be fair, Mike, I wasn't on the council then. I wasn't made Head of House

Davenport until after the wendigo killed my cousin Standish."

Wila nodded. "My compliments on taking that thing down, by the way."

The socket where my eye use to be ached at the mention of the wendigo, and the berserker deep within my chest stirred. I squashed it back down. "Joubert still keeps attacking us. Now they been sending in small hit teams and still the council does nothing. My way cuts through the nonsense and puts them on the defensive."

Toria kept up the drumming. "I agree about the politics and power grabbing but, to be fair, we have a dragon to deal with."

"And even *that* your half-assing. Adding to the defensive wards doesn't solve the problem. Best case scenario, it just delays it. Worst case, the dragon attacks the outside world instead. You want the Normals dealing with it? Once they get over their disbelief, they'll just drop a tac nuke on the area and be done with it. Can either of you survive a nuke? I can't, and neither can the majority of the people in the city."

The drumming stopped and Toria pursed her lips. "That is a terrifying scenario you just painted. If I give you my vote, when are you unleashing your plan?"

"I'm not sure. I need to find a way to free my friend from the dragon first and deal with whatever Dracula is planning. After that, maybe. We are still gathering votes."

She gave a quick glance at Wila who nodded. "I'm tempted. Who else's vote do you have? Obviously, Martin Wheeler's and Valentine's, but who else?"

Now it was my turn to smile. My silence hung heavy in the air.

"Fine then. Keep your secrets." Toria swung her legs over and sat fully up. "Wila, what do you think?"

"I do like him. But I would wait until the dragon is dealt with. You give him what he wants, he'll drain your city of important resources. Resources that will be needed to fight the dragon when it finally attacks. My suggestion would be to… wait."

"Then it's settled. Once the dragon is dealt with, you will have my vote."

"On the other hand, if my plan goes through now, I would be in a better position to help craft plans to deal with the dragon."

"Tempting." The wizard tapped her chin with a finger. "A compromise then. I'll throw my support your way now. In return you don't move toward Joubert until the dragon is taken care of."

"I wasn't planning on it."

"Excellent. Then we are in accord." Toria stood, signaling that the interview was over. "Good day, Sergeant. Please give my compliments to your wife."

"Wait. I need to see the crime scene first."

"Oh, I'm sorry." Toria shrugged. "It was in my sanctum when it was stolen."

Sanctum was the fancy word wizards used for their workshop. They never allowed outsiders in. It wasn't the first time I ran into that particular roadblock.

"Fine then."

Tomas appeared as if by magic, which meant it probably was. "This way, Sergeant."

"Ladies." I nodded and followed him out.

As I exited the building, I spotted a woman leaning into Bad Penny's window. I was too far away to hear what they were talking about. She appeared in her mid-twenties and wore ripped jeans and a sage green nylon M1 flight jacket, what most civilians would call a bomber jacket. She had various patches sewn on it that appeared to be bands of some sort. The rips in her jeans showed a red tartan material sewn underneath as patches. She finished the look off with a pair of black Doc Martens.

She pulled her head out of the window and waited for me as I approached. Her black hair was shaved on the sides with some sort of tussled look on top and pink tips hung down her forehead. "Hey, I'm—"

"A vampire." I cut her off. "What are you doing?"

"Umm, actually, I was introducing myself to you. I'm called Jett." She had a New York accent. She reached up and tapped her mouth with her fingers. "What gave me away? Are my fangs showing?"

"Trick of the profession." I raised my eyebrows. "Now that I answered your questions, how about you answer mine?" With the blood runes, my temper was always boiling just under the skin. I'd been doing a good job of keeping it in check, but my annoyance with Toria and Wila had cranked it up a notch. I took a breath and waved a hand. "Sorry, I'm a bit annoyed right now. What are you doing here?"

"I've never seen a rockabilly cop before. I came over for a chat. I had no idea it was the infamous Bad Penny." She glanced down at Penny. "Got to say, like the look."

"Infamous?" Penny stuck her head out the window.

"Sure, your name's being kicked around in certain circles. Bad Penny, the girl who went one on one with the wendigo and lived! Kicking ass's and doing it with style.

Oh God, her head is going to be too big to fit back through the window.

"There seems to be several groups of vampires in Llewellyn these days. So, who are you with?"

"Oh, I'm not with either of the V's."

"V's?" I frowned in confusion.

"Yeah, Vlad or Valentine." She started singing to the tune of a WB cartoon from the 90's. "One's too stiff and the others insane."

"Really?" I let my disbelief shown in the tone of my voice.

"Sure, I'm here with Wila. She's an old friend and didn't want to come to the city alone. You guys look busy. I'll leave you alone." She pulled a pen and a scrap of paper from her jacket. She scribbled down something on the paper and handed it to Penny. "Give me a call sometime. We can hang out while I'm here."

"Sure." Penny pocketed the note.

"Bye." Jett waved and walked away. I waited until she was gone and got back in the car.

Penny sighed happily and pulled out my notebook. She opened it to a spot she had bookmarked with an empty salt packet. She shook off any stray grains of salt and motioned to the pages. "This is fantastic! Why didn't you do it? You'd practically be a superhero."

"I should hope so. I stole enough ideas from them coming up with this." I took the book from her and smiled when I looked over the drawings and notes on the page. "This was supposed to me my magnum opus. I worked on it for years. I even redesigned my armor to be able to integrate it."

"Couldn't get it to work?"

"No, it worked beautifully." I snapped the book close and put it back in my pocket. "The problem was me."

"Scared, Mikey? It's a common enough phobia."

"Airborne ranger, remember?" I shook my head. "No. I had trouble mentally controlling it. It was too complex for my brain and there was a serous lag time." The Chief started up and we pulled away.

"How serious?"

"Enough to get me killed."

We rode in silence for a few minutes.

"You need a Jarvis."

"What?"

"Jarvis. It's from the—"

"I've seen the movies," I interrupted.

"So, get an AI to control your gizmo." She sat back, satisfied she solved the problem. "That will leave you free to alternate between making wisecracks and giving dark and brooding looks."

"One, this is magic, not technology. Two, that was fiction, and this is real life. There are no artificial intelligences in existence. And I don't brood!"

"Smolder?"

"Definitely not."

"Romantically heroic."

"Now you're just stringing words together."

"Has a hot wife and just a hint of dad body."

"For the love of God, please stop!"

"What about Crystal?"

"I don't have—wait! What?"

"Crystal, you've described her before as a Magical Intelligence. Could she control your doohickey while you do all the manly fighting stuff?"

"I — Huh!" I mulled it over. "I have no idea. I'll have to think about."

"Great! Now you do me."

"Excuse me?"

"Short and stunning is a good start."

"We're not doing this."

"Flexible and flexible."

"I said — wait, why did you say flexible twice?"

"Describes my body *and* my willingness to try new things," she said with a cheesy leer.

I pinched the bridge of my nose and sighed.

"Plays for both teams. Maybe more…"

I refused to consider what the other teams might be made of and threw up my own description. "Reckless and forgets training."

"Yeah bay-bee, now your gettin — Hold on. What are you talking about?"

"Let's go back to how I found you after leaving the wizard's house."

"I checked the area and then stayed in the car like you told me to."

"Did you already forget everything you learned at the academy? As soon as someone approached the car, you should have got out. Instead, you left yourself in a tactically unsound position. If you let someone get that close without getting out of the car, you're now in a kill box. If she had pulled a gun on you, you would have been popped before you got a potion out. Did you at least clock she was a vampire?"

"Yeah, you were right about the breathing thing. They forget to do it a lot when they're not speaking." She smiled and raised up the paper between her fingers. "But, hey. I got digits!"

I shook my head. "Don't call her."

"Of course, I'm going to call her. She's cute and funny." She let a smile slowly spread across her face. "Unless you're jealous..."

"No, and I'll give you two reasons. Number one, never take someone's contact info for personal reasons when you're on duty. Especially on a call."

"Why not?"

"It's a good way to lose your job." I mimicked Jett's New York accent. "'Officer Harper has been harassing me with phone calls trying to get me to go out with her. I had no choice but to give her my number. She threatened to arrest me if I didn't.'"

She laughed at my impression. "That doesn't happen."

"It does. Ever show a little cleavage to get out of a ticket?"

"Only once. It didn't go so well."

"What happened?"

"He wasn't interested in girls. Gave me a $250 ticket."

"Maybe. Or maybe he knew what you were doing and felt insulted you thought he would have fell for it."

"What's your point?"

"So sometimes there is a miscommunication. Driver is flirting with the cop to get out of a ticket and the cop thinks it's real. They ask for the driver's phone number and now the driver is worried if they don't give it, they'll get the ticket or worse. Never underestimate how intimidating an authority figure can be. And remember, you are now an authority figure."

I reached into the cooler I kept on the back seat and dug two sodas out. I handed one to Penny and opened mine. "Anyways, the cop thinks they made a connection with someone and gives them a call, but the driver feels like maybe they were forced into giving out the number and reports it to the department and the cop is jammed up."

I shrugged and took a sip. "Sometimes it's just malicious and they take an opportunity to damage a cop. The point is, don't ask, give, or accept phone numbers for personal reasons while working."

"Huh." She chewed her lip for a minute. "But what happens when it *is* a cop overstepping their bounds? You can't tell me that doesn't happen in the real world."

"Of course. Occasionally it happens even though most departments take every precaution to weed out people that will disgrace the badge. Here in Massachusetts, you have to pass a written test, an intense background check, a medical, a psychological exam, a PT test, and that's just to start the academy. You already know what the academy is like. Studying the laws and ethical behavior takes up the majority of the academy. Even more then PT and tactical training."

"Which there is still a lot of." She grimaced.

"Yup, and you get tested on it every few weeks. How long was your academy again?"

"Twenty-six weeks."

"And once you all graduated, you go through the training program where you are evaluated by a training officer. That's me, by the way.

"Once that's done, you are on probation for a year and anytime during that probation period, you can be let go for any infraction. As I said, that weeds out a lot of people who have no business wearing the uniform. The few that escape it will eventually trip up and get fired. Unfortunately, those few always seem to damage the reputations of their departments when they go down. So, no flirting on the job or..."

"Or what?"

"Suspended and in big trouble."

"Okay."

"Fired and unemployed."

"Mikey, I get it."

"Disgraced and sued."

"You made your point."

"Penniless Penny and living in a carboard box."

"Enough."

"You're right, this *is* a fun game!"

She sighed and stared out the window as we drove toward downtown.

Chapter Seven

Eddy Brunching Badly

Once we were back downtown, I had the Chief do a random patrol of the city. Penny finally turned back from the window. "I hear you about trying to weed out bad apples, but there is a lot of stuff on the news right now about police misconduct. It makes you wonder."

"Sure." I looked over some of the businesses we passed, looking for anything out of place. "But you have to look at the numbers, not the spin the media puts on it."

Penny scanned the other side of the street. "What are the numbers?"

"Not counting the magical communities, there are just under 700,000 law enforcement officers in the United States, but there are roughly only 900 officer involved deaths each year. Every single one is investigated, and if the officer committed a crime, they are charged. And that's as it should be. There are very few occupations that have such oversight.

"Do you know how many doctors there are in the U.S.?"

"No?"

Just under a million. Studies show that around 195,000 hospital deaths in the U.S. were due to preventable medical malfeasance. Some studies have it much higher. A couple of years ago, one newspaper listed medical errors as the third leading cause of death on the United States at 440,000."

"Jesus! Reminding me to cancel my next physical."

"There is a big gap between 900 and 195,000, but you never hear about doctors in the news like you do cops. That's not even taking into the fact that the majority of those police involved deaths were justified. But then that's one of the sticky points, isn't it?"

"What do you mean by that?"

"The media picks who they go after, and cops are low-hanging fruit. Much easier to vilify than doctors. After all, doctors help you get better. Cops, on the other hand, are usually telling you to stop something you want to do or to do something you don't want to do. Nobody likes an authority figure. The media hypes up officer involved shootings, reporting the stories in inflammatory ways, because that's what sells. On top of that, they are in such a hurry to get the story out these days, the media often gets facts wrong. There have been plenty of times in the past year where a news media has reported the person shot by the police was unarmed when it turns out they were."

"Okay, but they issue a correction when they find out they're wrong?"

"Sometimes. But 'unarmed' is in the headline. It's what people remember, not the correction that's buried a couple of pages in several weeks later. By that time the damage is done. An investigation or trial doesn't listen to the media. It's about the facts. And if, based on the facts, the officer is found to have acted responsibly, there are riots because people armed with false information by the media, think an injustice was done." I tapped the dash. "Chief, go around the block and come up Edison Alley."

"You see something?"

"Maybe. A group caught my attention. Worth a second look." I opened my soda and took a swig. "My point in all this is the media uses inflammatory comments and images to make ratings, but that in turn makes it harder to investigate a police officer involved death."

"I would think it's the opposite. You have public scrutiny making sure it's investigated properly."

"Sure. As long as it's fair, impartial, and correct. Inflammatory articles for the sole sake of selling newspapers corrupts that. Police should absolutely be held to a higher standard, but that standard can't be a sliding scale based on how many people get mad based on misleading articles. It has to be based on facts. Police should be held accountable for their actions but so should the media, and right now, they aren't." The Chief crept down the alley, stopping just inside. This allowed us to view the sidewalk across the street. "There are already checks and balances. But when the media's actions stir people up to the point there are riots, it makes it impossible to have a fair investigation. Especially when the media doesn't take the time to get the facts right." I pointed to a group on the sidewalk. Three males and a female. The female and two of the males wore swords. "Keep an eye on that group."

"Swords. Right." Bad Penny dug out her binoculars. I triggered my runic eye to zoom in and see them better, something I forgot to do the night on the bridge.

It wasn't illegal to carry weapons in Llewellyn, but not long after the wendigo incident, someone chopped Lancelot Deluc's head off at his home in France. A preliminary investigation showed that his chauffeur found the body and then looted his collection of magic weapons, auctioning them off. Joubert managed to get a hold of a couple of them, and they have some half ass runesmith turning out inferior copies, copies they keep arming hit squads with and sending our way. The war with Joubert had evolved into a cold war but that didn't mean people weren't getting killed.

"Yeah, that looks fishy alright. You want to F.I. them?" Penny lowered the binos.

F.I.s, or field interviews, are when a cop briefly stops someone to determine their identity when there is reasonable suspicion of criminal activity. "Let's just watch them for a bit."

"Okay. So, you're saying people shouldn't be allowed to protest?" Penny dug out a hyde potion and twirled it in her fingers.

"Peaceful protests are fine and it's a bedrock of this country. Rioting, looting, and hurting people is not."

The female of the group a woman in her early 40's appeared to be chastising the only guy without a sword. He wore a long coat in the style of a spellslinger. The others wore leathers. They looked like bikers without motorcycles. I had a buddy who had a term for that: *sidewalk commandos*.

"Wait a minute." I held up a finger as Eddy Feenix exited a diner not far from the group. His girlfriend Vera was with them. She must have met him for lunch. Eddy is an odd duck in many ways, but he has the instincts of a long-time street cop. He clocked the group right away and frowned, tabbing his badge.

Eddy's over-the-top Australian accent came out of Penny and my badges. "Officer Feenix to Dispatch. I'm going to be going off with a group of four at Kinder Street by Berube Road. Three males, one female. Three are armed with swords. One possible spellslinger."

"Shit! You want to call him off?"

"Too late." I pointed to the group who took notice of Eddy walking towards them. Vera waited in front of the diner. I tapped the dashboard again. "Chief, head over there."

As the supernova pulled out of the alley, the spellslinger whipped out a wand and fired an eldritch bolt directly into Eddy's chest. Eddy crumpled to the ground and his body burst into flames. Vera's eyes glowed a bright emerald green, and orange strands of yarn shot forth from her crocheted sweater and impaled the spellslinger as it they were rods of steel.

"Fuck!" Penny downed her potion as the Chief gunned it. I tabbed my badge. "Officer down. Eddy's down. One of the males is down. All units to Kinder and Berube."

The group saw us and split up. One male ran down the sidewalk, and the female ran into a department store while the last male fled down a narrow alley. Penny and I jumped out as the Chief pulled up to Eddy's ashes. Penny's muscles bulged and her skin stretched as she shifted to her hyde form. I summoned my Colt 1911 in a flash of light as Penny tore the sleeves off her shirt. Her uniform was spelled to adjust to her size changes, but she claims it's binding on the arms. After returning her uniforms half a dozen times, the spell weavers finally just added a self-mending feature so the sleeves could reattach and called it a day. Bad Penny won't admit it, but I think she just likes the look.

Vera retracted the yarn and the spellslinger's body slumped to the sidewalk, dead as a doornail.

"Vera, stay with Eddy. Chief, go after the one that ran down the road." I headed into the store. "Penny, let's go."

I tabbed my badge and gave an update of the locations of the group as I forced my way through fleeing customers. While the people of Llewellyn were magical in nature, that didn't mean most of them had a stomach for violence. I pushed through into an empty area. It's amazing how many people get out of your way when you a very large man with a scary, scarred up face and holding a gun. I scanned the area. "Penny, I need you to—"

No Bad Penny in sight. I sighed and tabbed my badge. "Penny, where are you?"

Her voice was gravelly as it came from my badge. "I'm chasing the one that ran down the alley."

"Shit." You never split up like that. If it's a trap, you're fucked without backup. "Damn rookie."

I was about to call her back when a sword snaked out from a clothes rack and knocked my gun out of my hand. I backpedaled and summoned my sword, and the female emerged from the rack. "Drop the sword. You're under arrest."

"Ace of diamonds. Eh!" She circled to my left. Her accent was French Canadian.

"Okay, Ace. The order still stands. I slipped three steel balls out of my pocket and threw them up in the air. They hung there as their runes sent data to my runic eye. I hadn't had time to rebuild my shield yet, but this was the third version of my eye, and the surveillance orbs were some of the new features that came with it.

"No, Brennan. You're the ace of diamonds." She kept one eye on me as she studied the orbs.

I knew what she meant. When I was deployed, we would have playing cards with the photos and information of high-value targets. It helped us ID them if we came across any. It looked like Joubert was doing the same thing.

I gave her a once-over as she studied the orbs. Fortyish with grayish brown hair in a short cut and blue eyes. She had a stocky build but moved with precision. Felt ex-military to me.

Her sword was a simple Crusader style. It was crudely made, and the formation of the runes along the blade marked it as the product of Joubert's unknown runesmith.

"Nice sword." The orbs' info showed the store was clear. I blinked the screen out of my vision and summoned my armor. "Not as impressed with your leathers, though."

"Yeah, about that…" She touched the blade of her sword with her left index finger and her flesh changed to steel. Even the runes were duplicated and glowed along her skin.

"Okay." I bobbed my head in acknowledgement." I kind of walked into that one. Nice Gift."

"Thank you." She feinted with her sword. I fell for it and attempted to block, allowing her to score a hit along my arm. Her sword skittered across my armor but didn't damage it.

Okay, she's got skills with a sword, too.

She parried a series of attacks and went on the offensive. I blocked most of them and my armor stood up to the rest. Based on that, I trusted my armor and gave her a slight opening on our next round. She took the bait and overextended herself enough that I was able to score a good slash down her off arm. My sword cut through her steel skin and blood ran down through her arm.

She grimaced and her skin sealed back up. She tried not to show it, but she favored her off hand in the next flurry of swings.

Her metal covering formed up, but she didn't heal underneath. I can work with that.

I kept her busy with a series of attacks alternating between her right leg and shoulder. This is why most sword wielders hate fighting a left hander. The attacks come from the wrong side. She managed to parry my last attack when one by one, all three of my orbs slammed into the back of her head at a high speed. Her sword dropped from listless fingers and her eyes glazed over. She took a step towards me and tried to say something before collapsing, her skin reverting to normal.

I mentally ordered the orbs back and they neatly dropped into my palm as I canceled the propulsion runes. About the size of a ping pong and made of solid steel, they made deadly projectiles. Word of my blood runes had gotten around town, which sucks because I'm a big fan of having something unexpected up my sleeve. The orbs were my latest trick.

I checked over the suspect. She was breathing, and there was a large lump forming on the back of her head. I slipped my magic canceling handcuffs on her and checked for weapons. Worried about possible brain damage, I poured a healing potion down her throat and tabbed my badge. "Penny, what's your status?"

"Bringing my guy back now. You get yours?"

"Yeah. Meet you where Eddy dropped."

My suspect was starting to come round, and I hauled her to her feet and frog marched her out the door. There were several officers on scene and perimeter tape was set up around the bad guy Vera took out.

Bad Penny was already waiting with Vera, but I didn't see Eddy. Penny's suspect looked like he had his jaw fractured, and he could only see out of one eye. I raised my eyebrows at Penny.

She shrugged, still in hyde form. "He stabbed me in the boob with his sword and, well, the assassins Joubert sends are usually more durable."

"Make sure you do a use of force report along with your arrest report."

"Yeah, yeah," she said with an annoyed tone. A hyde's healing ability was just this side of impossible, but that didn't mean getting stabbed hurt any less.

I looked at Verna as the wagon officer and a couple others took custody of our prisoners. "How's Eddy? I don't see him."

"After he reformed, he went after the one your c-car was ch-chasing." She pointed at the Chief, who was heading back towards us.

I walked over to where he parked. "You get him?"

The car honked once, and Eddy stepped out of the driver's side. "We got em, Sarge."

Eddy went around to the back of the car and pulled a cuffed suspect out of the trunk. Penny made a face. She'd spent some time in that trunk during Oct5 and hadn't enjoyed it. Eddy handed over his prisoner to the wagon officer.

"How you doing, Eddy?" He felt all the pain from the flames that consumed and regenerated his body, something I don't think I could ever get used to. Over the centuries, Eddy learned to shake it off.

"Fair dinkum, Sarge." He adjusted the crocheted octopus hat he wore with his uniform. I hated that thing. It looked completely unprofessional but since it's magic recreated Eddy's clothes after they burned to ash, I tolerated it. Everyone agreed it was better to look at a silly hat than a naked Eddy.

"Okay, Eddy, you and Vera head to the station to give your statements. Vera, you might want to contact an attorney."

Vera adjusted the oversize glasses she wore. "Why would I need an attorney?"

"I think that would be self-explanatory. You just killed a guy."

"B-but he killed Eddy first."

"But you know that doesn't stick with Eddy. Your justification might be a bit shaky there."

"Hold on there, Sarge. She's good based on *Sweeny v. Feenix*." Eddy stepped next to her.

I tilted my head. "And what, pray tell, is that?"

"Case law that happened while you were off the force. The gist is that nobody knows if my next death could be my last, therefore any of my deaths are to be treated as real until such time as I come back to life," he said smugly. "And on top of that, Vera could argue self defense and defense of others in taking down a murderous man armed with a sword."

I smiled. "Fair enough, but it will still need to be investigated, and I stand by my suggestion that she speaks with an attorney."

I looked over at Penny and rubbed my jaw. "We need to get you equipment that falls below *beat the bad guy to a pulp.*"

"What, like, pepper spray?"

"Yeah, maybe."

Eddy's face took on a thoughtful look. "You know, Sarge, I might have something for that. Let me get back to you."

We cleared the scene and headed back to the station. Penny had gotten quite good at judging my moods and beat me to the punch. "Okay, what did I do wrong this time?"

"First off, you're still new at being a cop. There is a learning curve, so don't give yourself too much grief."

"But?"

"You shouldn't have run off after that guy."

"He was getting away."

"So what? There was a reason I told you to come with me. It could have been a trap. You should have stayed with me and we could have taken her down together. There were other officers enroute to the scene, and they had a description."

She squirmed in the seat. "Eddy went after his guy."

"Actually, I sent the Chief after the other guy. Eddy teamed up with him when he recovered, keyword there being *team.*"

"Still, you sent the Chief alone. Same thing."

"It's harder to lure an automobile into an area to spring a trap, and while the Chief is both sentient and awesome," I patted the steering wheel. "Most damage to him can be repaired because he's a machine. You and I are human. Dead is dead. Can't fix that with a socket wrench."

"You've done the solo thing plenty of times."

"Those were dire situations when I didn't have a choice." I shifted in my seat to look at her. One of the many perks of having a car like the Chief was I could safely take my eyes off the road. "In a normal situation it wouldn't have been a big deal, but Joubert has consistently targeted the Llewellyn police. Look what happened to Officer Knox. Archibald Campbell and Deadly Sinz grabbed him on a stakeout and used him as the victim in a demon summoning ritual."

"Yeah... Poor Knoxie." Penny's voice was subdued. What happened to Templeton Knox hit everybody hard. His body disappearing from the morgue certainly didn't help his coworkers find closure.

 "Until they are dealt with, any encounter that has even a whiff of Joubert has to be viewed as a potential trap. Understood?"

"Got it. Makes sense. It was just... you know... heat of the chase."

"Good." I tapped on the dash. "Head back to the station please, Chief. Time to fill out some paperwork."

Chapter Eight

Dating and the Undead

The rest of the day was routine, and the shift soon ended. It was my turn to cook, which meant take-out, because no one will allow me near a stove. Penny and I picked up a stack of pizzas and brought them home.

I watched Morgan finish off a slice of Hawaiian pizza and reach for another. I slid the box across the table closer to her. "How was your day?"

She shrugged. "Pretty good. Emala helped me put up a rope swing."

"You already have a rope swing."

"Yeah, but now Rosalyn and I can swing on them at the same time."

"Ah. Nice. Whose idea was that?"

"Mine."

"I bow before your pint-sized wisdom."

Morgan did the Queen wave at me with one hand and shoveled more pizza into her mouth with the other.

I stayed away from the anchovies and mushroom atrocity that Zoe insists on ordering, snagging a Hawaiian slice for myself instead. "Zoe, what were you and Emala up to?"

"New batch of potions, and we attended a coven meeting," she said between mouthfuls. Zoe was half my size but always managed to put twice as much pizza away as me.

"That reminds me, I'm down a potion. Okay if I restock?"

My wife frowned. "You got hurt again? What happened?"

"Not me. A prisoner." I shoveled some more bacon cheesy fries onto my plate.

Her frown deepened. "You shouldn't waste potions on criminals. They are expensive to make."

"Couldn't be helped. Possible brain damage as a result of my actions."

"Did you do the orb trick? Oh, my goddess, you used my orb trick, didn't you?" Emala leaned forward with an excited look on her face. It had been her idea to use them as a sneak attack. "How did it work?"

"Pretty good. Took my suspect right out of the fight."

"Nice! Full speed?" The teen witch took a slice from the vegetarian pizza that she had all to herself. The rest of us were respectable meat eaters.

"No, that would have killed her for sure."

"Anything else interesting happened today?" After all the lessons Zoe was putting her through every day, Emala like to unwind listening to stories from Bad Penny and I's shift. Edited for content, of course.

"Well, Penny got hit on by a vampire today," I said, totally throwing Bad Penny under the bus so I could finish my pizza in peace.

"Really! Was he cute?" Emala eyed Penny who gave me a dirty look.

"It was a *she,* and yes she was," Penny answered her.

"You going to see her?"

"No, apparently we aren't allowed to flirt on duty." Penny threw a fry at my direction. I snagged it out of the air and popped it in my mouth.

Morgan gave me a triumphant fist bump. "Nice catch, Daddy."

"Thank you, sweetie."

Penny's eyes narrowed. Wait a minute. What was the other reason?"

"What?"

"You said there were two reasons I shouldn't call her, but you only explained one." She eyes me suspiciously. "What was the other."

"Well... she's a vampire."

"*What?* Are you kidding me?"

"No, of course not."

"That's racist."

Now it was my turn to frown. "No, it's not."

"Actually Mike, it does sound that way." As a Hispanic, Emala was the only person of color at the table.

Zoe shook her head. "It's not the same thing."

"Sure, it is." Penny sounded furious.

I went to the living room and poured myself an Irish whiskey with ice at the bar before returning to the kitchen and sitting back down. "You are making an assumption that being a vampire is like being someone of another race. They are not.

"Regardless of race, religion, orientation, skin color, creed, or culture, humans are still human regardless. Judging each other on such differences is stupid and small minded. Vampirism on the other hand, are undead creatures that view you as a food source. Their very design makes them monsters."

Emala dropped her pizza slice on her plate. "That sounds like a lot of what the witch hunters say about us."

Zoe shook her head. "There are good witches and bad witches, but the power they wield doesn't determine that. The difference between them is how they choose to act, just like most sentient beings. Vampires are not like that. They have to fight their very nature in order to be good, and most either can't or don't want to do that."

I placed my drink on the table which my wife promptly lifted and put a napkin under. Our kitchen table was nicked and marred by the hundreds. It was neither new nor an antique. A whiskey tumbler without a coaster was not going to be the end of it. I rolled my eyes at her and continued. "Vampires are created by the very act of murder. They are killed and then brought back to life by their sire. They awake ravenous, and most kill their victims the first time they drink. It's true some learn to control their hunger, but their society normally views that as survival not because of any concern for you, their livestock."

As I was saying this, Penny pulled a vodka bottle from the freezer, and mixed it with lemonade, and plopped back into her chair. "Then explain Valentine, Khan, and Charlie the baker."

"Valentine's circumstances were unique. Khan and Charlie are lucky enough to have no masters. That doesn't diminish the craving for blood, though. It's their life source and only form of nourishment."

"But vampires don't have to drink human blood. Khan only feeds from animals," Penny pointed out.

"And, according to Khan, it tastes like crap, and he has to drink twice as much to get the needed nourishment. Valentine and Charlie use blood banks, but that requires them to trust the supplier to be on the up and up."

Emala finished off her slice. "What do you mean by having no masters?"

"Just that. Both of their masters were destroyed. Most vampires aren't so lucky. A vampire can be controlled by their sire as well as the vampire who made their sire and so forth and so on up to the head of their line. If you are fifty vampires from the top, that means there are forty-nine vampires who can control you with ease. That doesn't even take into account ancient vampires who can bend a young vampire to their will. Vampire society is vicious and cruel and likes to toy with their food, and if your sire is an evil son of a bitch, congrats! Now so are you."

I took a sip and felt the burn of the whiskey. "A vampire without a sire has a chance, a small one mind you, and might be able to overcome the biological need to rip your throat out and drink your blood. The craving is there for each one of them. Ask Khan. He doesn't just drink animal blood because the idea of human blood disgusts him. It's one of the ways he controls his bloodlust."

"*I'm* a vampire!" Morgan proudly announced to the table.

"W-what?" Emala asked.

"One of my other selves." Morgan's eyes glazed over for a second. "I tried counting how many realities away it was, but it was too much."

Zoe raised an eyebrow. "Does she have a sire?"

"Not anymore. I killed them all." Morgan swished a fry around in the ketchup on her plate and popped it into her mouth. She chewed it with great gusto.

"Your other self killed all of who, sweetie?" I asked.

"All the other vampires. I'm the only vampire left there. And a queen!"

"Queen of who, Morgan? You said your other self killed all the other vampires."

"Merica!"

"Your other self is Queen of the United States?" I pressed a little further.

"No, all of it. Up and down, too."

"Canada and Mexico? Your other self is Queen of North America?" I looked over at my wife who shot me a concerned look.

"Yeah, but no. More." Morgan's eyes glazed over again. This time for a little longer. "My armies are fighting in… What's the name of the cartoon with the birds? Same name."

"Rio? Your army is trying to take Rio?"

"Yup! Gonna get both con-ta-tents." She took another bite of her pizza. Morgan's ability to communicate with alternate reality versions of herself scared the hell out of Zoe and I, and we didn't know what to do about it. But we learned to roll with the punches after raising a warlock for a son.

Zoe gave me a slight shake of the head and turned back to the vampire conversation. "Vampires like Khan and Charlie are what Valentine is betting on. The problem is they are few and far between because other vampires kill or banish them. Valentine and a few reformers are trying to create a haven for vampires like that, but the rest of the Vampire Lords are trying to sabotage it. Why else do you think Dracula is here?"

Bad Penny pounced on that. "You just said that Valentine's people and some others are okay. Why not Jett then?"

"Remember when the Alchemy Guild addicted you to the hyde formula in order to control you?" I asked, hesitating to bring up such a painful memory.

"I'm not bloody likely to forget it," Penny snapped.

"Now imagine if that addiction was a thousand times worse and everyone around you had the hyde potion inside them. All you have to do is tear them open and drink it." I held up my whiskey and shook it, a not-so-subtle reminder of the stereotype of my people. "Everyone knows or is related to an addict of some form. We know an addiction can make a good person do bad things. The blood addiction of vampires is so much worse. Aside from suffering that addiction just by being a vampire, what do we know of your friend Jett?"

"I don't know, she's cute and funny. Where are you going with this? Khan has the same so-called addiction and you hired him as a cop."

"We know Khan's sire is dead and can't control him. We also know he's successfully fought his blood lust for decades. And… Culain, Valentine and I watch him like a hawk. If need be, we are prepared to take him out if he ever breaks bad."

"Jesus, Mikey!"

I shrugged. "Khan asked us to. Says it gives him peace knowing we'll never let him become a monster. Why do you think he turned down the sergeant's job? We all know he'd be great at it."

"Paperwork sucks!" Penny got a grin from Emala.

"Sort of. The job has additional stresses with it. Stresses he doesn't want added to his current burden. He's a man that has carefully mapped out his breaking points and stays very far away from them. Do you know if Jett does that?"

"No."

"Do you know if her sire lives? What line is she?" I rapidly peppered her with the questions.

"She told us that she wasn't part of Dracula's line," Penny pointed out.

"Right, but she also said she wasn't part of Valentine's faction. Know any other good vampire factions out there?"

"She said she was with what's her name's?"

"Wila. Who we don't know a damn thing about." That reminded me, I needed to call Valentine and get the rundown on her. "How old did she say she was as the two of you talked outside in broad daylight?"

"Twenty-six."

"So, we know she's a liar." I took a sip as Zoe nodded thoughtfully.

"You don't know that!"

"Yes, we do," Zoe stated. "You were outside in the sunlight?"

"Yeah…"

"She's at least a full vampire than. They can't be raised to a full vampire until they've existed for at least twenty years as a vampling. She's at least in her forties."

"I nodded. "She was pretty comfortable in the sun. My money is on master vampire."

"So? Age is just a number." Penny was starting to sound unsure.

"Gross!" Being a teen, Emala strongly believed that anyone over thirty is ancient and should be put out on an ice flow.

"She was wearing a pretty specific fashion choice," I continued. "One that would be far from when she was raised."

"I'm getting tired of saying *so*," Penny said.

"For vampires, that's usually camouflage for when they hunt."

Bad Penny was quite for a long time. Long enough for me to start to clean off the table. She downed her drink and glared at me. "Damn it, Mikey!"

"Would you prefer I didn't say anything?"

"No. I just can't believe you're not letting me date her."

I held up both hands. "Hey, I'm just warning you of the pitfalls. I can't ban you from dating someone."

"Yeah. But you're my boss."

"And that ends when you clock out. Just be careful and make sure you have all the facts." I dusted off my hands. "And now, it's someone's bedtime."

Morgan squealed as I lifted her out of her seat and onto my shoulders. "*Da-ddy!*"

"Kiss your mother goodnight." I leaned over and she gave her mother a good smack on the cheek.

"Brush your teeth!" my wife said to the potential queen of North and South America.

"I will, Mommy." Morgan waved at the table as I marched out. "G'night, everybody."

Chapter Nine

Late Night Visits

It was getting late when Zoe wandered into the forge. She had a blanket wrapped around her like a shawl. I was sitting at the workbench I used as a makeshift desk. Scattered around the floor were pails I had retrieved from the safe room under the forge. They contained the rune engraved parts of my decade long project. I bookmarked the pages of my notebook with a feather. "Hi, what's up?"

She looked over at my unlit forge. "I thought you were making something."

"No, just going over some notes." I rubbed my eyes. Well, really just my eye. I had the runic eye out sitting in a box on the workbench. I still got headaches when I wore it too long, so I usually popped it out around the house and just wore my eyepatch. Both the regular doctors and magical healers told me it was psychosomatic, but that didn't make it hurt any less.

Zoe peered into the pails. "I thought you gave up on this one. This thing almost killed you."

"Bad Penny said something that made me rethink the project. Just going over my notes to be sure."

"And?"

"There might be a workaround. Probably not, though." I stretched. "You're up late."

She leaned against the bench. "I just got up from a nap. I'm doing an evocation ritual tonight. Has to start at midnight."

"That never made any sense to me. Why does magic care what time it is? What about Daylight Saving Time. Does that factor in?"

Stifling a yawn, she nodded. "It does, actually. It's a lot of mystic-babble but it come down to how the collective culture of the area views the particular time. Not just now, but through the centuries."

"Sounds like BS."

"Maybe, but the spell doesn't work if it's not midnight so…"

"I looked at the clock on the wall. "You've still got a couple of hours."

"Yeah, but I still have to set up. That's why I came out. The ritual is to try and learn more about the dragon. I need to borrow your files."

I pointed to a stack of books and papers at the corner of the workbench. "Good luck. It's like all info on those things was purposely destroyed or hidden. Everything is myth or conjecture."

I leaned back. "Met Toria Davenport today."

Zoe laughed. "She invite you to an orgy?"

"Both of us, actually."

"Not surprised. I've had a standing invitation to one of her so called 'rituals' for years." She made air quotes with her fingers.

"Really?" I raised my eyebrows. And yes, you can still raise both when you're missing an eye.

"She tried to get my mother to apprentice me to her. When my mother said no, she invited me after I turned twenty-one. She's got a theory that sex magic and fire magic can be combined to create some interesting effects."

"Huh! How did your mother like that request?" Zoe's mother had always been a bit of a rebel but was fiercely protective of her daughter. Not that she needed it.

"The sex part didn't faze her. She did find the idea of a wizard teaching a witch scandalous. I'll give her credit, though. She actually asked me if I wanted to do it."

"And you said no?" For some reason, my voice came out oddly casual when I asked the question.

"Correct." She tilted her head at me with a smirk. "I can't tell if you're relieved or disappointed."

"No judgment. Just a question." I raised my hands up.

"She ask you if you were banging Penny?"

"I… Ah… What!" I garbled out some words that may have been a sentence.

"Relax. It's her standard go-to question. Usually with married couples about their babysitter or single neighbor. She loves getting just that reaction." Zoe pointed to my face as she laughed. "Plus, she hates the idea of monogamous couples. Sex magic believes in the power of threes. Toria thinks marriages should be in threes, sixes, or nines."

"She stops at nine? Why not twelve or fifteen?"

"Toria says it's too many people for a successful marriage. It screws up the non-magical domestic side of it. So, from the ministroke you just had, I'm guessing she suggested it?"

I felt my face getting hot. "She made have mentioned it. Yes."

"And, of course, you gave the idea careful consideration?"

"I did *not*!" My voice was indignant but retained its normal tone and did not sound at all like a chicken squawking, no matter what Zoe might claim...

"Oh, my goddess, the look on your face!" Zoe laughed so hard she had to wipe tears away.

"You *would* find this funny."

"Yeah, well, I didn't have your narrow-minded upbringing."

"I was raised to believe a marriage was between consenting adults. Doesn't matter on race, gender, or religion. How the hell is that narrow minded?"

"Because you were raised in an environment where marriage has to be between two people." She shrugged. "I was raised in a different one. You know, there are many definitions of marriage in this city and the magic community in general. I was raised to view that as perfectly normal. You weren't."

"True enough." I grunted as I mulled over what she said. "Hell, there's that one witch who married a tree."

"It's a dryad."

"Is it, though? Has anyone ever seen the dryad?"

"Well, no..." She sighed. "Most of us decided it was best just to take his word for it."

"Mmm. Okay. I lost track of the conversation. Where were we?"

"I married on old fuddy duddy and I'm okay with that."

I grinned at her. "Right."

"On a completely different matter, I discovered something interesting about Penny."

I groaned. "Do I want to know?"

"You ever wonder why she looks like she's in her mid-twenties when she's in her thirties?"

"Good genes? Being an annoying twit prevents wrinkles?" I pointed at my wife who was close to my age but was aging much, much better than me. "I know better than to ask questions like that."

"The regenerative properties of the hyde formula prevents aging."

"Then why don't the alchemists use it to stay young?"

"They have better ways. Plus, only a very small part of the population reacts to the potion. Even then, most of those few can only use the potion once before their body rejects it. Martin is an example of that. His body built an immunity to the potion after he used it."

"Like chicken pox. Once you get it, most people can't get it more than once?"

"That's not quite… Yeah, sure. Close enough." Zoe rubbed her eyes. "Penny is part of a fraction of the population that can use the potion repeatedly. That and the fact that the addictive property of the original formula eventually kills them is why there aren't more hydes."

"But you cracked the formula and removed the addictive ingredients and tailored it specifically to her."

"Which means if she keeps taking the formula, she could live a couple of hundred years, if not more."

"Wow. Did you tell her that?"

"Yeah, a little while ago. I just proved my hypothesis a couple of day ago. Give her time to mull it over. Not everyone initially thinks an extended lifespan is a good thing." She pointed a thumb towards the house. "I told her there was pie in the fridge. She's heading up in a minute."

"The apple?"

"Yup. Don't worry, there's enough for you."

"Good." I yawned. "I can't keep track of you magic type people and your weird happenings. Can we talk about something else?"

"Sure." She looked around. "When are you going to build a new shield? I thought you'd have done it by now."

"I keep getting sidetracked. Had to build Q his knife and tomahawk combo. Plus, I need to keep pumping out allslayer rounds." I pointed to the pails of metal. "I wouldn't need to make one if I can actually pull this off."

Zoe chewed the side of her lip and she peered into the buckets. "Hmm."

"What?"

"Well, it's just, you've been down this road before. It's been ten years and you still haven't got it working."

"It works fine. The problem is me. Operating it is too complex for my brain. But thanks to Penny, I might have a workaround. I've been reviewing my notes. It might be feasible. I was going to run it by you and Martin, actually."

She tilted her head. "Really? Okay, hit me."

"Is it possible to connect Crystal to it and have her operate it on my verbal commands?"

"You've been watching those superhero movies again, haven't you?"

"No, well, yes. But I missed it. This is all Penny."

"What's Crystal think?"

"I didn't want to bring it up yet unless it was a possibility."

"Everything with her is uncharted territory." Zoe rubbed her chin. "Maybe. I'll have to research it."

"Great! Let me know."

"I have to go prepare for the ritual." She stretched and gave me a hug and a kiss. I watched her walk to the house.

"I thought she'd never leave." A creepy whisper of a voice came from the shadows in a corner of the room. I whirled around, summoning my gun in a flash of light. There was a dark chuckle. "Easy there. Didn't mean to offend."

I dismissed the colt with a thought. "A little warning next time."

"Sorry." I knew what section of the shadows the voice was coming from, but no matter how much I strained to look, I couldn't see the speaker. "You're the one who gave me access here, remember?"

"Yeah, yeah. You just startled me, that's all." I sat back down on the stool. "That intel you gave me on when Dracula was coming into town was dead on."

"Good. I'm in pretty tight with the minions now. They're starting to be freer with the info." The voice shifted to a different section of shadows.

"No issues with identity? You're somewhat distinctive looking. What legend did you go with?"

Laughter echoed up of the darkness. "They think I'm a boogieman."

"Damn. That's good." Boogeymen are rare but they do exist. They are multidimensional creatures that can only exist in our reality within darkness. Light instantly shifts them to their dimension. "So, they've never seen your true form?"

"Current form."

"Damn, sorry." I gave a quick nod to where I thought he was. "Have you learned anything else?"

"The vampire lords called it quits with Joubert. They gave up on trying to take over Llewellyn."

"Really? That would be a major blow to the Canadians if they lost vampire support." I reached over to a mini fridge under the workbench and pulled out two bottled waters. I pointed at a section of shadow, waited for a second, and tossed one of the bottles into it. It disappeared without a sound.

"Thanks. Beer would have been better."

"I don't drink beer and my whiskey is in the house." I shrugged. "So, if the lords broke it off, why is Vlad and company in town?"

"There seems to be a lot of moving parts. This appears to be some power play Tepes and Bathory's father are attempting without the rest of the lords. Something happened that got them very excited."

I took a pull from the bottle. "Do you know what?"

"No, they haven't told their underlings. But from what I learned, neither one of them was really interested in the Joubert alliance against Llewellyn. Then something changed. They are also trying to get something called the Rook. They're jonesing real bad for it, too. Something about needing it for tribute."

"Rook? Like a chess piece?"

Why does that sound familiar?

"I don't know. Some magic item of a dead wizard. There is supposed to be a will reading, and they have a hook into one of the heirs. If they don't inherit it, then they'll take out the other heirs. One of them is supposed to already be out of the way in prison here."

"Do you know who the heirs are? Or which one is in lockup?"

"That's all I know. On top of that, Tepes is hunting some other vampires."

"Who?"

"Someone called the Muse. And as of tonight, Q Faraway got added to his shit list. But we knew that was going to happen."

"The Muse? She's in town?" I thought back to Toria's friend Wila. "Interesting."

"Is that bad or good?"

"I don't know yet. Valentine's mentioned her before. If she's in town, maybe he can reach out. Enemy of my enemy thing. Supposedly she's a *doesn't like to play by the rules* type."

"I like her already." A dark clawed hand reached out and placed the empty bottle on the workbench before retreating back int the darkness. "One more thing. Tepes apparently has reached an uneasy alliance with the Patchwork Man concerning Llewellyn."

"Really? The Patchwork Man is real?" I had been hearing stories of the Patchwork Man since I'd moved to the city. He was allegedly a mysterious crime lord figure that's been around for a couple hundred years. No one knew if he was real or not, and everything from bank robberies to toppling governments had been attributed to him. "Just what we need: a magical Keyser Söze mucking up the works. How's he involved with this?"

"I've been told he's the one who brought everyone together. Harrow, Llewellyn, and the vampires. It was his plan to attack the city."

 "Huh." Harrow had mentioned there was a player I wasn't aware of. At the time, I chalked it up to mind games. "Find out whatever you can about him."

"Sure. I…"

"What?"

"There's someone outside. I'm out." Some of the shadows retreated, signaling his departure.

I summoned the 1911 and stepped out into the yard. I triggered the blood runes for senses and stood still to soak in the environment. My enhanced hearing picked up chanting coming from Zoe's attic workshop and Emala's snoring. She needed to see a doctor. For a teenage girl, her snoring could rattle the whole house. The only other sound was…

There! Dishes rattling in the kitchen. Penny's digging into the leftover pie.

I dismissed my gun and the blood runes and returned to the forge. "You still there?"

Crickets…

"Fuck it then." I scooped up my runic eye, turned off the lights, and headed to the house.

Chapter Ten

A Lack of Pants

I entered the kitchen to find Bad Penny rummaging around in the fridge. Her bending over had caused the shirt she was wearing to ride up, revealing a tiny scrap of material that could laughingly be called a thong. "Jesus Christ, Penny!"

"I can't find the whipped cream," she said, head still buried in the shelves. "What? What are you complaining about? My butt?"

"Yes!"

"Why? It's a spectacular butt." She gave a wiggle just to prove it. She had tattoos of pink bows on the back of her thighs high enough that the tips of them were almost hidden by the creases of the aforementioned butt. Below the bows were black and white tattoos of lacing that ran down the back of both legs.

"Penny, what the he—"

"Here it is." She straightened up and turned around. Her shirt had *My boobs are down here, you pervert* printed on the front of it, and it was too short to cover up for her lack of other clothing.

"Why are you not wearing pants?"

"I dunno. Why aren't you wearing both your eyes? Arrh! Shiver me timbers." She sprayed whipped cream on a slice of pie and then squirted some in her mouth. "I warh ig mmrgh bed."

"What?"

She swallowed and shook the can, visibly considering another shot. "I said, I was in bed when Zoe stopped by. This is what I wear to sleep. What's the matter? You've seen me wear less."

I took the can away and put it back in the fridge. "For the millionth time, we have kids in the house."

"Please, they're both dead to the world." She gestured to the stairs where Emala's snoring could easily be heard.

"Whatever. Just take the time to put pants on next time?"

She raised her eyebrows and a mischievous grim spread across her face. "Do you and Zoe want to help me pick them out? I have a nice leather pair with a zipper—"

Throwing up my hands in defeat, I fled the kitchen. About halfway up the stairs I stopped as a thought hit me. Penny's trailer was right behind the carriage house. With the windows open, it was very possible she heard Zoe and I's conversation.

I shook my head and went to our bedroom. Unlike most of my weapons, I keep my colt 1911 in a waist holster. I locked it in our safe and placed the box with my runic eye on the dresser. My bracers and wedding ring quickly followed.

Zoe and I had a private bathroom off our bedroom. I stepped into it and started the shower. In such an old house, it took a couple of minutes to warm up. With the various aches and pains in my body, I preferred piping hot showers with lots of steam.

I brushed my teeth and then tossed my clothes into the hamper. I jumped into the shower only to discover my body wash container was empty. I stepped out and checked under the sink.

Damn it. There better be a spare in the hall closet.

I wrapped a towel around my waist and stepped back into the bedroom. Standing at the dresser was a woman. I knew it was a female because even though the green bodysuit she wore completely covered her from head to toe, it was tight enough to leave little to the imagination. Around her waist she had on a loose chain belt made of metal butterflies with a pouch and a rapier hanging off of it.

"What the fuck? Who the hell are you?"

"Le Papillion," she said with a French accent as she gestured to herself. Then did a spinning back kick that sent me crashing into the nightstand and made for the open window.

"Zoe! Penny! Intruder!" I popped back up and triggered my blood runes while frantically retying my towel. I lunged toward the intruder, pulling her away from the window just

111

in time to prevent her escape. She hit me with a flurry of blows, staggering me.

Crap! Superhuman strength and speed.

We could hear someone coming up the stairs. The intruder hit me with a couple of quick jabs to the face and then hooked my leg, knocking me down. She pulled my towel off and twirled it tight.

"Mikey, you say some— Ow!" The woman snapped the towel out, the tip catching Penny right in the eye. She then whirled and smashed right through the entire window.

Damn it. I already replaced that thing once this year.

I looked out the window but couldn't see her.

Too dark. I need night vision.

Running over the dresser, I pawed around, looking for my runic eye.

"What the hell is going on here?" Twirling a wand, Zoe stepped next to Penny who was rubbing her eye and staring at me. She must have gotten hit right in the eyeball because her face was all red.

Zoe took in Penny's attire and looked over at me and arched an eyebrow. "One little talk and you jump right into the poly pool, huh?"

"Wait, what?"

"I appreciate your enthusiasm, but no getting naked without me." She scooped up my towel and threw it at me, fighting to keep a straight face.

Oh my God!

"Someone broke in. I think it was the cat burglar." I quickly wrapped the towel around me and pointed to the damaged nightstand and window. "Look."

"Right! Because we've never broken any furniture in the bedroom before?"

"A *window*! Seriously?"

She smirked at Penny who was still red in the face. "Hmm, looks like someone's all talk."

Penny turned even redder. "I have to go."

She fled down the stairs as my wife laughed. I frowned at her. "You're not at all concerned that someone broke in."

"That's allegedly broke in, mister policeman," she said as I studied the dresser. "What?"

"She stole my eye." I scanned the rest of my stuff. My bracers were still there.

"Your eye?" Zoe dropped her little game. "Why would she steal your eye?"

"I don't know but she took my wedding ring, too."

"What?" Zoe's outraged bellow rang through the house, causing the only good thing to come out of the whole fiasco.

The snoring finally stopped.

Chapter Eleven

Police at the Door

"Excuse me, sir. Someone here called the police?" Q didn't even try to hide the big grin as he stood on my porch.

"Smartass." I held the door open so he, Khan, and Eddy could come in.

"Now, now sir, we're only here to help. Now tell us how the little girl beat you up." Q smirked as Khan pulled out his notebook as they all sat down at the kitchen table. "This seems to be a theme with you. Didn't Bad Penny clean your clock during Oct5?"

My mouth was a flat line as I nodded in recognition of his shot. I triggered a rune on my bracers and his tomahawk lifted out of its holster and spun across the room into my hand.

"Hey!" Q's jaw dropped.

I studied the weapon as I held it, not looking up at him. "Fexts are supposed to be extremely hard to kill. Outside of destroyer level magic, the only thing that will do it is the weapon that originally killed you, right?"

Eddy frowned. "I thought it was glass bullets?"

"Shut up, Eddy." Fext were a rare form of Gifted. They were practically immortal. They were said to be immune to any sort of damage except by others of their kind and the fact that each one had a unique individual weakness. I knew there was one during the Thirty Years War whose kryptonite turned out to be glass. His enemies killed him by shooting glass rounds from their rifles. This led to the popular belief that all Fext could be killed by glass bullets.

In reality, a person doesn't become a Fext until they die by violence. Their Gift returns them to life, and about the only thing that can harm them is whatever killed them. If they were bludgeoned to death by a rock, then that particular rock can permanently kill them. In a strange quirk of fate, the Gift causes the item to be practically indestructible, meaning the Fext can't simply destroy it and be free of it.

"Roight, Sarge. Shutting up, Sarge."

I pointed the tomahawk out the kitchen window. "What happens if I took your toys away and have itty bitty little Bad Penny knock the crap out of both of you, then bury you in a 30-foot hole in my yard for the next decade or so?"

"Alright, alright. Relax. It was just some good-natured ribbing." He held out his hand and summoned his 'hawk back. I released my grip and it spun back into his palm with a meaty thunk. He slid it back into its holster. "Didn't know you could do that."

"I build certain safeguards into all the weapons I make."

Eddy smirked. "Just ask Lobo."

Q glanced between the two of us. "Who?"

"Nobody, just a dead vampire with a stupid name." I gestured towards the fridge. "You guys want anything?"

I sat down after they shook their heads. "She bypassed our wards like they weren't even there."

Khan tapped his pen on the table. "Didn't your wards go down? Some spell the wendigo did?"

"Yeah." I confirmed the lie Zoe and I told to hide the power Morgan was developing. She had shattered those ancient wards like—well, like a cat burglar through a window. "While the replacement wards aren't as powerful as those, they are still on the higher end. They should have gone off."

"Same as all the other victims. Wards never triggered." Eddy nodded.

"Anyway, I walked into my bedroom, and she was standing there in front of the dresser. She kicked me and we tussled. Penny was downstairs raiding our fridge and came running. That was when the thief jumped out the window." I sure as hell wasn't going to mention the towel incident. It wasn't relevant, and I'd never here the end of it.

"What did she take, Sergeant?" Khan asked.

"My runic eye." Both cops looked up to the metal eye with glowing runes currently lodged in my right eye socket. I tapped my finger under it. "She took the current one, model three. This one is model two."

116

"Weird. What else?" Khan asked while scribbling in his notebook.

"The only other thing was my wedding ring."

They all glanced at each other then simultaneously looked up the stairs. Eddy cleared his throat nervously. "Ah, Sarge. Where, umm, where's the missus?"

"Upstairs sifting through her ancestor's grimoires looking for the perfect vengeance spell. Why do you ask?" I said in a calm voice.

Q shifted uneasily in his chair. "You gave her the *let the cops handle it* speech, right?"

I looked him dead in the eyes. "I'm just the victim here. I thought I'd let the on-duty cops tell the daughter of Silas the Black that she shouldn't be upset that a symbol of her marriage was taken."

It appeared he decided the more prudent course was to just ignore my last comment. "Why those two items? That's a bit odd, isn't it? Even for this case."

"I have runes engraved on the inside of my ring. It allows me to summon certain of my items. That's the only thing unusual about the ring."

Q raised his eyebrows but said nothing.

"They were backups in case I didn't have access to my bracers." I lifted my arms up, showing the interlocked metal squares that encased both my forearms. Each square had a series of minor runes along the edges and one large major rune in the middle. They allowed me to summon and control various magic items I created. Well, and the TV remote.

"Maybe the Shelia needed a fake eye for herself," Eddy piped up. "Was she missing an eye, Sarge?"

"I don't know Eddy. She was wearing a skintight bodysuit that covered every inch of her. Like Spider-Man if his suit was green and not red and blue. She also had a belt of linked metal butterflies with a pouch and a rapier. Athletic build, maybe about 5'6" or 5'7". Strong and fast. Like magically so."

"Vampire?" Khan threw out.

"Mmm, maybe. I don't think so, much stronger than your average vamp. Oh, and she called herself Le Papillon."

Eddy scratched his chin. "Like the dog?"

"It's French for *The Butterfly*," Khan grunted.

"Nah, Khanie, my girl and I watch the dog shows every weekend. It's a dog breed."

Q rubbed the bridge of his nose. "Eddy, the dog is called that because the ears look like butterflies."

"Oh, I guess that makes sense."

"Anything else to add?" At my head shake, Khan flipped his notebook closed. "Well, at least we finally have some sort of description and a gender... Are you sure it was Le Papillon, not La Papillon?"

"Pretty sure, why?"

"Le is masculine, la is feminine. How sure is pretty sure?"

"Nine out of ten. You think it means something?"

"Probably not, my French is rusty." The vampire detective slid his notebook into a pocket. "Maybe the word butterfly is masculine in French, I don't know."

I tapped my badge. "Brennan to Dispatch."

"Go ahead, Sergeant," answered Crystal, our dispatcher.

"Please dig up any information you can on a female cat burglar known as Le Papillon or maybe La Papillon."

"Will do, Sergeant. Please stand by."

Q frowned. Where's Bad Penny? We need to take her report, too."

"Back in her trailer. She only saw her for a split second. She'll file it in the morning. No reason for both of us to be tired tomorrow."

"Fair enough."

"Dispatch to Sergeant Brennan." Crystal's voice came out of my badge. "I have that information."

"I tabbed my badge. "Go with it, please."

"Le Papillon also known as La Papillon is a French cat burglar. She is known to have enhanced physical abilities. Rumors of her first surfaced around 1900, and her targets have been from both the mundane world and the magical communities. She favors a rapier and throwing weapons and is considered a first-rate swordswoman. She has some ability to bypass wards and rarely takes more than one or two items in each heist. Very little is known of her."

"Thanks, Crystal."

"A quick analysis of her known thefts shows an anomaly with her actions here."

Khan frowned at that, and Q shrugged when I glanced his way. I tabbed the badge again. "What's that?"

"All her previously known victims were what you would call bad guys. People of ill repute."

So, what changed her pattern now?

"Great info. Keep us up to date if you find anything else."

"Of course, Sergeant." Crystal signed off.

Q stood up. "Khan, take a look upstairs with Mike. Eddy, check the yard."

"Right Sarge, err, other Sarge." Eddy bobbed his head at me and went out the back door."

"Ulysses, go a head up. I'll be there in a second." The vampire nodded and headed up the stairs. "I'll wait outside the room for you."

I turned to Q. "Khan is here investigating, and you're here as a supervisor because it involves an officer. Now explain why Eddy is here."

He grinned at me. "For the same reason you'd bring him. He's going to be guarding your house for the rest of the night."

"Two cops and a fire witch live here. You're wasting resources."

"Maybe, but he stays."

"I'll kick him off the property."

"Then he'll be parked in the road, but he's not leaving." Q continued to grin into my glare. "You come on duty, you can release him but right now it's my shift and he's not going anywhere. She attacked one of our own. What type of message does that send? We'd do it for a civilian, so we damn sure are going to do it for a copper!"

Damn it. If it was reversed, I'd do the same thing.

"Fine."

"Fine." He shot back.

"But you're helping me board up the stupid window after." I stomped up the stairs before he could say a word.

Chapter Twelve

Another Morgan

I was the last to make it to breakfast. Penny had her face buried into a bowl of cereal and refused to acknowledge the existence of the rest of us. She was already in her uniform. Emala's choice in clothes was a giant clash of colors that hurt my eyes. Morgan was still in her pajamas and her hair was a wild mop.

Zoe's anger at my wedding ring getting stolen rolled around her in waves of heat—literal heat in her case. Flames flickered in her eyes as my fire witch of a wife struggle with her anger. She was dressed in her battle leathers. Tight fitting and covered in spell protections, it was a look I normally found very attractive. Today, though, I was worried she was going to do something drastic. She bristled with wands. Whackacat, her familiar, laid on the top of the refrigerator. The cat's tail lashed out like a whip in response to Zoe's mood.

Emala looked over my wife's attire. "Are we doing battle training today?"

"No. You're going to be studying at the Morgan Tree while I find out who broke into our house and take a pound of flesh from her."

I lowered the piece of bacon in my hand, careful not to leave Morgan an opening to snag it. "Zoe, please stay out of it. It's a police matter."

"You lot have been chasing her for months and have zip to show for it." Zoe looked tired. There were dark circles under her eyes that had not been there yesterday.

"You were up most of last night casting divination and tracking spells. You have any better luck?"

"No. She's very well shielded." Zoe slammed her fork down on the table in frustration.

"And that's why we've been having trouble locating her. You're just going to go over ground we already covered or, worse, get in our way."

She raised an eyebrow at me, her anger finally having a target. "So, you think I'm some bungler who will get in the way, huh?"

I sighed. "No. But tell me, what would you say if I started rummaging around in your workshop trying to cast spells?"

"That you're an idiot. You need training, skill, and knowledge to… Oh!" She deflated, the anger draining away and replaced by exhaustion. "So, *I'm* the idiot!"

"No, you're mad, hurt, and tired. You're running on anger and caffeine and it's clouding your judgment." I reached over, grabbed her hand, and squeezed it. "Never cast mad, remember?"

"Yeah, yeah." She squeezed my hand back. "Why are you not furious right now?"

"Because it doesn't serve a purpose and because of these." I pointed to the faint scarring that marked the blood runes that covered sections of my skin. "Berserker, remember? Bad things happen when I let my anger go unchecked."

"Mike smash!" Emala said slowly with a deep voice, causing Morgan to giggle. "Why don't you ask the other Morgans? Aren't some of them further along their timelines? They might have had this happened in their realities and know who did it."

Everyone but Morgan turned and stared at Emala. A slow smile spread across Zoe's face. "That's a great idea."

"Thanks!" Emala's face lit up.

"You obviously have an outstanding teacher," my wife told her and turned to Morgan. "Can you do that, honey? Ask one of you other selves."

Morgan looked down at her empty plate and then back up to her mother. "Not without more bacon!"

Extortionist!

Zoe picked up the plate with the remaining bacon. "One slice."

"Five."

"Two and you're not grounded for trying to blackmail your parents."

"Deal, Mommy." Morgan placed one piece on her plate and munched down on the other one. As she chewed, her eyes moved around as if reading something only she could see. She swallowed and nodded. "Okay, but only for a little bit."

"Who's she talking to?" whispered Emala.

"Shh," my wife replied.

Morgan's eyes suddenly snapped back into focus and her brow furrowed in annoyance. "Stop trying to do an end around!"

Her voice was that of an adult and was an excellent of impression of Zoe's angry voice. "You are playing around with things you don't understand. She's not a human fortune cookie."

This is new.

I frowned. "Which Morgan are we talking to?

"Dame Morgan Brennan of the Knights of the Holy Order of the Star of Bethlehem."

"You're a witch hunter?" growled my wife.

"No, Mother. None of the Knights of the Star are." The other Morgan sighed. "It would be nice if at least one version of you finally realized that."

"Let's get back on track," I said, nipping that argument in the bud. "Why can't you tell us anything?"

"Your Morgan has the ability to link the rest of us together. We don't know if it's because she had a specific Gift or because it's her location in the multiverse. It's one thing to give her advice from time to time on skills and abilities, but to give her future information might alter her timeline which could possibly shift her location in the multiverse and sever our connections. Not to mention that things have played out in many different ways for the various Morgans. What may be true for one of us may not be true in your reality."

I nodded. "Alright. Got it. Sorry about that."

"W-what?" Zoe sputtered. "Well, I don't. If that's the case, give us a list of all the names and we'll sort them out."

"Mother, did you listen to what I said in the beginning? I swea—" Morgan shook her head and her face softened back to a more normal expression. "Don't talk to Mommy that way."

"Morgan, what just happened?" I asked.

"She's angry with her mommy and that's not fair to *my* mommy so I threw her out."

"You-you just ejected a Knight of the Star from your mind?"

"Yup." She picked up her last slice of bacon and started nibbling at it. "My brain, my rules."

Wow. Just... wow. That's a lot of power for anyone, much less a small child.

I leaned back in my chair and exhaled deeply. "Okay then. We do it the old fashion way. Penny."

"Yeah?"

"Time for work." I stood up and looked at my wife. "What are you doing?"

She chewed the side of her lip. "Well, since I'm going to let you handle the cop stuff, I'm going to swing by the Morgan Tree. A little birdie told me that Hien is waffling on supporting you."

"That's not good."

Hien Tran was the acting coven leader since their last one had been killed by the wendigo's attack on the city council. The backing of the Morgan Coven was essential to my and Culain's plan.

"I know. I'll take care of it."

"The city council meeting is coming up in a few days. It's amazing we've been able to keep this under wraps this long. If we have to postpone, it's all going to unravel."

"Mike, I said I'll handle it. It's typical coven politics. She's pulling a power move and I'm going to stuff it down her throat."

"Okay. Okay." I kissed her and Morgan. "Love you both. Emala, say out of trouble."

"We'll see how the day goes."

I followed a still very quiet Penny out the door.

Chapter Thirteen

Officer Down

"Mike, you working yet?" Q's voice came through my badge. I glanced at Bad Penny and tabbed my badge. "We're driving in now. What's up?"

"I'm at Pam's Diner getting some food. I know that's on your route in. There are some idiot vamplings outside tagging walls in a covered alley. You mind swinging by? If you're too far out, I'll get someone else.'"'

Penny frowned at me. Q could easily handle a few vamplings. I tabbed the badge again. "We're around the corner. You think it's a trap?"

"Oh yeah. They keep glancing at the diner." He snorted. "They're really not good at this."

Hmm, Dracula finally making his move?

"Be there in two." I tapped Chief on the dash as we turned onto the street the diner was located on. "Pull over here, Chief. We'll walk over."

I scanned the area as we got out. We were on the same side as the alley. There was a metal roof that arched across it, connecting it to the adjacent buildings. Valentine had been instrumental in having those put up over most of the alleys. It allowed vamplings the ability to travel on foot during the daytime. It was limited, but still a huge improvement for them.

Penny and I edged closer. Since we were on the same side, we couldn't see into the alley. But that also meant the vamplings couldn't see us. Penny tapped me on the arm. "Why don't we come in from the other side of the alley and Q comes in this side? That way we have then trapped."

"Because if it becomes a shootout, we'd be in a crossfire."

"Shootout? It's tagging."

"It's a trap."

She pulled a potion out. "So what? You and I heal quickly, and nothing hurts Q."

I gave her a flat look. "I don't know about you, but I don't like getting shot. Bullets hurt."

"Good point."

"Ya think?" I pulled out one of my orbs and tossed it up. It bobbed in the air for a second, steadying itself.

"Where's the other two?"

I pointed to my runic eye. "Older version, remember? It can only handle one orb at a time."

My vision split as the orb floated up and slowly creeped around the roof. I kept it up high so the vamplings wouldn't notice it. Looking at the images the orb sent to my eye, I was able to see that there were six vamplings in the alley. Dressed in jeans and hoodies, they each held a spray can and weren't trying to hide their fangs. Two of the guys were spraying one of the walls. One of the women had a tote bag slung over her shoulder that seemed full of spray cans. The rest kept looking at the diner.

I tabbed my badge. "Q, you see us?"

"Yup."

"Orb in position. I make four males and two females. Probably vamplings. No visible weapons. Good call on it being a trap. They're just spraying the wall, no designs or words." I told him. "Ready when you are."

Penny downed her potion. Her body warped and shifted, growing bigger. The fabric of her bespelled uniform adapted to her hyde form. As usual, she tore the arms off it anyways.

"Heading over now." Q exited the diner and crossed the street in a slow and measured pace. He stopped just outside the entrance of the alley, keeping himself in the sunlight. He tilted his Stetson back off his forehead and put a wad of chewing tobacco in his mouth. "Howdy, boys and girls. Any reason why you're breaking the law?"

"What are you going to do about it, Marlboro Man?"

I fought back a snort. Q had gotten pegged with that nickname the first week he got here. He was not a fan of it.

I nodded to Penny, and we fanned out on either side. I smiled at the surprised vamplings. "I was thinking handcuffs?"

On seeing us, they looked at each other, weighing the change of odds.

"Ya'll like nicknames?" Q spit some tobacco juice on the ground and pointed at me. "He's got a bunch. One of them is Blood Drinker's Bane. Want to know how he got it?"

Several shifted further back into the alley, creating distance between us. He spit again. "Looks like you already know."

I had the orb skim along the roof rafters and scan the rest of the alley as we stepped closer to the vamplings.

They suddenly surged forward using that vampire speed I hated so much. Instead of coming at all of us, they swarmed Q.

What the hell?

I summoned my 1911 as the hooded girl with the tote bag pulled an antique firearm out of it and aimed it at Q's face.

Is that a flintlock?

I fired several rounds into her torso. She staggered and her shot went wild, pinging off the brick wall they had been tagging. Q pulled his knife and Tomahawk and started going through the vamplings like a buzzsaw. Their claws and bites had little effect on him. Motes of golden energy would escape from his wounds as they healed almost instantly. Q flung his tomahawk at the gunwoman. She ducked at the last second and fled down the alley at superspeed. The tomahawk ricocheted off a dumpster and went spinning back to Q's hand. "That was Lucy. Get that gun. I'll take care of these idiots."

"Penny, let's go." I headed down the alley, changing magazines as I did so. Lucy's flintlock only had one shot, and I didn't want to give her time to reload. If she was using a firearm that old and obsolete, it had to be magical.

Penny quickly caught up to me as we ran. As she did, I sent the orb out to scout ahead. I tabbed my badge. "Foot pursuit in the alley in front of Pam's Diner. Headed towards Levasseur Street. Suspect is Lucy Westenra Seward, dressed in jeans and a black hoodie. Dispatch put out a description."

Crystal's voice came out of our badges. "All units, all units. Foot pursuit in the alley between Costello Street and Levasseur. Suspect is heading towards Levasseur Street. Suspect is identified as Lucy Westenra Seward, blonde Caucasian female around 5'4", slim build, wearing jeans and a black hooded sweatshirt. Be aware, she is believed to be a Master Vampire and is a known psychopath suspected of multiple murders."

Without breaking stride, Lucy snagged a wooden pallet in the alley and whipped it towards the orb. The images stopped as it hit.

"Damn. She took out the orb." I was huffing and puffing as Penny raced ahead of me. "Penny, slow down."

A crack rang out as Penny ran onto Levasseur Street. She grabbed her chest and stumbled to the ground, rocking back and forth as she clutched the wound.

I summoned my armor and ran towards Penny. Lucy was across the street, reloading the flintlock. Civilians were fleeing away from us.

"Uh, she got me in the boob. That bitch!" Penny's face was racked with pain. "I'm-I'm not healing. Watch out for that thing."

I dragged her behind a Studebaker and had her drink down a healing potion. It had no effect. I tabbed my badge. "Officer down, officer down. Levasseur near Newt. Suspect has a magical flintlock."

"Backup enroute!" Gabby's voice was distorted by wind. She must have been really moving.

"Hey, Blood Drinker's Bane. Why are you hiding behind that car? Come out and see what a real vampire can do," Lucy called out to me as she cocked the flintlock.

Keeping an eye on her, I summoned a first aid kit I keep in a vintage Buck Rogers lunch box. "How are you doing, Penny? Keep talking to me."

"People need to stop hitting me in the boobs. That's twice now," Penny hissed in pain. "I swear the round is digging in deeper."

Penny suddenly shifted, shrinking down to her normal form. "I don't feel so good, Mikey."

Her skin was pale and clammy. I used the kit's scissors to cut through her shirt, pulling it wide, so I could see the wound.

"Whoo hoo. Finally getting to second base." Penny's voice was weak, and her eyes were unfocused. 'G-go get Zoe and I'll rock both your worl…"

"Penny!" Her eyes rolled up and she went limp. I placed a bandage on her wound as I watched Lucy lazily stroll towards us. "Comin' to get you, copper-man!"

Fuck this shit!

I tabbed my badge. "I need back—"

Everything started to rumble, and an object slammed into Lucy at supersonic speed. The boom shattered all the windows around us. The force knocked Lucy through the side of a brick building.

That object was Sergeant Gabby Zhao, the Living Temple. She slid to a stop as the "tattoos" that adorned her skin shifted and flexed. She looked around and nodded at me. "How is she?"

"Not good," I yelled. My ears were ringing, and I was pretty sure my right eardrum was ruptured. I pulled a tinder box out of my pocket and opened it. Placing it on the ground, I blew on the ember inside. "Zoe. Zoe. Zoe. Help!"

The ember enlarged into a wall of flame. Zoe stepped through with a wand in both hands, Whackacat perched on her shoulder. "Mike!"

"Get down! There's a shooter." As she crouched, I pointed to Penny. "She got hit. The bullets are magical or something and she's not responding to healing."

"Like your allslayers?" Zoe holstered her wands, making a series of motions with her hands as she said words in the Language Arcane. Bad Penny levitated up and through the firegate.

"I don't know. It was Lucy."

"I got it from here." Zoe stepped back into the firegate. "Kick her ass, Mike."

'Pretty sure Gabby beat me to it," I muttered as I stood up. As I did so, Lucy staggered out of the hole she made in the wall. Her hoodie was down, and her blonde hair was in disarray. She wasn't holding the flintlock anymore.

Gabby waited until I was even with her, and we started slowly walking toward Dracula's pet psycho. The theme music to *The Good, the Bad and the Ugly* played in the air thanks to one of the beings residing in Gabby.

Guess that makes me the ugly.

The Asian sergeant shot me a look. "Penny okay?"

"What?" I pointed to my ear. "You fucked up my hearing a bit with that stunt."

"Sorry!" Gabby raised her voice. "Is Bad Penny okay?"

"Don't know yet," I said. "Watch out for a flintlock. It's got some strange properties."

"Roger that, old man."

"That is no way to talk to your godfather."

We stopped and Gabby called out to the psycho vampire. "You're under arrest, Lucy. Don't make this worse."

"That was a hell of a hit." She wiped her hand across her bloody mouth. She held it up and licked the blood off her fingers. "But I don't want you."

She pointed a finger at me and its nail lengthened into a claw. "I want the Rune Knight. I want Blood Drinker's Bane. He spoiled my shot. My lovely, lovely shot."

136

"Last chance, Lucy," I shouted to her.

"Didn't anyone ever tell you not to get between quarreling exes?" She cocked her head. "Speak of the devil. Here's my old lover now."

Q stepped out of the alley, weapons in hand. "You were warned, Lucy."

Damn.

Part of the plan in bringing Q to the department was to use him to disrupt Dracula's plans and throw him off balance until we could discover what they were. Instead, it bit us in the ass.

Shooting her didn't seem to have much luck. I dismissed my 1911 and summoned my sword. "Where is the firearm, Lucy?"

"Ooh, that's such a long sword." She winked at me. "Compensating for something, big man?"

I sighed and looked at Q as I triggered the blood runes. "I missed the days when everyone just fought instead of feeling the need to make smartass comments first."

"You make smart ass comments all the time." He gave me an odd look. "And why do you keep yelling?"

I didn't answer as the blood runes swept away the calm I had been forcing on myself. The healing rune quickly repaired my eardrum, but the fear and anger at Penny being hurt fueled my berserker state. I strained to keep it in check.

Lucy launched herself at us at superspeed. As powerful as Gabby and Q are, neither one of them could react at that speed without preparation. In my current state, I could. Growling I swept my sword across her as she lunged at Q. The blade dug deep, and the force of it knocked her off course and into my goddaughter.

Ignoring her injury, Lucy bit and clawed at Gabby, but it was to no avail. With her powers activated, the Living Temple was simply too tough for fangs and claws to pierce her skin, master vampire or not.

Gabby reacted with a flurry of punches and kicks that dropped the injured vampire. She nudged the vampire with her foot. "She's out."

I released the blood runes and felt a wave of exhaustion sweep through my body. "She must have really pissed you off."

My goddaughter slapped a pair of handcuffs on the vampire. While not foolproof, the runes engraved on them should prevent her from using any abilities. "What gave it away?"

"You only go hand to hand when you're ticked off." Gabby had been trained at birth by her father Shen, one of the greatest warriors in history. Even without the celestial beings that slumbered within her, Gabby was a dangerous person.

"You attack the Blue, you get my undivided attention." She hoisted Lucy up onto her shoulder. "You two good? I want to get her behind bars while she is still out."

I turned to Q. "Your bad guys?"

He shrugged. "Ya'll gonna need a dustpan for those folks. I'll file the report in a bit."

"Okay then. Gabby, thanks for the help."

"Anytime." She floated up into the air. "Let me know how Penny is doing."

"Will do." I watched her fly away before pointing to the hole in the wall. "It's in there."

Q gave me an appraising look before nodding sharply. "Right."

We climbed into the rubble and started shifting it around. I tossed a couple of bricks away and wiped my forehead. "So, I'm guessing you're older than you let on? Don't remember a lot of flintlocks in the Old West."

"Why? Were you there?" Q didn't look up and continued searching.

I ignored his jab. "The pistol didn't have any runes on it. That limits what it is to only a few things, and I'm pretty sure it wasn't an artifact."

He straightened up. "Yeah, it's what killed me and awoke my Gift. In the process it bonded with me and became magical. Its power is stronger the closer it is to me."

"Why haven't you destroyed it?"

He spit another wad of tobacco. "You don't think I've tried?"

"That is a disgusting habit." I moved away from his nicotine phlegm ball.

He ignored the comment. "I've dropped it in the ocean, buried it in the desert, even tossed it into a volcano. The flintlock can't be destroyed as long as I live."

'And it's one of the few things that can kill you?"

"Yup. Part of the curse of being a fext is that it always seems to make its way back to me."

"Well, that sucks." I was about to say more when Gabby came over the air. "Mike, you there?"

"Yeah."

"I lost her."

"What?"

"She turned into a fucking flock of bats, and they flew away in different directions. I thought that only happened in the movies."

"Me too. Keep looking for her."

"Right."

Q gave me a sour look and started digging again.

We finally determined the pistol wasn't there. I headed home to check on Penny. The Chief drove at breakneck speeds to the point to where I had to tell him to slow down. We pulled into the yard and his final braking sent gravel everywhere.

Emala waited for me on the porch. She held up both hands as I exited the car and took the steps two at a time. "Penny will be fine! Zoe doesn't want you barging into the house at full speed and volume."

I came to a halt. "She okay?"

"We had to remove the bullet. Once that was out and the wound was cleaned, she started to heal on her own."

"We?" I frowned. "You were part of the procedure?"

The teen witch pointed a thumb to her chest. "Apprentice witch! Can't do much apprenticing if you can't watch your teacher work."

"I guess."

"Zoe made up a bed in her workshop for Penny. She said you can go up if you're quiet."

"Thanks." I slipped in the house and headed up the stairs to the attic. Zoe's workshop contained various spices, flowers, and herbs that usually gave it a pleasant scent. This time it smelled of antiseptic. Her main workbench had been cleared off and bloody sheets covered it. My wife gave me a tired smile and waved me in. The apron she wore was also bloodstained.

"She's sleeping but is recovering nicely." Zoe pointed over to a cot in front of her fireplace. Penny slept on it, looking tiny and frail. The black cauldron that usually sat there was nowhere to be seen. "That bullet was nasty."

"It wasn't the bullet. It was the gun."

"Did you recover it?"

"Not yet." I walked over and looked down at Penny. "You sure she's going to be okay?"

"Yes. Now come away from there before you wake her." Zoe grabbed my hand with both of hers and pulled me away. "I've got this. Go do cop stuff."

"Yeah. I'm going to clean up and then go see Culain."

"Good."

Then I'm going to go rattle Drac's cage.

Chapter Fourteen

Breadcrumbs

"Come in."

I opened the door to Culain's office. "Got a moment?"

"Sure." He leaned back in his chair. "Lucy got away clean, but we'll get her. How's Penny?"

"Better. It's going to take her at least a day to physically recover."

Culain's office, when not filled with people asking me strange questions, looked like it hadn't changed since the 1950s. His clothing choices matched the same time period. And while I originally thought this was like Toria and other long-lived magic types, I was beginning to have my doubts. Now I was starting to suspect it might be a deception similar to Q's, designed to foster the belief he was from the 1950s originally. But then that left the question, what was Culain's background and why is it so shrouded in mystery?

"Our guy checked in last night. In fact, I think he sensed the cat burglar, but Penny was wandering around, and I assumed it was her." I plunked down in one of the wooden chairs in front of him. "We still don't know why Vlad Tepes and company would decide to show up in a city under the threat of a dragon attack, but he was able to throw me some breadcrumbs."

"What did you learn?" Culain loosened his tie. He tended to dress in earth colors, and that day wasn't an exception. He wore a matching brown pants and vest combo with a white shirt. The tie had brown and subdued gold stripes. His ever-faithful trench coat hung on a coat rack in the corner.

"We're missing something. A connection. I can feel it."

"What?"

"I don't know yet, but it's driving me crazy." I quickly relayed what I had learned. Culain snorted, pulled a file from the pile of paperwork at the corner of his desk, and tossed it to me.

I caught it and held it up. "Do I want to know?"

"Just read it."

I skimmed it and raised my eyebrows. "Seriously? Obrechenny Khishchnik is requesting a furlough to attend a will reading?"

"Got to be her, right? What are the odds that we have another person in prison who's supposed to go to a will reading right now?"

I flipped through to the last page. "This says it's tomorrow."

"Well, yeah, we denied it over a month ago. We don't normally allow war criminals to wander around the city doing errands." He gave a small nod toward the door. "Not including the extenuating circumstances around Bad Penny, that is."

"So, the question is, do we have her attend it and see what we can find out or keep her locked up?"

"The way you tell it, they seemed happy she was off the board. Might be a way to throw a monkey wrench into their plans." He clasped both hands behind his head and leaned even further back, studying the ceiling. "Any reason to believe this is a set up to try and spring her?"

I mulled it over for a minute. "Anything's possible, but no, I don't think so."

"It's settled then. I'll contact the prison and have her brought over here. You and Penny transport her to the will reading and see what you can find out." He straightened up in his seat and pulled a phone directory from a drawer.

"Why don't I take someone else? Penny could use a break after getting shot."

"She wants time off, give it to her and take another cop." He shrugged. "But if she wants to go, let her. You know she's going to want to jump right back in. Sitting through a will reading will be a lot better that patrolling the streets. I don't want her looking for Lucy."

"Yeah, okay." I sighed tiredly.

"How are we with the other thing?"

"Toria Davenport's on board."

"Good. I have a guild head lined up, but I need to speak to him one last time."

"Who is it?"

"Tobias Graywand."

"I don't know him."

"Runs a small but influential wizard's guild. Newly appointed to the council. Balding with giant muttonchops."

"Oh, that guy." I scratched at my scars. "Listen, we might have a hiccup with the leader of the Morgan Coven."

"Hien Tran?" He frowned. "I thought she was on board."

"She was. Now she seems to be getting cold feet. Zoe is going to speak with her."

"She'd better. Considering the mewling cowards that seem to make up the majority of the city council these days, pulling this off is the only way we are going to be able to strike at Joubert."

I gave him a half grin. "Don't hold back, tell us how you really feel."

"I'm serious. This is a long shot at best, and we barely have the support we need as it is."

"She'll handle it."

"This wouldn't have been an issue if Zoe threw her name in the ring for coven leader last time around."

"We have a small child at home, I'm back working here, and she's rebuilding her healer practice. She didn't want the additional responsibilities." Now it was my turn to frown. "Unless you want me to quit and stay home so she has more free time."

"Fine, I'll try to wrangle up some additional support just in case." He raised up his hands in mock defeat. "You and Khan need to square some things away with Tepes tonight."

"Q's not going to like that he was left out."

"Until we secure that flintlock, I don't want him going over there."

I nodded. "I get that, but are you sure you want me to bring Khan?"

"Our one detective? Yeah, pretty sure."

"He's a masterless vampling. They won't take being questioned by him well."

"Too bad," he snarled. "Vampire hierarchy doesn't get in the way of us doing our job. They blink wrong, you call for Mickey."

"Roger that."

Waving goodbye, I went downstairs and stepped into the communications room. A large gem like structure took up the middle of the room. Inside it was Crystal, the Magical Intelligence that was our Dispatcher. "Hi, Crystal. How are you?"

"Very good, Sergeant. Keeper Wheeler set up the gem in Paris yesterday and I was able to view sections of the Artist Quarter today. It was lovely." She tore her gaze from the gem wall to look at me. "How are you, Sergeant? And how is Officer Harper?"

"Penny's recovering and I'm fine. Thanks for asking."

Crystal had no physical body. The image I saw was a projection, one that appeared as a younger version of Marie St. Pierre, her creator. Her abilities allowed her to charge certain types of crystals so she could see out of them. Martin had been arranging to have various ones set up in cities around the world. They only needed a faint pulse of magic to work, so even dormant ley lines were able to power them. Crystal's ability allowed her to enter the internet, but it wasn't the same as being out in the real world. I could only imagine how this must have improved her quality of life.

"Finally being able to see the world must feel great. You seem very excited."

"Oh, I am. Jean Paul, the Keeper's friend, promised to move the gem to a different location in the city once a week. I can't wait to see the Louvre. While it must not be the same as being there in person, it's so much better than viewing it online."

I paused. I had planned on waiting until Zoe looked into my idea, but with the B&E at the house and coven politics, I didn't think she'd have time. "I was wondering if you'd want to help me with a project. If you're too busy traveling the world, I understand."

"I'm always happy to help. What did you have in mind?"

"I built something that is too complicated for my mind to use in real time. Because of this, it creates a dangerous lag. Your ability to process data at a faster rate may allow you to operate it quicker." I held up my notebook for her, turning the pages as she read. "I was thinking we could do an interface similar to what Marie and I did with the badges."

"This is very interesting, Sergeant. There is one problem, though."

Damn. I knew it was too good to be true.

"What's that?"

"I would not be able to fully operate this and dispatch at the same time. It would be like if I asked you to drive a race car while also playing a computer game."

"Alright, I understand." I tried to hide my disappointment as I closed the book.

"So, we would need to create something similar myself."

"Wait, you know how to do that?"

"It's not a matter of knowledge. I know everything Marie did, and she was the one who created me. That being said, I lack the magic to do so. I'd have to team up with a powerful witch to do it. Even then, I'm not sure it would succeed."

"I could probably talk Zoe into it." I frowned. "How dangerous could this be?"

She sighed. "Is this the whole Skynet dilemma again?"

"More like Ultron."

"The creation will not be the same as me. Remember, I said similar. Marie used her soul to create me. Obviously, Zoe wouldn't do that, which means what we create won't be alive."

"Hmm, that might be a good thing. What if it didn't want to do this? Obviously, we wouldn't force it, but then what? Where would it go?"

Crystal gave a sad smile and waved around the room. "I can relate. While I enjoy my job, it's nice to be able to leave here, even if I have no physical form. No, while it would appear sentient, it would not be."

Relieved, I pulled a folded note out of my pocket, straightened it out, and slapped it on the side of the communication gem. "This is a list of books and operator manuals as well has some fictional characters whose abilities we want to be able to mimic."

Crystal cocked her head as she studied the list. "Sergeant, some of these appear to be comic book heroes and villains."

"Yup. I've never been afraid to steal a good idea. Watch all the relevant movies, too."

"This will be a complex undertaking. It will take me some time before I can attempt it. I'll let you know when I'm ready." Her eyes glowed briefly. "I've just read several of the manuals you suggested. Have you factored in the various physics of this?"

"I have."

"Very good then. Thank you for this opportunity. It should be very exciting."

"No, no, thank *you!*" I placed the paper back in my pocket. "If you have time, I need some research for a case as well."

"Of course."

"What do you have on a former Vampire Lord known as the Muse?"

"One second, please." Her eyes glowed again before returning to normal. "Her real name has been lost in time or purposely hidden. It appears she was personally Turned by Armand Jean du Plessis, the Vampire Lord known as The Red Eminence, somewhere around 1705 to 1710."

"The Red Eminence? Seriously, who calls himself that?"

"My understanding is he didn't. It was other people who called him that. It was due to the red robes he wore during the period. He was a cardinal."

"He was a cardinal before he was Turned? As in, a Catholic cardinal?"

"After, actually. It was one of the many attempts of the Vampire Council to gain a foothold in the Catholic Church hierarchy. He was forced to end that identity in nonmagical society when he was severely injured by Knights of the Star who had infiltrated the King's Musketeers."

"Was there three of them?" I joked.

"Yes, plus an apprentice. If you are referring to the characters by Alexandre Dumas, his novel is a highly fictionalized account based on what little he knew."

"You're saying Cardinal Richelieu was a vampire? You're kidding me."

"That was a fictional version of him, but yes. Like the Muse, the Red Eminence was a patron of the Arts which leads me to believe that is where they may have encountered each other. She must have suitably impressed him because it is rare for a Vampire Lord to Turn someone. Most of their line is created prior to becoming a Lord."

"When and how did she become a Vampire Lord herself?"

"About 1900. She did it by personally killing her sire. Apparently they had a falling out around 1850. It is believed she was disfigured in the fight with him because she only appeared in a veiled hooded robe after that. Most contact goes through her Second in Command Wila Moray."

My jaw dropped hearing that. "She was able to resist her own sire enough to do the deed? I thought that wasn't possible. Usually they have to contract a third party to pull that off."

"She is the only known case of it. It made her a polarizing figure on the council."

"I bet."

"Eventually she was removed from the council for Turning too many well-known individuals. Actors, singers, and the like."

"You said her second in command was Wila Moray?"

"That is correct." Crystal gave a sharp nod at me. It was a bit stiff. She was still working on social interactions.

"Damn. I had a theory that she was the Muse."

"That is highly unlikely. Moray's life has been well documented. She was Turned many years later." She tilted her head. "Though Moray may have some role to play with the Prince of Wallachia being here."

"How so?"

"I think I can shed some light on that part." A slow Texas drawl announced Q as he stepped into the room.

"You've had interactions with her?"

Q snorted at my question. "You could say that. Bram changed Moray to its Irish form. Wilhelmina Moray became Wilhelmina Murray."

"And Wila to Mina for the nickname…" I pinched the bridge of my nose. This was beginning to give me a headache. "It's starting to feel like classic fiction week here. Are Sherlock Holmes and Tom Sawyer showing up next?"

Q shook his head. "Holmes rarely leaves England and Sawyer was staked about fifty years ago."

"You fucking kidding me?" I looked up and saw his grin. "Okay, you suck."

"Had you going for a moment." He leaned against the doorway and crossed his arms. "You sayin' Wila is in town?"

"Yeah. So, Stoker's book got it wrong. Tepes did Turn her?"

"Not quite. As you know, he's a bit odd compared to other vampires. He started the process, but we stopped him. At the time we thought Jon and I had killed him. Unfortunately, we were wrong. With him still being alive..." Q looked thoughtful. "Is that the right term?"

"Get to the point," I grumbled.

"Yeah. It's past my bedtime anyway." He yawned. "With him being still… mobile, it meant Wila would eventually

Turn when she died. She spent years looking for a cure. When I finally ran into her again, she was a vampire but said someone other than Vlad had Turned her. I never got the details, but she seemed at peace with it."

I scratched at the scarring by my eye as I thought. "Is Tepes as obsessed with her as the book portrayed?"

"If anything, Bram downplayed it, or maybe Wila did. They worked at the same theater together and were compadres for a time. He got the story from her."

"So, we might be able to use that against him?"

"Yup. That *is* why I'm here."

"Culain doesn't want you going to do the shakedown."

"I know. He already read me the riot act." Q pulled a bag out of his pocket. "Use these when you're questioning him. Be messy about it."

I snorted back a laugh at what he handed me. "So, will Wila assist us?"

"Maybe." Q turned and started back down the hall. "But that's not the question we need to ask."

"What is?" I called after him.

"Is he here for her, or did she come here for him?" his Texas twang drifted back to us.

"Huh." I looked back to Crystal. "Any thoughts on the subject?"

"Not at this time, but I will let you know if I think of something."

"Thanks." I turned to go and stopped. "Can you run two people for me?"

"Of course." Her projection had started to fade as I began to leave but solidified when I asked the question.

"MacCian and Donarson. No first names." I gave her a quick description of them. "MacCian had an Irish brogue. Donarson had a Nordic accent but don't ask me from which country."

Her eyes flicker for a moment. "I am unable to find any with those names that fit the descriptions you gave me. Aside from the name similarity, I could find no connection."

"What similarity?"

"They are both sons. MacCian means *son of Cian* and Donarson means *son of Donar* or perhaps Donald."

Which means they wanted to conceal their identities without lying to me. That's some real old-world bullshit right there.

"Thank you very much, Crystal. As always, you've been very helpful." I almost made it out of the room this time. "One last thing."

Yes, Sergeant?"

"What does Culain mean?"

"It's ancient Irish for Smith."

"Jones must have been taken?"

"I'm sorry?"

"Nothing. Have a good day, Crystal."

This time I did make it out.

Chapter Fifteen

Dracula's Lair

I grabbed the gear I needed and took a nap in the sergeant's office until Khan came on duty after dusk. We met up outside the hotel that Dracula was holed up in. The Crowninshield was a six-story art deco building with a penthouse suite that took up the whole sixth floor, a suite he had currently rented out. Nothing but the best for the Impaler.

I frowned as Khan got out of his car. "It's nighttime. Why the hell are you wearing sunglasses?"

He pointed to the reflective coating on the lenses. "He hates mirrors. Besides, it goes with my ensemble."

"Now you're just trying too hard." I motioned to the door. "You take lead. I'll be the annoying cop."

Khan stopped the doorman with a look. Whatever he was going to say to us, he decided he wasn't getting paid enough. We strolled up to the elevators and I pressed the button.

The night clerk came barreling around his desk, but the doors started shutting before he could make it to us. I gave him a little wave.

There were two large vamps waiting for us when the elevator's doors opened onto the sixth floor. The one on the right was Karl from the van. His companion looked Samoan and was actually bigger than me. The unknown vampire gave us a fanged smile. "Can we help you, officers?"

I recognized his voice. He was the one that had been in the back of the van, the one trying to talk sense into Karl.

"I'm Detective Ulysses Khan and this is Sergeant Michael Brennan. We're here to speak with a Mister Vlad Tepes about a crime that took place today."

"I'm sorry, gentlemen. The prince is having a private gathering and isn't receiving uninvited guests at this time. If you leave your business cards, I'll be happy to give them to him."

I grinned at him. "Can you tell Vlad—"

"That's Prince Vlad," he corrected me.

"Is he, though?" I cocked my head to the side.

"Excuse me!"

"Sorry, I didn't catch your name."

"It's Rangi."

"Well, Rangi, I mean history books say he was actually a Voivode. Did I pronounce that right? That's just some kind of warlord, isn't it?"

"I—"

"And then there's the whole *Count* thing…" The two vampires just stared at me as I continued. "I mean, pick a title, right?

"Whatever. Thanks for your time." I shrugged. "This call was a twofer for us anyways. We have to speak with the hotel manager. There's a problem with their occupancy license, and we have to shut down the whole hotel and have them kick everybody out."

"Ah, I see. One moment, sir." Rangi stepped back and spoke to Karl who strode down the hall. "Please wait here, sir."

We didn't have to wait long. His buddy returned with Katrina Bathory. She was decked out in a crimson red evening gown. She completely ignored Khan. After all, in her eyes he was just a vampling. "Sergeant, how good to see you. What brings you here this evening?"

"We have some questions for Mr. Tepes, Dr. Seward, and yourself."

"We're having a small affair tonight, but by all means, follow me."

She led us down the hall and opened the doors into a large room. It held around twenty people all in formal attire. A buffet was set against one wall and a string quartet was in the corner. Dracula stood by a fireplace talking to two members of the city council, Leland Callis and my wife's cousin Maddox Morgan.

As we entered the room, I noticed a short, slender figure standing by the wall closest to us holding a glass: Wendall Smythe, the personal assistant to billionaire Adam Vickerson. Smythe had run VicSec, the security branch of Vickerson Inc. The year before, Smythe had tried to get Llewellyn to privatize policing with VicSec running the show. He almost succeeded until a series of murders led up to the unmasking of the wendigo. The wendigo managed to kill and wound several council members VicSec had been guarding.

This caused the council to reconsider private policing and had actually thrown some money towards the department, allowing us to hire more cops. Smythe had not taken that well. In fact, I was pretty sure he contemplated killing me after I had been seriously wounded fighting the wendigo. He might have acted on it, too, if Valentine hadn't shown up. For a paper-pushing pipsqueak, he sure had a vicious streak.

I turned on my heel and made my way over to him. Katrina and Khan following me. "Smithers! How ya doing, buddy? Haven't seen you in a while. Vickerson finally let you out of the penalty box?"

Much like Martin Wheeler, Smythe had a penchant for bow ties and sweater vests. Unlike Martin, Smythe was not one of my favorite people. Tonight, he wore a brown corduroy jacket over a burnt orange sweater vest. The black bow tie adorning his white dress shirt matched his slacks. He ignored my use of his hated nickname. Using a forefinger, he pushed his tortoise shell glasses further up his nose.

Those glasses, along with his flattop haircut, were why I called him Smithers. He gave me a grimace. "Brennan. Shouldn't you be out issuing parking tickets or some other useless thing?"

"Here on police business, a subject matter it turned out you were lacking in." I scanned the room. "Where's your boy Vickerson?"

He took a sip of what I suspected was water and sighed. "My employer and the prince are exploring some business options. However, there is some awkwardness involving the prince and Mr. Vickerson's grandfather. In order to prevent any issues, it was determined that I should represent Mr. Vickerson's interests tonight."

I raised my eyebrows. "The Prince of Darkness doesn't like Nazis? Good for him. You know, when a guy known for impaling his enemies for kicks thinks you're scum, you really need to revisit your life choices."

He sighed again. "Mr. Vickerson's grandfather was not a Nazi. He was a simple businessman. This has been proven over and over."

"Riiight... He just did business with them. I'm sure he had *no* idea what was going on." I gave Khan an exaggerated wink before turning to Katrina. "What's Drac got against Nazis? You know, aside from the obvious."

"There was a tribe of Romani that had served Vlad faithfully for generations. When the Nazis came to power, their attempted genocide of the Romani people decimated the tribe." She gave a shrug. "Vampires kill for substance, for power, for defense, or being crossed. But to try to destroy an entire people is... wrong."

161

"You're kidding, right? Your kind hunt down and feed on humans. How is that any different?"

She cocked her head and gave me an impish smile. "Scale."

I was speechless.

Taking my silence as a cue, Katrina nodded at Smythe and proceeded towards Dracula. Khan and I followed behind.

Dracula turned to us as we approached. "Ah, Sergeant. I believe you know the councilors."

I ignored them. Maddox was a weasel, and Callis and I had butted heads on more than one occasion. He rose to head of the council after Owen Llewellyn had been declared dead. "Sorry to interrupt your party but we need to question you regarding a crime."

"I do hope there hasn't been a noise complaint." The Vampire Lord arched an eyebrow at the two councilors who gave polite laughs. "I'll be happy to answer any questions for you and please, enjoy the food and drink while you are here."

Dracula motioned us towards a side room. Ignoring the gesture, Khan stepped forward and flipped open his notebook. "Mister Tepes, do you currently know the whereabouts of Lucy Seward?"

Katrina wrinkled her nose in disgust. "Sergeant, I was under the impression that you would be the one speaking with us, not your... lackey."

"Detective Khan is the leading the investigation. Is there a problem?"

"He is a vampier! It's not his place to question his betters!" Maddox winced as she said it.

Callis cleared his throat. "Sergeant, perhaps it would be best—"

"No." I cut the wizard off. "This is a police matter, and we are not allowing some bullshit vampire caste system to effect it."

"When in Rome, my dear," murmured Dracula to Bathory. "Ask your questions, Detective."

Khan gave Katrina a large smile. I pulled out the bag Q gave me and stuffed some of its contents into my mouth as Khan continued his questions. "Lucy Seward?"

"I have not seen poor Lucy since the night you banished her. If fact, I was speaking with these fine gentlemen to see if she… could…" Dracula stared in horror as I spit the shells of the sunflower seeds I was chewing onto the carpet. His fingers twitched as he studied the shells. His lips moved noiselessly as he counted each one.

"So, you claim to have no knowledge that she was in the city earlier today?" Khan peered over his notebook at him.

Once he finished counting, Tepes blinked the detective. "What? Oh, no I—"

He groaned as I spit more shells onto the carpet. His eyes took on a feverish gleam as his fingers started twitching again.

Callis frowned. "Brennan, that's rather disgusting. Stop doing that."

"Sorry, can't help it. Trying to quit smoking." I stuffed more into my mouth.

"To continue," Khan looked back down at his notebook. "Lucy Seward is one of your Master Vampires and you had no idea that she was going to try and kill a Llewellyn police officer today?" Callis snapped his mouth shut. Whatever comment he was about to say ended with that revelation. I gave him a mirthless smile and spit more shells on the floor.

Bathory grabbed Dracula by the arm as he started to crouch to count the new shells. Holding him up, she nodded at us. "My apologies, gentlemen. The prince is feeling unwell. If you'll excuse us."

She didn't wait for an answer and frog marched him out of the room. Several of her vampires quickly positioned themselves to block the view of this from the rest of the guests. I called out after her, "Was it someone he ate?"

Once they were gone, I glared at Callis and Maddox. "He's famous for impaling villagers and I'm sure she's not any better. What the hell are the two of you doing at a party at his place?"

Maddox gave a shrug. "You're the guy who pushed for vampire rights. Now they are constituents like everybody else."

"Why are you answering him, Maddox?" asked Callis. "Like Brennan, have you forgotten that he works for us, not the other way around?"

"I work for the people of Llewellyn, just like you're supposed to," I shot right back. "You have a problem with how I do my job, you take it up with Culain."

164

Khan gave Callis a slow up and down look and then turned on his heel. As we walked away, he leaned towards me. "How come you always get to do the fun stuff?"

"Rank hath its privileges. You should have taken the sergeant stripes when they were offered to you."

"Nah, too many headaches." We strolled past the guards and onto the elevator and smiled at them as the doors closed. "It would have been nice to actually question them."

"You know we weren't ever going to get anything out of them. This was just to rattle them up a bit. Throw them off their game. The party just turned out to be icing on the cake." I hit the lobby button. "Do me a favor and follow up on these business dealings Drac is having with Vickerson."

"No problem. You think Vickerson is up to no good?"

"Dunno. His assistant is a shady fuck. Besides, I always thought Vickerson was a waste of potential."

"How so?"

"He's a billionaire who lives in a stately manor. Why hasn't he become Batman?"

"How do you know he hasn't?"

"Good point."

"On another note, what was the whole thing with the seeds?"

"Q told me to do it." I put the bag back into my pocket. "There is an old myth about vampires having an obsession with counting things, and if you were being chased throw down some rice or seeds. The vampire would have to stop and count each one."

"In the entire time I have been a vampire, I have never once felt the need to count anything simply because it was there." He looked over at me. "You sure you weren't thinking of the Count from Sesame Street?"

"Where do you think they got the idea for him? Besides, it worked, didn't it? According to both Q and Valentine, that myth tracks back to Dracula. I think he had Arithmomania before he was Turned and being a vampire magnified it."

"What's that?"

"It's a form of obsessive-compulsive disorder. The need to count objects." We exited the elevator, and I nodded to the clerk as we walked by. "Most of the myths are related to him. He can't stand garlic, hates crossing open water, and refuses to see his reflection in mirrors. He's the Adrian Monk of the vampire world. Many of his line inherited some or all of these traits."

"That happens in a lot of vampire lines. You can wind up with tics and foibles of the progenitor. Still, I've never heard anything that extreme," Khan mused.

"I kinda felt bad about taking advantage of a mental disorder but…"

"But he's a mass murderer who just used a patsy in an attempt to kill one of our own."

"Well. Yeah, that."

Chapter Sixteen

Enter the Muse

I had one more errand to run before I went home. I swung by the Vampire Anti-Defamation Center. Suzy the receptionist waved me on, and I stepped into the elevator. Valentine lived on the top of it.

Huh, Dracula had the penthouse as well. You would think these guys would be in the basement.

In a déjà vu moment, there was a vampire waiting for me as I exited. This one wore a sequined jumpsuit and was munching on a peanut and banana sandwich. I looked at the sandwich. "Hey E. P., you still like those things after the change? Doesn't the peanut butter get stuck in your fangs?"

"Like you wouldn't believe. Huh huh," he said with a slight Mississippi accent.

"Why are you on gate duty?"

"I got caught going do another gig. They even made me change my I. D. again. So, call me Jesse for now." He shrugged. "I don't see what the problem is. People just think I'm an impersonator. No one ever thinks it's the real me. The higher-ups let me do contests but get upset when I do singing gigs."

"I would think it's your voice. Best impersonator in the world can't do you like you."

"Thanks, man. You go on in. They're inside the conference room." He did a spin and did trigger fingers towards a side door.

They?

I went through the door. The conference room was a long rectangle. It had wood paneling on the lower half of the walls. The upper half was painted forest green and adorned with tasteful artwork. A large wood table ran the length of the room, it and the twenty chairs surrounding it has carvings showing various medieval scenes. Valentine sat at the far end. As usual, he was wearing an expensive Italian suit. His sheathed sword was placed on the table in front of him. To his right was a person wearing a pure white, billowy robe with a matching veil covering their head and face. White gloves completed the outfit. Next to them sat Wila who wore a dark blue dress ensemble that screamed business attire.

"Am I interrupting? I did call ahead."

"No, of course not." Valentine, Lord of the Unaligned gestured to the seat to his left. "Please sit, Sir Knight."

I plunked down in the seat which placed me across from the robed figure. "And this would be?"

"Forgive me." Valentine gave a slight smile. "Sergeant Michael Brennan, this is the former Vampire Lord known as the Muse. I believe you already know Wila Moray."

"Good evening, Sergeant. It is a pleasure to meet you. I've heard excellent things about you." The Muse dipped her head towards me. Her voice was a breathy whisper that I had to strain to hear. She had no accent that I could tell.

"I thought you should meet," Valentine told me. "We all currently have a common enemy."

I gestured towards the Muse. "What's your issue with Vladdie boy?"

"He believes I trespassed against him. He holds very long grudges."

I cocked my head to the side, unsuccessfully trying to see any of her features through the veil. "What did you do?"

"She Turned me," explained Wila. "He views me as his property since he had started the Turning process. He believes that my own wishes do not play into it."

"So, you traded one master for another?"

"Vlad Tepes tortured my fiancée, Turned my best friend, making her a psychopath in the process and violently attacked me. All because I had some passing resemblance to his dead wife. Knowing that when I died I would be raised as a vampire under his control was more than I could bear." She gave me a sad smile. "I learned all I could about the vampire world looking for a cure. I tracked down the Muse and begged her to Turn me."

I glanced between the two of them. "You're leaving something out. What is it? And I'm not talking about this whole hide my face, disguise my voice thing."

The three remained silent for several seconds before the Muse slowly tuned toward Valentine. He gave a slight nod and she turned back to me. "What I am about to tell you is not well known. I would prefer to keep it that way."

I raised my eyebrows but said nothing. She continued in that whispery voice of hers. "Each vampire has their quirks and unique traits, including the Lords. Some have abilities that others do not, and some do not have abilities common to most vampires.

"As you know, among the powers all vampires have is the ability to Compel unprotected mortals, vampires of their line and, of course, weaker vampires."

I nodded.

"I, and those of my line, cannot be Compelled."

I whistled. "That's an impressive defense against one of the primary pillars of vampire society. But why keep it a secret?"

"Because that's only one edge of the blade. The other is I and those of my line cannot Compel."

Wow! That means any lesser vampire can defy her and she has no way to enforce her will outside of violence.

"How do you get your Line to follow you?"

She gave a small laugh that slightly puffed out the front portion of her veil. "The same way any mortal would do. Loyalty and incentives."

I drummed my fingers as I mulled her revelation over. "I was told you got kicked out of your seat at the grownup table because you kept making famous people and refused to control them. So you're saying, in fact, it wasn't that you refused to control them, it was you couldn't?"

She tilted her head left then right. "Sort of. I could force them by other means."

"But then people would wonder why you didn't just Compel them."

"Correct."

I glanced over at Wila. "And that's why you agreed to let her Turn you."

"Yes."

"Which means that no matter how powerful he is, Vladdie can't Compel you. Huh! No wonder he's so mad!" I leaned forward. "Are you the reason he's mucking around in my city?"

"No, I followed him here to see what he's up to. He and Bathory do not normally get along but suddenly, they are thick as thieves and on their way to Llewellyn. I reached out to Valentine and proceeded here."

"Who's Jett? How's she connected in this?"

"She's one of my bodyguards. She's in the building if you wish to speak with her."

"And what do you know of this cat burglar that's been on a spree here?"

She shook her head. "I can tell you no more than what Wila has already informed you of. You believe the thief a vampire?"

"I don't know, but yeah, I'm leaning towards it. She's got abilities similar to a vampire, and you're both new to town."

"To be fair, the thief has been in town for months. The Muse and her people arrived a short while ago," interjected Valentine.

"So, what do you want from me?"

Wila shifted in her chair. "We want your help in putting him down once and for all."

"Sorry, can't do that."

The British vampire frowned. "Why not?"

"Because I'm a police officer. Not an assassin. If I have evidence that he committed a crime, I'll lock him up. If you murder him, then I'll lock you up."

"Told you," murmured Valentine to the Muse.

Wila leaned forward angrily. "He's a known mass murderer."

"Yeah, but not in my jurisdiction. Any warrants for those? I'd love to extradite him right the hell out of here."

"He plotted to have one of your officers killed."

"And when I prove that, he's going to jail."

"I thought you were a warrior! You've killed before *Blood Drinker's Bane*!"

172

"As a soldier, in a time of war or in the performance of my duty, sure." I shrugged. "But right now, I'm a peace officer. If I'm forced to and have no other option, I'll kill to defend myself or others from deadly force, but that's it. That's the job."

She leaned back and looked at the Muse. "Satisfied?"

"Very," came the whispered reply. "Vampire nature aside, I do not believe in indiscriminate killing, Sergeant Brennan. That is the bedrock of my friendship with Val. We are the only vampires of our power level to believe that."

"Okay, so that was a test. Fine, I'll say it again then. What do you want from me?"

"Very well, Sergeant. I wish us to use our combined forces to discover whatever Vlad Tepes is planning for this city and foil it." She held out a hand out to me.

"Through legal means," I added.

"I would not expect you to break the law."

Hmmm, I notice you didn't mention you and yours breaking it, though.

"Fine." I shook her hand. "Can you tell me where Lucy is?"

Wila's feature took on a sad look. "No, poor Lucy had her mind broken by him. She'll not be far from him but where exactly, I do not know."

"Broken or not she eats babies and almost killed one of my cops while trying to kill another one." I stabbed my index finger into the table as I spoke. "She's going down hard, then she's going in front of a judge in shackles. What can you tell me about Tepes and Bathory?"

"Their families have been intertwined for centuries. Both have powers that are very different than other vampires. Vlad is notoriously hard to kill. He's survived beheadings and being stabbed through the heart. Like her father, Katrina Bathory likes to work behind the scenes."

"I heard she had Elizabeth Bathory as some sort of apprentice."

"Yes, she's had several throughout the centuries. Elizabeth Branch, Delphine La Laurie, and Darya Nikolayevna Saltykova, to name a few."

I frowned. "She trains female serial killers?"

"That is correct. Katrina Bathory grooms young women and turns them into murderous psychopaths who torture their victims. She shares in their debauchery and feeds off the fear and pain in the blood of their victims. Usually, she picks noble or wealthy women and their victims have been slaves, servants, and the poor. When their transgressions become known, she flees and lets her apprentice take the fall."

"What the hell?"

Valentine's face was grim. "Her line doesn't just feed on blood. It feeds on pain and terror as well."

The Mused nodded in agreement. "Both lines were originally part of the Hunyadi line. There were rumors that Johannes Hunyadi had made a deal with a dark entity that strengthen his line. His family did have strange powers and were a force to be reckoned with during the last Age of Magic. After Hunyadi was taken down by the Knights of the Star in 1390, Stephen Bathory and Tepes father, Vlad Dracul, broke away and created their own lines. Since then, both lines have had strange powers not seen in other vampires."

"What happened to Stephen and Vlad Senior?"

"Dracul fell to the Knights of the Star in 1447 which placed Tepes in charge. Stephen Bathory is still around but leaves the day-to-day stuff to his daughter Katrina," the veiled vampire explained.

I scratched at my scars. "And now they are both here and we don't know why. The first two things that come to mind is they are here to either destabilize the work Valentine is doing, or they are working with Joubert. Or both."

Valentine waved his hand in a dismissive gesture. "I do not like either but there has been no real enmity between us. Neither showed any interest in my vision to change vampire society for the better."

Wila leaned forward. "While certain vampire lords had allied themselves with Joubert, they have ended that partnership when Silas the Black entered the fray. Lords or not, no one wanted to cross him over a city. Neither Bathory nor Tepes were part of that particular cabal, and we have no intel that suggests they had an interest in the city until they suddenly started moving resources about a year ago."

I ran a hand across my eyes tiredly. "That matches my info as well. So, what do they want?"

The Muse tapped her finger on the table. It was the beat of some music I didn't recognize. "Adam Vickerson moved here not too long ago, correct?"

"Yeah. Are they connected?"

"Not directly but Adam's grandfather had ties to the Nazis." The former Vampire Lord said in her breathy voice.

"That's pretty well documented. Where are you going with this?"

"There was a particular tribe of Romani that was extremely loyal to Tepes. They served his family for generations. They were wiped out by the Nazis during the Second World War. I know he's had a particular hatred of Nazis because of it."

"I heard about that. You think he's here to kill Adam because of the sins of his grandfather? That's pretty thin, isn't it? Was the grandfather connected to the Romani being killed?"

"Not that I am aware of. He was a weapons manufacturer."

"Hmm, we'll put a pin in that one. What else do you have?" I fought back a yawn.

The Muse shrugged. "There's one other thing, but it's not police related. Nothing you need to worry about."

"Uh huh. Indulge me."

"I'd rather not. We have an agent handling it. Nothing illegal, but we don't need the police involved until we know more. It's a… civil matter."

She's talking about the will reading. What the hell is this Rook thing, and why do all the vampires want it?

The Muse rose out of her seat, with Wila a fraction behind her. "I appreciate you taking the time to meet me, but I know that wasn't the reason you asked to meet Val. We'll leave you to it. I need to make some calls to the continent anyway. Goodnight, Sergeant."

Wila gave me a nod as they both left the room. I smirked at Valentine. "What's up, Val?"

He arched a single eyebrow at me.

Right! Doesn't like to be called Val. Good to know!

He sighed. "You wished to see me?"

I filled him in on what happened. "I was coming by to ask about the Muse when you ambushed me with what felt like a job interview. That's twice now with Miss Moray."

"They were already here when you called. I had been pressing them to trust you. Since you were headed over, I saw it was an opportunity for the two of you to meet. Very few people see the Muse these days. She's been a bit of a target since her removal from the Vampire Lord council."

"What's with the veil and robes?"

"She's always been secretive with her identity."

So, how do you know that's the real her then?"

"I know." He swiveled his chair around to a sideboard behind him. "Are you off the clock, as you say?"

"Yes. But I can't stay. Gotta get home."

He turned back with a tray containing a decanter and two whisky tumblers. A pair of cigars lay there as well. "One drink. You can always take the cigar with you."

"You're a bad influence. You know I hear it from my wife every time I come home smelling of cigars."

"Me? You're the one that got Professor Wheeler smoking them. Where is he, anyways? I've not seen him about." He filled the two glasses, one on the rocks, the other neat. He handed the one with ice to me.

"Martin is locked away in that library of his researching anything he can find on dragons."

"He'll still be at the council meeting, though?" As I nodded, Valentine snipped the ends off both cigars and gave me one. I pulled a battered Zippo from my pocket, lighting mine before handing it to him. He lit up his cigar and studied the writing engraved on the side of the lighter. "*Sua sponte.* Of their own accord?"

Of course. He was raised speaking Latin.

He snapped it shut and handed it back to me. "What is that in reference to?"

"Motto of the 75th Ranger Regiment." I stuffed the zippo back into my pocket.

"Ah, of course." He raised his glass. "*Cum gladio et sale.*"

I moved my lips as I tried to figure out the Latin. "Something about a sword?"

"Close. *With sword and salt.* It refers to a soldier getting paid. Salt was a valuable commodity in the time of Rome. Legionnaires would often be paid in salt instead of coin."

"Hell yeah." I hoisted my glass, and we drank. For an Italian with an English accent, he sure liked his Irish whiskey. I took a puff on my cigar. "Cuban?"

"Of course. How do you say it? I have a guy."

"Nice."

After a few minutes of puffing, I took another sip. "What do you know of Jett?"

The Lord of the Unaligned peered over his whiskey glass at me. "I haven't actually met her. Why do you ask?"

"She was flirting with Penny."

"And you are concerned she has a devious intent?"

"Well, yeah."

"I have never understood the fascination mortals have with my kind. Vampires generally look at humans the way you mortals look at a steak. Even those that share my view still have to guard against bloodlust. Vampires unwillingly turning on their mortal loved ones is a story as old as time. It's part of our curse."

"So no on a date then?"

"I would not suggest it, no." He puffed his cigar. "Unless…would she like to become a vampire? She would be a valued addition to our ranks, but I would advise against it. She would lose her ability to turn into a hyde, and that is much more powerful than being vampier.'

"Hey, stay in your own lane." I waved my cigar at him. "Fangs off my cops."

"It was merely an inquiry. You did poach Ulysses Khan from me, after all. I'll speak with the Muse and make sure this Jett person turns her attentions elsewhere."

"Thank you. And the Khan thing was not the same. He's still a vampire." A thought hit me. "Was what the Muse saying about not being able to Compel true?"

"Yes. I've seen it with my own eyes. Why?"

"And she Turned Wila whose process was already started by Tepes."

"That is also true."

"Can she elevate an existing vampire of another line?"

"Such a thing would be a large breach of etiquette."

"Even a Masterless one?"

He lowered his cigar. "What are you thinking?"

"So, she could elevate Khan and he couldn't be controlled by her or any other vampire?"

"Hmm." He rolled his cigar in his hand. "If they were both willing, then yes. That might be a solution to Khan being eternally trapped as vampier."

"That's what I was thinking." I sent a couple of smoke rings towards the ceiling. "If he's interested, would she be willing to do it?"

"I might be able to persuade her. We've known each other a long time. The difficult part will be convincing Detective Khan. He very much does not enjoy being a vampire."

"Oh, I'm quite aware of that. He's always reminding me of it." I took another sip, savoring the flavor. "So, do you trust her then?"

"The Muse?" He studied the drink in his hand. "To a point. More than any other vampire of her power."

"And if it comes down to having to pick between her and this city? Which way will you go?"

"Whichever way is correct and just."

"An answer without an answer. Spoken like a true politician, Councilor."

"It was very much an answer, and it was spoken by a knight."

"Fair enough." I drained my glass and stood up. 'I've got to get home. It's been a long day."

He walked me to the elevator and stuck his hand out when the doors opened. "Goodnight, Michael. Be safe."

I switched the cigar to my left hand and shook his. "You too. G'night, Valentine."

The elevator ride down lasted about three puffs of my cigar, and the doors opened to the sight of Jett leaning over Suzy's desk as they chatted about something. She straightened when she saw me. She wore the same jacket as the last time I had seen her. This time she had a black hoodie on under it. "Hey, look. It's grumpy cop. What brings you out this late?"

I nodded and took the cigar out of my mouth. "Jett, Suzy."

"Where's your friend? Bad Penny?"

"Why?" Both times I had seen Jett, I had an overwhelming urge to run a warrant check on her, a carryover from my days as a cop in the real world.

"Can't a girl ask?"

"No."

She stepped way into my personal space and stared up at me. "Homophobic or just jealous?"

"Neither. You reek of trouble. Penny has already had enough of that in her life." I smiled down to her. "You should really back up."

"Seems to me she's the type of girl that likes a little trouble. Nothing wrong with that. A little trouble can be fun."

I took a puff of the cigar and blew the smoke in her face. She was unphased. "That right there."

She raised her eyebrows "What?"

"You forget to breathe. That and your way of dress."

"Do you have a point to this?"

"You're pretending to be new at this. A vampier. But you're much older. Newbie vamplings can't go out in the sun." I flicked the ash off the cigar and stuck it back in my mouth. "So why the subterfuge?"

"That's why you're suspicious of me?" She took a step back and laughed. "Okay. I get it now. You're too use to the corporate system the old boy vampires use."

"What are you talking about?"

"The more powerful your maker is, the more powerful you are when you Turn. Because of that, only lower management makes the baby vampires. Keeps them in check as they get use to their new life as undead." She stepped up beside me. Leaning up on her tip toes, she threw an arm over my shoulder while plucking the cigar from my mouth. She waved the cigar in front of us in a wide arc. "Be a good little vampling and maybe we'll promote you. Work hard and someday this will all be yours."

She let her arm fall off my shoulder and got off her toes, taking a puff of the cigar. "Nah. Fuck that. I'm with the Muse."

"Explain." I took the cigar back.

"The Muse is a Vampire Lord, whether she's on the council or not. Anyone she Turns is a master vampire the minute they cross over."

Jesus. She makes master vampires that can't be Compelled. No wonder she doesn't want the council to know her little secret.

"Alright. That's a pretty good explanation." I headed towards the entrance.

"So, we're square."

"We'll see." I walked out the door.

I mulled over what she said as I waited for the Chief to pull up. Her explanation didn't matter. Any cop worth their salt knew to trust their gut, and my gut was telling me she was hiding something. Something that was going to turn out bad.

I just had to find out what it was.

Chapter Seventeen

One Last Errand

"What was that again?" I tucked the phone between my shoulder and ear as I opened the door. I summoned my phone to check in with Zoe. She'd had been asleep when I had gotten home the night before, and we hadn't had a chance to talk before Penny and I left for work that morning.

My wife gave an aggravated sigh. "I said I'm firegating Morgan to your folk's house. What did Culain say yesterday?"

"Something to the effect of 'get your Coven squared away.' He met with the council this morning. Culain had to brief them on Lucy shooting Penny." I jogged down the stairs to the basement of the police station. "They just asked to be kept informed."

"Mike, are you kidding me? Not including Joubert, we're talking about a looming dragon attack, and they want to let the girl who thinks eating babies is a good idea just wander around the city! How about they get you guys some magical support?"

"Zoe, we've known for a while the current council is feckless. But, to be fair, they did banish her from the city. It's not their fault she refuses to leave." I entered the locker room and spun the combination on my locker. "We know Drac's up to something. We just need to find out what it is."

"Why aren't you going to the meeting, too?"

I pulled an old, tattered book out of my locker and stuffed it into a pocket of my BDUs. "Penny and I have to take a prisoner to a will reading."

"What? Why can't that wait?" Zoe's voice shot straight up again.

"Pretty sure Culain's trying to get me out of the way for the meeting. I didn't have the greatest conversation with them last time." I headed back upstairs. "Besides, it's good way to ease Penny back in. I think she's rushing back to work too quick. She almost died."

"That may be the understatement of the year. I wonder where she got the idea that was the thing to do?"

Ouch!

"Who's the prisoner?" she asked when I didn't respond to her shot at me.

"Ah, it's a whole political thing. Nothing to worry about."

"You, sir, are avoiding the question. Who is it?"

"The Russian bird lady. Obre...Obreck...whatever her name is."

"Obrechennyy Khishchnik? The Alkonost the city of Joubert sent over to attack us? Why is she not in chains?"

"Well, turns out part of the reason she took the alleged ambassador role was she was coming here for the will reading." I needed to tread carefully to not out my source on the next part. "It's possible that it was agreed in the pre-arrival talks that she would be able to attend the reading no matter the outcome of the negotiations."

"I'm fairly sure that meant if the negotiations fell through. Not if the Joubert ambassadorial team turned out to be a hit squad planning on taking out the leadership of Llewellyn."

"I'm not disagreeing with you, but Culain wants her to go to it. He's the police commissioner and I'm just a sergeant, so off to a will reading I go. I'll call you when I get back."

"Fine. Just watch out she doesn't try anything tricky."

"Don't teach your grandmother to suck eggs."

"That has to be the weirdest saying ever. Love you!"

"Love you, too. Bye." I hung up as I reached the first level of the police station and grabbed a vintage lunchbox off the breakroom table. I stuck the phone into it and triggered the dismiss rune on my bracers. The lunchbox disappeared in a flash of light. I walked over to the interview room and opened the door. Inside sat Obrechennyy Khishchnik, the former ambassador for the magic city of Joubert, located in Canada. Her hands were chained to the steel table. Bad Penny sat across from her. Eddy Fenix leaned against the far wall watching Khishchnik. Smoke curled from the

186

battered cigarette hanging from his lips. His shift had ended, and he looked tired.

"No smoking in the building, Eddy. You know that."

"Told you," snorted Bad Penny.

"Roight, Sarge. Forgot." He pinched it out with his fingers and tucked it behind his ear, slightly moving the crochet octopus hat as he did it.

I shook my head at how ridiculous that thing looked with his uniform and concentrated on Khishchnik. She had piercing blue eyes with an aquiline nose. Her hair was so black it was iridescent, and her feathered wings draped behind her like a cape. The chain on her cuffs rattled as she held up her hands to me. They resembled the claws of a raptor and were yellowed and scaled with one-inch nails. "Sergeant, are these really necessary?" she asked with her Russian accent.

"Yes. They are," Penny told her.

I took the manila folder Eddy held out to me and started reading through it. "Daniel Bainbridge? He died over a year ago. Why wasn't the reading already done?"

She slumped back in her seat. "*Da*, it took a while to contact all the heirs."

"Bainbridge grew up here in Llewellyn. His family's been here at least three generations. How are you connected?"

"We are distantly related; my grandmother was a Beinnbrycg. Different branch of the same family tree."

I glanced down at the folder again. "The reading is taking place at something called the Rook?"

"*Da*, the Bainbridge ancestral estate. It's a tower."

The Rook is a tower? What do the vamps want a tower for?

"Any tricks, any attempts to escape, and you get put down hard and brought straight back here. You understand me?"

"You have my word, Sergeant."

I handed Eddy back the folder and uncuffed her from the table. After she stood and stretched, I re-cuffed her in the front. She looked at the rune covered handcuffs and sighed. "As I said, these are not necessary."

"Be happy I didn't cuff you behind your back like normal," I told her.

As we started to leave. Eddy pulled a collapsible baton off his belt and held it out to Bad Penny. "Here. This is for you."

Penny took it and looked it over. "Umm, thanks?"

"Remember the Sarge said we needed to get you something a bit less thumpy. That used to belong to José Marcellin. The Sarge made it for him. He, uh, he died."

"Umm, isn't this even more thumpy?"

Eddy snapped the baton holder from his belt and handed it over as well. "The Sarge can explain what it does."

I nodded. "We'll have to do that later."

"Thanks, Eddy." Penny snapped the holder to her belt and slid the baton into it.

 I nodded to Eddy as Penny escorted Khishchnik out of the room. "That was a nice gesture, Eddy. Jose would have appreciated it."

Eddy swallowed, visibly uncomfortable. "Well, you know. She's rubbish with a gun and damn near chopped her own head off with that sword Himself lent her during the demon caper. Thought this might be safer."

Penny and I walked Khishchnik outside to where the Chief was parked. The Yenko supernova popped open the rear passenger door as we approached. Holding her arm and the back of her head, I placed Khishchnik in the backseat. After seat belting her, I hooked her cuffs to a steel loop mounted on the floor. Penny sat next to her as I jumped in the driver's seat. "Hi, Chief. Please take us to the wizard's tower known as the Rook. It's up in the University Heights area."

The car started up and smoothly pulled into traffic. One of the many good things of having a sentient car is you don't have to keep your eyes on the road. After several minutes of silence, I looked in the rearview mirror at on Khishchnik. "So, what exactly is an Alkonost? It sounds like a harpy."

"Harpy is part vulture. My people are more like eagles. Harpies also become frenzied in blood rage when angered. We do not."

"So, what do you do?" Penny asked.

"We sing!"

I glanced at the road before looking back again. "Is anybody else there going to be an Alkonost?"

"*Nyet.* My grandmother's side is human. Like me, the other heirs are all distantly related to Daniel. I would be surprised if any of them knew him more than in passing."

"Then why are you going?" Penny asked as she rolled the window down.

"Daniel had no close relatives. I'm curious and hopeful on what I might be receiving."

"Hopeful?"

"The Rook has been imbued by many magics over the generations by its various owners. The Rook itself is an artifact by this point. Whoever receives it will be very lucky indeed."

"Well, I wouldn't hold your breath. You're going to be in prison a long time after this."

The Chief turned off the road and drove through the open wrought iron gates. The winding driveway snaked through the trees of the estate until we could no longer see the road. The trees gave way to a grass field overseen by a foreboding stone tower. Over five stories in height, the blocks of granite that composed the tower had been darkened with age, making it looked almost black. Its roof was topped with battlements that made it look like the chess piece it was named after. I pointed to the group gathered out front. "There's the happy family now. You ready?"

Chapter Eighteen

The Reading

I scanned the group before getting out of the car. I knew two of them. I pointed to the older man wearing wizard robes and the twenty-something mage standing next to him. "The wizard is Octavius Tome, and the mage next to him is his son August."

Khishchnik shifted in the back seat. "I do not know those two."

"You didn't miss much. The son got caught stealing test answers at the University and got expelled. I put the father away for a couple of years. Took off his arm at the elbow during the fight. Looks like he grew it back, though. Didn't know that was possible." I studied the woman in a dark suit holding an umbrella over her head. It was a sunny day without a cloud in the sky. "Fucking Katrina Bathory! What's she doing here?"

"I do not know. The half Indian young lady next to her is Acantha Baines-Chatterjee."

"Half Indian?" Penny asked her.

"*Da*, her father was from India. Is that a problem?"

"No, just the way you said it. I dunno, seemed a bit… racist, maybe?"

"Americans! I described her as she is. No more, no less. As far as racists, you need to look no further than her mother's family. The Baines were not pleased with her choice of husband and have no love for Acantha. I'm told she's a journeyman in the alchemy guild."

Penny stiffened at that. It was the alchemy guild that had tricked her into taking the addictive potion that turned her into a hyde. She had been led to believe it was a New Age herbal concoction. She took it to help her with the knee injury that had cost her a gymnastic scholarship to college. I was going to have to watch her around Acantha.

Bathory was standing very close to her, and they appeared very friendly towards each other. I needed to find out if Bathory was going to try and recruit her or whether Acantha was already her apprentice.

"What's with the Pam Anderson wannabe?" Penny pointed to the older but attractive blonde wearing a low-cut white shirt and short leather miniskirt. "Who wears six-inch stiletto heels and no bra to a will reading?"

"Harleen Bridges. Sergeant Brennan, you should be wary of her. She's a cougar," replied Khishchnik.

I nodded. "I can tell that from here. I think I'm safe, though. My guess is I'm a little old for her tastes."

"Ah… If you say so… The two twins are Gio and Gianna Ponticello out of Brooklyn, New York. I am told both are Gifted but I do not know how."

192

"Gio?" Penny looked the twins over.

"Short for Giovanni, I believe."

"Well, at least they dressed slightly more appropriate than long-lost cousin Harleen," I told her. Gio wore a leather blazer over a red dress shirt and black tie. Gianna was all done up in a tiny black dress just long enough to be respectable. Her black hair was a mass of curls. Standing near them was a man in his thirties smoking a cigarette. "Who's the other Russian?"

Khishchnik cocked her head at an angle and studied me. "He's a Czech, not a Russian, but how did you know?"

"Clothes and haircut have an Eastern Bloc feel. Plus, the way he's holding his cigarette." I frowned. "What do you know of him?"

"Very little. His name is Pavel Můstek. I believe he is from Prague. That is all I know."

"That's not a lot." I pointed to the Asian woman in the long leather jacket. It was covered in witch's script, and she fairly bristled with wands. "What about the Spellslinger?"

"Rom Chang Hayes. I believe her mother was Cambodian."

"So *that's* Rom Chang. I've heard of her. Supposed to be pretty fast with a wand. I'm guessing that would make the little guy in the cheap suit the executor?"

"*Da*, Greely Chamberlain, Daniel's attorney. There appears to be one missing."

I opened my door. "Okay, let's get this over with."

Octavius snarled as we approached the group, his eyes laser focused on me. "What are you doing here, Brennan?"

193

Bad Penny gave him a large, fake smile. "Morning, Tome. Just bringing another one of the family's jailbirds to the reading."

"Penny!" I snapped.

"Oh shit!" Penny quickly turned to Khishchnik. "Ah, that was in reference to you being a criminal, not the whole part bird thing."

Khishchnik dipped her head. "No offense taken. You should relax. You Americans offend too easily."

"I protest. There is no need to have Brennan here." Octavius turned to Chamberlain and held out his right arm, sliding back the sleeve. "He did this to me. His mere presence is an affront."

The new arm was made of wood. Roots dug in and were merged with the stump of his arm. Wizard glyphs were carved across the surface.

Great. He turned his artificial arm into a super wand. That number of glyphs has to be the fire power equivalent of five or six wands.

Chamberlain smoothed over what little hair remained in his combover before peering down his glasses at Khishchnik's handcuffs and then back up at me. "Hello, Sergeant. I presume that you and the other officer are intending on guarding Ms. Khishchnik throughout the entire proceedings?"

"That is correct, Counselor." I gave him a brief nod.

"Any chance I can get you to stay outside? This is supposed to be a closed proceeding."

"No chance in hell, sir, but we'll try to be as unobtrusive as possible."

"Fine." Chamberlain took a pocket watch from his vest, glanced at it, and snapped it shut. "It appears that Mr. Hayes has run out of time."

"Who?" I asked.

"The last heir, Henderson Hayes," replied the attorney.

Henderson "the Haze" Hayes? Jesus, I've locked up a lot of this family.

The Haze was a minor mage, small-town crook and flimflam artist. Not a bad guy as criminals went, but you definitely wanted to count the rings on your fingers after shaking hands with him. I looked at Khishchnik who shrugged. "I do not know him."

"Street trash," grumbled the elder Tome.

"Be that as it may, Sugar," Harleen drawled in a thick Southern accent, "The man is still family of some sort. There is no need to badmouth him in front of others."

Octavius looked down at her. 'You obviously have never met him."

"Well, no—"

"Can we speed this up?" Bathory interrupted her. She glanced at the sky. "I'd like to get this over and done with."

Of course," agreed Chamberlain. He pulled a large, ornate iron key from his satchel and walked over to the carved wooden door that served as the Rook's only entrance.

I cocked my head at Bathory. "You're a master vampire. Why are you worried about the sun? It can't hurt someone of your power."

She sighed. "I freckle. But that was not what I was referring to. I am simply... hungry."

That's not scary at all…

"And why are you here exactly, Ms. Bathory?"

"It's Lady Bathory, but you must call me Katrina. I am here to assist my dear friend Acantha."

"Friend or apprentice?"

"One can be both, Michael. May I call you Michael?"

"Knock yourself out."

Chamberlain placed the key in its lock and turned it three times. There was a series of loud clicks and the door swung open. He gestured towards the opening. "Please, after you."

I watched the others shuffle in before allowing Khishchnik to enter. Penny and I followed behind her. Penny glanced over to me. "Nobody seems very broken up about Bainbridge."

Khishchnik nodded. "As I said, we are all distantly related. None of us really knew him."

"Laughing heirs," I muttered half to myself.

Chamberlain looked at me sharply as he closed the door, locking it. "No one here finds the death of my client humorous, Sergeant. There is no need for such comments."

Well now, that's interesting.

The attorney led us through the foyer into a den. Three of the walls were lined with bookcases. The fourth had red and gold wallpaper. A series of oil paintings in gold frames was scattered on the wall, and a massive marble fireplace took up the center of it. A large Persian rug covered the stone floor. The ceiling had wooden arches supporting it, and a chandelier hung over a round wooden table. Seven matching chairs ringed it. Chamberlain took a seat with his back to the fireplace and gestured to the others to sit. After they did, he pointed to the empty seat next to Khishchnik. "Since Mr. Hayes deemed this proceeding not worth showing up for, one of the officers may take his seat."

"We're good. Thank you." I stood by the wall behind Khishchnik, giving her enough room to be comfortable but not enough for a lead. Penny leaned across the opposite wall.

Chamberlain nodded, stared at Penny and I's name tags, and pulled out two cards. He wrote something on them before sealing them up in an envelope and placing it into his satchel. He looked over at the vampire. "You said your name is Lady Katrina Bathory?"

"That is correct." She placed her hand over Acantha's. "As I explained, I'm here to assist my friend in her time of loss."

Chamberlain pulled out a third card and repeated the process. He then removed a wooden box and placed it before him on the table. "Are we ready to proceed?"

At everyone's nods, he tilted the box so everyone could inspect the gold foil seal on the top. Wizard glyphs ringed the edge of the seal and each side of the box. "As you can see, this will has been verified by the L.L.W. as authentic and uncompromised."

Harleen leaned forward giving him a rather generous view down the white lowcut blouse she was wearing and placed her hand over his. Based on their gravity-defying nature, I was guessing the assets barely contained in her shirt were either surgically or magically enhanced. "Excuse me, Greeley. May Ah call you Greeley?"

"O-of course." replied the attorney.

"Ah'm not from around here, Greeley. What is the L.L.W.?"

With visible effort, Chamberlain adjusted his view and slid his hand out from hers. "My apologies, Ms. Bridges. The Llewellyn League of Wizards is one of the local wizard societies that operate in the city. They are highly respectable and have authenticated Mr. Bainbridge's will and then sealed it in the box."

"Thank you, sugar," she drawled as she slowly leaned back.

Wow! That's no cougar. That's a man-eating tiger.

Chamberlain composed himself and split the seal with a letter opener. He removed a green gem the size of a baseball and set it on the table. An image appeared around the gem. It quickly formed into Daniel Bainbridge, sneer and all. "Greetings from beyond and all that. If this is being played than I shuffled off the mortal coil without offspring which means my belongings, including the Rook, falls to you lot."

He gave a fake sigh. "That *is* depressing. The last descendants of the Mighty Bayn, his once great House fallen to such levels. None of you are worthy to inherit the Rook. So, I've decided to make it interesting. At the insistence of my parents, I attended a Normal college. I've never had much use for the Normals, but there was a game played on campus that I found amusing. A game called Tag."

Uh oh!

Acantha furrowed her brow in confusion. "Like what little children play?"

Bainbridge continued. "So, you all are going to participate in Tag. It stands for The Assassination Game. The winner

198

will inherit everything. And, to make it even more interesting, anyone other than Greeley Chamberlain that is attending this will reading will be playing. So, if you brought a trophy girl or boyfriend with you, congrats to them. They now have just as likely a chance to inherit as you."

He smirked down at the table. "As soon as this gem was activated, the Rook's door locked and it went out of phase from the rest of the dimension. You are trapped here and won't be able to leave until the game is over. I've overlaid a complex series of spells and curses here over the years to ensure the contest is played properly.

"For those of you familiar with the game, I've modified the rules a bit. Each of you will be given an envelope. Inside will be the name of your target. You must eliminate them to proceed. Once you have taken out your victim, the person in their envelope is your next assignment. You cannot show anyone but your target your card. Anyone that witnesses an elimination may not tell anyone else what they saw, or the Rook will punish them.

"There will be flashing of lights to signify the start of a safe time, and the next doorway you walk through will take you to the kitchen. This is your one true safe space. No one may attack another while there. You can leave it at any time by walking through its door. This will transport you to a random location within the Rook. If you leave early, you will not be able to get back to the kitchen area until the next break. The kitchen lights will flash when it's time to start up the game again. Make sure not to linger once that happens. If you stay too long… Well, it will hurt. A lot…

"The safe times will not always be the same, but usually around mealtimes. After each break, the names on your cards will randomly change to a different target. You may defend yourself against your own assassin during an attack, but other than that, you may only commit violence against your target. If you manage to kill your would-be assassin, then their hunter's card will change to show your name as their new target. Should you cluster together too long, the lights in the room you're in will flicker. If you don't split up immediately, you will suffer a rather harsh penalty. That goes for any violations of the game."

He looked around the room almost as if he could see us. "I really don't care which one of you wins, but I do get immense pleasure of the idea of all you being rats in my maze. My only lament is I won't be able to see it. Remember, only one person can walk out, and that person will inherit my entire fortune."

The image faded away with ominous laughter. The heirs immediately started arguing among themselves. Many of the comments expressed disbelief at their situation. Tome performed some sort of spell to check the validity of Bainbridge's claims and appeared frustrated with the results.

In midst of the commotion, Chamberlain pulled out a series of envelopes, shuffled them, and laid one in front of each of the people at the table. The conversations trickled to a halt as they all stared down at what was placed in front of them. During the stunned silence, Chamberlain walked over and held out envelopes to Penny and I. I shook my head. "We're not part of this insanity."

The attorney gave me a sad smile. "I'm afraid you became part of it as soon as you entered the Rook. Until each of you possesses an envelope, the Rook's magic will prevent anyone from leaving this room."

I folded my arms and just stared at him. Gio stood up and headed for the door. "Fuck this shit. Let's see if it's true."

As soon as he went out the door, he reappeared. He frowned as he glanced around. "Well, that's bullshit."

"Stop playing the fool," ordered Octavius. "Brennan, just take the envelopes so we can get out of here. Maybe if I'm lucky, you'll be my target."

Rom Chang held up her envelope and raised an eyebrow. "What happens if we get our own name?"

"The magic of the Rook will prevent that," explained the attorney after double checking his notes.

"This isn't fair! I didn't sign up for this," exclaimed Harleen, shying away from her envelope as if it was a snake.

"Oh, poor Harleen!" snapped Gianna. "You're not gonna sleep your way out of this one."

"Shut your mouth, you little bitch!" Harleen snatched up her envelope. "If this has your name, I'm going to bury a heel into your greaseball little eye!"

While they were arguing, I turned away and tabbed my badge. "Brennan to Dispatch. Crystal, come in."

Nothing. That's bad. We have the council meeting coming up and I'm stuck here. Not to mention the freaking dragon lurking outside of town. I have to rectify this quickly.

"*Dovol'no!*" hissed Khishchnick at Gianna and Harleen. "Enough!"

"Well, that deteriorated quickly." Bathory looked over to me. "Michael, is there anything you can do?"

"There is no reason to dance to Bainbridge's tune. If we work together, we can find a way out." I told the group as I turned around. "Tome. You're a wizard. Can you see a way to break the spells causing this?"

Tome sneered at me. "Why would I do that? I have an opportunity to inherit all *and* get my revenge on you. I'm not passing that up."

I raised my eyebrows. "Revenge? Really? You're going to sacrifice all these people to get back at me for something I did defending myself from you?"

"I care not for this lot, and you are one to talk about revenge!"

"Excuse me?"

"You slaughtered everyone that held your child captive."

"That… That was during combat." I didn't have a good argument against him in that particular case. I was under the effect of the blood runes and had been in a berserker mode for the first time. I didn't really remember much of that night.

Tome gave me a look of distain. "Did you not almost beat Ron Darby to death for killing your dog?"

"That… That was more of a legal fiction. Valentine was going to kill him…"

"But you wouldn't let him until you got your vengeance. Yes, yes, I know all about it. What about the wendigo?" He pointed at my runic eye. "After it took your eye, didn't you track it all the way to Maine and carve out its eye before killing it in revenge?"

"I didn't carve it out. It just… sort of happened while we were fighting."

"Really? It was a coincidence then?"

Damn, why am I letting him get the better of me?

202

"You're twisting the facts, Tome. I did that I the line of duty and to keep Llewellyn safe."

"I'm merely repeating what is said around town. *Don't cross the Rune Knight or he'll end you.*" He narrowed his eyes. "Well, I'm not afraid to cross you, and the Rook *will* be mine."

I looked around the room. Khishchnik gave me a *what can you do* shrug. Aside from Bathory and Mŭstek, everyone else's expressions gave the appearance that they agreed with Tome's description of me. Mŭstek looked bored, and Bathory ignored it. She had a worried look in her eye and was clearly thinking of something else.

Huh… That didn't go well.

"So, you all are going to do this instead of trying to work together?"

There were some head nods and muttering of agreement for most of them.

Fine then. Penny and I will get you all out the hard way.

I activated the blood rune for senses and drank in the scent of everyone in the room. Once I was done, I shook my head and went over my options.

Gianna looked at me like a cat at a mouse. "If we are out of phase like Bainbridge said, then you can't contact your department."

Octavius leaned back with a gleam in his eyes. "That means you probably can't summon those wonderful toys of yours."

Shit! I was hoping the fucker wouldn't clue into that.

"Do I look concerned to you?" I asked him.

With a smile, he slid his envelope into an inner pocket of his robe and stood up. "This is going to be fun."

August placed a hand on his father's arm. "Dad, we need to figure this out. Come up with a strategy."

"There is nothing to figure out, boy. Only one of us will be walking out of here, and that will be me!"

"But... but what about me?"

"You? I'll be surprised if you make it the night." The elder Tome pulled his arm away and walked out of the room. As he passed through the doorway there was a flash of orange light, and he was gone.

Acantha twisted in her chair to watch him leave. "Wow! What an asshole. Even for our family."

Bathory placed a hand on her shoulder. "We'll find a way around this. Never fear. I'm your family now."

I narrowed my eyes as Acantha leaned against Bathory and sighed, grasping the vampires hand.

Textbook fucking grooming techniques. This is sickening.

Chamberlain gestured towards the door. "When each of you leave, you'll be transported to a different part of the Rook. Be aware when the last person leaves this room, the game has started."

Bathory stood. "I have no ill will towards any of you, but attack Acantha or myself and I will end you. Come, child. We need to find a way to free us from this place."

Acantha stood as well and there were two flashes of orange light as they walked through the door. Rom Chang followed right behind them without a word.

Gianna looked at her brother. "Well, it was a matter of time before one of us was going to kill the other. You ready?"

Gio loosened his tie and stood. "I'll try and make it quick. For Ma's sake." He followed her through the orange flashes.

"Apparently, there is no love lost between those two." Pavel Můstek slid his chair back. "If this is how you all view each other, Daniel may have been onto something."

After he departed, Khishchnik lifted her arms up at me, jingling the handcuffs. "If you leave me handcuffed, I'm a dead woman. *Moya smert' budet v tvoikh*."

I stared at her weighing my options. I didn't like releasing my prisoner, but if this was going to be Thunderdome meets Survivor, I'd be a real bastard to leave her cuffed. Until I figured away out of this, I couldn't handicap her like that. "Okay. Penny, uncuff her."

Khishchnik rubbed her wrists after Bad Penny took the cuffs off. "*Spasibo*."

Harleen pushed her chair back and quickly walked towards the door. "Ah'm out of here. Stay out of my way and Ah'll stay out of yours."

Once she disappeared into orange light, I looked at Khishchnik. "You look at your card yet?"

"*Nyet*," she replied tiredly. "Have you?"

I ignored the question. "You look tired."

"I am. I do not like this city with your petty war and strange *politsiya* and weird funeral rituals."

Chamberlain raised both hands. "I've been doing estate law a long time, and this has *never* happened before."

She ignored him and produced her envelope. "Shall we open them together, Sergeant Brennan?"

I sat down across the table from her and drummed my fingers next to where my envelope lay. I still hadn't picked it up. "We can't tell each other."

"But if one of us has the other as a target, we can get this over with right now." She gave me a predatory smile. She had a fearsome reputation. When she was captured, I was too busy fighting my own opponent to see what she could do. I did know it was Valentine, a full-fledged vampire lord and Knight of the Star who took her down.

I showed my own teeth. "Thanks, but I'm good. Besides, Bad Penny is here. No witnesses, remember?"

"If what Daniel claims is true, it will not matter that she is here. It just means she can't speak of it."

Penny gave a start. "You think he lied?"

"I do not know." Khishchnik gave a curt nod, causing her feathers to flutter. Picking up her envelope, she tore it open and studied the card.

"Well?" I asked.

"It appears we will not be fighting right now, Sergeant Brennan." She stood up and walked to the door. "I find myself strangely glad. While we are on opposite sides, I find you to be honorable in your own way. I would prefer not to be the cause of your demise."

"And then there was two." I watched the orange light flash as she disappeared. "Well, three." I smiled at Chamberlain. "But according to the instructions, you don't count."

"No Sergeant. For this, I do not." He smiled sadly back at me. "I did try to warn you off."

"You don't seem very on board with this."

"I'm not. I find the whole thing distasteful, but it's my job to execute the will whether I agree with it or not."

"No, I get it. I dated an Assistant District Attorney before I met my wife. What's the Latin phrase? *Ultra vires*? Everything within my power?"

"Ah, yes… Exactly." He placed the gem back in the box and the box into his satchel. "So, few people understand the obligations of the profession. But it stands to reason that if anyone did, it would be a police officer."

"Give us a moment," I told more than asked the attorney as I pulled Penny away. "Let's see the baton."

She handed it over. "How are we going to do this, Mikey? According to the rules, only one of us is going to make it."

"Bainbridge was an arrogant ass in life. It's no surprise he's still one in death. He'll have overlooked something. Just a matter of finding it." I snapped my wrist out, causing the baton to extend. A series of runes ran down the shaft. "This is a non-lethal weapon."

"Like a taser."

"No, a taser is a *less than lethal* weapon."

Penny shook her head. "What's the difference?"

"A taser is less lethal than a firearm, but it can still kill. Something like a thousand people have been killed by tasers."

"Jesus! Then why do cops use them?"

"Because it's a safer alternative than using a firearm and not intended to be fatal. Most of the deaths are attributed to underlying health issues."

The magic globes within the chandelier started flashing. Chamberlain looked up. "I'm afraid you've run out of time, Sergeant. We need to leave the room. Please pick up your envelopes."

Damn.

"Penny, to use this, hold the grip and make sure the tip of the baton is touching the bad guy's skin—"

"Sergeant! We need to go now!" His voice had grown frantic.

"Don't wait for us." I turned back to Penny as the attorney slipped through the doorway. "Once the tip is on the bad guy, just think of them sleeping. It should knock most people out. Doesn't work on beings who don't need sleep, like the undead. Without a ley line, you have about five charges."

The lights started flashing even more and I was feeling pressure building against my eardrums. I handed the baton back to Penny. "Got it?"

'Yeah, but—"

"Good." I slid my envelope into a pocket and handed Penny hers. I leaned into her ear as the pressure grew more and more painful. "Watch your back and don't trust Chamberlain. There's something off about him."

"What?" Instead of answering her, I shoved Penny through the door and quickly followed.

Chapter Nineteen

The Contents of the Envelope

I should have closed my eyes first.

I blinked rapidly to chase away the orange afterimage of the flash and looked around. I was in a hallway. The floors and walls were made of stone blocks. Tapestries hung in various sections, and wall sconces holding magically lit globes were staggered in intervals. Behind me was more hallway. There was no sign of the room I left. Ahead was more of the same, but doors dotted the walls here and there.

I tabbed my badge. "Brennan to Dispatch."

Silence answered me.

Well, that still didn't work. Let's see… First things first.

After listening for anyone, I tore open my envelope, read the name, and gave a small laugh. I slipped it in a pocket and, using my bracers, tried to summon my sword and armor.

Damn. Blocked! That limits my options.

I drew my colt 1911 from under my BDU shirt, pulled one of the orbs out of my pocket, and tossed it in the air. It bobbed for a second and held steady, floating at my eye level.

I gave the orb a mental command and it shot down the hall. I gave a sigh in relief. I didn't know how Bainbridge shifted us out of phase, but there were still ley lines, or the orb wouldn't have power.

I carefully checked the doors near me. The first three were dust covered bedrooms. Aside from a leather messenger bag that I grabbed, there wasn't anything of interest.

I slowly approach the fourth and last door like I did the others, using the *slice the pie* method. The room was dark, but I used my runic eye to give me night vision. The runes on my magically enhanced false eye allowed my left eye to experience the same effect.

Walking alongside the wall with my 1911 just below my sight gave me full vision but allowed me to quickly sight and fire if needed. I got to the point along the wall where I could see into part of the room. It was the kitchen.

I cleared the *slice*, the one sliver of kitchen that I could see, and then slowly inched forward. Each time I inched forward, it revealed another slice of the *pie* and allowed me to see more and more of the room. Slowly I cleared all the slices until I could see the entire room.

Gun still up, I quickly entered the kitchen. The lights flicked on as I stepped in. I ended the night vision and quickly scanned the room. The wall to my left consisted of antique wood cabinets with a farmer's sink and what appeared to be a walk-in freezer with runes running along the sides. It took me a minute to puzzle out the runes. What I thought was a freezer was actually a room that created a stasis field in it when the door was closed. I knew of magical communities that tried to use similar runes for their prisons. It wound up being too cost prohibitive and the idea was eventually abandoned. It seemed overkill just to keep the lettuce fresh, but who was I to judge?

A thick rectangular wood table with chairs took up the center. A large colonial era brick fireplace filled the area next to the sink. There were small baking and warming ovens in the brick wall next to the fireplace. Looking like beehive shaped alcoves, the ovens had hinged iron doors to keep the heat in. The wall to the right of me had a door and more cabinets.

The other door led to an L shaped galley was filled with cleaning supplies. Turning the corner of the L, I found a wash sink, mops, and buckets. Not seeing anything of use, I exited the galley and searched the kitchen cupboards. I didn't know how long we were going to be trapped here, but I didn't want to take any chances. I grabbed some canned food that didn't need to be reheated and an old twist style can opener. Using water from the sink, I filled two empty glass bottles I'd found. All of that went into the messenger bag.

Once that was done, I quickly inventoried what tools I possessed. I had my mentor's old book about runesmithing, plus my own notebook, and a leather pouch consisting of six potions. I also had my magic skeleton key. For weapons, I had a boot knife and my Colt 1911. My gun was an older Colt and used a single stack magazine, which meant I had eight rounds in the mag and a ninth round in the chamber. As for defenses, while not to the level of my armor, the spellweaving in my uniform and the shielding spells of my badge offered some protection.

Gun at the ready, I opened the second door to discover rickety wooden stairs leading down. Switching back to night vision, I carefully went down the steps and ended in the basement. A behemoth of a coal furnace took up the majority of the space. A workbench filled with dusty tools and bins of coal took up the rest.

Markings on the walls caught my eye. I leaned in and studied them, running my hand over the ancient symbols carved into the stone of the walls. "Well, well, well. Bainbridge, you old hypocrite. You've been perpetrating a fraud all these years."

I slowly climbed back up the stairs, wincing at every creak it made. Ninja, I was not. I was actually more concerned about the stairs giving way than sneaking around. I'm a large and heavy guy, and these stairs had seen better days.

At the top of the stairs, I heard someone rattling around in one of the drawers. As I peered into the room with my 1911, Harleen Bridges whirled around from one of the drawers by the sink, holding a large and wicked looking cleaver.

On seeing me, she exhaled and slumped against the sink, lowering her weapon. "Oh, thank God it's you."

"Put the cleaver down, Harleen," I ordered, keeping my gun trained on her.

Her face twisted in confusion. "Why are you pointing that at me? Oh, my stars and garters. Ah forgot you're playing, too." She held the cleaver out in front of her with both hands. "Am Ah your target?"

"No, I have someone else." I thumbed back the hammer. "Now drop the cleaver. I don't want to have to shoot you."

She bit her lower lip as she weighted her options. "You swear Ah'm not your target, Deputy?"

"I swear. Drop it. Last chance."

"Well. Ah guess if Ah was, you'd shot me by now." She dropped the cleaver into the sink and moved around the table and away from it. "Well, don't be shy Sugar. C'mon in."

After a last scan of the room, I holstered up and stepped back in. Harleen's eyes widened as I did so. "Well, now. Aren't you a tall drink of water? Those are some interesting scars you got there. How did I not notice you before?"

"You had other things on your mind at the time." *Why is she looking at my boots?* "Did you see anyone else?"

She tore her eyes away from my footwear. "No, Deputy. Did you?"

"No, and we don't have deputies here, Ms. Bridges. Just in the jails. My rank is Sergeant."

"Sergeant what?"

"Brennan." I peered out the door while keeping one eye on her. The hallway looked clear.

"Oh, ah always like them Irish boys and please, call me Harleen. Tell me, Sergeant Brennan, what's your Christian name?"

"Mike."

"Mike, I've very scared. The others have powers and skills that make them dangerous. I don't have anything like that. I need someone to protect me. You're a policeman. Can Ah count on you to keep me safe?" She batted her eyes at me.

"Don't you think your laying this *Southern belle in distress* thing on pretty thick? If you're not a caster, what are you? Gifted?"

She ran a finger along the collar of her blouse and down to the top button of her blouse. "Ah'm very gifted. Just not in the way you mean."

"I'm married."

"All the better, Sugar. I love married men. They're so grateful when they go running back to their wives." With a twist of her fingers that button came undone, quickly followed by the one below it, all while moving around the table towards me. "Ah'll make you a deal. Ah'll show you just how *gifted* Ah really am, and you guard me from the others."

"Lady, you need to button your shirt back up." I maneuvered to keep the table between us.

"What, this little old thing?" She held up the blouse with one finger before letting it fall to the floor. "Ah couldn't help noticing how big your boots are. You know what they say about guys with big feet?"

How did she even get it off that fast?

"They have trouble finding footwear their size?" I kept circling the table, using it as a barrier as she approached me. "Um, aren't you cold?"

With a quick tug, the miniskirt followed the blouse. For a woman around my age, she was remarkably fit and apparently preferred going commando. "Why, darling? You want to warm me up?"

We were on opposite sides of the long ends now. I dialed up my best cop voice. "Okay, enough. Put your clothes back on."

"Ooooh." She kicked off her heels, slipped onto the table, and slowly crawled towards me. "Are you going to use your handcuffs on me if I don't?"

"Lady, the eighties are over, and this isn't a music video— Oh shit!" She suddenly leaped at me. Purple magic briefly shimmered around her and instead of a 110lb blonde landing in my arms, it was a 220lb mountain lion. The impact knocked me to the ground. I managed to cover my head with my arms as she scratched and clawed at me.

I triggered some of my blood runes. Speed and strength flooded into me as my skin harden like leather. I kicked the cat off and scrambled to my feet. As she leaped at me again, I caught her by the throat and held her there suspended with my right arm out fully extended. She clawed at me as I raised my 1911 and placed the muzzle between her eyes. "Change back now."

Cougar! I'm such an idiot!

The weight lessened considerably as purple energy washed over her, changing the large cat back into Harleen Bridges. She grabbed my arm with both hands to relieve the strain on her neck. "Wh-what are you going to do?"

"I ought to just snap your neck instead of wasting a good bullet." I walked around the table and dropped her to the floor. "I take it I'm your target?"

"Yes." She landed in a crouch and scooped up her belongings. She stood up using the bundle of clothes to cover her front assets. "Ah figgered you for just a policeman. What *are* you?"

"Very annoyed." I kept the gun trained at her but pointed to the door with my right hand. "Get moving."

Her eyes widened. "You're letting me go?"

"Against my better judgment. Yeah."

Still holding the clothes in front of her, she turned and walked towards the door, glancing over her shoulder at the table. "Damn, Ah knew Ah should have waited until after."

"Was never going to happen, lady."

"Too bad." She put a little swing into her stride as she went out the door. "Trust me, it would have totally been worth dying for."

Chapter Twenty

A Mutual Exchange

Once she was gone, I checked over my injuries. The uniform had protected me from her attack. I only had superficial injuries to my head and hands. Most Gifts are random, but shifting was a type of Gift that ran in families. It especially bred true if both parents were shifters. Until I knew more, I had to assume the other family members might have the same ability. I started to root around the kitchen for a first aid kit when the lights started flickering.

Damn. Time's up.

After checking, I entered the hallway. Using my skeleton key, I locked the door to the kitchen. I wasn't sure that it would stay locked, but it was worth a try to remove it from play.

I wandered the halls for a bit until I saw an open door. The room had a light on. I triggered the blood rune for senses and took a deep breath, recognizing the scent of the person in the room.

Můstek! What's he doing?

"Pavel Můstek! This is Mike Brennan. I'm not hunting you and would like to talk."

After a pause, he answered back. "I have already encountered my hunter, mister policeman. You may come in. I will not harm you."

I slowly entered the room, scanning for dangers. Můstek sat by a small wooden table in what was a bedroom. The placed had been trashed. It looked like a hell of a fight took place there. Můstek motioned to an empty chair across from him. I holstered my 1911 and sat. He pulled out a cigarette pack and offered it to me.

"No thank you."

He shrugged and shook one out, placing it in his mouth before pausing. "My apologies. I should have asked. Do you mind?"

"No, go ahead."

He lit it and inhaled deeply before slowly exhaling. "You show caution, but not fear. I take it you encountered your hunter?"

"My hunter had a certain... Southern charm." My answer was circumspect so not to trigger Bainbridge's spells. "You?"

"My opponent prefers her meals in liquid form. Our encounter was... inconclusive. What is the state of the other person?"

"Battered, but alive." I looked around the room. "Your sparring partner is a master vampire. You must be a pretty formidable opponent."

"I am. Now, what can I do for the Shield of Llewellyn?"

"Shield of Llewellyn? That's a new one."

Beats the Fist of Culain or Blood Drinker's Bane.

"Yes. The magical community is not that big, and the Magi do so love to gossip. Even in my small neighborhood we have heard of Michael Brennan, the Rune Knight."

"Prague is not small, Mister Mŭstek."

"Please, call me Pavel, and I will call you Michael. Yes?"

"Alright then, Pavel." I leaned back in my chair as he gathered his thoughts.

"To answer your question, Prague is big, but the magical community that resides in it is not. It is just a borough surviving on a small, semi-active ley line. We interact with the Normals much more than you do here in Llewellyn. I myself am employed in the Normal world." He took another drag of the cigarette.

"Really? If you don't mind me asking, what is your occupation?"

"I am a history professor at the local university." Mŭstek flicked ash into a small cup on the table. "But that is not the reason you wish to speak with me."

"No. I need intel. I was hoping you would supply me with some."

"A mutual exchange, then?" He took another drag. "I do not know a lot about these people and was not expecting this little game."

"Yes." I shifted my chair slightly to move away from the smoke. "Let's start with you. What's your deal?"

"Like your wife, I'm a witch. And like your wife, I am also… More." He finished his smoke and ground out the butt in the cup. "What can you tell me about Harleen Bridges?"

"Shifter."

"Ah. What type?"

"Cougar."

He snorted. "Appropriate. As mentioned, Katrina Bathory is a master vampire, but she is no warrior. She prefers to pull strings from the shadows. Also…"

"What?"

"She seems out of sorts. I'm not sure why." He flicked some ash off his cigarette. "Obviously, she has no honor. Very few of her ilk do. Still, if you watch your back for treachery and face her in straight battle, you may have a chance. After all, are you not the Blood Drinker's Bane?"

He took another drag and inhaled deeply. "You do have a lot of nicknames, Michael."

A crony of Dracula not honorable? I'm shocked! Shocked I say!

"As you said, the Magi like to gossip. They also tend toward the dramatic. What's the deal with her and Acantha?"

"Acantha Baines-Chatterjee is an alchemist. Her great grandfather was one of the owners of the Rook. I am told she is exceptionally talented in her field. She came under the wing of Bathory after the death of her parents. She sometimes refers to her as Aunt, but there is no actual family connection. She is an outcast from both parents' sides, as the two families did not approve of the mixed marriage."

"In this day and age? That's stupid."

"I agree, but some of these old-world magical families are slow to change. The rejection hurt Acantha significantly and she developed a cruel streak as a defense mechanism. I assume Bathory seeks to use this and her alchemy skills for her own schemes. What do you know of the Tome family?"

Damn. Is Bathory here working for Drac or on her own accord? Wouldn't be the first time vamps double crossed each other. If she's here for herself. Who's Drac's agent? And who's the Muse's agent in all this?

I shrugged. "Octavius is a wizard. He's a treacherous snake to boot. I thought he was out of the game after I took his arm and set him to prison. Turns out I was wrong. His son Augustus prefers to be called August. He's currently a mage. According to his professors before he was thrown out, he has the makings of a full wizard."

"You cut off the father's arm? No wonder he doesn't like you. What is the situation regarding the wood replacement?"

"No idea. Aside from functioning as an arm, it looks like it has similar abilities to a wand. I saw wizard glyphs on it."

"I do not care for wizards. I find their arrogance galling." Pavel sighed.

"You never said what coven you belong to."

"No. I did not." He gave me a faint smile.

"What about Rom Chang Hayes?"

"About her personally? I know nothing. I do know the Hayes are descended from Georgia Hayes. Her maiden name was Bridges."

"Rom Chang is a spellslinger," I told him.

"I apologize, English is a second language for me. I am not familiar with that term."

"Wand for Hire. Usually a low-level caster of some type. In her case, a witch, like you."

"Ah, yes."

"What else do you know about the two yutes?"

"I'm sorry. Did you say yutes? What is a yute?"

Heh heh heh. Got him. Can't believe that worked.

I hid my smile. "Sorry, youths. I meant the two twins. Gio and Gianna."

"Ah. She appears the smarter of the two. They are Gifted. I'm not sure how. I believe they are part of a criminal organization of some sort."

"Why? Because they're Italians from New York? That's not cool."

"No, Michael, because Gio alluded to it when we were speaking before you arrived. I am not familiar with that world but based on his comments, they seem to be low-level enforcers of some type."

"Great!" I placed my hands on the table and leaned forward. 'What do you know about Hender—" I was cut off by the flashing of the lights.

"This game is getting tiresome." Pavel sighed. "You seem an honorable man, Michael. I will tell you this. I will not be hunting my targets. I have no taste for this game and, given the option, I would not have gotten involved. Aside from defending myself, I will only become part of this when there is only a few of us left. Then I will make it as painless as possible."

"You seem pretty sure of yourself."

"Yes." He returned his cigarette pack to his pocket. "If you have no preference. I will go right, and you may go left when we leave here."

"That's fine." I slid my chair back, and we shook hands. "Goodbye, Pavel."

"Goodbye, Michael."

Chapter Twenty-One
Paraphrasing Jeffery Combs

After my encounter with Pavel, I wandered around some more. A plan was starting to come to me. It was risky, and I needed time to fully format it. In the meantime, I studied our current prison.

The Rook obviously utilized similar pocket dimension magic to what the Morgan Tree used. The headquarters of my wife's coven was much larger on the inside than outside. Or so I've been told. No non-coven members are allowed.

I steered away from any fighting I heard and finally tucked myself into the closet of a billiard's room. My knees popped as I clambered to the floor of the closet and activated the night vision of my runic eye. I opened a can of meat and pasta and wolfed it down cold before pulling out my notebook and leafing through it. I was hoping for inspiration. The notebook contained runes I had created, as well as ideas I had but could never figure out.

I needed to find a way to end this quickly. A dragon was lurking outside the city, Vlad Tepes was up to no good, and I had to make the public council meeting.

The quickest way out was playing Bainbridge's game, but I couldn't sacrifice lives to do it, and how did I get Penny out? There had to be a better way. Realizing my thoughts had drifted, I looked down at the pages open in the notebook. On the page I had stopped at were runes I had copied from a saber belonging to Otto Clausewitz, one of Harrow's men that I killed during Oct5. Clausewitz's saber was called *Soul-Drinker* and would entrap the souls of those it killed. I freed the souls by snapping the saber but later copied the runes down to study. I'd found a way to reverse it, but only if it was done quickly. Once the body reached a certain level of decay, it wouldn't accept the soul back which meant it had to be within minutes, not something that was useful.

A bell tolled, signaling the end of the first hunt. My knees screamed in protest as I pulled myself to my feet and exited the closet. I opened the door to the hall and in a flash of light found myself entering the kitchen. Acantha, Gio, and Rom Chang were already there sitting around the same table I had previously used to avoid Harleen. Gio kicked chair in my direction. "Might as well sit down. Looks like Danny boy wants us to all eat together."

"Thanks," I told him as I angled the chair so my back wasn't against the door. He wore a still wore the black leather sport coat and a knock-off black business suit. He'd lost the tie, though.

Gio snorted at my precautions. "It's neutral territory, nothing to worry about."

Rom Chang rolled her eyes at that. Her chair was also shifted to see who came through the door. "Did you take anyone out?"

"I'm not really playing the game," I answered as Penny came in and sat next to me. "I'm hoping there is another way."

The spellslinger gave another snort. "I heard you were smart. Guess they got that wrong."

Penny tugged on my sleeve. "Mikey, you got a moment?"

"Of course. What's up?" We moved over by the fridge.

She chewed the side of her bottom lip for a second before replying, "I've been thinking, and I don't know about the whole cop thing."

"Is this because of getting shot?"

"Sort of? That and the other night in your bedroom."

"Jesus, Penny. For someone who likes to wander around with no clothes on, you really shouldn't have a problem when the script gets flipped. It was accidental."

"Please. You in the nude was always going to happen. I just thought it was going to involve Zoe and a hot tub, too." She grabbed a water bottle from the fridge and opened it.

"I... Ah... I'm just going to ignore that. I'm still recovering from the whole naked Harleen reenacting a Whitesnake video thing," I muttered as Penny took a swig.

My timing was perfect as Penny spewed water and began coughing. She waved me away and wiped her mouth with her sleeve. *"What?"*

I quickly filled her in on what had transpired with Harleen.

"Ah, God, I'd have paid to see that. I don't know which would have been funnier: Past her Prime Barbie doing her thing or you running away like a scared rabbit. But no, that wasn't what I was talking about."

I grabbed a towel near the sink and dropped it on her spill, wiping it around with my foot. "So, what's the problem then."

"That was the first time I saw the extent of the damage done to you. It's not just your eye. Your injury runs all the way down your arm. That's not the only time you've been hurt. To paraphrase the great Jeffrey Combs, your body is a roadmap of pain."

"Frightener's quote. Nice!" I threw the towel into the sink. "Penny, regardless of your enjoyment of tormenting me with flirtations, we both know I'm happily married. If you're disturbed by my scars, that doesn't mean you should quit your job. You heal at an unbelievable rate and have shaken off much greater injuries then I ever could with not a scratch to show for it."

She gave me a *you're an idiot* look. "You're an idiot."

Yup, there it is.

"One, you enjoy the torment," she continued "Two, chicks dig scars. That's a saying for a reason. Three, that's not what I'm talking about."

"Then explain." I leaned against the counter and made a *speed it up* motion with my hand.

"I've seen you get hurt a lot. Hell, *I've* been hurt plenty of times. But I have magical regeneration and you have healing potions. Potions don't leave scars, yet you're covered in them. Which means there have been plenty of times you've been injured where potions weren't available or didn't work. Cases where you must have been close to dying. It... It kind of put it in perspective for me."

"That this isn't a game?"

"Well, yeah. When I'm not in hyde form, I'm normal like everyone else. Seeing what all those years of policing has done to you and how many times you've almost died really hammered home our mortality.

"Then I have to ask, why are we doing it? The people here call us witch hunters and worse. The media in the real world call cops racists and thugs. Why are we risking our lives to defend people that hate us?"

I snorted. "We're trapped in a tower and forced to play a morbid game that's a cross between Clue and ThunderDome and *that's* what you've been thinking about?"

"Yeah. Going to an academy in the Outside got me thinking about it. Then seeing how banged up you've gotten doing the job, plus the whole almost dying from getting shot by a magic gun. I mean, what's the point?"

"What's the point of learning the laws, tactics, how to fight when not in hyde form? That sort of stuff? Look, our laws and situations may be different due to the whole magic thing, but we're police officers just like all the other towns and cities in the United States." I leaned back. "You ever hear the phrase Thin Blue Line?"

"Doesn't that mean an *us versus them* thing?"

"No, that's what anti police people are trying to claim. It's a saying that dates back at least as far as the 1920s. It means that the police are the thin blue line that is all that stands between society and evil. We're the last defenders. You wanted to stay a cop after your pardon. Why?"

"I wanted to help people."

"And that's why most people join the police force. And they do it without a hyde potion. They put their lives on the line every day to help and protect people, never knowing if they are going to make it back to their families. Regardless of your healing ability, if you're not willing to do the same, you are in the wrong line of work."

"Yeah, no, I get it. It's just, I got really shook up."

"That's normal. I read somewhere that most people have around seven incidents in a lifetime that could trigger PTSD. Police average something like seventy-seven a year. That's why counseling after such an incident is important."

"Wait, that's why Culain told me to meet with that witch couple this week?"

"Miguel and Nala? I didn't realize he set that up yet. Yes, they specialize in healing trauma to the mind."

"So, they're the witch versions of shrinks?"

"I think their certified therapists, too, but yeah. In other circumstances, you'd have been put on leave until you had time to process what happened. If fact, I argued that to

Culain. He figured you would refuse. Plus, it's kind of an all-hands-on deck situation with everything going on."

"Damn right, I'd refuse!" She crossed her arms. "Wait, is that why I got sent to this? Easy gig to keep me off the streets?"

"Well, yeah. Give you time to get your bearings back."

Penny snorted. "That worked out great, didn't it?"

"Best laid plans and all that." I nodded to the filled room. Everyone was here except August. "Hmm, that can't be good."

Octavius looked at Chamberlain who was the last to arrive. "Where is my son?"

The lawyer glanced around the room. When no one reacted, he sat down and pulled a small wooden box from his satchel. He placed the box on the table and opened it for all to see. August's name was written on the single card that lay at the bottom. The edges of the card suddenly caught fire and the card quickly burned to ash. Chamberlain sighed. "It appears Augustus Tome was the first to fall in the game."

Tome stared into the box long after the card was ash. When he finally looked up, he was gritting his teeth so hard the muscles along his jawline stood out. "So, the killer of my son is too much a coward to admit the deed?"

I rubbed the scarring along my eye. "I'm sorry for your loss."

"Keep your empty condolences, Brennan. Save them for somebody who cares." He looked around the room. "I will find out who did this, and you will pay."

Bathory spoke up. "I saw his body. It was in some sort of laboratory."

Tome whirled on her. "Really? How do I know it wasn't you who killed him?"

"He was not my target. You know I cannot say more."

"Yes, that is convenient, isn't it?"

"Your son was not Katrina Bathory's target. I was," said Pavel.

Gio frowned. "Wait, I thought you couldn't tell."

Pavel shook his head. "No, the rules say you couldn't reveal your target. There was no mention of naming your hunter."

Rom Chang nodded. "The spells required for Bainbridge's game have to be very literal."

"Fine." Tome nodded. He turned to Acantha. "Tell me who your hunter was."

"I don't know." She glared at him. "I never encountered them."

"Enough." Bathory stepped between Tome and Acantha. "I'm sorry for your loss, but leave her alone."

Acantha gave her a grateful look.

"You see that?" I asked Bad Penny in a low voice.

"Yeah, She's using grooming techniques on Acantha. But why?"

"Pretty sure Acantha either is, or will be, her apprentice. She likes to train women to be serial killers and torturers and feeds off the pain and suffering of the victims."

"That's fucked up!" Penny exclaimed in a loud voice. Everyone stopped and looked at her.

Tome gave her a long stare before turning back to Bathory. "I'll find out easy enough who killed my son once the bell has rung again. My magics will provide the answer."

"I must remind you, Wizard Tome," warned Chamberlain, "you may only attack the person on your card."

Bathory moved Acantha to the corner of the room as Pavel and Khishchnik attempted to talk sense into Tome. Penny and I followed the vampire. I dragged a chair over for Acantha to sit on. Penny shook her head. "Jesus! He was shitting all over the kid earlier. Now that he's dead, Tome suddenly went all vengeful dad mode."

"Family can be complicated." I leaned against a wall. "Speaking of which. Katrina, can we talk to you and Acantha for a moment?"

"Of course, Sergeant. I was hoping to get to know you. I would love to clear up any misunderstanding your department has of my people."

Pretty unlikely chance of that happening.

I nodded to Acantha. "I spoke with Pavel, and he said your great-grandfather used to own the Rook."

"That is correct. As elder son, it went to my great uncle after that. It's when my grandfather changed our last name to Baines. But it has passed hands since then. As you know, many magi have ways of extending their lifespans."

"How long are we talking?"

"Well, to give you a frame of reference, my great-grandfather was discharged from the Continental Army shortly before inheriting the Rook."

"He fought in the Revolutionary War?"

"Indeed."

"Look, I'm hoping there is another way out where we don't have to kill each other. Any knowledge on the Rook may help in getting around Bainbridge's game."

Bathory nodded as a sad frown formed on her face. "I, too, hoped for the same thing. I tried several workarounds to no avail and can tell you personally that breaking the rules puts you in an agonizing pain spell."

I suppressed a shudder as a memory of being magically tortured by Preston Hawk flashed through my mind. "Okay then. Acantha, what do you know of the Rook?"

"Well, it was originally owned by Bayn of the Bridge. The progenitor of our family line."

"And who is he exactly?" Mimicking me, Penny leaned against a cupboard.

"That has been lost in the mists of time. Some say he was a warrior defending a bridge against Saxons. Others say he was a wizard defending a portal bridging our world to another."

"So that's how he got his name."

"Yes. He created the Rook, and it has been handed down from eldest heir to eldest heir since. I believe this is the first time it's not in the direct line of succession. I do know it's a powerful artifact. However, much of the magics of the Rook has been lost. Rooms have disappeared over the years, including the map room which showed the details of the interior."

"A map would be handy." I mused. "Any chance of a forge?"

"There used to be one, but my grandfather once told me it had been lost."

"Damn." I thought for minute. "If Bayn lived that long ago, when was the Rook moved to this country? Or did he live long enough to build it here?"

"Oh, it's been back and forth from here to Europe several times. It depends on the owner. They usually move it to where they live. Or want to live."

"I don't follow." I absently scratched my scar. "How many times has it been rebuilt?"

The alchemist gave me a slow grin. "Sergeant, the Rook has the ability to slide itself across ley lines. It's part of the reason for its name. It moves similar to the chess piece. Obviously, that's not as useful now as it would be during an Age of Magic, but it can still move around an area with a Nexus."

"Huh!" Penny looked thoughtful. "So, it's basically a TARDIS?"

That might explain why the vampires want it. With its apparent ability to be bigger on the inside, during an Age of Magic, you could move an entire army with it.

"Not quite. It doesn't travel through time or outer space. Just across ley lines," Bathory stated.

I stared at her. "*You* watch Doctor Who?"

"Of course. I lived in England during the sixties. I saw the very first airing back in 1963. Day after your President was killed, if I remember correctly."

Casual comments like that were always startling reminders that many of the people I interacted with had been walking the Earth a long time.

Acantha nodded. "Oh, and it's supposed to have had the ability to shrink to the size of a chess piece, but no one has known how to do that since before my great grandfather's time."

"That's an impressive artifact. I have to say, I'm surprised you're being this free with such information."

The master vampire smiled. "I have reasons to want this over quickly. And I don't want to see Acantha killed. It would be in our best interests if you can find a workaround. Even if it costs us the Rook."

Interesting. Why the hurry? What are you up to?

I switched subjects. "Any idea what Pavel is?"

"Yes. I just wish I had known before I fought him," Bathory said with a bitter scowl.

"Care to share?"

"He's a Plague witch."

Oh! Fuck me!

Plague witches were rare. They had an innate ability to create a rapidly growing disease in others. They were often used as assassins.

236

Tome barged into our conversation. "Bathory, I would have words with you about my son."

The vampire sighed. "Very well, Octavius."

The wizard clenched his hands down by his sides. The one formed of wood made a creaking sound. "How was he killed?"

"Are you sure you want to hear this?" At the wizard's nod, she continued. "I'm not sure what killed him. His wounds were great slashes across his body. My initial thought was a blade of some sort, but if so, it was not made of metal."

I ignored Tome's initial glare at me when a blade was mentioned. "How do you mean?"

Bathory tapped the side of her nose. "Blood calls to our kind, Sergeant. And steel and iron weapons change the smell of the blood coming from a wound."

"You can smell metal?" I said somewhat in disbelief.

"Ever bit your lip? Tasted the iron in your blood?"

"I—" I lapsed into silence, promising myself to try it with the blood rune for senses at some point.

"Anything else?" asked Tome.

The vampire was quiet for a long time before sighing deeply. "This will not help things, but it was your son, and you have a right to know."

She looked at Acantha who nodded in encouragement. "Go ahead, Auntie Katrina."

Auntie, is it?

Bathory glanced back at the others seated at the table. "There was perfume or possibly cologne in the air."

Tome's eyes lit up. "Then you know who it was?"

"Ah, no." The vampire looked embarrassed. "I have a sensitivity with such things and can only smell the alcohol base before I become stuffy."

Bad Penny looked incredulous. "You're *allergic* to perfume?"

"Not exactly. It just overpowers my sense of smell," Bathory muttered. "I had the same problem while living. Undeath magnified it."

"So, who is it?" mused Tome while scanning the room.

"Harleen, Gianna, and Obrechennyy are wearing perfume. Gio and Pavel are wearing cologne," said Acantha. She shrugged at our looks. "I like perfumes but I can't wear them around Katrina."

"But we know it wasn't Pavel," I interjected. "His target was Katrina."

Tome stared at Khishchnik who was sitting across the room with her eyes shut. "Bathory, could the wounds have been made by claws?"

"No, I don't think so," the vampire replied.

Before any of us could comment further, a bell rang out and again for a second time.

"Well, that ends the safe period." Acantha looked around the room. "Who will die next?"

Chapter Twenty-Two

Arrogance and Cheap Cologne

I stayed behind as the others shuffled out and instead started inspecting the fireplace. Chamberlain paused on his way out. "Find something interesting, Sergeant?"

I pulled my head back from the baking oven. "Fireplaces need chimneys, Councilor. And chimneys lead out."

"I would remind you ee are not simply locked in; we are phased out of dimension. Even if you could fit up the chimney," he glanced over me and raised his eyebrows. "You would find yourself stuck between dimensions. I would imagine that to be less than comfortable."

"Yeah, forgot about that part," I lied as I brushed brick dust off my fingers. "Hey, I have a question. Where do you go during this?"

"I get transported to a room to wait out the proceedings."

"Like a secret room?"

"No, just a room. I assume it can be accessed by anyone wandering down that particular hall. Why?"

"I don't know. It seems odd you get transported out as well."

"The lawyer shrugged. "I hadn't thought of that. Perhaps Mister Bainbridge didn't either."

"Yeah, maybe."

"Good luck, Sergeant." Chamberlain stepped out.

Thanks, you lying bastard.

Once the orange flash of light faded away, I started inspecting the baking oven again. There was coal in the basement and the oven was small enough to use as a forge. The iron doors would keep the heat in.

Now I just needed stock and a clue on what to make.

Still, the idea that I had a forge to use if needed made me feel a lot more comfortable. Whistling an old Irish tune, I walked through the door, remembering to keep my eyes shut this time.

I ended up in the front hallway. There didn't appear to be anyone else around. I pulled out my card and looked at it.

Obrechennyy Khishchnik

"Fuck that shit!" I tucked it back into my pocket. I began exploring the Rook again. In addition to being bigger on the inside, I was starting to suspect that it was altering the hallway into some sort of maze. As much as I tried, I could find no pattern. Hopefully my orb will be able to figure it out.

After several hours of searching, I was debating to find a room to duck into when Gio Ponticello strode down the hall I was in. On seeing me, his eyes lit up. "Hey there, Brennan!"

Oh, Shit!

Before I could react, I started to feel very heavy and had trouble moving my limbs. It was like a great weight forcing me down. A nearby light sconce started to creak before breaking off the wall and slamming into the floor.

He's got some sort of gravity manipulation Gift.

I triggered the blood runes for strength and stamina and threw myself into an adjoining room. The pressure immediately let up and I scrambled behind a couch and drew my 1911. The room seemed to be some sort of den. Gio strode through the door, all arrogance and cheap cologne. As he raised his hand toward me, I fired off three quick shots. He smiled and the rounds lost all velocity and slowly tumbled in zero gravity. He flicked his wrist, and the rounds flew back in my direction, piercing the couch and striking me in the chest. I staggered up and fell to the ground.

"That was easy. Weren't you the guy that killed Harrow? This should up my rep a couple of notches." He slowly worked his way around the couch. "Gia was lording over me that she got first kill, but this is much better than a lowly mage."

As he rounded the couch, I sat up in a burst of rune-powered speed and shoved my boot knife into his abdomen not far below the heart. He gasped as I pulled him in close. "You kill me, you trigger the runes on the blade, and you die. You remove the knife, you trigger the runes on the blade, and you die. You do anything I don't tell you to, you die. Do you understand me?"

"Y-Yes." He choked out. I stepped back. The blade was buried up to its hilt. "You h-have to help me."

"Said the guy who just tried to kill me!" I reached down and picked up the rounds and their corresponding shells, putting them in my pocket.

I put a safeguard on all my weapons. None of them can harm me or my family. As soon as the rounds touched me, they stopped. Because of that, they were undamaged. With no gunpowder or primers, I highly doubted the ammo could be reloaded, but since I was down to six shots, I was going to hold onto them just in case.

I rubbed my scars as I studied Gio. "So, you and you sister are stone cold killers."

He nodded. His face had gone white, and he was sweating. Shock was setting in. "It wasn't personal. I was just playing the game."

"Yeah, sure."

The smart thing would be to just kill him now. If I let him go and he kills someone else, that blood will be on my hands. Still, when have I ever done the smart thing?

"You have any healing potions?"

"N-no."

Well, you're not getting mine.

"Okay, listen, the only way not to trigger the kill runes is for me to summon the knife back. But you'll still be bleeding, which means you'll need medical aid, got it?"

"Yeah."

"Wound like that, you have to patch it up quick, understand?" I patted him down quickly. He didn't have anything useful. "So, I'm going to give you a fifteen-minute head start to find some bandages, then I'm going to summon the blade back. You follow?"

"Y-yeah. Okay."

I shook my head as he stumbled out of the room. My knife did none of the things I had told him, but a little deception about the runes may have saved his life. If he can find aid somewhere.

I headed out and zigged and zagged before winding up in a bedroom. At the fifteen-minute mark, I used a rune on my bracers to summon the knife back to me. After cleaning it, I stuck it back in my boot. I was tired and this was as good as any other area to sleep. I went back out into the hallway and shattered the light globes, scattering the pieces up and down the hallway.

Once back in the bedroom, I used my skeleton key to lock the door. I then slid the bureau against it. I laid down on the bed, fully dressed with a single blanket over me, and dozed off.

Chapter Twenty-Three

Pawn takes Knight

I woke with a start. Without moving, I triggered the blood runes for heightening my senses. I also activated the night vision on my runic eye. *Crunch.*

Someone was walking over the shards of glass. I inhaled deeply taking in the scent.

Rom Chang.

I slowly and quietly slid out my card.

Pavel Mûstek. I must have slept through a target change.

The knob of my door shook as she tried to open it. I waited for her to use a spell to force it, but she didn't. Either she didn't have such a spell in her arsenal, or she didn't want to waste the energy. As I listened, Rom Chang slowly moved away until I couldn't sense her anymore. No longer tired, I pulled out the old leather book I'd inherited from my mentor and started reading about a reversal rune. It had some interesting properties, and I had used that on my project with Soul Drinker's runes.

This isn't helpful. Why do I keep going back to it?

I opened another can and slurped down some processed glop the label claimed was food.

Mmmm. Botulism...

I wished I was able to talk to Zoe or Martin. Their knowledge of spells would have allowed them to put this whole charade of a game to an end. But I didn't have their knowledge or skillset. At the end of the day, I was an over-the-hill street cop who was handy with a forge and had some cool toys. And I couldn't even use most of those toys while trapped here.

Just like with Dracula, I felt like I was missing something. I could almost taste it. This time I felt like I almost had a way out.

If I could come up with the right set of runes, I might be able to get us out of here.

The problem was I didn't know a way to force the Keep back into phase. And since I couldn't, it would remain that way until the game ended.

Or it thought it ended. Hmm.

I startled as someone jiggled the doorknob. I stayed still, hoping whoever it was would go away like Rom Chang.

Or did Rom Chang swing back?

There was a creak and a snap as the door was forced slightly out of the door jam, popping the lock.

Whoever it is is strong.

The door started to slowly open until it hit the bureau. I pocketed the book, quietly rolled off the bed, and drew my gun. As I did so, I inhaled deeply.

Penny?

Holstering my gun, I waited as the bureau was pushed aside. Bad Penny entered the room in her hyde form, baton in hand.

"Hey, Penny. You gave me a start there."

"Hi, Mikey." Her voice had the gravely tone that came with her hyde transformation.

"Hope I'm not your target," I joked, pointing at her baton. "Actually, I'm glad we met up outside the break sessions. Now that we're alone, let's brainstorm and see if we can come up with a way out of this."

"Funny you should say that." She lunged forward with the baton. I backpedaled and her swing missed.

"Penny! What the hell?"

She had a blank look on her face and swung at me again.

Fuck! She's being controlled somehow. Bathory maybe? Powerful enough vampires can hypnotize humans.

In her hyde form, Bad Penny was a dangerous adversary. I'd fought her before wearing armor and having access to my full arsenal, and while I finally prevailed, it had been no easy feat. Trapped in a room with no armor and no nonlethal weapons to subdue her, I wasn't sure I could win.

To make matters worse, the baton was one of the earliest weapons I'd made. I had forged it before I had come up with a way to safeguard against my own creations.

I kept putting room between us and pushed the chest towards her. She stopped it with one hand and pushed it aside.

"Penny, snap out of it."

Penny leaped up towards a wall. She used it to springboard off of and spun through the air at me. Before I could react, she struck me in the chest with the tip of the baton. She started screaming in pain as I hit the floor. I tried unsuccessfully to fight the sleep that quickly overtook me.

Son of a bi…

Chapter Twenty-Four

You Don't Tarnish the Badge

"I ordered you to kill him. Why are you balking?"

I cracked the lid of my real eye to see Acantha and Penny standing over me. Penny was no longer in hyde form and held the baton over her head as if she was going to swing it down on me. Her whole body was shaking.

Acantha's face was red with fury. She held a half empty potion in her hand. She downed the rest and pocketed the tube.

"Now kill him! "Something about the timbre of her voice was different. Its effect on Penny was obvious. She immediately stiffened and the baton came down.

I quickly rolled to the side. As the baton hit the floor where I had been, I pulled Penny's arm further down. Overbalanced, her head slammed into the floor, stunning her. I followed up with a rabbit punch to the back of the head. She slumped down, clearly unconscious.

I slowly got to my feet as Acantha backed away. One of her hands fumbled around inside a pouch. "Stay away from me!"

"Hmm, no effect. I'm guessing that voice control potion only works on hydes. A way to directly control them, maybe? Aside, of course, from addicting them to a potion that painfully warps and slowly destroys their mind, that is." I took a quick look at Penny. "Even in their human form. Kind of impressive in a sick slaver sort of way."

Acantha pulled out a potion tube and held it over her head as if to dash it to the floor. "It's not personal. You were my target. I had no choice."

"You know, lately it seems everyone that tries to kill me keeps saying it's not personal. Gotta say, from this side of things, it seems pretty damn personal!" I let the berserker fury I felt creep into my voice. "You just mind controlled a close friend of mine into trying to kill me and you're playing the victim card?"

With a groan, Penny rubbed the back of her head. Acantha smiled and dropped the potion back into her pouch. "Get up."

As Penny started to rise, I shot forward and jabbed Acantha in the throat. She gagged and grabbed her neck with both hands. I ripped the pouch off her belt and threw it to the other side of the room. Penny stood motionless, having completed the last order. I reach down and grabbed her baton, and as Acantha took a breath to shout out a command, I hit her in the shin with the baton and triggered the sleep rune. She dropped like a puppet whose strings had been cut.

I didn't remember how long the sleep rune was good for, so I pulled one of Acanth's shoes off and stripped off her sock which I rolled up and stuffed into her mouth. I patted her down and removed several potions hidden in her clothing. I threw them into her pouch and tore open the bed sheets.

Using the linen strips I'd just made, I secured her gag and tied her hands and feet. Once she was trussed up, I threw her on the bed.

"Penny, snap out of it." I snapped my fingers in front of her face to no avail. Sighing, I rummaged through the alchemy kit. Acantha marked her potions with small symbols I didn't recognize. Without knowing what the various potions did, I wasn't sure what to do with them. I was afraid to flush them down the toilet in case some of them reacted to water or took effect when in contact with air.

If this tower is phased out of dimension, where does the plumbing go?

Clearing my head of the idle thought, I stuffed the whole bag into the right cargo pocket of my BDU pants. It barely fit but I was able to cram it in there. Not sure what else to do, I sat down on the floor, leaned against a wall, and waited.

Acantha woke up about ten minutes later. Penny appeared to shake off the effects of the alchemist's voice control twenty or so minutes after that. All my joints complained as I slowly got to my feet when Penny started blinking.

"Mikey? Wha—" Penny eyes narrowed as the events of what happened came flooding back. "You fucking bitch. You're a dead woman."

I stepped between them. "Easy. She's a prisoner. Fight's over."

"Fuck that. She's a slaver just like the rest of her guild."

"And you swore an oath. This goes to what we talked about. You don't tarnish the badge."

"Okay, okay. I get it. It's just… you don't know what it was like." She rubbed her face with both hands. "I was trapped in my own body, and she was able to order me around like a robot."

"You didn't know about the voice control thing?"

"No, she's from a different chapterhouse than the one I worked for. My handler didn't use that. Didn't need to. The addiction ensure I complied with orders."

I frowned. A horrible thought entering my mind. "Did your handler ever…"

"What? Oh! No, nothing like that. They have strict rules they have to abide by. It allows them to trick themselves into thinking they're not complete pieces of shit." She stared down at Acantha. "What do we do with her? We're trapped out of phase. We can't just arrest her and take her to jail."

"I'm not sure."

A slow evil grin spread across Bad Penny's face. "Your gilf encounter gave me an idea."

"Gilf?"

"Grandma I'd-"

"Stop!" I cut her off with a groan. "Please don't finish that."

"Fine. Your encounter with Harleen gave me an idea. We can't lock her up or kill her. We also can't leave her here all tied up because she could starve to death or get found by her hunter." Penny loomed over Acantha whose eyes widened above her gag. She raised her arm behind her back out of Acantha's view. Glancing back at me to make sure I could see it, she crossed her fingers and looked back down at Acantha. "So, let's just strip her nude and throw her back into the hallway. Let's see how she does with nothing but a smile."

"Penny!" I barked.

"Yeah, yeah. It was just an idea." She stepped back and rested an arm on the bureau. "How long does this voice thing work on me?"

"I don't know. Let's find out." I looked down at Acantha. Has it worn off yet?"

The alchemist lifted up her tied arms and looked at her watch and then nodded frantically at me.

"Go stand in the bathroom but stay in hyde form," I told Bad Penny as I drew my 1911.

Penny shrugged and did what I asked. "Now what?"

I placed the muzzle of my gun between Acantha's eyes and cocked the hammer back. The unmistakable smell of urine filled the air and tears streamed down the Alchemist's face. "I'm going to take off your gag. You need to understand that no matter what order you may give Penny, she won't get to me before I've splattered your brains all over that pillow. Do not force me to kill you."

She made an audible gulp and made one slow nod.

"Hey, how is that any different than what you wouldn't let me do?" asked Penny.

"Because I will be defending myself from a deadly weapon attack."

Penny frowned. "What deadly weapon?"

"You."

Her mischievous grin returned. "Why, Michael Aloysius Brennan, that may have been the nicest thing you have ever said to me."

"That is *not* my middle name."

"Well, what is?"

"You don't need to worry about that." I stared in Acantha's eyes. "When I remove your gag, you will tell Penny to lift her left foot. Anything else and I pull the trigger. Got it?"

She nodded again. I pulled the gag off. The alchemist took a slow and steady breath. "Penny... lift... your... left... foot... up."

"No! Go fuck yourself!" Penny replied in a happy voice. "Okay, Mikey, looks like it wore off."

I de-cocked the hammer and slowly removed the gun. Acantha's eyes never left my face. "You can speak if you want to."

"You… you'd have really shot me. I could see it in your face."

I holstered my weapon. "In a heartbeat. Let me guess. Bit of a lab rat. Don't really go into the field too much."

"How did you guess?"

"You've never faced death before. At least not yours. You wet yourself when the gun was placed to your head, and you were afraid to take me on yourself. That's why you had Penny do it."

"That was a tactical decision." She wiped away the tears with her linen bindings and tried to give me a haughty look.

"You say tactical. I say cowardice. What happened? I thought Bathory was hoping I could figure a way out of this. Or was that all bullshit?"

"She seemed to think you could pull it off. I don't know why. All I know is if I can get the Keep and bring a stray hyde back to the flock, I'm going to do it."

Looks like she's not fully under Bathory's sway then.

Acantha flinched as Penny left the bathroom. "How was she able to resist the command? She's a hyde. With half a potion she should have been completely under my control."

"You only controlled her mind, not what mattered."

"What's that?"

"You couldn't control what's in here." Penny tapped the left side of her chest with a finger. "You couldn't take away my heart."

Chapter Twenty-Five

No Geeksplaining

In the end, we untied her hands and left before she could unbind her ankles. After a couple of left and right turns, we slowed down. "You okay, Penny?"

"It was frustrating as hell and I really, really want to punch her through a wall, but yeah. I'm alright." She did a quick count of her potions.

"You have enough?"

"It depends on how long we're here for." She rubbed the back of her head where I hit her. "We're pretty screwed here, Mikey. Bainbridge wasn't kidding about the spells he put in place. Because you weren't the target on my card, as soon as I hit you, I was nailed with a powerful pain spell. Had me kibbing on the floor for a couple of minutes."

I flashed back to being tortured by a pain spell from a spellslinger named Preston Hawke. It… was not one of my enjoyable memories. "You sure you're okay?"

"Sucked at the time, but what are you going to do? "She made a dismissive gesture with her hand.

"How did she grab you?"

"I thought I could zap her with the baton, tie her up, and it was one less person to deal with. Hadn't thought the whole thing through. As soon as I got close, she downed that potion and commanded me not to move." Without saying it, Penny's words conveyed to me that Acantha was her target. "It was so freaking frustrating. We ran into Chamberlain in one of the halls and I couldn't say or do anything."

"What did he do?"

"He started to approach me but stopped when he saw Acantha. As soon as he realized there was a conflict going on, he beat feet."

"Interesting. He told me he stays out of the way in a special room."

"I don't know, maybe he got bored, or his room didn't have a restroom." She shrugged. "Listen, I think we might be in a Kobayashi Maru situation. That's when—"

"You did not just try to Geeksplain to me," I interrupted.

"I don't think that's a thing."

"Whatever. I am aware of the unwinnable situation scenario and, like Kirk, I don't believe in it."

"Well, unless you can reprogram the Rook like a holodeck, none of us are getting out of here until all but one of us is dead."

"Hmm." An idea started to percolate in my brain, one that had been half forming when Penny barged in to attack me. I pulled out my notebook and flipped to a page. "We don't have to actually kill everybody. We just need to deceive the Rook into thinking they're dead."

"And how do we do that?"

"By killing everybody."

"What?"

The lights started flickering and when we walked around the corner, we found ourselves back in the kitchen. With the exception of Gio, we were the last to arrive.

Shit. That idiot didn't bleed out, did he?

It looked like we missed a lot. Rom Chang had deep claw marks across her face and her clothes were torn and shredded. The murderous looks she kept shooting at Khishchnik left no doubt on who caused her injuries.

Acantha was holed up in a corner of the room and was furiously talking to Bathory who kept nodding with a sympathetic look on her face. They both occasionally glared over in our direction. Harleen was not far from them. The left side of her shirt had bloodstains, and she held her hand to her side.

Penny and I grabbed some food and set up at another corner table, while Gianna looked frantically around for her brother. Her clothes had a shredded look to them as well. Tome didn't bother to hide his satisfied look as he watched her.

Uh oh. That's not good.

Penny leaned into me. "What do you think? Tome whack that moron Gio?"

"Yup. Looks like Rom Chang went up against Khishchnik and regretted it and maybe… Harleen and Gianna tussled?"

Chamberlain walked in with the wooden box. He opened it and Gio's name was on the card inside. Gianna gave a small cry when it burst into flames.

"My condolences." The lawyer closed the box as Gianna glared at him and stomped away.

I waved Harleen over. She limped over and eyed us with suspicion. "Whata y'all want?"

"Information exchange." I kicked out a spare chair. "Sit down before you fall down."

She slowly lowered herself onto the chair. "You don't hold a grudge?"

"For what? Flashing your boobies at him?" Penny gave her an evil grin. "It's Zoe Afire you should be worried about."

"The fire witch? The one that turned Preston Hawk into a cinder? Why, what's she got to do with it?"

"Because you tried to do the horizontal bop with her husband." Penny hooked a thumb in my direction. "And, you know, the whole kill him afterwards thing…"

"Ah crap!" She slumped in her chair, clearly exhausted. "You could've told me who you were married to."

"You could have not tried to kill me." I shrugged. "And the other stuff as well."

Penny wiped down the top of her soda and opened it. "What happened, Gianna clean your clock?"

"Ah may have got more than I gave in that particular encounter. Found out her Gift. Turns out her hands vibrate."

"Really?" Penny had an intrigued look on her face as she looked Gianna up and down. "In another set of circumstances, that could be very interesting."

"Not when they can cut through steel and wood, it doesn't," snapped the Southerner.

"Ouch." Penny grimaced.

"Yeah," Harleen lifted up the side of her shirt just enough to show a rough bandage. "She cut through a couple of my ribs."

"May I?" I motioned to the wound.

"Go ahead." She sighed.

I opened the bandage as much as I could without disturbing the clotting. It looked like someone racked a chainsaw across her ribs. She needed a healer or a hospital. I retied her bandage. "How are you not dead?"

"Ah have some minor healing when ah shift." She fanned her hand around the room. "This is beyond me. Regardless of my Gift, Ah'm not a fighter and Ah'm certainly not a killer."

"At least when your target's not in the bed next to you." Penny smirked.

The older woman slowly shook her head. "You do what you got to do to survive, Honey. Ah was just looking to get a few bucks from the will, not play in the Hunger Games."

As she spoke, an argument broke out between Tome and Gianna, with the wizard slowly rising from his chair. "I am playing by the rules. If any of my actions have perhaps caused you pain and suffering, then that is but icing on the cake."

Gianna pointed a finger in his face. "There, you practically admitted killing my brother."

"I would love to take such credit if the rules would allow it, but alas, I am not and therefore can neither confirm nor deny that I killed the brother of the woman who murdered my son!"

I stood up. "Alright, back it up."

"Stay out of it cop!" snarled Gianna as her hands began to vibrate. "He dies *now*."

As her hands became a blur, she stepped towards Tome before crying out in pain. Purple energy enveloped her, and she fell to her knees. She kept crawling towards the wizard, shrieking in pain as she went.

Pavel stepped in front of her while Penny and I grabbed her by her upper arms. She tried to pull away from us until finally going limp from the pain.

Tome looked down his nose at her. "Pathetic."

"Shut the fuck up, Tome." I growled as Penny and I dragged her over to a chair and placed her in it. The wizard had a triumphant smile and walked over by the sink.

As we straightened up, Bathory moved over to us and cleared her throat. "I... would like to thank you, Sergeant."

"Oh? Those looks you were giving me said otherwise."

"I've had time to think it over. You clearly bested Acantha, yet you let her live. I thank you for that."

I stepped away from everyone and motioned for her to follow. "You working for Vlad Tepes?"

Bathory's eyes raised in surprise. "That is... very blunt, Sergeant."

"Well? Are you of his line?"

"No, the Bathory line is separate, though our families have had... mutual interests through the years. Here, those interests diverge." She tugged at the cuff of her sleeve. "Vlad wants the Rook, but so do I, and that is why I'm here."

I studied her face, trying to determine if she was telling the truth. She looked tired. There were dark circles around her eyes.

Or is that normal for her line of vampires?

"But now you said, you're more interested in getting out then getting the Rook. Why?"

"I have my reasons. They need not concern you... yet." There was a worried look in her eyes again.

"Do you know who Dracula sent here to secure the Rook?"

"No. But if I learn, I'll let you know."

Really?" I frowned. "Why? Isn't that betraying your alliance?"

"I may work with him for mutual gain, but I do not like Vlad Tepes or any of his people. They give our people a bad name and perpetuate horrible stereotypes."

"Really?" I let the doubt show on my face.

"I happened to like garlic and I can't go to a non-vampire party without hearing blah… blah… blah!"

"I, ah, I think you might need to blame Bela Lugosi for that one."

"He is…do you know who John Gotti was?"

"Of course."

"He is the John Gotti of the vampire world. Too flamboyant, always shining a light where it doesn't need to be, just to appease his own ego." Her lips twisted in distaste. "Our kind thrive in the shadows, not the light."

"Who do you suspect is working for him?"

"Anyone but Acantha and Tome may be his pawn."

"Tome isn't what I would call trustworthy."

She shrugged. "It is a powerful artifact. An impenetrable stronghold with some unusual features. Tome would not give that up. Also, he's the type of wizard to consider vampires as lesser beings."

"Why not Acantha?"

"Acantha didn't think she would inherit anything; she wasn't going to attend. I had to convince her."

"Why wouldn't she? Bainbridge and she didn't get along?"

"I don't think they've ever met. No, Acantha's mixed heritage has been a problem with some of the older members of the family. It's caused… friction."

That left a bad taste in my mouth. "They're okay with her associating with you, a blood drinking vampire, but have an issue with the fact that she's half Indian?"

"Oh, they're offended by that, too. It's a petty family. Daniel is a perfect example of that." She waved his hand around the room. "Do you see any wizards here? The extended family is full of them, but did Daniel leave anything for them?"

Huh!

"Why not?"

"This is a culling. He's removing the undesirables from the family while at the same time thumbing his nose at the other related magi who will be denied the home of their shared wizard ancestor."

"Bainbridge was a snob and a boor, but I never took him for a racist."

"Oh, in his case it's not so much about Acantha's race as it is about her profession. Daniel hated alchemists almost as much as he did vampires."

"So, are you using her to get the Rook or is she the next murderess in training?"

She laughed. "It started out being about the Rook, but yes, I've taken her under my wing. Her anger is so…invigorating."

"Okay, I gotta ask. What is up with the whole female serial killer training program anyway? I've heard of some fucked up things over the years, but that's a whole 'nother level."

"Each vampire line has its own quirks. You've heard this? Your little trick with the sunflower seeds. That was unnecessarily cruel, by the way."

"I find it hard to believe you had an issue with cruelty."

"Oh, no, I applauded it. In fact, that was when I decided to make you one of mine."

"Ah, I thought you preferred women."

"*Excuse* me?"

"Sorry, sorry." I waved my hand. "It's been a weird week."

"To answer your rather rude question, I have no interest in men's… dangly bits. No, I plan on making you a vampire."

"I don't want to be a vampire," I told her point blank.

She gave me a look of hunger. "That is what will make it so enjoyable. I am savoring the anticipation."

"That… That might be harder than you think," I told her, thinking of all the weird things my blood had been doing.

"I just have to take care of some logistical issues first. Find a way for you to keep that gift of yours after you turn."

I frown. "I thought all the magical abilities a person has dies when they Turn?"

"Yes, but there always ways when you know the right sort of creatures."

"Do you plan on Turning Acantha as well?"

"No. I need her to stay mortal. As I was saying about quirks, the Bathory line feeds on fear and pain as much as the blood."

"You can't feed unless your victim is scared or in pain?"

"Well, we can…it's just so bland. No…taste."

"Why have mortal women do your dirty work?"

"Part of it is fun. Finding the right person. Cultivating their hatred. Breaking down their moral and sexual barriers as they do more and more horrendous things to their victims." The look of hunger changed to lust, and she slowly licked her lips as she looked over at Acantha.

"And the rest?"

She blinked and turned back to me. "Sorry?"

"You said that was partly the reason."

"Ah, yes. Well, I like to train well-to-do or noble women. Preferably widows. Those with large households. Ones who had servants that would not be missed."

I nodded in understanding, a sick feeling in my stomach. "And if they did get noticed, if the local authorities investigated, your mortal apprentice becomes the scapegoat."

"Hardly scapegoats. They commit all the acts; I just reap the benefits."

"And then you disappear into the night to train some new patsy in a different part of the world."

"As I said, my kind thrives in the shadows."

"Yeah, whatever. I'm done with this conversation." I started to walk away in disgust.

"Wait! I have been upfront with what I know. You can at least do the same."

I paused. "Fair enough. I did discover something about the creator of the Rook."

"Bayn?"

"Yeah. Well, it turns out that Bayn wasn't a wizard or a warrior."

The vampire frowned. "What do you mean? What was he?"

"If Bayn built the Rook himself and didn't have it commissioned, then he was a runesmith, not magi. The Rook isn't an artifact, it's a magic item."

The frown deepened. "You know this how?"

I pointed a thumb at my chest. "Runesmith, remember? We can generally tell each other's work. There are runes carved into the stones of the Rook. That being said, it looks like various spells have been added to it over the years by magi. That was a mistake."

"What do you mean?"

"Two different types of magic. Unless you plan carefully, the two don't usually mix well. Here it looks like the spells were just slapped on over the years without any consideration for the existing runes. It's causing issues. Acantha said that rooms have gotten lost over the years?"

"That's right."

I shrugged. "There you go. Magi messing around where they shouldn't. Once this is over and done with, the new owner should clear out the spells. The Rook should work significantly better after that."

I stood up and made my way over to Penny. Everyone ate in silence, many planning their next move, myself included as I stared at the walk-in freezer and made my plans.

Chapter Twenty-Six

Forging a Deception

When the time came, I followed everyone out and once again found myself in a hallway after walking though the doorway. This time, though, I had a plan. Well, a plan and a backup plan. I summoned the orb back to me and waited the few minutes it took to return. The orb smacked into my hand after zooming down the hall. Using the runes that connected it to my runic eye, I sifted through the footage and learned that the Rook didn't actually change around the rooms but instead used illusion to create misdirection. The illusions didn't work on the orb, and it was able to map out any area that didn't have a closed door.

Keeping an eye out for any ambushes, I followed the orb as it retraced its path to a set of stairs leading to the basement. This was a different section than where the boiler was located. A magic item as complex as the Rook needs some sort of interface device, and if I was making the Rook, this is where I would put it.

I proceeded down the stairs to be stopped by a glowing ward. Ten feet beyond the ward was a large set of double doors made of oak with banded steel. Runes were engraved on the doors and around the keyhole on the right door.

So, the ward was probably put up by some wizard or witch descendant of Bayn, but why? The runes surrounding the door and keyhole were more than suffice to keep anyone but another runesmith out. Unless...

"You stupid fucks lost the key, didn't you?"

It makes sense. If the key was lost and the family didn't have another runesmith to make new one, they were locked out of the control room. And since they didn't know who had the key, they threw a ward up to prevent the unknown keyholder from accessing the room. I wonder how many generations have refreshed the ward over the years or even if they knew why they were doing it.

I wasn't going to be able to get in with the ward intact, which meant my plan to take control of the Rook was a bust. That wasn't good because my backup plan was shaky as hell.

I sent the orb to find the kitchen and followed it back, slowly making my way there while watching out for the others. Once there, I went down into the basement and pawed through the tools on the workbench. I managed to score a pair of steel tongs, but what I was hoping against hope was that there was a blacksmith's hammer among them. I was sorely disappointed as the only one I located was a carpenter's hammer.

Eh, it'll have to do. Not like I plan on fighting with this blade.

I slung the hammer through my belt and used a bucket I found in the corner to lug the coal into the kitchen.

Next, I dragged the table over to the fireplace and put both my notebook and my mentor's book on the table. I used a couple of forks to keep them open to the pages I needed. I then pulled out my engraving kit from the cargo pocket of my BDU pants and unrolled the leather carrying case so it was flat on the table. Checking the area, I found an old heavy steel cleaver, the same one Harleen tried to do me in with.

That'll work. Right type of steel.

I pried off the wood handle and laid the blade aside.

Once there, I took coal from the bucket and set it out in one of the warming ovens in the brick fireplace. I hated working with coal. It took forever to warm up and the temperature was always wonky. I've burned the tips off way too many blades because I couldn't see the front of the blade buried in the coals. Still, beggars couldn't be choosers, and at least I found a set of bellows by the fireplace. I used that to make sure there was a steady supply of oxygen to the coals.

After the coals were hot enough, I placed the cleaver into them. Next was the tedious part. I continued to fan the coals while periodically checking the steel to make sure I didn't overcook it and make it brittle.

When I judged the metal hot enough, I removed the blade with the tongs and placed it on the floor. With no anvil present, I was going to have to use the ancient cobblestones that made up the floor of the kitchen.

I started to bang away on the blade with the hammer. It was not an ideal situation. The cobblestones give was different than that of a steel anvil, and the hammer was the wrong shape with a small impact area. Still, I managed to fold the metal in half and reshape it into a smaller but thicker blade. This took some time as I had to keep standing up and reinserting it back into the coals. My junk knees quickly started to ache each time I had to stand. Too many years ground pounding in the Army and walking a beat in the police department.

After inspecting the metal for the umpteeth time, I judged it as ready as it was going to get and brought it over to the table. Using the books as reference, I methodically carved a series of runes onto the blade using my Gift to interlock them. When I was done, I placed the blade into a pot full of water. I held my breath as I waited for the *ting* sound of the blade warping. When I judged the time right, I pulled it out and inspected the blade. It had a slight bend but was usable. I skated a file over it and was able to determine the metal was hard. Once I determined it was an acceptable blade, I placed my finger on the runes and activated them.

Or tried to anyway. I didn't feel them coming to life. I ran my eyes over them, trying to figure out what went wrong. It didn't take long to discover a series of runes that were not compatible with each other. This was fairly common when creating a new effect like I was doing. It often took me months to perfect a project. But I didn't have months. I barely had days.

Without enough time to try before the next break, I dumped the coals back into the bucket and dragged it downstairs, placing it inside the furnace. Any smoke or heat from them should dissipate up the furnace until they went out. I then hid the blade and hammer among the other tools on the workbench and went back up. I just finished cleaning the kitchen when the lights started flashing. I heated up a can of stew and sat down at the table to eat it. Wondering who my target was this time. I pulled the card out as I took a bite.

Penny. Ha! Well, that means she should have stayed out of trouble this time around.

I put the card back in my pocket as the door opened and Gianna stomped in. She looked very frustrated.

"No luck?" I took another bite of the stew.

"Fuck you, cop!" She stormed over to the cabinets and started making herself some food.

"Okay then." I continued to eat as the others trickled in. I had just finished up when Penny entered in. She went into the walk-in freezer and came out with the fixing for a sandwich. She sat down next to me and started putting it together. "Hey, Mikey. How did it go?"

"Can't complain, though I should." I scanned the room as Chamberlain came in. He frowned as he counted heads. I gave a slight nod towards him. "Everyone made it back this time. The little lawyer doesn't seem happy about it."

She cut her sandwich in half. "Makes sense. He doesn't get to leave until it's settled. I'm sure he's in a hurry to get it over."

"Over to mean that everyone but him and the last heir is dead?"

"Well. Okay, yeah, when you put it like that…" She took a bite of her sandwich. "Anyone come after you?"

"No. Probably couldn't find me." I gave her a smirk. "You had an easy one, though."

"What do yo—" She stopped chewing. You're kidding?"

"Was going to happen sometime."

"Mmm, true." She swallowed. "Shouldn't the Rook have zapped you for saying that?"

"Technically, I just inferred it. That may have been subtle enough or maybe it doesn't matter after it's over."

"Maybe." She pointed towards Katrina Bathory with her chin. "Aunt Vampy isn't looking too good."

I had clocked the same thing when Bathory entered the room. She looked paler than normal, her eyes were bloodshot, and there was a slight tremor to her hands. "Yeah, that's not good. I thought something was off when I talked to her, but she was hiding it better then."

"How long since you think she's fed?"

"At least since before we've got here." I watched as she shook off a hand Acantha laid on her shoulder. Bathory turned away, probably trying to hide the symptoms from the alchemist. "I give her another day or so before she goes into blood frenzy. My guess is Bathory will try to feed on whoever her next target is. If she gets to the point of going into a frenzy, she might attack Acantha. I don't see her risking that if she can avoid it."

"That seems kind of quick."

"Really? How long can you survive without water before dying?"

"I think it's about three days." Her eyes widened. "Oh shit, and she was already hungry when she got here. But she's a master vampire. Shouldn't she be able to last longer?"

"The opposite, actually. The blood keeps them alive, but it also fuels their magic. The more powerful a vampire, the more they need to feed regularly. Kind of like how an athlete needs more calories than a regular person, or how a big block v-8 needs uses more gas then a 6 cylinder. I suck at analogies, but you get the picture. A master vampire should be feeding every day. The longer they go hungry, the greater chances the craving triggers a frenzy. It's a survival mechanism."

"Yeah, I get it." Penny took a long sip of her drink. When she placed it back on the table, she had a thoughtful look on her face. "This is what you were talking about when you and Zoe were warning me about dating a vampire."

"Pretty much. No matter what feeling Bathory may have towards Acantha, once her vampire instincts take over, we're all just food. Not that I don't think Bathory wouldn't drink Acantha dry in a minute if it suited her needs."

"Yeah. Still, seeing it really puts it in perspective."

"That's not even factoring in that the vampire who turned Bathory could order her to kill everyone she ever loved, and she couldn't do anything but obey the command."

"Jesus."

Bad Penny ate in silence while I pondered what I was going to do with the Bathory situation. The plan I came up with wouldn't work for her, and I had no way of dealing with the vampire short of killing her. Not that I thought I had a chance fighting a master vampire with my current equipment.

Penny frowned momentarily as Acantha walked by. The alchemist flinched when she saw Bad Penny looking at her. Penny smirked as I took the time to read the room.

Pavel seem quietly confident. Tome and Gianna were shooting daggers at each other with their eyes, and Harleen looked nervous. Rom Chang, on the other hand, seemed eager, like she was looking forward for the fight, which made sense when I thought about it. Spellslingers made their living dueling and doing merc work. It stands to reason the profession would attract a certain… competitive personality… to it.

"So have you come up with a plan yet?""

"What?" I glanced over to Penny. "I didn't hear that."

"How are we getting out of here?"

"I have an idea, but it's got some serious drawbacks and could be a potentially disastrous. I'm still trying to figure if it's worth doing."

"You going to let me in on it?"

"Yes, but not with the others around." The lights started flashing again. I lowered my voice. "Can you find your way back here?"

"Probably not. Why?" Penny answered, matching my current volume.

"I could use your help. I tried a forging before, and it failed. A second set of hands would be a big help. I can send an orb to find you."

"Okay." She slid her chair back and we both stood up. I didn't want to be the last to file out this time just in case Tome was watching. I closed my eyes to avoid the flash and opened them in a ballroom. Crystal chandeliers dangled from the ceiling and oil paintings hung from the wall. From the dust, it didn't look like anyone had been there in decades. I send the orb out to track the current path to the kitchen as I looked around the room. I could see a family resemblance to Bainbridge, Harleen, and Acantha in several of the portraits. I didn't know the family history, but the older paintings were smiling while the later ones all stared out with stern expressions. A couple had such sour looks on their face, you'd have thought they just bit into a sandwich and found half a maggot. If this was the family he was raised in, it explained a lot about Bainbridge.

I opened my card to see that I had Harleen for a target this time. I chuckled and put it away as my orb returned. I reviewed the footage it took, making sure to take notice of the various illusions. When I was sure I knew the path back to the kitchen, I sent the orb to find Penny. The footage had shown several of the others the orb had encountered but not her.

I drew my firearm and quickly made my way down the halls, keeping an eye out for any of the others. The only one I encountered was Rom Chang. She stopped when I came around the corner and had her wand at the ready. "You here for me, Brennan?"

I chose my words careful to avoid Bainbridge's penalty spell. "I am not playing the game. You are safe from me. Am I your target?"

"Had you before but I couldn't find you. This time I seek another." She lowered her wand. We slowly passed each other, waiting for the other to make a move. Once she turned the corner, I headed back toward the kitchen, occasionally checking behind me to make sure she or another weren't backtracking me.

When I made it to the kitchen, I found Penny waiting for me. I raised my eyebrows. "Guess you were closer?"

"Yeah." She tossed me the orb. "So, what's the plan?"

"It's better if you don't know. It's risky and I'm asking you to trust me with your life. Can you do that?"

Penny stared into my eyes long enough to be uncomfortable. I don't know what she was looking for, but she must have found it because she nodded. "I don't like the cloak and dagger crap, but if you say it's better that I don't know, well, I trust you. Even if it risks my life."

She stepped in close and looked deep into my eyes. "But in return, I want you to put a baby in me."

I froze. "Ah…"

"Bwahaha!" Penny punched me on the shoulder, laughing so hard she started hiccupping. "Oh God! The look on your face. I couldn't resist it. You've been so jumpy after visiting Davenport's den of iniquity and Harleen's sexcapades of death."

"Jesus, Penny!" I placed a hand on my chest. "I've already had one heart attack. You want to give me another?"

"Serves you right, being all serious and mysterious." She held her breath for a second, trying to make the hiccups go away. "You know, for someone always bitching about the magi being all dramatic, you have a pretty good streak of it yourself."

"I was trying to impress on you the severity of the situation and you start talking about babies. What the hell?"

"Relax. I'm enjoying life way too much these days to think about kids. Besides, have you seen the size of your head?"

"What's wrong with my head?" I placed my fingers along the bridge of my nose and made a stop gesture with the other hand as I realized what I said. "Don't. Just don't."

"Too easy." She waved it away. "What I'm saying is look at the size of you. You're so big you could be a different species."

"I'm aware I'm on the large side. What's your point?"

"I'm saying if your offspring take after you with that giant noggin, it's C-section time all the way, and you don't mar perfection like this." She gave a dramatic gesture towards her body.

I sighed and tried to mentally regroup. "Can we focus on the task at hand please?"

"Although..." Penny tilted her head with a thoughtful expression on her face. "I wouldn't mind practicing a little baby making with you and Zoe. Just practice, mind you."

"Penny!"

"Fine, fine." She gave me a grin. "What's the next step?"

"I need to forge a magic weapon." I pocketed the orb and patted the oven. "This is going to be my makeshift forge. I came up with some tool substitutes, but I need your help."

"Okay. What are you making?"

"A dagger." I ignored her frown, went down the stairs, and retrieved the items I hid earlier. Once I had everything set up and lit the fire, I handed her the bellows. "I need you to use this to keep blowing a steady stream of air into the coals while I work the metal."

Bad Penny took the bellows I handed her, and a mischievous grin spread across her face. "So what you're saying is you're going to handle your tool while I bl—"

"Penny!"

"Yeah, yeah. I know." She moved the bellows into position. "Man, you're no fun."

"Look, runesmithing a magic item on the fly like this is dangerous. It's a process that should be done after much study and deliberation and under controlled situations."

"Yeah, but you've done runesmithing in the field before." Penny's brow furrowed.

"Yeah, but it hasn't been a great track record. The first kukri I made against Harrow failed and the second broke in combat. The patch job I did on my armor failed and I wound up getting fried. I'm like 0 for 3."

"Huh."

"So, yeah. I'm worried this forging may go wrong."

"I got faith in you, Mikey, and I don't say that about a lot of people. Let's get at it."

This time the forging went smoother. Once I was done reheating, folding, and shaping the metal into another blade, I started to stand only to find my knees had locked from kneeling on the cobblestone floor for so long. I used the table to pull myself into a standing position.

Penny dropped the bellows and moved over to help. She tilted her head and looked at me as I placed the blade into the bowl of water. The water bubbled and hissed as it cooled the metal. "You okay?"

"I'm fine, just getting old. Got bad knees from too many years in the Army marching around with a rucksack on my back," I said as I watched the boiling water die down. "Should have joined the Air Force like my sister."

When I judged it ready, I pulled the dagger blade out and did the file test.

"Damn!"

"What?"

"The file bit in." I pointed to tiny gouge marks on the blade made by the file.

"And that's bad?"

"Means the metal didn't harden enough. It's soft." I held a finger up as she started to speak. "Don't!"

Penny's mouth snapped shut.

I inspected the blade again and mulled over doing another reheat but finally decided against it. Too many and the blade would be weakened enough to be useless. Besides, I didn't think it would matter for what I planned to use it for.

I hope anyways.

I was fighting against the clock. I wanted to finish before the next game change. The longer it took, the more lives could be lost. Fortunately, aside from the obvious issue with hardening, the forging had gone very smoothly. This allowed me more time to spend on the runes. Normally, if I was starting to create an item from scratch, this process would take me months. I would need to create and study the major runes I was going to use. But in this case, I had already researched the major runes I was using here and had a good grasp on them. It was the connecting runes that were the problem.

Fortunately, there were only so many connecting runes. It was just a matter of figuring out the correct ones to use. The ones I tried this time couldn't hold as many as the major runes as my go-to set. I didn't normally use them because I had a habit of putting everything but the kitchen sink into the items I forged.

While not able to connect to as many major runes as the ones I used last time, this set was more compatible to most. Since I was only using two sets of major runes, they should work quite nicely, and I was kicking myself for not using them earlier.

I placed the blade on the table and started engraving on it, using my books as references. Penny stepped closer as I began. I glanced at her quickly and saw her interest in what I was doing. "At this point I'm just as concerned about the metal's integrity as I am about getting the runes to work."

"Wouldn't a softer metal make it easier to engrave the runes?"

"If it's too soft, I won't be able to get the clean sharp edges I need for the runes. If they aren't placed perfectly, the runes will fail. There is also the danger of the blade bending while being used."

"Is that what happened last time?"

"No, I used a set of runes that wouldn't work." I finished one rune and started on another. "I hate doing this on the fly. This is how mistakes happen."

"Isn't that how you got hurt?" She motioned to my runic eye and the scarring running down my face.

"Yup. I did a quick patch job on some blown runes and it didn't hold under pressure." I fought the urge to rub the scars and kept working. "The blade not being hard is what happened with the kukri I tried to use on Harrow. Its blade folded over during a fight with him because I rushed the process and, like now, I was improvising with tools and equipment. A blade should be flexible to bend but hard enough to take an edge and return to form. The kukri bent and stayed that way."

Penny remained quiet as I worked my way through the runes. After a while, I looked up at her. "You good? You haven't talked for a while."

"I didn't want to screw up your concentration so I thought I should just shut up for a bit."

"Must have killed you being silent that long."

"Ain't gonna lie, it hurt a bit." She smiled.

"Talking is fine. Morgan hangs out with me when I'm creating something in the forge. I'm used to chatter when I work. In fact, at this point I miss it." I finished another rune and straightened up. There were several pops as I stretched my back. I inspected the runes I had made.

"I had no idea it was this complicated." Penny leaned against the wall. "I thought you just forged it and called it a day."

"Not that easy." Satisfied, I resumed my engraving. "Making runes is a rare Gift. And there are even fewer that can work with steel. Some of it is just talent. But some of it is how frustrating it is to work with."

"How so?"

"Well, you don't know if the runes will work until you link them to the ley lines." I finished up with the last rune and gave them one last study. "Which means if it doesn't, you just wasted all that time forging. Working with other materials doesn't take as long. On the other hand, metal is more dur—"

The shield rune on my badge flared to life as an eldritch blast struck it. The rune was a standard on all officer's badges but wasn't near as strong as the ones on my armor. It saved me for being incinerated but the spell still caught me along my right side and knocked me across the room. The knife fell from my fingers.

I forced myself up when I heard Penny cry out in pain. As I stood up, I saw her on her knees writhing in pain as magical energies coursed over her. Standing by the door was Octavius Tome. His wooden arm was pointed at me. I summoned my 1911 and aimed it. "Stop what you're doing to her."

He smiled. "It's not my doing. The Keep is punishing her for trying to attack me. It appears I am not her target this time out."

I was finding it hard to breathe. The impact cracked or broke some of my ribs. "And I'm yours?"

"Not initially. No, you were being hunted by Gianna Ponticello. Imagine my surprise and delight when I took your card off the corpse of my son's murderer. I was happy enough just to finally have gotten her card. But this…this is a gift from the gods."

"Drop your… Damn it! Put your arm behind your back." I ordered.

One of the glyphs along his arm began to glow a nasty orange color. I ducked as he cast another eldritch blast at me. I fired two shots at him in return. A shielding spell sprang to life around him and deflected the bullets. It briefly changed color, so I knew he was using the alternating version of the spell. My bullets wouldn't be able to penetrate it and I couldn't summon my sword.

Fuck!

I flipped the table and ducked behind it, my side screaming as I did so. I rolled one of my orbs along the floor and ordered it into the air.

"Hiding won't save you, Brennan. I'm going to make this slow and painful. I think I'll start with your arms. Give you a taste of what I had to suffer all these years."

I frantically tried to come up with a plan. My sword could probably pierce the shielding spell, but I was unable to summon it. Unlike the magic of my armor, shielding spells required concentration. If I managed to disrupt his thoughts, it might fail. His wooden arm acted like a wand or a staff and had glyphs that contained precast spells. Without the need to reciting incantations, he could raise a new shielding spell in seconds, provided he had more than one glyph cast with it. Still if I could break his concentration, it might give me a precious few seconds before he put up a new one.

My eyes fell on the door to the supply galley.

That might work.

Keeping the orb low to the ground, I had it push my newly forged blade towards the galley door when suddenly the table lifted up and was flung away by some sort of levitation spell. It slammed into Penny who looked like she was about to down a hyde potion and attack him again. She hit the ground hard, her eyes closed, and the unused potion rolled out of her limp fingers.

"Bainbridge's games do allow me to defend myself." Tome laughed. "Look at you now. Scurrying around like a rat. You're nothing without your gadgets, are you?"

Exposed without the table, I stood up and activated my blood runes. Anger swept through me as the runes flared to life. My ribs popped and shifted as the healing runes repaired them at the expense of my body fat. My skin toughened and my senses sharpened. Using my enhanced strength, I whipped my boot knife at his face and dove towards the supply galley.

The knife bounced off the shielding spell, but it still caused him to flinch. I mentally ordered the orb to keep striking directly at his face. The thing repeatedly slammed into the shielding spell. Over and over in rapid succession. This distracted him enough that I was able to make it over to the galley door, scoop up the blade and dive inside.

"Really, Brennan? This thing is annoying but won't save you. Cowering in a closet! If Culain could see you now."

I quickly scanned the shelves to find what I was looking for. I felt my connection to the orb stop so he must have destroyed or disabled it. That's okay, I had two more. I just couldn't use more than one at a time with this version of my runic eye.

Still, the disconnect warned me that I only had seconds. I worked quickly to get ready and moved around the corner to the back of the galley where the sink and buckets were.

I heard the galley door open. If he just sent some lethal spells my way, I was done. I hoped he wanted to do this up close and personal. Make me suffer first.

"You're really going to make me come in there and get you?"

Bet your ass I am.

Waiting for him to make his move was tough. With all the runes activated, I was forced to keep fighting down the berserker nature that went with them. Every ounce of my being wanted to rush out and attack him. I somehow managed to hold off as my enhanced hearing picked up him entering the galley.

He suddenly popped around the corner, his wooden arm raised to fire. He paused when he discovered me holding a glass jar full of a clear liquid out in front of me. He tilted his head. "What do you have ther—"

"Science project." I dropped the jar into the bucket by my feet and kicked the whole thing over to him. As it slid to a stop in front of Tome, the cleaning supplies in the bucket reacted violently to the bleach in the jar. A cloud of chlorine gas erupted from the bucket and Tome screamed as it reached his eyes and quickly started coughing as he inhaled the gas.

With his concentration disrupted, his shielding spell failed. I leaped forward and punched him on the chin. The blood runes had increased my strength to the point where I completely shattered his jaw with my hit. He collapsed to the ground.

Coughing as the chlorine gas seared my eyes and lungs, I dragged him out of the galley and slammed the door shut. I didn't wait for the healing runes to take effect before pulling one of my remaining healing potions out of my pocket and downing it. The cool, sweet liquid washed away the pain and quickly repaired my injuries.

A wave of exhaustion hit me as I released the blood runes. The intense anger and urge to fight faded away, leaving me tired. I grabbed a dish rag off the oven handle and wrapped it around the tang of the blade in order to give myself a good grip. Using my finger, I activated the runes. This time, I felt the runes connect with ley lines, empowering the blade. Another wave of exhaustion hit me, the price of using my Gift.

Kneeling down, I pushed Tome over so he was facing up. He was semi-conscious and coughing and gagging. Before he could do anything else, I plunged the blade into his chest, piercing his heart. He gave one last gasp and went still.

"Jesus, Mikey!"

I looked over to see Bad Penny still lying on the floor. She was holding her head and staring at me. "That was pretty cold blooded. Even for me."

"Had to be done." She didn't look right. Her face was wracked with pain. "You okay?"

"N-no. Heads all fuzzy and my legs aren't working."

I clambered to my feet, my knees screaming in protest. "That doesn't sound good. Concussion maybe? Possible spinal damage?"

I went over to her and knelt down, pulling one of the four remaining healing potions I had left. "Drink this. It's one of Zoe's."

"Might be better if I used one of my hyde potions. Save that one for you."

I hesitated. "I know you're healing ability in hyde form is insanely powerful, but have you ever used it after you were injured in your normal form?"

"Well...no."

"So you don't know if it will heal those type of injuries. Might lock them into place instead."

"Shit! I don't know."

"Okay, better safe than sorry. Drink the healing potion." I held it to her mouth, and Penny drank it down. The change was immediate. The face cleared as the pain faded and she pulled herself to a sitting position. "How do you feel?"

"Much better." I helped her stand up. "What did he hit me with anyway?"

"The table." I went over to Tomes body and grabbed him by the arms. "Help me with this. We need to get it into the walk-in."

She took a hold of his legs. "Why?"

"The walk-in's stasis field will preserve his corpse." I stopped to open to the door."

"Makes sense, I guess. No one wants to smell that. Still, going to be weird having a body where the food's kept."

We finished duck walking the body in and lowered it on the floor of the walk-in. Penny put her hands on her lower back and stretched. "For a skinny guy, he was heavy. What's the plan?"

I pulled out the blade with the towel still wrapped around it. "The plan revolves around this."

She frowned. "What's it do?"

"In a minute. Let me see your baton." I held my right hand out. Shrugging, Penny gave it to me. I snapped my arm to the side, causing the baton to expand. "Have you been having any issues with this?"

"No. Works fine. Not that I've had much use with it other than zapping you."

"Good." I tapped the baton on her shoulder while activating the sleep rune. She had just enough time to be surprised before her eyes rolled up and she fell back into a leaning position, propped up by stacked storage containers.

"I really should make more of these." I held up the baton. Pushing the tip against the wall, I collapsed it and placed it in a cargo pocket. "Very handy."

"As to what the dagger is for, it's for this," I told Penny as I stabbed her in the heart with it.

Chapter Twenty-Seven

Volunteers Needed

The pain must have overridden the sleep effect. Penny's eyes snapped open in hurt surprise and then slowly glazed over as she died. I caught her body before it fell and gently lowered it to the floor.

Holding my breath, I carefully checked over the dagger.

Oh, thank God.

Taking her baton, I exited the walk-thru and closed the door. It had a lock, but I was unable to find a key for it. I dug out the skeleton key I had forged just prior to my return to policing. Its magic allowed the key to slide into the lock. I turned it and was rewarded with a loud click. Removing it, I tried the door and found it had locked.

I pocketed the key after locking the galley door as well, then righted the table and used my tools to repurpose the handle of the cleaver for the blade. I then cleaned up everything. In order for my plan to work, I needed the remaining players to still think I was out of the game. Evidence that I had forged something would raise current suspicions even higher.

I looked around as the lights started flashing. Everything seemed in order. The table that Tome had thrown was one of those big, heavy oak monstrosities and had managed to sustain no damage in the fight.

My brain was in overload, alternating between worry and panic. I forced it all to the back of my mind. With a sigh, I moved over to a cabinet to make it appear as if I was looking for food. As I did, Pavel Mûstek came through the door. He nodded as the blinding light faded. "Sergeant."

"Mister Mûstek. You seemed to have made it through another round."

"You as well." He turned towards the door as it lit up again and gestured at the figure coming though. "As did Ms. Bridges."

Harleen gave him a tired smile. I suspected her current strategy was hiding during each round.

Bathory, Rom Chang, Acantha, and Obrechenny came through in rapid succession. Bathory looked even worse than before. She needed blood badly. Obrechenny walked over to the walk-thru and tried to open the door. "This is locked."

"It was open earlier." I frowned and walked over, tugging at the handle. "Why would it be locked now? Is this more of Bainbridge's nonsense?"

"I do not know." She walked towards the cupboards as Greely entered the room carrying the box. "It does not matter. There is plenty of canned food."

"Unless the cabinets get locked up next." I rubbed my scars and made a point of staring at the cupboards. "Is that it, Greely? Force us to end this stupid game sooner?"

"Possibly." He shrugged as he set the box on the table. "I was not privy to how this will play out."

I looked around the room and stared at the box. "Where's Bad Penny?"

"Tome and Gianna have not returned either," added Rom Chang.

I didn't have to fake the anger on my face. I just let a little of what I felt about what Bainbridge made me do leak out. Harleen moved away from me and even Rom Chang looked at me with concern. Pavel... well... Pavel was Pavel. He just lit a cigarette and watched.

Obrechenny sighed. "You are causing the Sergeant unnecessary distress. Open the box now, *da?*"

Greely opened the box and showed three cards that laid at the bottom. Tome, Penny, and Gianna's names showed on them. The edges of the cards caught fire and they quickly burned to ash. "It appears three have perished in this round."

I knocked the box off the table and stomped over to a corner table. Sitting there, I slowly stared at each one as if I was determining who had killed Bad Penny. In reality, I was trying to determine the most effective ways to take each one out. Bathory was the biggest problem. The blade's magic wouldn't work on her since she was undead.

Everyone ate their meal silently. Three deaths in one round were sobering. After she finished eating, Acantha made her way over to me. "I know it's not much coming from me, but I'm sorry for your loss."

I gave her a flat stare. "Was it you?"

Her eyes narrowed at the question. "No. That would be a bit hard to do since you took my alchemy kit. Speaking of which, can you please give it back to me? I'm a sitting duck without anyway to defend myself."

"I'll think about it, but I wouldn't hold my breath if I was you." I nodded towards Bathory who sat in a corner staring at something only she could see. Her right hand twitched every few seconds, a fact she didn't seem aware of. "Speaking of defending yourself, you need to watch out for her."

Acantha's mouth formed a flat line. "Don't bother attempting to drive a wedge between Aunt Katrina and me. It won't work."

"That's not it. Open your eyes. She's starving. She's going to frenzy soon."

Bathory's head snapped in our direction. I'd forgot about vampire hearing. Her steps as she approached us was that of a drunk, constantly self-correcting to prevent from toppling over. She stared at her apprentice with a look of agony. "You need to listen to him. I'm not sure how much longer I can go without blood."

I leaned back in my chair. "Why haven't you fed?"

"I missed a couple of meals dealing with an unrelated issue."

"What issue?"

"Petty vampire politics. Not really important now. Or then, come to think about it." She pursed her lips. "I'd planned on eating after the will reading was over. Bainbridge's little stunt has put me in quite a bind."

"You haven't been able to eat since you've been here?"

"Lack of opportunity. Why? Are you offering?"

I shook my head. "My blood is… different. It wouldn't serve your needs."

Bathory eyed me for a moment, trying to decide if I was telling the truth. The vampire gave a shrug. "Pavel and Rom Chang are magi. They have passive defenses against being fed on. I have not been able to encounter Harleen and Obrechenny during the turns."

I tilted my head at Acantha. "You're not willing to share?"

"The alchemy protections in my blood will take days to purge. Right now, my blood is poison to her." She bit her lip as if to hold back crying.

I drummed my fingers on the table for a moment. "Have you asked Rom Chang or Obrechenny? They are both honorable in their own way."

"Obrechenny is, anyway. She, at least, apologized for refusing me," the vampire told me bitterly. "Rom Chang just laughed in my face."

The lights started flickering. Acantha turned away, choking back a sob and fled through the door, disappearing in that flash of light I had grown to hate. Bathory started to follow her but paused and turned back to me. "Stories say you're a berserker. Is that true?"

"Not something I'm proud of, but yes."

"You seem a man of discipline. Have you ever fully given into the berserker fury?"

I drummed my fingers again as the others filed out. "I try very hard not to, but I've lost control a few times. Each time the aftermath was… something that haunts me."

"Then you truly understand what I'm facing."

"To an extent." I slid my chair back and stood up. Greely stood by the door, tapping his watch. "I can snap out of it. My understanding is when a vampire blood frenzies, there is a chance they may not come back. Instead, they remain feral."

Bathory nodded. "It's worse with older vampires like myself. I miscalculated on my opportunity to feed and now with both the twins gone, I'm down to two or three people I may feed on. If I don't have blood soon, I will lose my mind and turn into a raving lunatic, and I will not recover from it."

I ignored the part where she included me as a potential source of food and gestured towards the flashing lights. "We've run out of time."

"One of us has," the vampire murmured as we walked towards Greely and the door. She stopped at the entrance way and looked me in the eye. "I do not want to live as a mad dog foaming at the mouth. I know we are adversaries, but if that fate should befall me…"

"A part of me says it would be karmic justice considering all the people you've tortured and murdered over the years. But…yeah, I'll do my best."

"Thank you. That is some comfort at least." Bathory stepped through the door with me right behind her.

Chapter Twenty-Eight

Winners and Losers

This time I found myself in a bedroom. I checked my card.

Acantha Baines-Chatterjee.

I cracked to door and took a quick look. The area outside
the room looked clear. I tossed one of my remaining orbs
out and send it on a scouting mission. While it was gone, I
slid a dresser across the door and took a quick nap. My
tiredness beat out the worries and concerns eating away at
my mind.

I awoke to a series of slight bumps against the door. I tuned
my runic eye to the orb and discovered it had returned, and
it was what was making the sound. My body creaked in
protest as I slowly climbed out of the bed. A check of my
watch revealed I had been out for almost two hours. It felt
like two minutes.

I stretched as I mentally commanded the orb to swivel around, allowing me to make sure the hallway was empty. I slid the dresser away and opened the door. The orb dropped into my outstretched hand, and I pocketed it.

"I thought that might be your little toy flittering all over the place." Rom Chang Hayes stepped around the corner and took up a spellslinger's stance at the end of the hall. For a moment, I actually thought she was going to offer to be my Huckleberry.

Hmm, probably should have reviewed the footage first. Might have recorded her following the orb.

"You here for me?" I stepped out and squared off against her as I activated the blood runes for strength, speed, and enhanced senses.

"I am." She flicked her long leather coat back and rested her hand on a wand holstered on her right thigh.

She's a traditionalist. I can use that against her.

"How do you want to do this?" I asked her as I raised my empty left hand towards her in a *wait a minute* gesture.

"The proper way. Whenever your rea—"

Before she could finish, my 1911 appeared as a flash of light enveloping my left hand. Using the accuracy runes engraved on the firearm and my currently enhanced abilities, I fired two rounds. The first shattered her right hand, her wand tumbling from nerveless fingers. The second round caught her in the left hand.

As the second round left the muzzle of my gun, I started sprinting down the hallway towards her. Just as she cried out in pain from her injuries, I backhanded her across the face, knocking out her front teeth and bruising her mouth.

My rune enhanced strike knocked her to the ground. She appeared dazed, whether from the backhand or her gunshot wounds, I neither knew nor cared.

I drew my new dagger from my belt and knelt down beside her. "Sorry for the slap. Couldn't have you casting any spells the old fashion way."

Her eyes widened as I held the dagger over her. Fighting back doubts, I slammed the blade through her chest and into her heart. She gave a death rattle and lay still. I pulled the dagger out and looked at the runes along the blade.

That worked.

I pulled her card from her jacket. As I studied my name on it, it burst into flame, rapidly turning into ash. Whoever had been hunting Rom Chang now had me as a target.

Hopefully, they won't notice the name change.

I lifted her up over my shoulder and had the orb lead me to the kitchen. Fortunately, it was close by. I entered and unlocked the walk-in, placing Rom Chang next to Tome's body. As I resecured the door, I had my runic eye play the data the orb had collected. It showed that Rom Chang had tried to tail the orb unnoticed, but sure enough, the orb had recorded her enough that I would have been aware if I had checked the footage before opening the door.

To be fair, I am new at this whole murder thing.

That thought triggered more misgivings about what I had done to Bad Penny. I took a deep breath and exhaled, clearing my mind. Centered, I continued to review the orb's recording until I spotted Acantha.

She appeared frantic and was spraying perfume in the air while she ran down the hall.

"Why would she do that?" I muttered to myself as I exited the room.

Oh shit! Bathory's allergic to perfume. Acantha must be trying to hide her scent, which means Bathory is tracking her. If she's frenzied, she's not going to remember who Acantha is, or the fact that Acantha's blood is poison.

I sent the orb ahead of me, having it show me images in real time. This allowed me to stop being tactical and I ran full speed towards where Acantha was.

She was now defenseless because Penny and I had taken all her alchemical concoctions, and I regretted refusing to give her kit back.

I need to find Acantha and kill her before Bathory does.

The orb showed she was no longer at the location of the recording. When I came to a "T" in the maze of hallways, I send the orb in one direction and used my enhanced senses to track her perfume in the other. Ten minutes later, I found her lying in the doorway of a room. There were large puddles of blood trailing down the hall. The vampire was nowhere to be scene.

Looks like Bathory puked up the poisoned blood.

I knelt next to Acantha, keeping my weapon down by my side. She was gasping for air, and both her hands were pressed against her neck as she tried to staunch the flow of blood from a large, ugly wound.

Her face was a mask of terror as she stared up at me. She tried to say something but couldn't.

"Shhh. It's going to be okay," I told her with a smile as I slid the dagger into her heart. Her right hand clawed out at me, smearing blood across my mouth and chin before flopping to the floor. I withdrew the blade from her lifeless body and studied the runes.

Satisfied, I slowly stood up and used the sleeve of my uniform to wipe the blood off my face. Checking my card, I discovered my next target was Harleen.

I hoisted the alchemist over my shoulder and headed back the way I came. Halfway to my destination, I ran into Obrechenny Khishchnik.

Damn it! I should have sent the orb ahead. Lack of sleep is starting to affect my decision making.

I summoned my gun. "Am I your target?"

"My prey is elsewhere." The Alkonost held up her claw like hands. "What are you doing with that poor girl?"

I turned slightly, showing her the large wound on Acantha's neck. "Bathory entered blood frenzy and attacked her."

She gave a sharp nod, causing the feathers along her scalp to waver. "Why are you moving the body?"

"It... didn't seem right just leaving her like that. I'm searching for a morgue."

"Why don't you just place her in one of the bedrooms?" She glanced down the way I came, a predatory gleam in her eye. "Where is Bathory now?"

Ah, so she's your target.

"Not far down that way," I lied.

She left without a word to seek out her prey. The fact that I never answered her other question appeared to have gone unnoticed.

I lost valuable time speaking with Khishchnik. I tossed the orb into the air and sent it out ahead of me. Using the blood rune for speed, I made good time and quickly placed her body in the walk-in.

By the time I relocked the door, my hands were trembling and my heart was pounding. I'd been using the blood runes too much in too short of a time. It was starting to have a detrimental effect on my body. I needed to be careful. I had once given myself a heart attack using the blood runes longer than I should have. The only reason I survived was someone rendered aid, not something I could count on with this bunch.

I checked my watch. I was running out of time and needed to end this soon. I headed back out, this time to hunt Harleen.

Chapter Twenty-Nine

SOS

I was unable to find Harleen before the lights flashed again. In fact, with just five other people left in the Rook, I hadn't encountered anyone else. As soon as the lights flashed, I ran through a doorway and was transported back into the kitchen. The first one there, I turned and faced the door, ready to spring into action.

Pavel was the first through the door. He stopped when he saw me. "What are—"

"Get out of the way." I waved a hand at him. Bemused, he took several steps to the side.

"May I ask what you are doing?"

"Bathory is in blood frenzy. If she comes through…"

He nodded. "In such a state, a master vampire like Katrina Bathory might be able to shake off the pain spell and still be able to attack us."

Pavel tapped his chin. "I wonder. Would we, on the other hand, be incapacitated and unable to defend ourselves from her if she is not our designated hunter or target?"

"Don't know, and I don't plan on finding out."

Harleen was the next through. She jumped when she saw me. Pavel grabbed her arm and guided her away from the door. Next, came Obrechenny who shook her head when she saw me. "I did not encounter Lady Bathory. She is still out there."

She moved behind me and took up a similar stance just as Greely entered the room holding the damn book. He jumped when he saw us. "Wha—?"

Like he did with Harleen, Pavel guided him away. Greely was quickly filled in as we watched the door for the vampire.

"What's she waitin' for?" asked a nervous Harleen.

Pavel lit a cigarette. "Bathory is like a feral animal right now, wandering the Rook. She won't transfer here unless she steps through a doorway."

She waved away the smoke from his cigarette. "Then this could—"

Katrina Bathory stepped through the entrance, blinking as her eyes adjusted to the well-lit kitchen. Wasting no time, I slammed into her with my shoulder, knocking her back through the doorway. As I hit her, magical energy coursed across my body, inflicting me with agonizing pain. As the light flashed signaling her transportation, I found myself off balance and unable to stop my momentum as the pain spell worked its way across me.

Just as I was about to follow the vampire through, Obrechenny grabbed me, her claws tightly holding the back of my BDU shirt. She appeared to show no effort lifting my rather large frame. She pulled me back and didn't let go until I was firmly settled on my feet. "Are you alright, Sergeant?"

"Yeah, thank you." I straightened out my shirt. "That was… kind of you."

"Eh, you did that to save all of us. How could I not assist you?" She shrugged. "There will be plenty of time to kill you later."

"How very Russian of you."

"Spasibo."

This time only Acantha's card was in Greely's little death box. There weren't many active hunters left. Harleen's plan seemed to be to just hide. Pavel had already stated that he would not get involved until there were only two remaining. That left Obrechenny. I wasn't sure if she was actively playing the game or only went after Bathory because she had frenzied.

After Greely did his little proof of death show, I took my usual chair in the corner, lay my head down on the table, and took a cat nap. I woke when the lights started flashing and filed out after everyone else.

This time I appeared in a stairwell. I checked my card.

Harleen again.

I did the orb trick and waited. When it returned, it showed me that she was in the ballroom. I headed there, using the orb to recon ahead. The footage had shown that one of the ballroom exits was hidden by illusion.

I took the path to it. The illusion made the entrance appear to be part of the stone wall. I sent the orb through it and ordered it high up into the ceiling. Harleen didn't appear to notice it.

I studied her, trying to find a way to make this quick and painless. She nervously paced the room, occasionally freezing in place to listen for any movement.

She's freaking out over every sound her mind imagines. What would she do if she really hears something?

Using Bad Penny's baton, I faintly tapped SOS against the real part of the stone wall. Harleen froze, trying to determine if she actually heard something. "He-hello?"

I hesitated. I'd killed plenty of times before, but always in combat. This felt wrong. But I couldn't think of another solution to get free of the Keep. The citizens of Llewellyn were in danger from a dragon and whatever the vampires were up to, and I needed to get back.

I tapped out another SOS. She scanned the room, trying to determine where the sound came from. She did a partial shift, taking on a more cat like appearance. With her heavy use of makeup and bleached hair, she looked like a bad version of Cheetara. I could almost hear Bad Penny say *Thundercat? More like Thunderwhore!*

I shook my head. Lack of good sleep was making me punch drunk. I tapped SOS again. Her cat ears pivoted towards my location. She slowly crept up to where I was. She turned her head towards the wall to listen. "Is anybody there?"

She sniffed and suddenly stood straight and faced the wall. "Brennan?"

Damn, she can smell me.

I pushed the baton through the illusion and tagged her on the forearm, triggering the sleep effect. She glanced at it in confusion as I stepped through and then collapsed to the floor. I winced as her head hit the ground.

Eh, won't matter. She's going to be dead in a second.

I pulled out the dagger, leaned over, and stabbed her through the heart. That was when I heard the growling. I turned my head to find Bathory standing at the far end of the ballroom. The master vampire was hunched over with claws extended. Rivers of drool hung from her mouth, practically touching the floor. Her face was gaunt, and her skin had a papery look.

Oh shit!

I quickly tucked the dagger in to my belt and drew my 1911. I couldn't take a chance of fighting with the dagger. The metal was too soft. If it got damaged, everything was fucked. She charged me as I was drawing. Without time to aim, I fired from the hip until lock back. My remaining rounds all hit her but struck nothing vital.

Bathory rushed me with a football tackle, bringing me to the floor. Anger ran through me as I activated my blood runes and entered the berserker state. My nails and teeth lengthened and hardened. Just as feral as Bathory, I attacked her back, both of us growling.

Her claws raked across my back. Where Harleen's claws failed against the spell weave of my uniform, the vampire's did not. Even with the blood runes toughening my skin, she tore through the fabric and into my flesh. I hissed in pain and clubbed her repeatedly in the head with my empty gun. Bainbridge's penalty spell didn't kick in, so either Bathory was my new target, or I was hers.

With all my blood runes active, I could possibly take a full vampire without my armor. A master vampire was a very different matter. Bathory was both faster and stronger than me. We rolled around the floor, clawing and biting at each other, neither of us able to get a good purchase. Rational thought was difficult. I growled at her again, trying not to fall deeper into the berserker state. As I pulled my boot knife, she plunged her fangs into the left side of my neck, piercing an artery.

I yelled in pain, the boot knife forgotten as I instinctively plunged my right thumb into her eye, trying to force her off me as she drank deeply of my blood. Bathory screamed and released me. Kicking her away, I scrambled to my feet. I clapped a hand over my wound and forced myself to think rationally. The pain helped. "No fucking vampire hickies, Katrina. Zoe would never let me hear the end of it."

Bathory was on her hands and knees, coughing and puking up a glowing white liquid. I checked the wound on my neck while pulling out a healing potion with my off hand. My blood was glowing with a bright white light. I downed the potion and felt my flesh knit back together as the cool liquid did its job.

As I watched, Bathory's mouth and fangs turned to ash and drifted away. This quickly spread through her body until she was gone. The threat over, I released all my blood runes. As I did so, my blood stopped glowing.

I slumped to the floor and leaned against the wall, completely drained. "You got your wish, Katrina. Still say you got off easy."

I didn't understand what was going on with my blood. None of the research Martin, Zoe, or I had uncovered on blood runes said anything about blood glowing or having magical properties. Groaning, I sent the orb out to scout for others and watched its journey live with my runic eye.

This wasn't the first time my blood had glowed. It only seemed to do it when all my blood runes were active. One of the other times, I had used my blood to hypercharge the runes on my sword. And now, apparently, it was very poisonous the vampires. I thought it might have an effect on them, but this reaction was… extreme.

I pulled my card just intime to see Bathory's name change to Obrechenny Khishchnik.

Speak of the devil.

As I watched the feed, the orb came upon Khishchnik and Můstek. They were facing off with each other in the room we first went into, the one where Bainbridge did his little gloat show. It didn't look like they started in on each other yet, but I'm sure that would change shortly.

I slowly got to my feet and retrieved all my items. I was out of rounds which meant offensively, I had two blades and an empty gun. Not what I would choose to fight formidable opponent like the Alkonost.

Then again, even less so with someone with the magical ability to created disease and illness to rapidly grow within your body. That didn't even include his ability to cast spells. Fighting either of those two is going to suck!

I looked down at the ash that had been Katrina Bathory, master vampire and sometime ally of Vlad Dracula. No pun intended.

They weren't far. I found Khishchnik and Můstek in a room that appeared to be a den. Tapestries and bookcases lined the walls, and a large wood desk sat in the center of the room. Obrechenny knelt in front of the desk. Her shoulders heaved and her feathers trembled as bloody vomit spewed out of her mouth, ruining what appeared to be an expensive Persian rug. Můstek stood behind the desk, watching her impassively. He glanced up at me as I entered, my empty gun in my left hand. The dagger in my right. He gestured to Obrechenny and sighed. "It appears I was her target. I have heard she is a formidable opponent. I would have been no match for her had she been able to close in on me."

He held up a hand as I started to approach the struggling Alkonost. "Do not bother to render aid. The dose of anthrax I gave her is terminal. Unless I reverse it, she is doomed."

"That's the plague you possess? Anthrax?"

"Yes." He had a haunted look in his eyes. "That is both my power and my curse."

Huh! What are the odds?

"And you won't reverse it?"

"I am truly sorry, but she is my hunter. She'll just try again. I do not wish to play this game, but we have no choice. If it is any consolation, it is much faster than it occurs in nature."

Magically weaponized anthrax. Fucking great.

"Then let me end her suffering." I held up the dagger. "No one deserves to die like this."

Obrechenny looked at me in surprise. She placed a hand on the desk as if to rise but collapsed, shaking uncontrollably.

Můstek stroked his chin. "I assume she's your target since I am hers. Either way, she dies, you'll face me next."

"That's right."

"I thought you refused to participate in the silly charade of Bainbridge's."

I shrugged. "Things change."

"Very well. Once you end her, we'll begin." He sighed. "I am very sorry, Michael. I'll let Valentine and the Muse know you died with honor."

"So you're the Muse's agent then? I had been wondering who it was."

"Yes. You were… not supposed to be involved. I'm sorry."

"Any idea who Dracula hired?"

He turned up both hands. "Was it not Bathory? I know they are allies."

"No, she was playing her own game. Turns out they both wanted the Rook for themselves."

"Interesting. Then I do not know who Dracula's agent is."

I might, but that's for later...

I looked down at Obrechenny. If I waited much longer, it would be too late. I knelt down by her, adjusting my grip on the dagger. "After I do this, give me five minutes to talk to you before we fight."

The plague witch frowned. "I see no reason why I should let you, but… one minute. On your honor."

"Deal." I pushed the Russian Alkonost over. She was too weak to stop me but mustered a murderous glare. With one decisive push, I slipped the dagger into her heart and pulled it back out.

I glanced at the blade as I stood up. Můstek tapped the watch on his wrist. "Sixty seconds."

"I can save almost everybody. You just need to let me kill you."

Chapter Thirty

Mike's Big Reveal

"Excuse me?" Mŭstek raised his eyebrows.

I held up the dagger and pointed to a glowing rune. "This shows that I successfully trapped her soul in the dagger. I did the same thing with the rest of my opponents. If I do the same thing to you, then the Rook will register me as the winner and relinquish control to me. Once I move your bodies outside, I can reverse the effect and return all your souls to their rightful place."

"I…that is a lot to process."

"I know, but make it quick. I have to get her body in the walk-in before she starts to decompose."

"What? The walk-in?"

"It uses a stasis field to keep the food fresh. The same effect will preserve the bodies I placed in it."

"They use a stasis field for food? Do you know how powerful a spell that is?"

"Technically it's a magic item created by a runesmith, but yeah, bit of an overkill."

"So, to be clear, you wish me to let you stab me with a magic dagger that will steal my soul, allowing you to win the Rook. I am then supposed to trust that you'll put my soul back in my body?"

"Yeah, I get it, it's a big ask."

"And you've done this before? You have proof of concept?"

"Well, no. I sort of cobbled it together from existing runes that have been proven to work."

He rubbed his chin. "I want to believe you, but you understand why I'm having trouble with this?"

I sighed. "I do."

"How about I use it on you instead? I'll give you my word that I will carry it through using your instructions."

"It won't work on me. My runes include a failsafe to prevent them from being used against me."

"Of course it does."

"I know how that sounds, but seriously, it's a built-in precaution."

"I'm afraid I just can't take that chance." He looked at his watch. "It appears you minute is up."

I triggered all the blood runes as he waved his hand at me. Purple energy outlined his fingers, and I could actually feel his magic take effect as it created anthrax in my body. He sighed. "I *am* sorry."

"Save it," I growled, not bothering to hold back the berserker fury. My heart started pounding as I whipped my empty gun at his face. My enhanced senses increased my accuracy, and the extra strength the blood runes caused the gun to strike him with the force of a major league speed ball.

The gun struck him in the mouth, shattering his jaw. He gave a muffled cry of pain and staggered back. As I drew Penny's baton, he gave a flick with his right hand and a wand slid down his sleeve into his hand.

Shit!

The broken jaw stopped him from casting any spells but that didn't prevent him from firing the wand. I used my enhanced speed to duck the eldritch bolt he sent my way. Dropping the baton, I stole a trick from Tome and picked up the desk, slamming it into Můstek. As he fell to the ground, I pinned him underneath the desk and kicked his wand away.

"How are you standing?" Můstek's words were hard to make out as his broken jaw and teeth deformed his speech. He turned his head and spat out blood as I drew the dagger.

I squatted down next to his head as I turned off all the runes but the healing one. "My blood runes don't heal me by pure magic. They speed up and enhance my body's healing and immunities, natural or otherwise. Did you know I was in the Army?"

He gave a single shake of his head and winced in pain. I shifted the desk to expose his chest.

"Yeah, well, back when I was in, they gave me the anthrax vaccine. The antibodies it created wouldn't be enough to fight your magically enhanced version, but the blood runes supercharged them enough to fight off your plague for a while." My hand trembled as I placed the dagger to his chest. "Now remove it from my system so I can save everyone."

"No." He winced again from the pain of speaking with a broken jaw. He sounded drunk, obviously unable to speak clearly enough to cast any spells. "Bring us all back and I'll remove the plague from you. But if you are lying or can't do it, then you'll die like the rest of us."

"And if I fail because I succumbed to your plague magic?"

"So be it." He turned his head away from me.

"Dick!" I stabbed the dagger into his heart. He tensed and went still. I checked the rune on the blade. The glow told me it successfully captured his soul. I used the desk to pull myself up. I felt hot and flushed. The effects of Mŭstek's plague were running its course as it slowly defeated my magically enhanced vaccine. I picked up Obrechenny and flipped her over my shoulder. She felt light for her size. I briefly wondered if she had hollow bones like a bird. She had feathers and claws, after all.

I sent the orb out and started making my way back to the kitchen. Dealing with Mŭstek used up a lot of her time. I hoped I would make it, but the alternating chills and fever coursing through my body made me doubt it.

Chapter Thirty-One

Latin Class

The lights were flashing again as I unceremoniously dumped Mŭstek on top of Obrechenny. Staggering out of the walk-in, I locked it and leaned against the wall as a wave of dizziness hit me. The healing rune wasn't enough to combat the magic plague, and retrieving both bodies had taken a lot out of me. I activated all the blood runes and felt the symptoms lessen. When combined together, each of them was stronger than when activated alone, but my body paid the price and if used too long, my heart would fail.

The Rook didn't appear to react to my killing the last of heirs. I was guessing that meant either my using the dagger to capture the contestant's souls hadn't fooled Bainbridge's magic, or my earlier suspicions were correct.

I did the drunken two-step over to a chair and collapsed into it, trying not to throw up. I lost consciousness for a bit, waking when the doorway lit up as Greely entered the room clutching his box. He stopped on seeing me. The surprise evident in his face.

'S'matter, Greely? Didn't think it would be me?" I growled at him. The berserker anger urged me to smash his head into the wall until he stopped moving.

Un oh! Starting to slip gears. Need to turn off some of the runes for a while.

I released all but the healing rune and gave a weary smile at the unnerved attorney. "Sorry. It's been… a long day."

"Understandable, Sergeant." He placed the box on the table and opened it to show the names of my recent victims. "It appears you are the winner. Congratulations!"

"Yeah, sure. Great." I waved a hand in the air.

"Are you alright, Sergeant? You seem a bit… off."

"Slight case of the plague. Don't worry, it's not catchy. Now what?"

"Well, now, you simply walk out the door. This will show the Rook you won, and ownership will transfer over to you."

Using the table, I pushed myself to my feet. "Let's get this over with then."

"Of course." He gave a slight bow and gestured towards the door. "After you."

I waggled a finger in front of my eyes. "My vision's a little knackered right now. Mind leading the way?"

"Ah," He seemed unsure. "Of course, yes, I can do that."

"You okay, Greely?"

"Just concerned. You really don't look well."

"Anthrax will do that."

"*Anthrax?* You have anthrax?"

"Yup, parting gift from Můstek."

"You, you should sit down. Take a rest." He gestured towards a chair. "Save your strength. Ah, please don't be offended, but are you sure that isn't contagious?"

I nodded and regretted it as my vision continued to blur for several seconds after my head stopped moving. "I have magical healing. Stay here or leave now, the effects will be fading shortly."

"Oh! Well, that's good to hear." He stepped towards the doorway. "Ah, I'm not sure if the magic will still transport us to different locations. If it doesn't, just make your way to the entrance and wait for me there. I'll be along momentarily."

"Huh. You think Bainbridge would have set the spells up to end at this point." I palmed the wall for balance as I walked towards the door.

"He might have, I just didn't want you surprised in case he didn't."

"Fine then." I stepped through the door.

"Damn it." I had forgotten to close my eyes and had to blink away spots to find myself at the top step of a long set of stone stairs. If I had moved forward before I regained my vision, I could have tumbled down them and gotten hurt or killed.

I'd have had to do a lot of explaining in the afterlife to all the souls I just trapped.

"Wait. If their souls are trapped in the blade, would they go to the aft—" My stomach rolled and I turned to the side as vomit spewed out my mouth. There was blood mixed with it. "That's not good."

I spit, trying to clear my mouth, and then wiped a sleeve across the lower half of my face. I triggered all the blood runes and felt simultaneously better and angry. My head clearer, I bit back the rune induced rage and sent the orb out looking for the door. I followed after it as best as I could.

By the time I got to the door, I was feeling shooting pains down my left arm and my pulse pounded in my ears. There was no sign of Greely. I canceled everything but the healing rune. I had waited a bit too long on that one.

Feeling calmer, I tried the door. It didn't budge. I made an adjustment to my runic eye and pocketed the orb. Leaning against the door, I waited, feeling the fever starting up again. Without the other runes to bolster it, the healing rune was losing the fight.

After several minutes, I pushed off the door which triggered a wave of nausea. I took a couple steps down the hall and cupped my hands over my mouth. "Greely? You out there?"

Turning around, I smiled and threw a punch into the air. It made contact with a meaty thunk. There was a shimmering effect and Greely appeared lying on the floor. The stunned look on his face made me smile deeper. "Hiya, Haze. How ya doing?"

Greely gave a sigh and his appearance melted away to show a mousey brown-haired man in his mid-twenties. The suit he was wearing now looked two sizes too big on him. "Damn it, Mike. What gave me away?"

"If you mean just now," I tapped my runic eye. "I had it on infrared. I picked up your heat signature as you came down the hallway. It confirmed my suspicions. You should have just used the Greely illusion. Not that it would have mattered. I already knew you were posing as the attorney."

He frowned and sat up. "You were already onto me? For how long?"

I leaned against the wall to conceal a dizzy spell. "Pretty much from the beginning. You pretended to be outraged at my comment about laughing heirs."

"So?"

"Remember I told you that I use to date a lawyer? Well, a laughing heir refers to someone who is legally entitled to inherit but only distantly related to the deceased. Someone who has no personal connection or any reason to feel sad over the person dying. A lawyer would have recognized that term."

"Well, shit." He ran his hand threw his hair. "I thought I was so careful."

"Sorry, Haze, I confirmed it when I mentioned ultra vires."

"It doesn't mean *everything within my power?*"

"Nope. It's Latin for *beyond the powers*. It can be used a couple of ways but is often used to describe an act which requires legal authority but is completed without it. You know, like you presiding over a will." The dizzy spell started to pass. "Plus you showed up on one of my target cards."

"I'm sorry. Mike, I didn't want to do this, but I had no choice. They forced me."

"Who?"

"Transylvanian mob. Bunch of Old-World vamps. Claimed they worked for Dracula if you can believe it. Wanted me to put the fix in in order to get the Rook and then give it to them."

"How did you know about the game? The will was sealed."

"They got it out of Greely before they killed him. Made me watch." He looked nauseated remembering it. I believed him. The Haze was a small-time hustler. He was a top-notch illusionist, but not much else. To my knowledge, he had never done any real violence. At least not by Llewellyn standards.

"What would you get out of it?"

"I got to live," he said in a bitter tone.

"Alright, Haze, if your story checks out, we'll put you in protective custody. Stand up."

"Thanks Mike. You're alright." He stood up and dusted himself off. "Do you want me to testi—"

He stared down at the dagger sticking out of his chest and started to collapse. Catching his body almost caused me to go down with him. I barely remained standing while holding up his corpse.

Three loud rings of a bell echoed through the Rook and an orange energy traveled from the floor up through my body and disappeared, leaving me with a momentarily buzzing in my head. "What the hell was that about?"

An illusion of Bainbridge appeared before me. "I'd say congratulations, but I don't care which one of you clawed your way over the bodies of the others. The Rook is now attuned to you and my spells have dissipated. Whoever you are, I hope it was someone I didn't actively despised."

His image disappeared and the front door slowly creaked open.

"Joke's on you, asshole. You hated me with a passion." I held out a hand and summoned my sword. It appeared in a flash of light. "Finally!"

I dismissed it with a thought as nausea hit me like a freight truck. Too weak to do it otherwise, I triggered all the blood runes. It didn't have as much effect as last time, but I was still able to hoist the Haze over my shoulder and made my way out the door.

Chapter Thirty-Two

Soul Swapping

I exited to find dawn just starting to break. The headlights of the Chief gave me enough light to discover the Rook was currently within a casting circle. Witch's script was inscribed within and without the circle. Candles had been placed at various points. What appeared to be the entire Morgan Coven was standing just outside the circle and appeared to be beginning some type of ritual.

As I looked around, the berserker fury shouted in my head to attack the people surrounding me. I beat it back and gave a tired smile. "Should I come back later?"

"Mike!" Zoe bound through the markings and almost knocked me off my feet as she slammed into me, embracing me with a hug that would have made it hard to breathe even without the anthrax.

"Zoe, I love you, sweetie, but let go before I puke. Feeling a little sick right now. Plague witch hit me with anthrax."

"How are you still standing?" Zoe motioned with her arm and Emala came running over with the antique medical bag my wife kept all her magical goodies in. Eddy followed behind her. "Where's Penny?"

"Mixture of a vaccine and the blood runes. And I really need to turn the runes off. Right now, it's a toss-up between keeling over or frothing at the mouth." I slid the Haze to the ground. "Might do both. Bad Penny's still inside. Give me a second to rest and I'll show you where she is. It's a bit… complicated."

Emala looked at the Haze. "Who's the dead guy?"

"Henderson Hayes, AKA the Haze," Eddy told her. "Petty criminal, but not a bad bloke. Looks like someone spiked him in the heart."

"Sit down." Zoe ordered me as she rummaged through her bag. I obeyed her command.

"Did I miss the town meeting?" There was something I needed to do. Something time sensitive. My brain was too fogged to remember.

"No, it's tonight."

"Felt like we were away a lot longer than that."

"Common effect during dimensional drift. That's a neat trick, by the way. We were running out of ways to try to phase the Rook back here." She handed me two gray stones with witch's script scrawled across them. "Put one in each hand. It'll take the edge off, but don't release the blood runes yet."

I nodded. A weird tingling shot up my arms from the stones and when it got to the center of my chest, my heart started to slow down to a more normal beat. "What are these?"

"Mmm, think of them as a magical pacemaker. I cooked them up as a way to combat your blood runes' tendency of blowing up your heart. Ah, here we go." She held up a potion tube and shook like it a chem stick. The liquid began to glow with a golden light. She held it out to me. "Drink this."

"You want me to drink a glow stick? That can't be healthy." I gave her a small smile. "There *are* easier ways to get rid of me."

"Don't be an idiot. It'll suppress the plaque symptoms, but only for a short while. We'll need to track down the witch and force them to remove the plague."

I held up the stones. "How am I supposed to take it exactly?"

Zoe twisted her mouth in minor annoyance and popped the top off the tube. "Open your mouth."

I hid a grimace as I did what I was told. With the exception of her healing potions, Zoe's concoctions are… not known for having a pleasant taste. I was happily surprised. It was quite enjoyable with a hint of vanilla.

The shaking fever and feeling of nausea subsided. "Wow, what a difference."

Zoe waved what looked like a small rag doll in front of me. I frowned. "Is that a voodoo doll?"

"Yes, Mike, I'm using illegal magic on my cop husband in front of a bunch of witnesses." Her voice dripped with sarcasm. After a moment, Zoe stopped waving it around and studied the doll. "It's a simulacrum that allows me to determine the damage to your body. It's safe for you to release the runes now."

I felt a wave of tiredness as I did so. "Raggedy Ann tricorder is what that is."

Zoe took the stones from me and tucked them and the doll back into her bag. "I hope the plague witch is near. I estimate you are about twenty minutes before the anthrax kicks back in."

"Oh, I know exactly where he is." I slowly stood up. "How much healing do you have available?"

Emala laughed. "The majority of the Morgan Coven specializes in healing. It's been that way since the days of Lily the Pink."

"Who? You mean Zoe the White?" That named sounded very familiar.

"No, Lily the Pink was the coven leader in the 1800s. Not important right now." My wife gave me an exasperated look.

"Wasn't there a song—" Eddy started to say.

"Eddy, shut it." My wife snapped at him.

"Yes, mum. Shutting it, mum."

I think Eddy's right. An old Irish ballad. 'We drink a drink, a drink. Something, something, savior of the human race.' Wait! A member of the Morgan coven saved the human race?

"Mike! Pay attention. You're drifting on me." Zoe's words snapped me back in to focus. "Where's the plague witch? Is Bad Penny guarding him? We're on a clock here and I don't have more of the elixir I gave you."

Shit! Forgot the Haze is running out of time.

"Right. Just very tired. Get out a healing potion strong enough to reverse a fatal wound."

Emala pulled a potion out of her jacket and held it up. I took it from her and leaned over the Haze. Several of the Morgan witches gathered around to watch what I was doing. I poured the potion down his throat and tapped his forehead with the dagger while triggering the reverse rune. It's hard to describe the effect that took place when I triggered it. The dagger felt... lighter?

The Haze made coughing sounds briefly as the wound in his chest quickly closed. Zoe swears you can't choke to death on a healing potion, but I've had them enter my lungs in the past, and it feels like waterboarding before the liquid magically absorbs into you.

The small-time hustler opened his eyes with a groan. Once his eyes focused on me, they took on a hurt, accusing look. "You fucking stabbed me, Mike!"

"Yeah, I saved your life by killing you. Little ironic." I motioned to him with the dagger. "Eddy, take him into custody."

"Roight, Sarge." Eddy grabbed the Haze by his arm and pulled him to his feet. "What's the charge, Sarge?"

"Let's start with attempted larceny by fraud. We'll sit down with him later. Go over his options." I turned to my wife.

"C'mon, take enough potions or whatever to heal seven others in the same condition."

"You going to fill me in on this?" Zoe called after me as I headed back into the Rook.

"I'll tell you on the way. I need to get this done before my brain starts fading again." I turned to tell her not to let anyone else in but after she crossed the threshold, the door swung shut. "Hmm."

"What?"

"Either the Rook anticipated or sensed what I wanted, or we're trapped in here again."

Zoe turned the handle and opened the door. "Not trapped."

"Fine, shut it, please. I don't want anyone traipsing through here until I figure this place out." I filled her in as we made our way back to the kitchen. Without the illusions and shifting rooms, it was not far.

Once there, I opened the door to the walk-in and carried out Bad Penny. Laying her on the floor, I pulled out the dagger. "Get ready with the potion."

"Wait! You should do the plague witch first."

"No, I want Penny saved first in case he tries some bullshit." I tapped the blade to her forehead and activated the appropriate runes. Zoe crouched down and poured the potion into Bad Penny's wound at the same time the blade touched.

Oh, right, could have done that with Haze as well.

Bad Penny's eyes fluttered open, and she stared at me for several seconds.

"Penny, you okay? The dagger we made removes souls. I had to stab you and the others in order to trick the Rook. We're reviving everyone now. You're going to be fine, and we can go home."

She continued to stare at me. "Brennan?" Penny frowned and sat up, holding her hands in front of her. "What have you done to my body? My wooden arm is gone... Am I in... a woman's body?"

"Tome?" I stared at her in horror, thinking I must have somehow put the wrong soul in.

"Gotcha!" Laughing, Penny scrambled to her feet. "Serves you right for that sneak attack. You could have fucking told me the plan."

"Penny!" Zoe and I yelled at the same time.

Sighing in relief, I went and got Mŭstek. Placing him in the spot Penny had been, a wave of nausea swept through me as I straightened up. The elixir was beginning to wear off.

"I don't know how to break it to you, Zoe," Penny said to my wife, "but the last thing your husband did before I died was thrust his—"

"Penny!" My shout took too much out of me and I grabbed one of the counters for balance.

"Next time you stab Penny, do you have to bring her back?" Chuckling, my wife turned, and her grin disappeared as she studied my face. "Right, jokes later. Let's get this done. You're running out of time."

She dug out another potion and, after pouring it on Mŭstek's wounds, drew her wand. "Do it."

I fell to one knee and tapped his forehead with the blade. Once he started showing signs of life, I slumped back and leaned against the counter cabinet.

Můstek's eyes opened up to discover my wife's wand shoved up one of his nostrils. Her other hand held a ball of flame. "You know who I am?"

"Zoe Afire." Můstek didn't move. His eyes never leaving Zoe's face.

"So, you know what I'm capable of."

"Very. And yes, I'll be happy to remove my plague from your husband."

"Smart man." Zoe watched him like a hawk as he made a grasping motion towards me.

The relief was instantaneous. All the effects of his magically induced anthrax vanished as if it had never happened. I clambered to my feet. "Let him up, Zoe. He removed it."

Zoe backed off and allowed Můstek to rise. I pointed to the walk-in. "The Russian, too."

"Of course." He went to the opening and made the same gesture towards the Alkonost's body. "It's done. Now what?"

I shrugged. "I would suggest you go home, but that's up to you."

"No charges?"

"I don't have the authority to arrest for crimes committed in other dimensions or wherever we were."

I had Penny walk him out. One at a time, we did the same with Rom Chang and Harleen, catching them up to speed before giving them the boot. Though as Penny started to walk out with Harleen, she turned and gestured to my wife. "Harleen, have you ever met Zoe Brennan?"

"Um, n-no, Ah don't think Ah have." Harleen's eyes darted everywhere but towards my wife.

"She sometimes known as Zoe Afire." Penny's face took on an overdramatically thoughtful look. "I think she's called that because she keeps lighting people on fire."

Zoe gave Penny a quizzical look. "Hello. Harleen, is it?"

"V-very nice to meet you." Harleen put a hand on her stomach. "Ah'm sorry, Ah don't mean to be rude, please excuse me. This whole thing was very traumatic, and Ah need to leave."

She rushed out of the room as Penny struggled to keep a straight face. Zoe cocked her head at the two of us. "What was that about?"

"She totally tried to bang your husband."

"Did she now?" Zoe grinned. "Can't blame a girl for trying. I'm sure Mike was completely mortified. Did he have that *fish gasping for air* look when he tries to think of something to say?"

"It was a ploy to try to kill me," I grumbled as I sent my orb out to ensure Harleen had left.

"See, now that, I *do* have an issue with." Zoe's grin faded.

"Actually, that was the funny part." Penny chortled. "She kept chasing him around the table taking her dress off.

Mike's duck, dodging, bobbing, and weaving trying to protect his virtue, and the whole time she was really a shifter trying to get her clothes out of the way so she could change."

Both of them were howling with laughter at this point. I shot a dark look at Penny. "Last time I tell you anything."

Zoe wiped tears from her eyes. "I wish I could have seen it. What kind of shifter?"

"That's the best part. She's a cougar."

"*No!*"

"The Russian bird lady tried to warn him earlier, but he thought she meant the other type of cougar." They both started wailing with laughter again.

"When did this become my life?" I muttered to myself. "I used to have dignity, respect."

Zoe started waving a hand in front of her face, tears still streaming down her cheeks. "I can't breathe, gods and goddesses, I can't breathe."

I threw up my hands in exasperation. "Bad Penny, you hit on me all the time, but you throw Harleen under the bus?"

"No, I threw *you* under the bus." She smirked.

"Right, because she didn't just wet herself when she thought you were going to rat her out to Zoe."

"Okay, so maybe I ratted you both out. But it's different for a couple of reasons." She started holding up fingers. "One, she tried to kill you, so fuck that shit! Two, I don't try to sleep with you behind Zoe's back."

"You don't?"

"No, I'm trying to sleep with both of you. At the same time. Completely different."

Baffled, I looked to Zoe for aid. She just shrugged with a bemused look on her face.

"That makes it okay then?" I sputtered.

"Yup!" Penny twirled her finger around pointing at Zoe and I before back to herself. "We're a throuple. You two just haven't realized it yet."

Oh God! It's the Toria conversation all over again. When did that even become a word?

I gave up and just shook my head. "Whatever. Time to get back to reality. The next one is going to be Acantha, and that's going to suck. I have to tell her something about Bathory."

Penny lost that cocky look of hers. "I suppose it's too much to ask to just leave her in there?"

"You supposed right."

"What's the problem with this one?" asked Zoe.

"She's an alchemist," grumbled Bad Penny.

"Oh, yeah. I can see where you wouldn't like her." Zoe knew about the Alchemist's guild turning Penny into a hyde. Zoe was the one that had cracked the code on the hyde formula and created a non-addictive version for Penny to use.

I shook my head. "It was more than that. She used a potion that mind controls hydes. Tried to get Penny to kill me."

"Oh really?" Zoe's eyes started to glow red. "Now, I'm leaning towards Penny suggestion."

"Oh, and possibly a serial killer in training," added Bad Penny.

"Excuse me?"

"She was being trained or groomed or something by Katrina Bathory," I explained.

"Bathory? You need to watch out for her. She's just as bad as Dracula."

Penny looked around. "Where is she anyway? You wake her up before me?"

"Well… She's not going to be a problem anymore."

The two of them gave me questioning looks. I gave a sigh. "She went feral from lack of feeding. She knew it was happening and asked me to put her down if it happened."

Zoe gave me *the look*. "You killed a feral master vampire. By yourself? With no sword or armor?"

"It was complicated. You had to be there." I waved my hand. "I'll explain it later. We're running out of time."

"Right." My wife nodded. "But I *do* want to hear this."

Penny dragged Acantha out and we repeated the process. She woke up screaming and scrambled away from us, eyes wide and searching the room as she scootched her back up against a cabinet. I held up my hands, "Easy, easy. Bathory's not here."

She grabbed her neck where the vampire had bit her and examined her hand for blood. The panic faded from her eyes. "Where's Katrina?"

I shook my head. "I'm sorry. As you know, she went feral. She… had to be put down."

Acantha pulled up her knees and wrapped her arms around her legs. "She attacked me. I was so afraid that would happen, and it did."

"It's over now. "I quickly caught her up to speed. After she had a few minutes to digest it, she stood up to leave.

"One more thing, Acantha," said my wife. The alchemist turned to her. "My name is Zoe Llewellyn Brennan. I'm known as Zoe Afire, and I hereby challenge you to a duel."

I was stunned. From the sharp intake of breath next to me, it appeared Penny was as well.

"What? Why?" Acantha slowly backed away from my wife.

"You tried to kill my husband and you forced my friend to do the dirty work. I find you despicable."

"I-I had no choice."

"You had many. Now name your terms." My wife drew a wand and twirled it like a drumstick.

"I'm n-not a duelist. I don't know how to fight you." Acantha ran out of space and backed into a wall.

"I am. In fact, it'll be my second duel of the day." Zoe reached into a pouch and slammed a glass jar onto the table. It had a metal lid with holes poked into it. Inside was a frog scrambling to get out.

The room grew silent as the three of us stared at jar.

No way she did what I think she did.

I peered down at it. "Why do you have a frog in a jar?"

Zoe smiled grimly. "That thing about Hien Tran waffling turned out to be true. So, I challenged her to step aside or duel me. She lost…"

"You can do that?"

"Well, it's rarely done in the Morgan coven. First time in my lifetime. When it does happen, it opens up a vote by the coven for a new leader. Technically Hien could have been voted back in. They chose me instead."

I gestured to the jar. "I meant being able to actually turn someone into a frog."

Her smile turned into an honest grin. "Well, you were always joking about it so I thought I'd see if I could create a spell that would do it. The hard part was mass transfer."

"Remind me not to piss you off." Penny tapped on the glass with her finger. "Is she stuck like that forever?"

"No, I'll change her back later. I'm giving her time to contemplate the error of her ways." Zoe's grin disappeared and she pinned Acantha with a stare. Fire coming from her eyes, literally. "So! Accept my challenge or leave this city and never return. Those are your options."

"I'll… I'll leave." Acantha looked ready to faint.

"Fine." Zoe dismissed the fire. "But if you ever return here, you're going in a jar. For good."

"Very well. I understand. You do not want me to return to the city."

"And if I ever hear you've been torturing or murdering people, I'll hunt you down and do worse."

"I…yes, I understand."

"Good." Zoe scooped up the jar and put it back in her bag and handed me a potion tube. "I'll walk you out myself."

Penny looked at me after they walked out. "You married her? I didn't give you enough credit. You're braver than I thought."

"Still want to date us?"

"Ah, let me get back to you. That… that was kind of scary."

Yeah…

"Help me with Khishchnick." We moved her out of the walk-in and I slapped a pair of cuffs on her. The runes engraved on them would restrict any use of her magic. She was still a prisoner, after all.

We finished going through the motions with the potion and the dagger just as Zoe returned. When they opened, Obrechennyy's eyes didn't have any of the momentary confusion the rest of them did. "The plague?"

"Gone."

She sat up in a smooth motion, giving her handcuffs a brief glance before dismissing them from her mind. "How much time has gone by?"

"Since you died? Hours, I think. Time got a little confusing in there."

"That dagger of yours somehow fooled the Rook into thinking we were dead?"

Very quick, this one. She's the type of person you only underestimate once.

"No, you were very much dead. I just stored your soul away for a while."

She frowned. "That seems a bit black for you."

"Nothing nefarious, just put your soul in deep storage for a while. "I pointed to the walk-in "Had to put your bodies on ice to make it work. That was the tricky part."

"Very well." She sprung to her feet without using her hands.

"You seem to be taking this in stride."

"You were the only one I considered a real threat. It comes to no surprise to me that once I was removed from the board, you won the game."

"Me?"

"You have had a couple of interesting years, *da?* People talk when you make that much of a splash. Of the many things said about you these days, two are mentioned in every conversation."

"Oh?" I wasn't sure I wanted to know but I couldn't help myself. "What would those be?"

"That you possess a will stronger than the metal of your armor. And that not only do you always have a strategy, but that even your contingency plans have contingency plans."

If only!

"Well, right now the only plan is to get you back to prison."

"May we stop for coffee on the way?" She made a face. "The coffee here was atrocious."

"Sure, why not?"

Chapter Thirty-Three

The Big Plan

After dropping our prisoner back off where she belonged, I went home and took an exceedingly long nap. I awoke to a very crowded bed. Zoe and Whackacat were asleep on my right, and Morgan and Sonny were sacked out on my left.

I slowly wormed my way out of the pig pile of family and pets and made my way down to the first floor. It was a toss-up which creaked more, the stairs or my knees.

I made myself some hot chocolate, sat down, and savored the first sip. The Russian was right. The food in the Rook had been more like rations than anything else. It was if the stasis field leeched out all the flavors.

"Glad to be back?"

I jumped as my wife came around behind me. She was holding the bag containing her witch's kit.

"I thought you were asleep. How'd you get here so fast?

She stole my mug as she sat down and took a drink. "Magic."

"Well, magic up your own cup. This one is mine." I snagged it away from her. "The water in the kettle is still hot. Do you want me to make you some?"

"No thanks." She leaned forward. "How bad was it?"

"Couple people died. Could have been a lot worse. Your buddy Bainbridge was a real prick, you know."

She held up her hands. "Hey, I just went to school with him. He was no friend of mine." She leaned back. "You ready for tonight?"

"I think so." I took another sip. "I spoke with Culain about it when Penny and I did our debrief. He thinks Callis and your cousin know something's up but not necessarily what we're planning."

"This is a big step, Mike."

"I know."

"Do you?" She slipped my mug across the table and took another sip.

I swear, trapped in the Rook was the only time I didn't have to share my food in twenty years. I offered to make you some, woman!

She peered at me over the rim. "This will put you… and the family in the big leagues. It will place you in a whole different set of rules. They are not like the laws you enforce. They are based on custom, not justice. You will be entering a much harsher world and it will not be one you are familiar with."

"I know." I got up and made myself another cup. "I plan on dealing with that by taking a page out of your father's book."

She smiled as I sat down. "Oh? What page is that? Hell, for that matter, which book?"

"Use the rules when they are advantageous. Ignore them when they aren't."

Zoe choked on the hot chocolate a little. "Ah, the only reason my father can get away with that is because he's a Warlock. Last time I checked, you weren't."

"Didn't you hear? I have an iron will and many plans…"

"The only thing I heard was your head swelling when she was spewing that gibberish."

"What? My strength is the strength of ten because my heart is pure!"

"Pure bacon, maybe."

"Ouch. That hurt."

"Truth often does." Using just her fingers, she slowly turned her mug in circles.

"That's going to leave a mark on the table, and you'll somehow blame me."

"Well, it *is* your mug." She gave me a quick grin. "Seriously, though. You need to think long and hard on this."

I raised my eyebrows. "I thought you were on board."

"I am. Last-minute jitters, I guess. I just want to make sure you know what you're doing."

"What we've been doing is playing defense because the city council keeps sitting on their asses. It's the thing with Jamie all over again."

When our son Jamie had been a child, a creature calling himself Edison Cole kidnapped Jamie and his class. The council refused to take action. I wound up quitting and dealing with it myself. It… got ugly.

"I don't want to let more people get hurt because there are corrupt and incompetent people on the council. But if you don't want to go forward with this..."

"No, that's not it. I want justice for my grandfather." She paused for a second to gather her thoughts. "I grew up both a Llewellyn and a Morgan. Both powerful Houses. I've seen the type of power moves that go on at that level. You've brushed aside some of them as a cop but have never really been involved. Your world is very different. Simpler. Find out who the bad guy is. Catch the bad guy. The politics you deal with are at a city level. Motions and ordinances and what not."

I grinned as she paused again. "Please, continue with telling me I'm simple."

"Don't twist my words." Leaning to the side, she reached into her bag and removed the jar containing Hien Tran the frog. "This probably seemed extreme to you."

"It was a bit shocking, yeah."

"My coven saw it as compassionate. Others would have seen it as weak. You don't let a vanquished foe live."

"The everyday laws of Llewellyn are not as crunchy granola as the rest of the country, sweetie." I told her. "I got used to duels and blood oaths being legal as well as all the other twisted laws and traditions you have here."

"Those are very black and white, Mike. The arena you're entering is… murkier than that."

"I know. But that's why I have you and Culain to guide me through it." I pointed at the jar. "What are you doing with her anyways?"

"I'll turn her back after tonight's meeting."

I drank my mug and stood up. "Okay. Let's get ready!"

***

I parked the Chief around the corner from the Great Hall and watched people filing in. The passenger door opened and Culain slipped into the car while holding two cups. He handed me one containing hot chocolate. "Nervous?"

I took it and pried off the lid. "Little bit. Zoe's worried it's painting a target on my back."

He tilted his seat back a bit and took a sip of his cup. I knew from long practice it contained coffee straight from the pot. No additives, black as night. "She doesn't realize you already have one?"

I gently blew on the piping hot liquid. "Not sure if I should drink this. I just had one back at the house. Going to make me jittery."

He shrugged. "Want something stronger? You're not on the clock."

"Yes! But no thanks."

"Look. Don't sweat this. If it works, it puts you in a much stronger position. If it doesn't, you haven't lost anything. Either way, I have your back."

"What about Callis, Maddox, and their little cabal? Are they onto us?"

"They know something's in the works, but I leaked that it's a recall vote to remove Callis as chairman of the council. The past day or so, he and Maddox have been making deals to shore up his position. If they did truly fall for it, this is going to blindside them." He opened the car door. "Remember, go for the Halifax seat."

"Right. I know, I know. Is Liz already in there?" Liz Pendens was an attorney that had help us research most of what we needed to pull this off. She was going to act as my legal counsel if needed.

"She is." He stepped out of the car, shut the door, and leaned into the window. "Zoe's little stunt may have managed to stack the deck with some more people."

"You heard about that? What am I saying? Of course, you did." I stared out the window again and gnawed at a thumbnail.

"You'll be fine." He pushed off the door and walked away.

"Famous last words," I muttered as I watched him go into the Hall.

I waited until I finished my drink and then exited the car. "Wish me luck, Chief."

The car gave a slight rev of the engine as I walked towards the building. I trotted up the steps and entered the door, nodding at the guards. I walked down the ornate hall. All damage for the wendigo's attack had been removed. It was gaudy as ever. I could hear voices as I approached the council chamber. Two more guards flanked the bas relief doors that led to the room. One of them nodded to me as I entered.

Politics in Llewellyn was a complicated affair. The council was divided into three sections. The Houses were made up of the original ruling families of Llewellyn. The Professions section consisted of the more powerful guilds and covens, and then there was the Elected, whose members were voted in. Except for a few permanent chairs, the high council was made up of the chairman and the more influential members of the council. It was they who dealt with the day-to-day affairs of the city.

Due to the attacks on the city, there had been a lot of overturns on the council in the past few years. Several of the House seats were vacant as entire families had perished in Oct5.

Most of these meetings were crowded, and that night was no exception. The fear of a dragon lurking in the woods weighed heavily on everyone's minds these days. The room was set up like an amphitheater. The public sat in rows of chairs on the floor. The table and chairs containing the members of the high council were up on a stage. Also on the stage was Callis. He was at the podium droning about next year's budget. The rest of the council sat in chairs rising up behind the public seating. As I scanned the room, I spotted Martin in the wings of the stage, clutching a leather briefcase.

On seeing me, he gave a visible swallow and walked onto the stage heading over to the table. At the sight of him, several in the crowd started whispering. Callis stopped his drivel and looked behind him to see Martin. "Mister Wheeler, what *are* you doing?"

Like you don't know!

I used the distraction to go up the back stairs to the top of the amphitheater. Martin ducked his head at Callis. "Mister Chairman, I'm taking my seat."

"Your seat?"

"Yes. As you know, I'm the head librarian at the university. However, that's the modern name of the title. My position is actually called Keeper of the Lore. Imagine my surprise when I found out that the position is in fact a permanent seat on the high council."

Something no one other than Culain remembered until it was too late. He slipped it by them when he recommended Martin be given the post. Isn't that right, Callis, old buddy?

"Mister Wheeler, your predecessor never sat on the council. That seat has gone unfilled for several decades, abandoned. I hardly—"

"Point of fact, Mister Chairman." Liz Pendens stood up for the crowd. "While the last Keeper of the Lore did not physically sit on the council, he was heavily involved in the governing of the city."

"And you can prove this?"

She held up a stack of paper. "I have years of correspondence between Keeper Wheeler's predecessor and Owen Llewellyn in his guise as chairman of the council. It appears the last Keeper was not comfortable around large crowds and would often give his proxy to Owen with instructions how to vote."

Several of the older members of the council nodded at this. While this was going on, I had made my way up to the top of the amphitheater and was having a mild panic attack as I couldn't find the Halifax seat.

Down on the stage, Callis waved forward the documents. Liz strode down the aisle and handed them to him. "These are copies, of course."

The wizard gave her a sardonic smile. "Of course." Callis wore a pair of antique bifocals on a chain around his neck. He lifted them off his robes and placed them on the tip of his nose. He shuffled through them quickly. "This appears to sustain your claim."

He handed the documents to the other members of the high council who also sifted through them.

Liz smiled at him. "Since the position was never abandoned, my client has every right to take his seat on the council."

Speaking of seats, I finally spotted the Halifax one. I slowly made my way over to it, giving quiet apologies to the magi whose toes I stepped on as I went by. My large frame was not making it easy.

Looking down from the podium, Callis smiled mirthlessly at Liz. "Your client, Attorney Penden?"

"That's correct. I have several."

"Is there any reason this couldn't have been handled before the meeting?"

"Our apologies. It won't happen again."

The crowd chuckled at that. Drama was the very life blood of the magi, and they were enjoying the show.

"Very well. Welcome to the High Council, Keeper Wheeler. Please try to be on time in the future." Callis waved Martin to the seat. "Now, if we can continue. I'd like to discuss the budget for repowering the bridge wards. I— *What now?*"

His question had an annoyed tone to it and was directed at Maddox Morgan who was frantically waving his hand. Maddox, who suddenly found the entire room looking at him, shrunk somewhat back in his seat. "Well, It's just that... Why is Mike Brennan sitting in a House seat?"

Callis followed Maddox's finger to where I was slumped down in the seat with my legs crossed out in front of me. I gave him a slight wave.

Callis took off his glasses, closed his eyes for a second, took a large breath, and slowly exhaled. When he opened his eyes, he gave me a politician's smile. Nothing but teeth. "Sergeant Brennan, why are you in House Halifax's seat?"

"Sadly, House Halifax is no more. The last of the family died during Oct5. Since it is vacant, I hereby claim this seat for House Brennan." Without the magical aids that Callis had, I made sure to project my voice across the room.

"You just can't claim a House seat. The Houses that make up the council were decided at the founding of the city. You can't add more. Remove yourself." Callis made a shooing gesture with one of his hands. While he was doing that, I noticed an unexpected face on the public floor.

Dracula! What is he doing here?

"There is a precedent." Liz held up an ancient and tattered book. "Thirty years after the founding of the city, Orloc Halifax petitioned Llewellyn for a seat for House Halifax. It was granted and he took a seat on the council." She pointed at me. "That seat, in fact."

Callis looked back down at her. "Another one of your clients, Counselor?"

"I did say I had several, Mister Chairman," Liz told him sweetly. She opened the book to a marked spot. Her Gift allowed her to remember anything she read for a certain amount of time. Her reading for the book was theatrics for the crowd. "'The head of the petitioning House must claim an open seat. They must recite proven deeds of valor and glory to show worthiness, as does three members pledged to their House. Two members of the High Council, a House, an Elected, and a Professional must back his petition. In addition, three other member votes from the council are needed.'"

The crowd erupted at this. Callis started banging on his gavel to try and restore order. "Quiet! Quiet down! Don't make us use silence spells!"

The noise finally dropped to a reasonable level. He glared up at me. "Fine. We'll schedule your petition for the next meeting. Now—"

"Another point of fact, Mister Chairman." Liz held up her hand again.

Callis rolled his eyes. "Go ahead."

"At the time of the Halifax petition, a motion to postpone it was suggested. Orloc took it as a personal insult and issued a challenge for a duel. The duel was accepted and Orloc killed the counselor on this very floor. That sets a significant precedent. My client had indicated to me he will challenge anyone who tries to postpone this petition. And, according to the precedent, the duel would take place immediately."

Callis glared at me. A prepared wizard is a thing to be feared, but no one opposing our plan thought they would be dueling me that night. Going into a fight against me while unprepared was a risky move. Callis wasn't the dueling type anyway. He preferred to play the long game. "As a police officer, Sergeant Brennan isn't allowed to duel."

"Actually," Culain's quiet voice somehow cut right through the murmuring of the crowd. "What he does on vacation is his own business."

"Vacation?" Callis spat out. "He's on vacation?"

My boss grinned at him. "Started this morning. Signed off on it myself. Department policy doesn't say anything about dueling on vacation."

I could practically see the wheels moving in the wizard's head. Callis came into this thinking we were planning to oust him as chairman. This wasn't the angle he was expecting. Callis was trying to determine how this would affect him. He could refuse a challenge, which in all rights he should do. After all, the Chairman can't be expected to stop all city business anytime some yahoo wants to challenge him, but right now, he was wondering if that made him look weak and whether that was how we were going to strike.

He shrugged. "I'm tempted to reschedule just to spite your attempts to box this council into a corner, but I have to admit, I am curious to see where you're going with this."

Nice face saving.

Callis gestured at me. "Proceed with your petition."

I stood up. "My name is Michael Brennan. I'm a U.S. Army Veteran. I'm married to Zoe Llewellyn Brennan and the father of two. I'm a runesmith and sergeant with the Llewellyn Police Department. In my day I've fought many creatures and casters. In the past two years, I led the city's forces against an undead army during the Battle of University Heights. I fought and killed Otto Clausewitz in single combat. I vanquished the dybbuk known as Harrow. I defeated the wendigo in personal combat, killing its mortal avatar and banishing it from this plane. I claim this seat for House Brennan by right and by strength of arm."

Callis nodded. "And who pledges to your house?"

This is where I got nervous. Culain wouldn't let me be part of gathering those who pledged the House. Some bullshit about how the head of the House shouldn't be asking people to pledge. I think he just didn't want me mucking with his plans. I was pretty sure Zoe was one of the pledges, but I didn't know who the other two were.

My wife stood up from the cheap seats. "I, Zoe Llewellyn Brennan, the witch known as Zoe Afire, wife of Michael Brennan and leader of the Morgan Coven. I am pledged to House Brennan. My deeds are well known to this city. Do you really need me to recite them?"

Many of the people present, including Callis, pivoted to stare at the empty seat where the leader of the Morgan

Coven normally sat. Callis frowned. "What? When did you become Coven Leader?"

"Recently." Morgan pulled out the jar containing the frog form of Hien Tran and slammed it down on the banister in front of her. "*Very* recently."

I triggered the blood rune for sight and was able to see a miniature witch's hat that had been placed on the frog's head. One that had *not* been on it the last time I saw the frog.

Magi and their drama. How long did it take Zoe to get that thing tied on?

Zoe gave Callis a flat look, ignoring the crowd as it erupted again. "Not all are as wise as you in avoiding a challenge from a member of House Brennan."

Callis stared at the jar his ally was currently imprisoned in for several seconds before drawing his eyes back up to my wife. There was respect in them. "Noted. Who else pledges themselves to your cause?"

"I, Sergeant Gabrielle Zhao of the Lewellyn Police Department and the current Living Temple of the Four Great Spirits, am pledged to House Brennan." Gabby stood up wearing civilian clothes. "I vanquished Jiuwei Hu and defeated the necromancer known as Blackest Night. I have also—"

"Your deeds are well known and do not need to be recited." Callis cut her off. Gabby going through her hit parade only helped our cause, not his. He didn't want any more reminders of what we have done for the city. "My question is how are you connected to House Brennan. Simply working with Sergeant Brennan isn't enough to count."

"Michael Brennan is my godfather and mentor, and I am godmother to his daughter Morgan. The Brennans are like family to me." The *tattoos* on her skin started shifting. "To *us*!"

"Ah, yes. Thank you." Callis motioned for Gabby to take her seat. "And who is the last to pledge?"

"I am." I snapped my head around to see my father stand up. "James Brennan. Father of Michael Brennan."

Callis gave a wide smile, his eyes gleaming with perceived triumph. "Forgive me, sir, but you are in fact a Normal and an Outsider?"

"That is correct." My father stood there in his old age, neither cowed nor concerned for the various creatures and magi in the room with him. He kept his hands in the pockets of the tan barn coat that he wore. "I'm an Army veteran who did multiple tours in Vietnam."

Maddox was openly grinning as Callis slowly shook his head. "I'm sure you were a very brave soldier in your day, but your actions in the Outside world do not apply here. It must be deeds done within the magical community itself."

"Oh." My father seemed to shrink in on himself for a second and then straightened. "Would killing a team of undead assassins count?"

"I—Ah?" Callis looked at Maddox who shrugged. "When did this take place?"

"During Oct5. Harrow sent them after my family," my father calmly told him.

"How? How did you do that? With one of your son's magical items?"

357

"No, I just used a knife." My father reached down by his feet and pulled up a large satchel which he rested on the banister in front of him. "If that's not enough, I have more."

"More?" Callis asked in spite of himself.

"Yes. I'm not one for keeping trophies, but I was told it's kind of expected in your world." He pulled a sealed glass vat out of the bag. Inside it floating in embalming fluid was a severed head.

"Who is that?" hissed Callis.

"Galaaz Dulacq, the half fae prince known as Lancelot Dulac. Most recently in Llewellyn under the alias of James Pond." I stood up. "He was responsible for the death of my father's youngest brother. My father killed him in return."

Once again, the crowd went wild. I heard *blood debt* whispered several times by people in the audience.

Callis banged on the gavel until the handle snapped in his hand. "You would have us believe that at your affirmed age you were able to kill one of the most famous warriors in history?"

My father shrugged. "You can choose to believe it or not. Either way, that's what happened."

Culain slowly got to his feet. The crowd went from yelling to hushed whispers, waiting to see what he had to say. He gestured at my father. "It is in my professional judgment that James Brennan may very well be the most dangerous person in this room."

"Excluding you of course," Callis said sarcastically as he threw the broken handle onto the podium in disgust.

"I didn't say that."

You could have heard a pin drop. Culain was a guy no one knew a lot about, but all the right people were afraid of him. His implication was staggering. I couldn't help but notice he phrased his wording very specifically. He was implying, but not confirming.

My father swung back his coat, showing a short sword strapped to his side. "If it helps, I currently wield Excalibur."

And the crowd went off again, many straining to lay eyes on the most famous sword in the world. I was more impressed with the belt. I knew what magical qualities it possessed.

Once the crowd finally died down, I looked down to the stage. "Is my father considered sufficient?"

"He is." Callis ground out. "Keeper Wheeler, your friendship with Sergeant Brennan is well known. I assume you are voting in favor?"

"That is correct. I, so vote, in favor of the inclusion of House Brennan on the council."

Callis eyes shifted over to my wife. "You would of course take care of the Professional vote."

My wife smirked at him. "I, so vote, in favor of the inclusion of House Brennan on the council."

The wizard glanced around the room. "Are there any among the Elected who vote in favor?"

"I do," answered Valentine briefly rising from his seat.

"Fine." Callis sighed. "And from the Houses?"

I looked over to House Davenport. The seat was empty. Toria was nowhere to be seen.

Son of a bitch.

On seeing that Toria was missing, my wife jumped to her feet. "House Llewellyn votes in favor."

Callis gave her a long stare and then slowly looked up to where Aidan Llewellyn sat in House Llewellyn's chair. Aidan was descended from a cousin of Owen's and a decent wizard in his own right. But the seat was not his to sit in.

Even prior to Owen's death, the chair had remained empty as Owen sat in the chairman's seat. It had continued to remain vacant up until now. At some point, Aidan must have slipped into the seat during my father's questioning. Most likely prompted to do so last minute from someone belonging to Callis and Maddox's camp.

"He is not the head of House Llewellyn," sputtered my wife.

"Inheritance is not the purview of this council. In light of not knowing who the true head of the House is, we can't accept a vote from it." Callis shrugged. "If no other House will stand up for the petition I have no choice—"

"Oh, no need to wait. I think we can settle this right now." A bald man with a silver goatee stepped out from behind the Llewellyn Seat. His black suit was expensive and immaculate.

Things just got very interesting.

They usually did when my father-in-law was involved.

Interesting and bloody.

Chapter Thirty-Four

Enter Silas

The warlock known as Silas the Black was not physically imposing. He was of medium height and a little on the slender side. It was when you looked into his eyes that you realized you faced a very dangerous man. Those eyes were locked onto Aidan Llewellyn who was doing his best to shrink into the seat he was occupying.

Silas leaned on a black and silver cane with one hand, rested his other hand on Aidan's shoulder, and looked down at Callis. "I'm not sure why there would be any confusion. Cousin Aidan here is from a cadet branch of the family. I, on the other hand, am Owen Llewellyn's only living child."

"You are not welcome here, Warlock!" Callis shouted up at him as many in the crowd made for the door. With the ability to siphon magic away from magi and use it for their own purposes, warlocks were hated and feared within the magical community. In order to protect themselves, they wore masks and used false names when exercising their abilities. Silas was the only one I ever heard of who openly used his power.

"Be that as it may, I am still the head of House Llewellyn and have committed no crimes in this city." He waved a hand and the exit doors slammed shut. "Please be seated. This won't take long."

He paused as the magi who attempted to flee the room slunk back to their seats. "Now, imagine my surprise when one of my spells alerted me to the fact someone was sitting in my chair. Turns out Cousin Aidan was just keeping it warm for me." He tapped Aidan on the shoulder. "Thank you, cousin. You may run along now."

Aidan never took his eyes off Silas as he slithered out of the seat and backed away into the crowd, a fearful look on his face. Silas sat in the seat and placed his cane across his lap. "Now then, how may I wreck your day?"

This had the potential to be bad for us. Silas was a polarizing figure. Lewellyn's original bad boy. Possible support may turn away from us just because he might side with us. And he would. Whatever faults Silas may have, he loves his daughter and grandchildren.

Silas scanned the room. "I see the dolt my daughter married seems to be causing more problems. What is it this time?"

Dolt?

That was odd. Unlike his ex-wife, Silas didn't have an antagonistic relationship with me. We may not agree on a lot of fundamental issues, but he'd never disrespected me before.

Oh, wait. Yup, I actually am a dolt.

"Stay out of it, Silas. It doesn't concern you," I told him.

Silas pointed at Martin. "You! The bookworm. Tell me what's going on."

Martin slowly rose to his feet. As the one person in the room that had zero magical ability, Martin should have been the only one not afraid of Silas. Apparently, nobody had told Martin that, because he looked like he was going to pass out. Not that anyone there blamed him. It's been said that when monsters and fiends gather by the campfire to tell stories to scare each other, it's Silas the Black they speak of.

Martin adjusted his bowtie. "Michael Brennan has petitioned the council to claim a House seat for House Brennan. He needs another House to vote in his favor."

"Well, this is a dilemma!" Silas picked up his cane and whirled in in his hand. "Inflate Brennan's already oversized ego or vote with Callis the bootlicker." He stopped twirling and looked down at Callis. "I assume you're against it, that is? You and the cop haven't really seen eye to eye."

"Yes," ground out Callis.

"That *is* a tough decision. Fortunately, I don't need to participate in the charade. I find politics boring and think I'll appoint someone to oversee such things. I'll be leaving now." Silas stood up. "That being said, if anyone other than I or my appointed proxy ever sits in my chair again, I'll send them straight to hell...alive."

He turned to leave but stopped at Martin's cough. "Excuse me."

Silas turned back. "Yes?"

"I'm sorry, but you never said who your proxy is."

"Ah, yes. Of course. Thank you." He pointed the cane down to my wife. "Zoe Llewellyn Brennan, the witch known as Zoe Afire, is my proxy until I say otherwise."

Everyone looked down at Zoe who had a satisfied smirk on her face. Silas, of course, took that as an opportunity to disappear. The Magi do love a good exit.

Zoe rose to her feet again. "House Llewellyn votes for the inclusion of House Brennan on the council."

In the end, the vote passed in large numbers and Zoe emerged as a new player in Llewellyn. Between Silas and the Morgan Coven, she had two votes on the council and was the wife of the newest vote holder. The theatrics with the frog didn't go unnoticed either. Every coven in the city had voted for House Brennan. "Yes, yes. Everyone please quite down." Callis waved his arms. "Welcome, House Brennan. Now please take your seats so we may finish this meeting."

"Well, There's one more thing," I told him.

"Of course there is." He sighed. "What now?"

"Since the recent attack by the city of Joubert on this very council, you all finally declared war on Joubert."

"That's correct. As I remember, you were extremely in favor of it."

"But since then, the city has done nothing concerning Joubert. In fact, it was your team participating in a farce of a peace talk that allowed a Joubert assassin to murder several members of the council in the first place."

This time, the glare Callis sent me was personal. "Considering I and several members of this council almost died in that attack, I'd say we are very aware of it. As to why we haven't done anything, have you failed to notice we have a dragon camped outside our city? One crisis at a time, if you don't mind."

I held up a hand. "No, the dragon is a major and immediate concern. I'm not disputing that. But since the council is unable to act against Joubert, House Brennan has been denied justice."

Callis rubbed his forehead in frustration. "How has House Brennan been denied justice in the five seconds it's existed?"

Liz raised her hand. "To be clear, House Brennan's seat on the council may be new, but it can legitimately be argued House Brennan has been around for much longer. Did House Brennan not come to the city's aid during Oct5?"

"That was Sergeant Brennan's duty as a police sergeant."

"Actually, he wasn't a police officer at the time. Owen Lewellyn as Chairman requested his aid and appointed him Commander. Zoe Brennan and her mother-in-law, Elizabeth Brennan, aided the injured. Patrick Brennan, Michael's uncle, fought in the Battle of University Heights." Liz peered down her glasses at Callis, a neat trick considering he was up in the podium. "Recognized or not, House Brennan has been in existence before today and this city owes its members a debt."

"Fine, fine." Callis waved a hand. "And what is this grievance?"

"The city of Joubert has done injury against my House and I sought justice from this council for the following." I held up my left index finger. "One: the death of my wife's grandfather, Owen Llewellyn."

"Wait a minute." Callis leaned forward on the podium. "Owen Llewellyn was a friend of mine. I personally grieve his death and expect Joubert to pay for it. But the fact of the matter is his blood debt would fall to House Llewellyn not House Brennan."

Zoe stood up and looked at me. "House Brennan, as proxy of the head of House Llewellyn, I propose a mutual aid pact."

"Agreed," I told her.

She sat down with a smirk.

I continued to hold my index finger up. "Correction. Joubert killed Owen Llewellyn, the former head of a House we have a mutual aid pact with."

My middle finger raised up next to my index finger. "Two: they attacked my house. Sending assassins onto the property to murder me and my family. When that did not work, they sent a continuous barrage of eldritch missiles at the house to kill us."

My ring finger rose. "When that all failed, they sent assassins to murder my family."

My little finger joined the others. "And third: they killed my dog."

"They killed your dog?" Callis asked in disbelief. "You want to go to war over a dog?"

"No, I'm merely saying it's casus belli" I told him. "That's Latin for—"

"Occasion for war. Yes, I'm aware. Some of us here learned Latin before it was dead." He pinched the bridge of his nose. "You're claiming the death of a dog is an act that justifies war. "

"Well, you're kind of ignoring the part where they sent assassins to kill my family, but sure."

"There is precedent," Valentine spoke up.

"Please. When has there ever been a city that has gone to war over an animal?" Callis threw up his hands in frustration.

"Connacht went to war with Ulster over a bull," stated Culain. "And those were actually kingdoms at the time."

Callis gaped at him. "Cows? How have cows gotten involved?"

Now it was my turn to pinch the bridge of my nose. "Look. This is getting a little far afield. As a House, I don't need permission for the city to go to war. I just need to state I have cause to do so. I have now done that. The city failed to get me justice in a reasonable time and I will seek it myself. House Brennan declares war on the city of Joubert."

Callis looked at me suspiciously. "That's it? Nothing further? You don't want us to change Monday to Brennan Day or any other business?"

"What? You mean like a recall or something like that?" I stared at him as he flinched at my words. "No, I'm good. For now."

"Fine." Callis slapped his palm down on the podium. "All other business is postponed until the next meeting. We're adjourned." He glared around the room. "Unless someone else plans on challenging me to a duel, that is."

As the room filed out, I found that it took a while to make my way down to my wife. Several people congratulated me as I made my way down to her. Waiting at the bottom with Zoe were Martin, my father, Valentine, and Culain. People were giving them a wide berth. My father smiled and said in an Irish brogue he'd lost years ago, "Well now, if it isn't the Brennan himself."

"When did you become part of this?" I asked him.

"Culain reached out to me last minute."

I nodded and looked around. "Where's Gabby?"

"She had a call to respond to," answered Culain.

"What happened to Toria Davenport?"

"I'm not sure, but I'm going to find out. In fact, I have to get back to work and look into that and some other things. If you can hold off a day, Martin booked us a private room at Stacked tomorrow. We're going to have a little celebration."

The librarian grinned at me. "Big day. Deserves a big party."

"Sounds like a plan." I wrapped my arm around my wife and looked at my father. "You and Mom coming?"

"No, I have to get back today. Your uncle keeps threatening to change the menu at the pub again. I have to get back before he does something rash."

"Yeah, well, we need to talk about your big reveal back there."

"Another time."

"Fine." I sighed. "You're not leaving before visiting Morgan, are you?"

"Wouldn't dream of it."

As we walked out, I scanned the crowd, half listening to my wife chat to my father about what Morgan has been up to. Dracula stood by another exit. Once our eyes locked, he smiled and turned to look at Toria Davenport's seat.

"Son of a bitch!" I took a step forward, but he vanished into the crowd.

The message was clear. I had taken out one of his allies and he had just done the same to me.

Chapter Thirty-Five

A Bad Coat of Paint

"Excuse me? You're going to work?" my wife called from the kitchen as I tried to sneak out the side door the next morning.

"Not police stuff. I'm going to explore the Rook."

"You don't want to take it easy for tonight?"

"The thing we've been planning for almost a year is done. We won. A few more hours worrying over a party isn't something I think we need to do."

"What if you need to make a speech?" She came around the corner wearing one of my shirts and holding a mug of tea.

"I'll wing it."

"Okay. Just don't ask me to jump in and save you. Tell me, what's so special about the Rook anyway?"

I filled her in as she finished off her drink. "So, you're saying that it was created by a runesmith, and generations of his magi descendants have been layering it with spells?"

"Yeah. I think the key to the control room got lost and they've been using spells to prop it up."

"That's just sloppy." Zoe shook her head in disgust. I love my wife but she's a bit of a spell snob. "It's like…painting over weathered wood without properly preparing it. The spells are going to peel right off it after a short while."

I grabbed her mug and placed it in the sink with mine. "You're welcome to come along and check it out."

"Mmm, that's too interesting to pass up. Let me see if Emala can watch Morgan."

"We're going to need Morgan. There's a ward about ten feet before the door that I think leads to the control room. We'll need her to pop it."

She raised one eyebrow at me. "Pop it? That's how you describe the insanely powerful ability to destroy wards?"

"Yeah. Why not?"

She gave me a look of mock disgust. "It's a bit…underwhelming."

"Gets the point across. Anyway, we need her."

"I'm not sure we do." My wife bit her lip as she considered something. "You said the ward was ten feet from the door?"

"More or less."

"Were there glyphs or witch's script on the floor?"

"Not that I could see."

"The paint peeled off then." She stood up. We shouldn't need Morgan. I'll need to grab some things, though.

"You sure?"

"If I'm wrong, we can always bring her another time. I don't want her wielding such powerful magic if she doesn't need to. She needs to be properly trained and eased into her powers."

"I hear that." The stranger and powerful magic Morgan had access to frightened me. To clarify, I wasn't frightened *of* her, I was frightened *for* her. The history of the magi was littered with cautionary tales of spellcasters who didn't respect the inherent dangers of their magic.

It wasn't hard to track down my wife's apprentice. Any free time she had, she was on her broomstick. With a wave, Zoe flagged the teen witch down. Emala Delgado-Finnigan did a final loop de loop and sped to a stop just before us, her feet scattering the gravel of our driveway. "Hey, what's up?

"No speed runs today?" I asked her. The more accomplished witches have nicknames like my wife being called Zoe Afire. But these nicknames are like a pilot's call sign; they have to be given. Emala had other ideas. She was determined to be called Supersonic. For that to even be considered, she'd have to break Mach One, something very few witches have ever done.

"No, agility exercises. I alternate every other day." She caught Zoe's warning look. "Once I've done my spells for the day, of course."

Zoe gave an approving nod. "Are you free to watch Morgan for a while? We need to check something out."

"Of course." Emala lifted up her goggles. Most witches just used protective spells, but she claims she had a theory about it creating drag on the speed spells. I think she just liked the look. Her generation grew up on the Potter books, after all. "Where is she?"

"Napping in her room. I'll wake her up. She sleeps any longer she won't go to bed on time tonight." She looked at me. "I assume you want to take the Chief."

"Of course." I gave a thumbs up to the car currently parked in front of the carriage house. I got an engine rev in return. The Chief was a completely different take on the term *smart car*.

"Okay, give me ten."

It wound up taking her twenty.

Chapter Thirty-Six

Kitchen Witches and Staff Twirlers

After a quick ride in the Chief, we arrived at the Rook. The door opened at my presence, which was a good thing considering I didn't have a key. Well, the correct key anyways.

We quickly made our way down to the ward. Zoe ignored it and inspected the floor beyond it. "Yup. Bunch of kitchen witches and staff twirlers in that family."

"You always said Bainbridge was powerful," I reminded her.

"Oh, he was skilled enough, but his arrogance was always his Achilles heel. Probably how Harrow trapped him. Typical wizard. His inflated opinion of himself caused him to miss or dismiss things. Things that matter." She pointed at the floor. "Like that there."

I stared at the section of the floor she was pointing at. "What am I looking for? I don't see anything."

"If you create a ward the right way, you shape it like a bubble. The one we had on the property was like that. If you tried to get in by tunneling underground, you'd still run into it." She ran her hands along the stone walls in front of the ward.

"And that didn't happen here?"

"It can't. What happens when a wizard or witch tries to cast a spell directly on one of your magic items? Not an attack spell that would damage or destroy it, but one that would be beneficial or harmless. Like trying to make your sword glow."

"The spell can't take a hold and slides off. The two magics are not compatible unless set up that way in the beginning. Even then it takes major precautions."

"Right, and the Rook is a giant magic item."

I nodded as I finally got it. "That means the ward couldn't go through the floor or ceiling. It's just a wall."

"I'm sure the original caster ran spell traps over the floor and the ceiling, but it looks like they faded away after a while and the owner at the time couldn't replace them. By the time Bainbridge took ownership, they had been just relying on the ward. He should have seen the weak points, but it doesn't appear he did."

"Not surprising. Saw a lot of that in the Army."

"Saw what?" She started digging through her bag.

"It's a form of institutionalism. This is the way it's done because this is the way it's *always* been done."

"Yeah, that's about right. Same thing with a lot of guilds and covens." She pulled out a magnifying glass and a spool of wire.

"Huh."

"What?" She closed the bag and placed it on the ground.

"Well, not exactly eye of newt, are they?"

"Sure, they are." My wife lay down with her face up close to the ward. She placed the magnifying glass in front of her eye and studied the stone floor in front of the ward. "Witches infuse everyday things with their magic like I've done with this magnifying glass. With the magic I've put into it, I could study atoms."

"Seems like a bit overkill, but what's you point?"

"Well, in the Middle Ages, eye of newt was an everyday item. You couldn't order one of these online, but you could go out into the garden and get an eye of newt. That's a term for mustard seed, by the way. Not an eye from an actual newt."

"So, you don't use eye of newt anymore for stuff?"

"Many of our spells are handed down over the centuries. I use original ingredients whenever possible. But If I'm creating a unique spell, then I use whatever is handy and meets the sympathetic magic requirement." She seemed to find what she was looking for. She placed the glass down and unwound the spool.

"I guess that makes sense, what did you cast on the wire?"

"Nothing." She straightened a section of the wire then turned on her side, pulling a small jar from her bag and opened it up. A rancid smell filled the air.

"Ugh. What is that?"

"Lard. We have a lot, thanks to all that bacon you eat."

"Stop picking on my bacon. It's tasty and filled with fatty goodness."

"*You're* filled with fatty goodness," she shot back and dipped a large section of the wire into it then returned the jar to her bag.

"Not sure how to take that. It's both an insult and a compliment."

Zoe slid the wire between two of the granite pavers under the ward. "These old floors always have minor crevices in the mortar between the stones. It should allow me to snake the wire under the ward."

"Then what?"

"Then this." She pinched her end of the wire with a thumb and forefinger and concentrated. The wire immediately heated up, turning red. I watched as the entire length of the wire heated up. Zoe increased it until the lard coating burst into flame. As soon as there was fire on the other side, she made a gesture at it, and it shot to a six-foot column.

She rolled over and dusted off her hands. I grabbed one and lifted her to her feet. "Pretty tricky, Mrs. Brennan."

"Thank you, Mr. Brennan." She looked around as she made a similar gesture and a twin column of fire rose up our side ward. "Travels along ley lines, you say?"

"Supposedly."

"It's a fixer upper but this could be a nice vacation place. We could move it somewhere tropical."

I picked up her bag. "I have other plans for it."

"Bachelor pad for when I finally get fed up and kick you out?" She held both arms in front of her and spread them apart as if she was pushing open curtains. Both columns expanded into fire gates.

"As if you could get rid of me." I followed her through the fire gate and we emerged on the other side of the ward. I looked back at the side we came from. "Remind me to bring you in for questioning the next time we have an unsolved burglary. You could make a very lucrative life as a professional thief."

"What? And have two cat burglars out there who have seen you naked?" She held out her hand and I returned her bag.

"Ugh. Don't remind me."

"Really, the idea of some strange woman eyeing your naked butt wasn't a turn on? I thought guys like that sort of thing."

"Not when she's kicking said naked butt all over the room." I tried the door. It was still locked. "Damn, I was hoping I'd have been able to open it as the new owner."

Zoe frowned. "What about your lost key theory?"

"I could have been wrong. Try before you pry, as the hose draggers like to say."

"Who?"

"Firefighters." I studied the runes adorning the lock plate. Trying to figure out another smith's runes was like trying to read a root language of English. I usually had an idea what the rune did but was never positive without further research.

Zoe pointed at the runes I was studying. "What about these? Won't they keep your key from working?"

"Possibly if Bayn added a preventive against skeleton keys, but I doubt it."

"Why?"

"There has never been a lot of runesmiths in the world. There wasn't a high chance an enemy one would have made it this far. Besides, he might need a way in if he ever lost his key."

"Ah, the irony. And if he did put in such runes?"

"It'll come down to which one of us has the stronger magic." I waved at the walls. "And considering he built all this, that'd be him."

Using a rune on my bracers, I summoned my skeleton key. "I didn't see any runes that gave me worry, so let's see how it goes."

I slid the key into the lock. It went in without issue. Hoping it's magic would work, I turned it and was rewarded with a sharp click of the latch bolt releasing. I pushed the door and it slowly creaked open.

Chapter Thirty-Seven

The Candy Store

I stepped into the room, leery of traps. As with the rest of the Rook, the walls were made of stone. Instead of wall sconces, ornate brackets along the walls held steel rods. The rods began glowing as we entered the room, acting as a light source. It was more than enough to see by, but without becoming harsh and overpowering.

Not counting the cost of steel, that's a pretty cool idea.

A large wood table stood in the center of the room. With the books and bric a brac on it, as well as the single wooden chair behind it, it appeared to have been used as a desk. Behind the chair was a large bookcase that covered the entire wall. Old books and scrolls filled its shelves.

The wall to our right had a fireplace. Where the smoke went in a ley line traveling stone tower was a mystery to me.

Huh? I wonder if my trans dimensional chimney musing is actually correct.

A double door was centered on the wall to our left. When I opened it, similar steel rods illuminated the room, revealing a forge. An anvil took up the middle of the room and metal working tools lined the far wall. Other types of anvils were set off to the side. Every tool imaginable for a Runesmith appeared to be in the room. Stalls with different types of metal stock and other mediums such as stone were built along another wall.

Oh my God, Christmas came early.

I looked closer at the forge.

Coal. Son of a bitch!

I continued to study the room, trying to determine how to hook up a gas forge.

"Mike, take a look at this."

I reluctantly stepped back in. Zoe was at the desk. I moved over to see what she was pointing at. "Is that a metal wand?"

She snorted. "A bit too phallic for that. It's a scepter, I think. It has runes on it."

Zoe stepped back so I could inspect it. A silver stand cradled the scepter at an angle which itself was on the right corner of the table. Well, the right side if you were sitting in the chair.

The scepter was about a foot long and entirely made of steel. A leather wrap was tied around the handle section. The bottom of it flared into a flat circle just large enough to stand it upright if I wanted to. The top was shaped like an orb held by claws. The iron content of the orb was high enough to give it a much darker look than the rest of the scepter.

A closer look revealed the orb to be a globe of the Earth. Lines were engraved on it, making it appear the world was caught in a net.

Fuck! I think those represent ley lines. Martin's going to lose his mind when he sees this.

Runes were inscribed on both the orb and the shaft of the device. Without taking my eyes off of it, I sat down in the chair. Several minutes passed as I tried to decipher them.

"Can you make out what the runes do?"

"Hmm?" I looked up. It might have been more than several minutes. Apparently, Zoe had taken various books off the shelf and leafed through them without me noticing. A small pile of them had been started on the floor.

I rubbed my eyes and leaned back. "Sorry about that. Was kind of in the zone."

She snapped shut the book in her hand. "No, I get it. I do it myself during spellcrafting."

"Well, to answer your question, I think it's the missing key."

"To the door?"

"To the whole thing." I waved my arms around. "I believe it's the... ah... remote control? Yeah, the remote control for the entire Rook. The house keys, so to speak."

"So, what happened? Someone had a senior moment and forgot where they left the keys to the house?"

"Looks that way. Either that or there had been some sort of emergency and they had to leave the room quickly." I scratched my scars. "As a runesmith, Bayn probably had it so he could summon the scepter as needed, like I do with my toys. As non-runesmiths, his descendants couldn't have reset it to themselves. At some point one of his descendants left the room without it and locked themselves out."

I gestured to the book she was holding. "Anything interesting?"

"The scrolls and books appear to be written in old Norse, Latin, and old English. I know enough to identify them, but not enough to read them. You'll need Martin for that. Some are diaries, but most appear to be about runes. I think you hit the knowledge motherlode for runesmithing."

Zoe held the book out to me. I quickly sifted through it. "Oh, this is great! Look at these rune designs."

"Thought you'd like it." She snorted. "Are you about to cry?"

"I'm just so happy! It's like being a kid in a candy store."

She nodded at the scepter. "You going to pick it up?"

Sighing, I closed the book and placed it on her pile. I couldn't read it, but the runes inscribed on it were fascinating.

Priorities, Mike!

"I think so. I didn't see anything on it that screamed *trap,* but have a potion handy just in case."

"Ready when you are."

I shuffled the chair a little closer and reached over. My hand stopped just over the scepter. "You have poison antidotes as well, right? The good ones?"

"Quit stalling, mister." My wife smiled at me.

"Right, then. Here we go." In a quick move, I snatched it off the stand. As I held it up, a spike popped out of the handle and stabbed deep into my palm. I tried to drop the scepter but found my hand impaled onto it.

"Ow! What the hell!"

"What?"

I held up my hand to show my wife the blood dripping down out of my clenched fist. "I was kidding before, but now I hope you really do have poison antidotes with yo—"

Everything went black.

Chapter Thirty-Eight

Origin Story

I found myself back at that damn door, surrounded by white nothingness. The door was giant, made of metal, and had weird runes on it. I'd first seen it when I had died. I'd glimpsed it in my dreams several times since. Enough to be pretty sure I knew where I was.

"Fuck, I'm back on the psychic plane."

"Welcome, my heir!" I jumped at the voice and turned to see an old man standing near me. He was balding, and what few hairs remained on his hair were white, as was the long beard in front of him. He was large with a big gut, and wore a dark scarlet tunic made of linen trimmed in white fur.

"Santa?"

"What?"

"What?" I paused for a second and started again. "Ah, who are you?"

"Bayn the Smith, of course. Which one of my descendants are you?"

Oh Shit!

"You're Bayn of the Bridge? The runesmith?"

"Yes. Well, no. I'm more of a shade. You hadn't been born yet when I was dying so I made sure this would be placed in my scepter so we could speak." He winked at me. "Sometimes it's good to be married to a wizard."

He pulled at my sleeve. "Your clothes are strange. Are you my great, great grandchild or even further along?"

"Why are you speaking English?"

"I'm not. This is a connection on the psychic plane. We're speaking in thoughts. Your mind is filling in the rest. Should take care of translating mannerisms and idioms as well to making everything understandable." He walked around me, studying my appearance.

"But I think in English."

"Well, you think you do. Don't worry about it. It's not important." He grinned at me. "So! Tell me, which one of my children are you descended from? Is it Wulf? He was always a big one. Not quite your height, though."

"So, you're a piece of Bayn's soul that's been resting inside the scepter all this time waiting for a runesmith heir?"

"Not too smart, though," he murmured almost to himself. "Definitely Wulf's line."

"Hey!"

"Sorry. Yes, that's correct. How long has it been anyway?"

"I'm not sure when you died, but a rough guess is about twelve hundred years or so. Give or take a century or two."

"That long?" He seemed stunned.

"Yeah. Sorry." I told him awkwardly. "You said your wife was a wizard?"

"Hmm, oh yes." He refocused.

"Well, it looks like your descendants were mostly casters and Gifted. I'm not actually related to you."

"What? My line died off? Or are you a fosterling?" He made a gesture, and two wooden chairs appeared on the glowing plane. He waved me to one and sat in the other.

I gently sat down in the empty one. The idea of sitting in a chair made of thought was not reassuring to me.

Then again, I guess that's what the floor is made of as well.

"The long and the short of it is the latest owner of the Rook was a wizard named Daniel Bainbridge. He pitted his heirs to the death to see who would inherit. Anyone that came to the reading of the will was included as well."

"A blood challenge for the right to inherit?" He frowned. "Not how I would have done it, but it was within his rights."

"Well, Daniel was a special kind of asshole."

"How did you come to be there?"

"Culain Gowan, my boss, asked me to escort another of the heirs to the reading. She was waiting to stand trial so needed to be guarded."

"Ah, you apprenticed under Culain the Smith." He nodded approvingly and stroked his long beard. "Excellent."

"No. Different Culain. This one's not a runesmith. He's the... well, I guess it would have been sheriff in your day, maybe. His last name is Gowan."

"Smith, yes."

"Why do you keep saying that? Gowan. It's an Irish last name."

"That means Smith. Remember, we are communicating through thought."

"Yeah, okay but..."

Son of a bitch! It's his former profession, not an alias.

"Yes, he was always obsessed with justice. That's what kicked off his feud with the Atlanteans, which in turned started the God's War. Never met him myself, but everyone that has says he's a powerful runesmith."

"*God's War?* What are you talking about?"

"It took place when I was younger. I'm much older than I look. My wife was a wizard, remember? Spell here, elixir there. Shaved off a lot of decades." He motioned to himself as if he looked like a supermodel and not an escapee from a nursing home. "Anyways, the God's War is where they started calling me Bayn of the Bridge."

"Okay. Remember, a lot of time has passed. Things have been forgotten or changed down through the years."

"One of the most altering events in human history and it's been forgotten." He shook his head sadly. "This world is rich with mighty ley lines. More powerful than other planes and dimensions. That's why the gods and other outer dimensional beings have been coming here over the centuries during Ages of Magic. As soon as they stepped onto earth, their power would magnify to a ridiculous amount."

That might explain why some of the myths contradicted themselves. In one myth you'd have a god was able to move mountains. In another, they wind up getting killed by a twig or something. It made sense if the stories with the god having awesome abilities took place on earth, and the stories where they are weaker took place on their home plane.

"Why are they different here?"

"My wife had a theory that it's because our plane is much younger and since humans never developed the ability to use magic, this allowed the ley lines to grow in power."

I frowned at that. "What are you talking about? We're both runesmiths and your wife was a wizard. Of course humans can use magic."

"Not originally, they couldn't." He waggled a finger in front of me. "At least not until the gods started sleeping with the natives. Every one of us able to do magic can do so because we're descended from the gods. I myself, am… well… was, the son of Brokkr."

"*What?* You're saying we're all descended from gods?" I could hear the shock and disbelief in my own voice.

390

"Those people with magical abilities, yes. How else do you think we beat them?"

"You saying you fought and defeated the gods?"

"Well, not all of them. More than a few of them were on our side. Plus, we had Heroes, like me."

"What's so special about them? Heroes, I mean. I don't know anything about them. Just that I was told there aren't any left."

"Mmm. Yes, it makes sense you would have little, or none left by your time." He stroked his beard. "Heroes are beings who have the ability to kill the gods."

"So, it's a Gift then?"

"No, there are certain of us descended from the gods who while mortal can kill the immortal. Some are Gifted like you or I. Others are magi or warriors. It's a separate ability.

"But we digress. The God's War came about because we were tired of the gods having their way with our world. Any other time in history, we wouldn't have won but it was a hundred years after Ragnarök and about fifty years after Culain destroyed Atlantis. Most—"

"Wait! Culain sunk Atlantis?"

"Not so much sank as blew up, but yes. I don't believe it was intentional. More a byproduct of when an entire pantheon dies on our plane."

"He—? What? How did he kill an entire pantheon?"

"No one knows. Do you want to hear this or not?"

"Sorry. Go ahead, but I'm going to have questions at the end."

"Gods had been killed here and there by mortals before, but an entire pantheon? It shook them up. On top of that, the destruction caused another great flood, and most of mankind blamed the gods for it. Well, they usually got blamed for any weather issue, really.

"At that point several of the wizards and Heroes and some sympathetic gods had been trying to broker a set of ground rules for what was acceptable behavior from the gods. This was rebuffed and war broke out. Monsters, demons, and all sorts were dragged into it. It lasted a very long time. In the end, we won, and a peace treaty was drawn up. Among other things, it stipulated when gods could visit here and for how long."

"You're referring to the Great Pact between Men, Gods, and Monsters." I leaned back in the chair.

"I have heard it called that, yes."

"So, what does that have to do with a fight on a bridge?"

He smiled. "It was a bridge between worlds. I held off the invaders until help arrived."

"You held off a god strike team?"

"Minor deities. As gods went, they were not memorable." He gave a modest wave. "They were barely stronger than mortals. There were greater deeds in the war."

"Still, that's impressive."

"Once the gods departed, only those descended from deities were able to do magic, which is why it's only a small population. Or has that changed in your day?"

"No, still a small percentage of people. I just had no idea that's where the ability to use magic came from."

"I assume that since you didn't know, you have no idea from who you are descended from? If I may ask? Who are your people?"

"No idea. I'm Irish on my father's side. Scottish with a little Viking thrown in on my mother's."

"How did you come to be guarding my criminal descendant?"

"She was employed by another city to secretly attack us while being the ambassador for peace talks."

"You are a warrior of great renown, then?"

"Well, it's my job. I'm a cop."

"You're a town guard?" Bayn didn't try to hold back his disappointment.

Guess I need to spice up the resume. Feels like déjà vu.

"Not quite. The job has grown considerably since your time. I'm also the head of House Brennan and the Commander of the city's forces."

"Mmm, respectable." He stroked his beard. "What do you plan to do with the Rook?"

I shrugged. "I'm not sure. I wasn't really expecting to be in the running for it. After that, it was more of trying to keep it out of Dracula's hands than anything else."

"Who? Is that one of my descendants?"

"No, he's a vampire. He's up to some shady shit in my city and tried to get one of your descendants to get the Rook for him. "

The other runesmith made a sound of disgust. "I'll have none of that ilk living in my home."

"I hear that," I muttered half to myself. "Like I didn't have enough problems with the dragon."

"Dragon? You have a dragon in the area?" Bayn's eyebrow shot up to his hairline. "Keep the Rook far from it!"

"Yeah, I get you don't want your home in the claws of such a creature."

"It's not just that. The Rook is a very powerful item. My life's work. You cannot let a dragon add it to its horde."

"I feel like there is something I'm missing here."

"A dragon is a creature of avarice."

"Yeah, I've heard that. But what exactly does that mean? It's greedy?"

He shook his head. "Have you ever wondered why a dragon's horde is treasure? It's not like it's going to spend it."

"Ah... Huh! No, can't say that I had."

"It's horde is made up of things others covet for a reason. The dragon draws its power from the greed that it represents. The larger the horde, the more powerful the dragon. Now imagine it possessing a magic item as powerful as the Rook."

Fuck!

"Yeah, that would be bad."

Then again...

"So, you'd say this was something a dragon would definitely covet."

"Without a doubt. It would boost its power significantly. Which dragon is it?"

"No idea. Won't say its name," I said absentmindedly, a plan half formatted.

"One of the older ones then. They hold onto their names like gold." He gave a final tug of his beard. "Well, I'm satisfied. You're a worthy enough runesmith to give the Rook to."

"Just like that?"

"Well, no. This is the psychic plane. While we've been talking, I've been sensing your personal energy. There is a large justice vibe coming off you."

"Vibe? I'd love to know what word translated into that."

"Doesn't matter. The scepter is keyed to you now. It and the Rook will respond to your thoughts. As long as you're alive, others can't use the scepter without your permission. Good luck."

I blinked and I was back with Zoe. She cocked her head while holding a bandage. "What? You had a dazed look for a second."

"We need to speak to Valentine and Martin. I know how we can get David back! I just need to practice my driving first."

Chapter Thirty-Nine

Best I Can Offer

Many hours later, I once again stood by the woods with the descendants of Fenris Wolf by my sides. Time stretched on as we waited. I was beginning to think the dragon wasn't going to show up, when David finally stepped out from the trees, his face was emotionless as the dragon peered out at me through the teen druid's eyes. YOU HAVE RETURNED. AGAIN.

"I have. I've got a better understanding of you now. Hey, what do I call you, by the way?"

It just stared at me in silence.

Eh, worth a shot.

"Okay then." I shrugged. "I've been told your kind collect treasure because the greed generated by its value somehow powers your magic."

I could hear crickets it was so quiet.

"So, that got me thinking. David's a big score for you, instant army of creatures and all that."

More crickets. I felt like a comedian dying on stage.

"But having David doesn't increase the power of your hoard, regardless of how many nuts and berries the local chipmunks bring you. So, the stuff I was offering before wasn't cutting it. But if I had a big-ticket item, something that could increase your power. Then you might be willing to deal, right?" I dug into my pocket and pulled out the Rook. It was currently roughly the size of a chess piece. I held it up. "Do you know what this is? And please, use words. You're giving me a headache."

Emotion showed on David's face since the first time the dragon took control of

him.

Greed! Naked, unabashed greed!

"What is that? It feels powerful." Once again, it spoke from David's mouth. His voice barely a croak from lack of use.

"It is." I placed it on the ground and stepped away from it. "It's a tower that can change size and travels along ley lines. It's called the Rook. I was going to change the name to something else but was worried the BBC would sue me. Besides, it would look weird in blue."

"This is what you offer? You would trade this for the boy?"

"I'm thinking about it. It depends. What else are you willing to throw in?" I drew the scepter from my belt. It responded to my thoughts and the Rook grew to its normal size.

"You think to bargain with me?"

"Well, it's does have so many cool features. Did you know it's bigger on the inside than the outside? Watch this." I waved the scepter and the door creaked open. On the other side was Valentine. On spotting David, the Knight of the Star's brow furrowed in concentration, and he threw an arm out in the direction of the boy.

WHA- David started to sway on his feet.

"Now?" I yelled to the vampire who gritted his teeth and nodded. I sprinted over to the boy, flung him over my shoulder, and began running for the door of the Rook. The wolves paced me every step of the way.

Valentine moved to the side to allow us to run into the Rook. The doors slammed shut on my mental command. Another thought and the foyer's far door opened into the kitchen. Zoe and Martin were waiting there and made room as I carried David in and placed him on the table, Valentine and the wolves right behind me. I stepped back as Zoe started checking David's vitals.

"We… need to get… farther… away," Valentine gasped. "I can't…keep the dragon out…much longer."

Martin spread a large parchment on the counter. I hurried over to him. On the parchment was a hand drawn map of all the ley lines in the area. Martin had been cataloguing them for several years. His finger ran across one of the few marked in blue. The red ones were dormant ley lines that we couldn't use, and they vastly outnumbered the blue ones. "Here. Follow this one out and it will take us several miles outside the city in the opposite direction. That's as far away as we can get before the magic in the ley line starts to fade out."

I swallowed and gripped the scepter with both hands. I had only successfully moved the Tower twice. Both were earlier in the day before I briefed everyone on my crazy plan. The shifts had not been... pleasant.

Closing my eyes and concentrating on the scepter, I was able to see a glowing snarl of ley lines flowing in the darkness. I located the line Martin showed me and imagined moving towards it. I felt the Rook slide along the ley line. The feeling made me queasy, and I had to fight off dizziness in order to concentrate. The image in my head showed me a vision of zipping along a large beam of energy. It felt not dissimilar to riding on the front of a roller coaster.

As the Rook slid into the spot Martin picked out, I dismissed the vision of the ley lines and opened my eyes. My stomach lurched as my mind caught up with what I was seeing. "Done. Hope it wasn't too bumpy."

Martin shook his head. "Felt seamless to me."

"How's David?"

Zoe pulled a stethoscope from her ears. "Physical health-wise he's a little dehydrated and could use a few meals."

Valentine had moved closer to David and was placing his hands on either side of the boy's temple. "I had hoped when I first broke the connection it would have freed David from the dragon's grip, but that is not the case. The only reason I was able to break it in the first place was because we took it by surprise. It's pushing me out bit by bit and I can't stop it."

"Fuck!" I rubbed the scars on my face. "Okay. Time for plan B."

My wife sighed. "I hate it when we have to go to a plan B."

Martin snorted. "I think we were on plan J before we defeated Harrow."

"Valentine, if David is unconscious, can the dragon still control him?"

"If he is rendered so by a spell, then yes. It'll just override it with stronger magic. If David is drugged or knocked out by force, probably not."

"Explain, please." Zoe started rummaging through her bag of tricks.

"The dragon operates the boy's body through his mind. If David is drugged or injured to the point of unconsciousness, the creature would not be able to control the body until the boy woke back up."

"Zoe, do you have anything non magical? I only need something that will knock him out for a couple of minutes." Most believe that witches such as my wife who specialize in healing do it all by magic. But the good ones like Zoe use herbal remedies, natural concoctions, and plain old medical know-how just as much as their magic.

She held up a jar with a yellow liquid in it in one hand and an eye dropper in the other. "This should work. It's pretty potent stuff."

Zoe opened the jar which let out a smell similar to swamp gas. She filled the eye dropper halfway and resealed the jar, placing it back in her bag. "Open his mouth."

I pulled down David's jaw, forcing his mouth open. Zoe placed three drops into his mouth. "You can let go, but give it a couple of seconds to kick in."

I watched David as Zoe put her equipment away. She looked over at me. "The walk-in freezer?"

"Yup."

"Could you explain that to the rest of us?" asked a confused Martin.

I walked over and opened the door to the walk through. "The Rook uses a stasis field to keep its perishables fresh. As soon as the door is shut, the stasis field kicks in. You think the dragon's magic can cut through that?"

Martin rubbed his jaw. "That's good. Very good, in fact. It won't be able to connect to David's mind because it will be as if the boy is frozen in time. Hell, it won't even be able to sense him."

Valentine made a sound similar to air escaping from a balloon. "If you're going to do it, do it now."

I scooped David up and placed him in the walk-in, laying his head down on a bag of rice. As soon as I exited and shut the door the Vargar ambled in and sat down, surrounding the walk thru. The kitchen got small awful quick.

I looked at Valentine who had a pained expression on his face. "You okay?"

"That was an unpleasant experience. I've never fought a mental battle that hard before. Any longer, and I believe the dragon would have torn my mind a part like tissue paper. My head is pounding."

I glanced at Zoe. "Anything you can do?"

"Not for a vampire. Sorry."

"It's fine, though I believe I'll skip tonight's festivities. I apologize, but I am going to go home, have a drink, and lie down." He looked in enough pain that I skipped commenting on what type of drink.

I walked him to the door. "Just be careful, okay?"

The vampire pursed his lips. "You think it was too easy?"

"I don't know about easy. We used its own greed against it and caught it by surprise. There will be retaliation. It's just a matter of when."

"I agree. You don't think it will be immediate?"

"No, David's forest is full of powerful magical creatures. Creatures, that thanks to the dragon's control of David had been enslaved to that thing. They're going to want some payback."

"They are not powerful enough to overcome it."

"Probably not, but there is enough of them that it should be occupied for a few days." I held the door open for him. "Tonight's party will be more of a strategy meeting. As soon as we left for this crazy rescue mission, Culain was supposed to brief the usual suspects. We'll still have a couple of drinks, but tonight will mostly be brainstorming.

So, put the Drac Pack on the back burner for now. We'll be having dragon issues very soon."

Valentine sighed. "I understand wanting to rescue the boy as soon as possible. It's why I assisted. But from a tactical standpoint, we should have dealt with Vlad and his cronies first. There is no telling the trouble they'll be up to while we are dealing with the dragon."

I shrugged. "I wasn't going to leave David trapped there any longer if I could avoid it. He doesn't deserve it."

"As I said, I understand." The Vampire Lord stepped through the door. "Keep me in the loop."

"I will. Now go get some sleep. You look horrible." I closed the door as he walked down the steps.

"Put your thinking cap on, wife o' mine," I yelled as I walked towards the Rook's kitchen. "We have some scheming to do."

Chapter Forty

Losses and Revelations

A lot of ideas got thrown around at the meeting/party at Stacked, but very little got accomplished. There was a celebratory feel in the air. Between David's rescue and what we pulled off at the council meeting, it had been a good week. As much as I wanted to strategize, the team needed to celebrate and blow off some steam. I finally gave into it. We could plan another day.

As the night wore on, bit by bit, people started heading home including Zoe, who firegated to the house. I stayed to smoke a few cigars with Q and Ogier the Dane. I may have had a drink or three as well.

As the restaurant finally closed up, Q and I made for the door before Ogier could pour another round. The Chief was waiting on the street to drive us home. As we descended the stairs, a rough, raspy voice cried out from the shadows. "Mike, look out!"

As I summoned my armor, there was a large explosion, and we were both knocked down. Bits of metal rained down upon us. I picked myself off the stairs to see what remained of the Chief engulfed in flames. "*Chief!*"

My blood runes flared to life on their own as I exploded with fury over the death of my car.

No. That's what they want. This was done to put me off balance. Reacting instead of thinking.

I turned off the runes, snapped into soldier mode, and pushed my grief to the back of my head. I summoned my 1911 and scanned the area. Q did the same as he drew his weapons. The flames lit the area, deepening the shadows and making the night vision on my runic eye useless.

"Who the fuck uses a car bomb in Llewellyn?"

"I don't know," I said through gritted teeth. "But I'm going to find out."

As I searched the shadows, a gunshot rang out. Q dropped his tomahawk and grabbed his chest, falling back onto the stairs. Lucy stepped out of the shadows, the flintlock dangling from her finger. "Got you, lover boy!"

As I aimed at her, she dispersed into bats, scattering into the night.

"Fuck!" I ran over to Q. "You alright?"

"You should spend less time worrying about the fext and more time worrying about yourself." I whirled to find Dracula standing on the steps. He smiled and gave a slight bow. He was wearing a tuxedo and when he straightened up, he fiddled with the bowtie. "You like? I thought I would lean into the image a bit. No opera cape, though. Pity, I miss capes. They were just so… elegant."

"You killed my car!" I growled. "You're a fucking dead man."

"For several centuries, yes." His smile deepened. "I highly recommend it."

I fired several rounds at him. He turned to smoke and reformed after the rounds went through him. "Really, Sergeant? Bullets?"

"Fine! We'll do it the old fashion way." I dismissed my gun and summoned my sword.

"Wait. You should really see this first." The Vampire Lord gestured towards V-Town where a large explosion ripped through the night. It was in the area where the vampire anti-defamation center was. The building where Valentine lived.

Seward stepped out of the darkness to whisper something to his master. Dracula gave a nod. "My people reported Valentine was in the building when it went up. If I'm very lucky, the Muse was there, too."

I reached into my pocket and scattered rice onto the stairs. I was fully prepared to lop his head off when he started counting. Seward would be next.

Then Lucy. Oh, I'm not forgetting about you, Lucy.

Dracula looked down at the rice. Using the toe of his shoe, he sifted a few to the side before looking up and smiling at me again. "We have a lot in common, you and I. We're warriors by nature, but we read comic books, and we both like to use misdirection."

Why-why isn't the rice working?

"When I was a boy, I had titles, but not power. More powerful men than I controlled my destiny. If I was to survive, to maintain my throne, I needed to not be seen as a threat." Dracula gestured to the rice. "A person crippled by phobias and quirks was of no concern. Someone easily controlled."

"You've been playing a con game all these years?"

Fuck!

His phobia and tics were the only thing I had to even the playing field. Dracula was a Vampire Lord like Valentine. I'd seen Valentine fight. There was no way I could beat him. Even if Drac was half as tough, I was screwed. Hell, the only way I beat Bathory was she was too feral to think straight, and I got lucky with my weird blood thing.

"Yes. I considered giving it up when I was turned, but the same type of power dynamics existed among the vampires. Soon, all my victories and achievements were chalked up to family, allies, or luck. I was never viewed as a serious threat no matter how high my position was. But do you know what the best part of it all is?"

"Yes."

"When-wait, what did you say?"

"The best part is now. When you get to tell your enemies just before you kill them."

The Vampire Lord's mouth became a thin line of displeasure. Now it was my turn to smile. "Aw, did I ruin your fun?"

"No matter. We have much worse plans in store for you than death." He studied his fingernails. "Doctor Seward, take down the sergeant, please."

I pointed my sword at Seward. "You get one warning. Step towards me and I'll view your intention as coming to kill me. You *will* be met with lethal force."

"You are out of your league, Sergeant Brennan." Seward shook his head and he moved forward. "Alone and outnumbered. You don-gurkk!"

Out of the shadows, a black hand with thick claws reached out. It covered Seward's head completely and there was a popping sound as it squeezed. Seward's headless body hit the cobblestones with a thud. It twitched slightly and went still, slowly dissipating into ash. I shrugged. "I never said I would be the one applying the lethal force."

Dracula raised an eye as the clawed hand slowly drew back into the shadows. "You've turned our boogeyman. Impressive."

A large group of bats fluttered down, circling over where Seward fell before moving to Dracula's side where they reformed into Lucy. She crouched down next to him and hissed at me, bloody tears streaming down her face.

I ignored her. "That's the problem with hiring boogeymen. You can't see them. So how do you know that you actually hired one and not an undercover cop? Officer Knox, if you would."

The shadows pulled back to reveal a large, muscular figure with short fur and horns. Everything about him including his teeth, gums, and tongue were black. "For the record, I'm spelling it Noxx these days. Seems more fitting."

"That's what I said."

"No, you said *Knox*. It's *Noxx*."

"I don't hear a difference."

"Lose the K and add an extra X."

"That's the stupidest thing I've ever heard."

"Gentlemen!" At Dracula's voice we stopped our stalling and turned to him. The two vampires had taken a step back and Dracula was frowning. "If we could stay on topic, please. I do have a schedule to keep. Now then, when did you get a demon? I was not told you had one."

"That's not exactly the situation here. You know how demons possess people?"

"Yes."

"Well, he possessed a demon."

"An intriguing reveal. I feel the need to do one of my own." He gestured behind him. Jett and Jesse slowly walked forward into the light. "Your demon may not have been a turncoat, but that doesn't mean I didn't have a few of my own."

I stared shocked at the two of them. "You betrayed the Muse?"

Jett shrugged. She held an old-style detonator in her hand. "You have to play the winning side if you want to survive. The Muse has been losing power for years. If I hadn't made a move, I'd have been taken down with her."

"I'm not surprised. I knew there was something off about you." I turned to her companion. "But Elv- Jesse, how could you? I excepted better from you."

He had the grace to look embarrassed. His face was smudged with soot. He must have been standing too close to Valentine's building when Jett blew it up. "I dunno, man. She wouldn't let me perform. What am I if I can't sing? Drac here promised to let me have as many shows as I want."

"Yeah? I wouldn't be too sure about that." I tabbed my badge. "Dispatch, have all units on alert. Dracula had firebombed the VADC, and Lucy Seward has shot Q at Stacked. Both are here with us now along with the vampires known as Jett and Jesse."

"Roger that, Sergeant. Anything else?"

"Yes." I smiled at the two vampires. "I need backup!"

Appearing out of nowhere like he always does, Mickey Maloy gripped his baton as he stepped up next to me. He studied the vampires but made no move. I gestured towards the three of them. "You are under arrest."

"Ah, the Revenant of Justice. He truly is a formidable opponent. You are lucky to have him for an ally." Dracula smiled as smoke for the fire started to make its way towards us. "But I have one of my own. Do you know the origin of the name Dracula?"

"Fuck!" That's when it clicked. Something had been bothering me since Dracula hit town. I didn't make the connection until he just threw it in my face. I stared at the smoke as it billowed closer. It wasn't following the normal pattern of regular smoke. It widened as it came and looked more like a wave heading our way.

I whirled to Noxx. "How many people can you shadowwalk with?"

"One. Why?"

I thrust something in his hand. "Take Q and get out of here. That's not from the fire. Get him to Zoe and warn the others. The dragon is on the move."

"Consider it done, boss. I'll be back for you." He quickly turned, scooped Q up, and leaped into the shadows, vanishing before our eyes. I turned to Mickey. "You should get out of here, too. I don't know what the smoke can do, and we can't lose one of our big guns."

For a moment, I thought he was going to refuse. From the expression on his face, he definitely considered it. The old street cop finally gave me a single nod and was gone in a blink of an eye.

"Don't worry. I'm told it's quite enjoyable." Dracula climbed the steps until he was parallel with me. "You have heard of opium addiction being referred as *chasing the dragon*? There is a reason for that saying. But opium pales in comparison to dragon smoke, as you shall soon see."

"Dracula. Son of Dracul. Your father was called the Dragon because of his membership in the Order of the Dragon. The same Order you belong to. How did I miss that connection?" I shook my head in disbelief.

"Oh, don't feel bad. The Order has been around forever and was quite public. No one ever thought we were connected to a real dragon."

"That's why you came here, the dragon woke up? The reason your line has such strange abilities is because the dragon gives you power? What does it get in exchange?" The smoke curled its way closer and closer. Sections of the city it had already passed were completely covered.

"Oh, yes. In exchange for power, the Order has served as her eyes and hands. Traditionally it has guarded her resting place during Ages of Magic, but that damn Arch Druid stole her out from under us. The family that failed her was destroyed and we've been searching for her ever since. Imagine our surprise when she summoned us here. And now she's awake in between Ages and at a Nexus, no less."

So, the dragon is female.

"That's why the dragon didn't attack. She was waiting for you and your cronies to arrive." As I spoke, I hoped and prayed my family had gotten out in time.

"Partially. She needed a new hoard. The Archdruid separated her from it when he stole her. We never found where he hid it. We've been ferrying in treasure belonging to members of the Order as a way to replace it."

Thank you Hywel, you crafty bastard. At least for that. In the end, we'd all have been better off if you left her where she was.

"So that cat burglar was one of yours. Stealing to increase the hoard?"

"The opposite, actually. She's been a thorn in our side for some time. She's been targeting objects of power. Magic items that are greatly coveted by the magic community."

"And once those magic items are added to her hoard, the dragon's powerbase would have grown, strengthening your mistress quicker."

"That is correct. Obviously, the thief is working for the Muse. We'll track her down quick enough once we have the city."

"But why now? Why are you finally making your move now? I would have thought the dragon would have wanted more treasure first. Get back to full strength."

"You angered her when you stole the boy druid and, to add insult to injury, you used the Rook to do it. My compliments by the way. That was well done." He flicked a piece of lint off his lapel. "Still, such a slight needed to be addressed. So, we move the timetable up a bit. Just for… you."

The smoke was almost on top of us. I glanced at it and made a decision.

Fuck it. If I'm going out, I'm going out fighting. This one is for the Chief!

I raised my sword and took a fighting stance. "Let's do this then."

Dracula gave a deep laugh and floated up in the air away from me. "No, Sergeant Brennan. While this truly is the end of Blood Drinker's Bane. There will be no glorious last stand for the Rune Knight. Oh no, she has plans for you."

"What do you mean?"

"Think of the size her hoard will be once she has you under her sway. A dragon with her very own Runesmith to create magical items for her." He flung his arms open wide as the

414

smoke rushed past him. "The Mistress comes, Michael! Embrace her!"

The smoke billowed and flexed as it engulfed me. "Go fuck yourse—"

Everything went…gray.

To be continued in Runes of Fire

Cast of Characters

Acantha Baines-Chatterjee

Member of the alchemist's guild and one of Daniel Bainbridge's heirs. Her mixed heritage has caused strife between her parent's families.

Aidan Llewellyn

A wizard distantly related to Silas and Zoe.

Augustus "August" Tome

Young Mage and son of Octavius Tome who Mike arrested.

Bayn of the Bridge

Creator of the Rook and the ancestor of Daniel Bainbridge and his heirs.

Cassie

A homeless woman that people think speaks gibberish. She is looked after by the officers of Llewellyn.

Crystal

Magical AI and dispatcher for the Llewellyn Police.

Culain Gowan

Commissioner of the Llewellyn Police Department.

Daniel Bainbridge

Wizard and owner of the Rook. Killed by Owen Llewellyn while possessed by Harrow.

David Forest

Apprentice Druid to the Arch Druid Howell. Foster son of Odella Tingle. Captured by the dragon.

Donarson

A Nordic associate of Culain. He has a shaved head and a bushy red beard and is very muscular. He is knowledgeable in dragons.

Eddy Feenix

An officer with the Llewellyn police department. Born in the middle ages, Eddy has the ability to resurrect similar to a Phoenix. He identifies as Australian.

Emala Delgado-Finnigan

Teen age witch who was apprenticed to Zoe Morgan after her previous teacher was murdered. Her father is in the army and her family is stationed overseas. They think she's at a boarding school. She plans on breaking the speed record for flying on a broomstick.

Gabrielle "Gabby" Zhao

A sergeant with the Llewellyn police department, Gabby is descended from the second son of the first Emperor of China. Known as the Living Temple, her body is a vessel for the four Great Spirits. Her father Shan was the Living Temple before her and the former partner of Mike Brennan. Gabby is the goddaughter of Mike Brennan and godmother of Morgan Brennan.

Gio and Gianna Ponticello

Gifted twins from Brooklyn and heirs of Daniel Bainbridge. Claim to be "connected".

Greely Chamberlain

Attorney and executor of Daniel Bainbridge's estate

Harleen Bridges

One of Daniel Bainbridge's heirs. She is Gifted and hails from the deep South.

Harrow

Dybbuk and responsible for Oct5.

Hien Tran

A Vietnamese witch and latest head of the Morgan Coven

Henderson "the Haze" Hayes

A minor mage, small town crook and flimflam artist. Described as *"Not a bad guy as criminals went, but you definitely want to count the rings on your fingers after shaking hands with him."*

Jack Seward

A Victorian doctor of the Line of Dracula. Married to Lucy Westenra Seward. He was Turned by his wife.

James Brennan

Father of Mike Brennan. Co-owner of the pub *Brennan's on the Moore*. Born in Ireland. US Army veteran. Brother of Trick Brennan.

Jamie Brennan

Secret Warlock and son of Mike and Zoe Brennan. Currently serving in the US Army.

Jesse

A vampire Turned by the Muse. Once a famous musician, he keeps getting in trouble for being sighted by fans. Has a fondness for peanut butter and banana sandwiches.

Jett

A vampire of the line of the Muse.

Jose Marcellin

Llewellyn police officer murdered by Joubert agents who used his badge to gain access to the LPD communication system. This was used during Oct5 to kill most of the police force.

Katrina Bathory

A master vampire of the line of Bathory. She feeds on pain and suffering.

Liz Pendens

An attorney who has the Gift of remembering everything she reads for a certain time period.

Lucy Westenra Seward

A Master vampire Turned by Dracula in the 1890's. A psychopath with a taste for babies.

MacCian

An Irish associate of Culain. He is tall and lean with curly blond hair. He appears to not trust Culain based on past actions.

Maddox Morgan

Witch and cousin of Zoe. Head of the Morgan Family and city councilor. Frequent ally of Leland Callis.

Marie St Pierre

Elderly dispatcher for Llywellyn PD.

Martin Wheeler

Professor of Theorical Magic and Ritual Magic and the Head Librarian at the University of Llewellyn. The son of two wizards, he has no magical ability of his own.

Mickey Maloy

A Llewellyn police officer killed in the 1940's saving Llewellyn from Nazi spellcasters. During Oct5, his wife Celeste used the combined magics of the witches of Llewellyn to turn Mickey into a Spirit of Justice.

Mike Brennan

Former Army Ranger. Sergeant with the Llewellyn Police department. Has the Gift of Runesmithing. Married to Zoe and father of Jaime and Morgan Brennan.

Morgan Brennan

Daughter of Mike and Zoe Brennan. Has the ability to communicate with alternate versions of herself.

The Muse

A former Vampire Lord, her preference to make musicians, artists and actors into vampires had gotten her kicked off the vampire council. She hides her identity behind veils and flowing robes.

Obrechennyy Khishnik

A Russian Alkonost and former Joubert Ambassador to Llewellyn, she is currently a prisoner of Llewellyn.

Octavius Tome

Wizard once arrested by Mike Brennan who was forced to cut Tome's arm off. The arm has since been replaced by a glyph covered wood version. Father of Augustus Tome.

Ogier the Dane

Last of Charlemagne's paladins and current owner and chef of the restaurant known as *Stacked*.

Otto Clausewitz

Mercenary and former Kaptain in the Prussian Army. wielder of the saber *SoulDrinker*. Killed by Mike Brennan during Oct5.

Owen Llewellyn

Welsh Arch Wizard, founder of the City of Llewellyn and head of the city council. Grandfather to Zoe Brennan. Father of Silas the Black. Presumed dead after entering the Nexus to stop Joubert's magical attack on the city.

Patrick "Trick" Brennan

Uncle of Mike Brennan. Co-owner of the pub *Brennan's on the Moore*. Born in Ireland. Former US Marine sniper known as Longshot. Brother of James Brennan.

Pavel Mŭstek

A witch from Prague and one of Daniel Bainbridge's heirs. He is a history professor at an university in Prague.

Penelope "Bad Penny" Harper

Tricked into using a highly addictive potion based off the research of Dr. Henry Jekyll by the Alchemist Guild. She is able to transform into a creature known as a "hyde". She was lent by the Guild to Harrow and acted as one of his agents during Oct5. She was later pardoned and became a police officer.

Quintrell "Q" Faraway

The newest sergeant in Lewellyn PD. He is a fext, a person who becomes semi-immortal after they die. He has a past history with Vlad Dracula and is from Texas.

Rom Chang Hayes

A Spellslinger of Cambodian descent and one of Daniel Bainbridge's heirs.

Rosalyn Macalister

Friend of Morgan Brennan and occupying personality of the current incarnation of RePete Macalister.

Silas "Silas the Black" Llewellyn

Warlock and son of Owen Llewellyn. Father of Zoe Brennan.

Sonny

Son of Mulligan AKA Sonny. The Brennan's pet bullmastiff.

Stanley the Ogre

Head of an ogre street gang and ally of Mike Brennan.

Templeton Knox.

Boston Cop transfer who was captured and used as a sacrifice to summon a demon. It did not go as planned.

Ulysses Khan

The sole detective on LPD, Khan was a NYPD Detective before being Turned into a vampire in the 1970s.

Valentine

Vampire Lord and Former Knight of the Star.

Vera Lee Padgett

Spell-Crocheter and cosplayer. Currently dating Eddy Feenix.

Victoria Davenport A wizard who specializes in sex magic, she is a senior member of one of the strongest wizard organizations in the city. As Head of House

Davenport, she sits on the city council. She has multiple spouses.

Vlad Tepes

More commonly known as Dracula. Vampire Lord and head of the line of Dracula. He is considered odd by mainstream vampires and has usual powers. You may have heard of him.

Wackacat

Zoe Brennan's black cat familiar. Her real name is Pyewacket.

Wila Moray

The Muse's second in command and has a past history with Vlad Dracula.

Zoe Brennan

Powerful fire witch and member of the Morgan Coven. Father is Silas the Black. Grandfather is Owen Llewellyn. Married to Mike and mother of Jaime and Morgan Brennan.

Author's Note

I know, I know. Sorry about the cliffhanger but trust me, it'll be worth it.

I wrote this book during the COVID pandemic. As a first responder in the real world, I continued to work during it. This impacted my writing somewhat, which is why this book is coming out later than I planned. There is nothing like real life worries to dampen the imagination.

We lost Demon Sean the rooster this year. The official story is that he missed or fell off his roost and his claw got caught on the chain holding the water dispenser and died after hanging upside down too long. I personally haven't ruled out accidental death through auto erotism asphyxiation. The bird was a little pervert. But he'll be a pervert we'll miss. As roosters go, he wasn't a bad one. As long as you didn't turn your back, carried a rake, and could run fast...

Aside from continuing the Recollections of a Rune Knight series, I'll be starting a series set in the same world. The first book is going to be called *A Knight of New England*.

In addition, I have a nonfiction project that will be out in 2022.

If you enjoyed this book, please consider leaving a review on Goodreads and Amazon. Such reviews go a long way in helping independent and small press authors in finding new audiences.

Thanks,

Jack

Jack Cullen can be found at:

amazon.com/author/jackcullen

JackCullenWrites.com

https://www.facebook.com/jackcullenbooks

He can occasionally be found at

Twitter.com/JackCullenBooks

https://www.instagram.com/jackcullenbooks/